CHARMED
CIRCLE

CHARMED
CIRCLE

CHARMED CIRCLE

by

SUSAN ERTZ

HARPER & BROTHERS
PUBLISHERS · NEW YORK

CHARMED CIRCLE

I

Is it here, i wonder, is it there, that with a light finger's touch, a word, a breath, things might have been made to take a different shape? At what point in time did that crystallization begin which set the pattern for our three lives?

This is how things were in an American family, lavishly provided for, miraculously blessed—could any group of people at any other place or time in the world's history have had such full and free control of the good things of life?—and steeped in mutual love.

Where to begin? Anywhere, anywhere at all. In New York, for instance. A scene can be chosen at random. Late afternoon. The father and mother and the three children at home in the library of their East Sixty-sixth Street house, with a fire burning and snow outside in the streets, cleared now and lying in heaps along the sidewalks—the cold sound of scraping has been going on all day—but blanketing the country, where they go very rarely. It is a warm, comfortable, well-furnished library, the sort of room people are happy to come into, sorry to leave. Over the mantelpiece is a portrait by Renoir of a dark-eyed young woman with her hair down about her shoulders, holding a small basket of flowers. It is the father who speaks first.

"Ruth," my father said, suddenly beginning to laugh at some recollection that struck him as wildly funny, bending over in his chair with a hand against his side. "Oh, Ruth, tell the children about the time Louise got into trouble with the London policeman, before she could speak English. You tell it much better than I do."

Louise was my mother's French maid, and my parents had engaged her when they were in Paris, on their honeymoon. She was with us for twenty-two years.

[1]

"When you've stopped laughing," my mother said, amused, "I'll begin." And she looked round smiling at our three expectant faces.

We had just left the furnished house we had been occupying in London, my mother told us, and were on our way to Paris. At Victoria Station Louise discovered that she had left her handbag, stuffed full of money and cherished articles, at the house. My father, with his dislike of haste or confusion, always saw to it that we were well ahead of time, so, as the boat train was not due to leave for half an hour, it was decided that Louise should quickly take a taxi and go back. When she got to the house she could not get the front door open—she had the right key, but it required a little knack, a little *finesse*, my mother said, to make it do its work—and neither could the taxi driver, who got down off his seat to help. So they went down the area steps to the basement and tried to force open a small window through which Louise believed she might crawl. A policeman walking slowly by saw them and asked them to give an account of themselves. Louise, by this time in a state of frenzy, could of course give none, and the taxi driver could only say that he'd picked her up outside Victoria Station, so the policeman got into the taxi and went back with them to verify as much as he could make out of the story, aided by Louise's frantic gestures. My mother laughingly described her own feelings when she saw Louise returning without her handbag, weeping hysterically, and escorted by a solemn policeman. The guards had blown their whistles and the boat train was just leaving, so my mother and Françoise, the nurse, went on to Paris with Clarisse and myself—Clarisse was a year old and I was two—while my father straightened matters out, retrieved the handbag and followed some hours later with Louise. As my mother told it, it seemed to us very funny indeed and we did not fail to remind Louise of it on many future occasions.

Every family, I suppose, has its folklore, and this is just one small example of the folklore that was so abundant in ours. My parents possessed to an unusual degree the faculty of being charmed and diverted by incidents in their own past and by the fortunate chance and circumstance of their meeting. All this they loved to share with us. No fairytales interested us as did stories of my father's unhappy boyhood and youth in the gloomy brownstone house in Thirty-fifth Street, just off Madison Avenue, and since demolished, or the fantastic early upbringing of my mother, of which I will speak later. There were stories in plenty, too, about our own early childhoods and the times and places of our births: first my own in New York in 1910, the son they had confidently planned for, then my sister Clarisse's in Paris in 1911, and finally my brother Julian's—he was fancifully called Giulio at first—in Florence, in 1914, three months before the outbreak of war. We were never better entertained than when our parents dipped into the ocean of past events and brought up odd, bright objects for our inspection. Nor did repetition tire us. We were wholly in love with all the circumstances of our lives, past and present. There was a glow over it all; even our illnesses, none of them serious, I believe, had, in retrospect, a magical quality.

Sometimes my mother, at our request, would read us extracts from the diaries she kept from her seventeenth year, when she considered herself ready to play an adult part in life. We listened entranced when she read aloud the entry she had made before going to bed on the very day on which she first met my father. She was then eighteen.

Paris. March 12, 1907. This is THE Red Letter Day of my whole life. This afternoon Aunt Sophy took me to Mr. Harper Brandon's reception. How thankful I am that I was wearing my new green velvet dress trimmed with beaver, and my green satin hat. Perhaps, though, it wouldn't have mattered what I had on. As soon as we were introduced, I *knew,* and I could tell from the way he looked at me that he knew too. His name is Myron Slade Prentiss and he comes from New York. He's the son of old Gideon Prentiss of Prentiss's Stores, who, Aunt Sophy says, is simply terrible, very rich, and as common as common can be. She says she can hardly believe this young man can be his son after all she's heard. I don't care whose son he is. *Je m'en fiche, je m'en fiche absolument.* He's the best-looking thing I ever saw in my life and so charming and so gentle, and he has the most enchanting smile. His manners are just wonderful. This is his third year in Paris as an art student but his father won't give him any money and he's nearly come to the end of his resources. He says he'll have to go home soon and eat humble pie, and I certainly hope he does because Aunt Sophy and I are sailing back to New York from England in ten days' time. He's calling on us here at the hotel tomorrow. Oh, how happy I am! Everything is beginning for me, I'm sure of it, and I think he feels that everything is beginning for him too. I don't know who else was there this afternoon, maybe nobody was. It would have been all the same to us.

This ingenuous record made us all resolve to keep diaries, but I was the only one who did.

And then a few days later:

[3]

March 15. Myron has told Aunt Sophy and me that he's written to his father saying he wants to go home and asking him to forgive him and take him into the business. He says he's admitted he was wrong and that he'll never be a painter. What made him decide to do this now, without waiting another day, is that he wants to marry me! He told us so yesterday, right straight out! Red Letter Day number two. I was too excited last night to write a word. Oh, I'm so in love! He has won Aunt Sophy's entire approval, so all is well.

The story of my father's rebellion more than two and a half years earlier against his father, old Gideon, was also a prime favorite. It followed the classic pattern that we have all met with either in fiction or in real life.

My father had confided in his mother that he wanted to study art, but she'd warned him that his father would never allow it. Old Gideon did not even want my father to go to college but expected him to go straight into the business on leaving school. This is probably what would have happened but for the fact that my grandmother got typhoid fever at about this time and nearly died. (But for some tainted fish or meat or drinking water, would we have been here? It seems improbable.) Believing she was on her deathbed she plucked up courage to extract a promise from old Gideon that my father should have four years at college before going into the business. Although she surprised herself and the doctor by getting well, old Gideon stuck to his promise. He chose Cornell, which he considered less "fast" than either Yale or Harvard, though my father would have preferred Harvard. Soon after his graduation he made up his mind to tell old Gideon about the career he had chosen for himself, and this must have taken considerable courage.

It was at the end of 1904, just before the turn of the year, a period that seemed to us children mistily remote. It was a period of carriages, cabs and horse-drawn buses, with here and there a smelly, noisy vehicle called a horseless carriage which aroused admiration and disgust about equally. The Spanish-American War of 1898, lasting six months, had been over long enough to be mainly forgotten, though it had aroused feverish excitement at the time. The country was solidly prosperous and looked confidently forward to more of everything that was good. Growth and expansion were to be seen on every side. It was a time perhaps unequaled in the world's history for the opportunities it offered to the healthy, the energetic, the young. My father and my grandparents were living in the big ugly house in Thirty-fifth Street that my grandfather had bought after bringing my grandmother to New York as a bride. He had wanted to live as near as possible to the home of J. Pierpont Morgan which was just around the corner, for Pierpont Morgan was one of the very few men my grandfather looked up to and admired.

Old Gideon—he was well over fifty when he married—was a poor boy from up-state New York. From the age of twelve he had had to work to support his widowed mother, so he had little education and no time at all for what he contemptuously called "book learning." He started work in a small general store on the outskirts of Schenectady. In ten years, thanks to the confidence his elders had in him and some cautious borrowing, he became the owner of the store and during the next ten years he succeeded in buying out the owners of half a dozen other stores round about. By the time he was forty he was head of a flourishing chain-store business, and at forty-five he installed his mother in a big house known locally as "The Pike Mansion," in Schenectady, with three servants. When she died he married Emily Slade, the gentle, nicely educated but penniless girl who had come to the house to do dressmaking for his mother. He sold the Pike Mansion and, with his wife and the furniture, came to New York.

Prentiss's General Stores now began a new era. Branches appeared in Brooklyn, the Bronx, White Plains, Newark, even in New York itself and later as far west as Pittsburgh and as far south as Atlanta, Georgia. My grandfather, his feet firmly planted on the financial ladder—shares in Prentiss's General Stores were soaring in Wall Street—opened a big office in Twenty-third Street, and as he was a man who detested walking, having had too much of it in his youth, was driven to and from his office every day in a carriage and pair with a colored coachman in livery on the box. He refused, later, to have anything to do with automobiles and fought hard against their use in the streets of New York.

There must have been much that was admirable about my grandfather but a great deal that was not. He spat freely and noisily indoors and out. (Indoors in spite of the presence of numerous brass spittoons he preferred to use the fireplaces.) He dunked his bread in his coffee, made loud smacking noises when he ate and was rude to servants, waiters—he never gave tips—and all whom he considered his inferiors. My father told us that they could only keep servants by paying them nearly double the usual wages. It seems doubtful that my grandmother can ever have loved him, though she may have admired his achievements, but to a girl in her unhappy position—she was the mainstay of an idle father and an invalid sister—marriage to my grandfather must have seemed the best solution to her problems, and he supported her father and sister until their deaths.

They first had a little girl who died in infancy, and then, in 1882, my father was born, to be his mother's comfort and delight. She brought him up to be as different as possible from my grandfather, and this, I imagine, was her legitimate revenge for the humiliations she had had to suffer. His unpleasant habits made her sigh and shrink and turn away her face, but during the whole of their married life, my father told us, she never once dared to voice a protest.

So one morning when my father was just twenty-two and was expected the following week to begin work at the office, he said to old Gideon at the breakfast table, "Father, I'm sorry to disappoint you, but I've made up my mind that I want to be a painter. I want to study art, either here or in Paris, though of course I'd prefer Paris. I shall never be any good at business. Will you please let me give it a try?"

His mother, who knew this was coming, sat trembling at one end of the table and old Gideon was dunking his roll in his coffee at the other end. As he shook the drops from it he slowly turned his head toward my father.

"That's enough fool talk," he said. "You're coming to the office on Monday."

"But, father," my father persisted, in his gentle way, "I really do want to study art. I believe I can be a good painter. It's what I want to be. In fact there's nothing else in the world I want to be."

"Then you can get out of my house in double-quick time," old Gideon said, and shoved his coffee cup at my grandmother to have it filled up again. Her hands shook so, my father told us, that she could barely lift the pot, and tears were starting to run down her cheeks.

"Well," my father said quietly but with a wildly beating heart, "if that's really the way you feel about it, all right I will."

"It is," old Gideon snapped. "Get out. Beat it. Skiddoo!"

"Oh, Gideon!" moaned my grandmother, and covered her face with her napkin.

"And I don't want to hear a word out of you," old Gideon barked at her. He drank his coffee in great noisy gulps and stood up. He was a stoutish man, tightly encased in his three-button, cutaway business suit and high stiff collar which barely allowed him to turn his head. His short gray hair and out-of-date General Grant beard seemed to bristle with fury. My father got up too, his legs almost giving way under him, but he tried not to show what he was feeling.

"Father," he said, holding out his hand, "won't you at least listen to what I—"

Old Gideon struck his hand down.

"See that you're out of my house before I get back. If you're still here I'll have you thrown out." And he went toward the door. As he passed my grandmother, who was sitting sobbing in a heartbroken way, he paused long enough to say, "I'll send the carriage back for you. Go out and buy yourself that fur cape you liked. And stop that noise."

Then the front door slammed behind him.

My grandmother helped my father to pack a trunk, her tears still falling, and then they drove to the Brevoort House, where my father got a room. My grandmother had no money of her own at all. Old Gideon paid all the household bills himself, and he allowed my grandmother to have accounts at Altman's, Lord & Taylor's and at Jaeckel's, the furrier's. Each night when they were undressing for bed he would take out of his trouser pockets all the change that happened to be in them and give it to her. But the year before, on my father's twenty-first birthday, in a sudden access of pride and generosity, the old man had deposited five thousand dollars in his name in the First National Bank of New York, and my father also had a few hundreds that he'd saved out of the allowance my grandfather had made him while he was at Cornell. So he was by no means penniless.

After booking the room and leaving the trunk, they drove to the Cunard office and my father got a berth—second class—on the first boat sailing for Europe, in four days' time. After that they drove to Jaeckel's, and chose a really beautiful mink cape which my poor grandmother didn't want and got little pleasure out of, but my father said it felt good to be spending so much of the old man's money.

My father told us he was sorry to leave his mother but apart from that very happy to be going to Paris, and to be getting away from the grim house with its hideous furniture, from the unpleasant old man and from the extremely dull life they all three lived there, for my grandparents had almost no friends in New York, and old Gideon never brought his business associates to his home. He was happy, too, to put behind him, forever as he believed, the horrid prospect of spending precious years "emptying waste-paper baskets at the office," as he put it. In addition to all this his best friend at Cornell,

Carl Frederickson, was shortly following him to Paris to study architecture.

"'Bliss was it in that dawn to be alive,'" my father quoted, smiling, "and never did a young man leave home more thankfully. Those unpleasant few minutes at the breakfast table changed my whole life."

The time that followed in Paris undoubtedly formed my father's tastes and did much to form his character. I have sometimes wondered if he ever really emerged from the enchantment of that place and period, so wholeheartedly, so absorbedly did he give himself up to it, so deep and ineradicable was the impression it made on him, and through him, though to a lesser degree, of course, on me. I too would have liked to be there. No gigantic outpourings of blood had yet darkened the scene. One could look on at gaiety, one could take part in gaiety, without being shamed by its opposite. The feeling of shared guilt which has now become our portion may someday bring about a new innocence, but that time is far off and I shall never see it. (I can never hear an old-fashioned Viennese waltz without feeling, "That is what life should be like," and Strauss's "Tales from the Vienna Woods" claws at my heart, and I remember the bodies of the youthful slain.)

My father of course fell in love with Europe; he was already in love with art. He was supremely happy and wholly unsuccessful, for it did not take him long to discover that a talent that had seemed considerable at school and at Cornell did not cut much ice at the École des Beaux Arts. But he learnt a great deal about his chosen subject, and especially about French nineteenth-century Impressionist painting. His simplicity and his readiness to learn, to admire and to enjoy, made him friends. He met many of the artists who were becoming known and many who were already famous, among them—for even then good luck attended him—Renoir and Cézanne, and of these fortunate encounters he never tired of telling us.

Cannily—and we felt we would have done the same—he wrote to his father once a week exactly as if there had been no break between them. He described to him what he did and saw—or at least as much of it as was good for their ears, for my father was attractive to women, young, good-tempered and gay, with the friendly gaiety, as I imagine it, of a charming dog. I am sure he fell in and out of love, and there was, I feel certain, a good deal more than friendship between himself and Madame Cléry, who gave him the Manet (a portrait of Victorine Meurend) to remember her by when she decided to marry a rich industrialist. It was she who first aroused his interest in the Impressionists and set him on the path he was to follow. I have seen a picture of her; she must have been a very pretty woman and had been left a widow at twenty-seven. I think she and my father must have loved each other, though perhaps not too seriously, and I do not doubt that my mother knew all about it, for she and my father had no secrets from each other. Whenever her name—she became Madame Druet—was mentioned, there was always a sparkle in my mother's dark eyes, and once or twice, when we were at home in New York at Christmastime, I remember seeing her mischievously place a sprig of mistletoe over the Manet.

I suppose those letters my father regularly wrote home to old Gideon kept the door slightly ajar for his return, if he should ever want to return, and early in the third year of his stay, he did. He had come to the end of his money, with which at first he may have been too liberal—and not even the most frugal living and such help as he would accept from Carl Frederickson, could stretch it out longer. And then, of course, he met my mother, and as soon as that happened he was eager to return. His final letter to old Gideon, mentioned by my mother in her diary, must have been a masterpiece of humility—and no doubt the old man was human enough to want his son home again—for two weeks after posting it he received a cable which said:

"Glad you have come to your senses take first boat home you will begin where you ought to have begun when you left school." Then old Gideon cabled my father the money for his passage.

When he got back to New York it was April but there was still ice floating in the harbor and a bitter wind blowing. Old Gideon and my grandmother—wearing her mink cape—were at the dock to meet him, and my grandmother cried with joy. The old man spat grandly to right and left, showing his satisfaction, walked proudly and was in good humor. He had grown much stouter, and although never a hard drinker—he allowed himself two whiskeys a day—his face was laced with fine purple veins.

"I didn't think, looking at him," my father told us, "that he'd live to be a hundred."

"A hundred!" I remember exclaiming. "But, father, that's terribly old, isn't it?"

He laughed.

"That's simply a *façon de parler*, my boy," he said. "What I mean is that I didn't think he'd live many years longer."

He made up his mind to get along as well as he could with the old man and to make his mother happy, and I am sure he succeeded in both. He soon confided to his mother the story of his meeting and falling in love with Miss Ruth Denniker in Paris, and she implored him to say nothing to old Gideon until he'd been in the office at least two years. This was only common sense, for the old man paid him little more than he paid the office boy and would have considered his son's matrimonial hopes a piece of gross folly.

So they waited, and not at all unhappily. Long engagements were not uncommon, and my father spent as much time as he could at the cheerful apartment in Twentieth Street facing Gramercy Park where my mother lived with her aunt, Miss Sophy Bligh. It was the time when the *Merry Widow* was taking New York by storm, and set everyone whistling, singing or strumming, and even set fashions in women's dress. (My father took my mother to see it six times.) Proudly, arm in arm, they would join the Easter Parade on Fifth Avenue, and regardless of uncertain weather and cold winds, my mother would wear a new spring dress, risking an all-too-probable aftermath of grippe or pneumonia. She scribbled away in her diary, sewed lace on underclothes and went to tea parties and receptions with her Aunt Sophy. She wrote, "It may be a long wait but I don't care. I'm so happy I'd wait forever."

My mother's early history was a very odd one.

Her mother, Miss Rebecca Bligh, was the elder of two wealthy sisters, orphaned daughters of a rich banker, who were born and brought up in New York. From her childhood, Rebecca seems to have gone her own way. Music was her passion, she cared for little else, and she worked hard at her piano as soon as she could read music, which was from the age of seven. But she developed an alarming strain of eccentricity, made unsuitable friends, and at seventeen disappeared completely for six months—it caused headlines in the papers—and had the whole police force of New York looking for her. When she reappeared she refused to say, and never did say, where she had been. When she was twenty-one and financially independent, she ran away with a violinist in a theater orchestra who already had a wife and family. A year or so later, as soon as he was free, she married him and became Mrs. Rudolf Denniker. She bought a house on Riverside Drive—it was then quite fashionable—and got together an orchestra of her own, and as most of the performers in it worked during the day, they did their practicing at night and often late at night and there were so many complaints from the neighbors that she was finally obliged to buy the houses on either side. At one time, my mother told us, there were as many as seven pianos in the house.

Mrs. Denniker became more and more eccentric and difficult to live with and when my mother, the only child of the marriage, was eight, Denniker left home and disappeared. He was never heard of again, and the supposition was that he had gone out West to begin a new life.

After he left, Mrs. Denniker's behavior grew still more odd and uncontrolled. She drank to excess, neglected the child, smoked cigars, wore trousers, and at one time had as many as five male members of her orchestra living in the house with her, so that the whole thing became quite a scandal. Her sister Sophy, who was still unmarried, persuaded her to let her take away the child, Ruth, and bring her up. Luckily for my mother, her Aunt Sophy was a very nice woman and she devoted her life to her niece. She took her to Europe, sent her to school for three years in Lausanne, gave her every advantage and a fairly sensible education.

When we were children, of course, we understood little of all this. We knew that our Grandmother Denniker's behavior was unusual without realizing, until we were older, just how unusual it was. She ran through all her money, giving large sums to musicians' charities, and died in some institution or mental home at the age of forty-five. A tragic story, and undoubtedly most parents would have suppressed a good deal of it, but it seemed wiser to my parents not to do so, nor to minimize the unpleasantness of our Grandfather Prentiss. We were sure to hear about it someday; besides, what had been had been; it was all part of a story that led to their present happiness and to ours, and if there was anything in it that caused them pain or embarrassment they were careful not to let us guess it.

The only effect her early years appeared to have on my mother was that they gave her a strong dislike for music. As my father was quite unmusical and hardly knew one tune from another, they were not conscious, I imagine, of any lack.

My father was a peculiarly fortunate man. Everything went well for him. Behind his pleasant blue eyes, in his gentle, hesitant manner, in his friendly smile there lay no expectation of any hindrance to his needs or wishes. He anticipated only what was agreeable. On the rare occasions when he encountered what was disagreeable, it caused him short-lived annoyance or hurt surprise, but these, together with their cause, were quickly forgotten. His hopes of being himself a painter—one of his very few disappointments—were soon canalized into a great enthusiasm for the works of the French Impressionists and a passion for collecting them, and these and his family kept him completely happy.

It was a part of his good fortune that he was even spared the necessity of breaking the news to old Gideon that he was secretly engaged and wanted to marry, for when he had been home less than two years, my grandfather was found dead in bed one morning from a cerebral hemorrhage. Father and son had, in the meantime, become wholly reconciled, and the old man had made a will leaving everything to my father unreservedly, appointing as his executor and my father's trustee, Sylvanus Dumont, of Dumont, Rowan & Dumont, the trust to terminate when my father reached the age of thirty. Inheritance tax in those days, as my father frequently told us in after years, was only five per cent, and old Gideon had died a very rich man indeed. My grandmother was not even mentioned in the will, but old Gideon knew well enough that my father would see that she lacked for nothing, as indeed he did. She lived with my parents—at least in the Sixty-sixth Street house, for they themselves were more than half the time in Europe—for the first eight years of their married life and then died, devoted to her daughter-in-law and delighted with her three grandchildren, all of whom she adored. I remember her very well; a frail, small-boned, sandy-haired woman with a pointed nose, a nervous little laugh and glasses which she fastened to her thinning hair by a fine gold chain.

Immediately after old Gideon's death my father sold the house in Thirty-fifth Street with everything it contained, installed my grandmother temporarily in a suite at the Murray Hill Hotel and took a room for himself at the Waldorf. As soon as arrangements could be made, he and my mother were quietly married at the Little Church Around the Corner in Twenty-ninth Street, which, as they had few friends in New York, seemed to them the most suitable place. Aunt Sophy Bligh was more than satisfied at the way things had turned out, and Grandmother Prentiss wept with happiness. Carl Frederickson was best man, and Sylvanus Dumont, who had already begun to play an important part in my parents' lives, gave my mother away. I shall have much to say about him later.

II

THE YOUNG COUPLE WENT, OF COURSE, TO PARIS FOR THEIR HON-
eymoon, and then made a tour of France. They must have been—
indeed I know very well they were—as happy as a pair of mating
birds on a spring day. While in Provence they made a special trip
to Cagnes where Renoir was then living in his pretty little house,
Les Colettes, for my father wanted above everything to persuade
him to paint my mother's portrait.

Renoir was then, and for many years before his death, half crip-
pled with arthritis, and my father has often told us how the brushes
had to be placed in his clenched hands. He spent most of his time in
his wheel chair, either sitting in the garden or at work in his little
"atelier" under the trees. He used to wear a funny old black hat,
green with age and turned up all the way round; his short body was
stiff and bent, and his white beard straggly and rough, but his lively
eyes were as keen as ever, and he charmed my mother and was
charmed by her. He agreed to paint her, but said that as he tired
easily he would not ask for many sittings. He spent four whole after-
noons working on the portrait. It is entirely successful and is in his
earlier manner, which is the one I like best. He chose to paint my
mother with her dark hair spread about her shoulders. Her girlish
roundness, her pretty pale face and velvet-black eyes must have
pleased him, for he painted them lovingly. The dress she is wearing
is pink, or at least that is the predominant color, but it is made up
of so many other colors that one marvels how the final one was ever
arrived at. She is holding a little basket of roses and these repeat the
color of the dress. Even without them one would have known it was
high summer, but I think that in Renoir's pictures it is almost always
summer.

Certainly my mother was the type he liked best to paint; broad
faced, round cheeked, bright eyed, above all, feminine. "I paint human beings as though they were fruit," he is quoted as saying, and

this is very true of his women and children. My parents brought the portrait back with them (it always hung over the mantelpiece in the library) together with three other Renoirs, two Cézannes, a Pissarro and a Monet, and these, with the Manet that he had been given by Madame Druet, were the foundation of my father's collection. It was a matter of great regret to him that he had not been able to buy Renoir's *"Portrait au Bord de la Mer,"* that picture of a *petite femme* sitting in a wicker chair against a background of cliffs, for it so resembles my mother that she might have sat for it. It was then in a private collection, and I was often taken by my father to look at it.

"If you ever marry, Halley, marry a woman of that type," my father would say, standing in front of it. "That is what a woman's face ought to be like. Full of sweetness, good temper and fun." And I knew he loved and coveted it.

So, out of their unpromising backgrounds, my parents emerge, triumphant, rich and very much in love. The scene is set for them as on a stage, the whole world is open to them. And to them were born myself, in May, 1910, during the appearance of Halley's Comet, and so named Halley, my sister Clarisse fourteen months later in Paris, and last, when Clarisse was two, my brother Julian. No children could have had happier childhoods or more loving care. Everything was in our favor. We were sufficient unto ourselves and fanatically devoted to one another. We made our own warm, deeply self-centered little world, taking from the world outside only what contributed to our enjoyment. The America of those days—I am speaking now of the period just before the First World War—seems to me to have been a land of strenuous, even strident vitality, possessed of a great wish to do well, to do better and better. The rich were exceedingly rich and unhampered, but, in theory at least, a child born even into the poorest family had a chance to make a good place for itself if it had the will. Let the rich get richer, some of the gravy, as someone has said, was bound to trickle down. Enterprise and hard work were bound to bring about at least a fair measure of equality. Utopia lay in the lap of time.

I like to turn to my mother's diaries and see that the novels she and my father were reading then were mostly English novels— though she speaks warmly of *A Modern Chronicle* by the American Winston Churchill—and most of the plays on Broadway were English plays. She and my father sometimes dined at Delmonico's— these occasions seem to have been to celebrate some special private anniversary—and liked to lunch on Sundays at the old Waldorf, Fifth

Avenue and Thirty-fourth Street, where my mother's favorite dish was breast of guinea fowl with paprika sauce. "Though," she adds, "nowhere is our cooking on a level with the best French cooking. It lacks delicacy."

She records in 1911 the fact that, Clarisse already being on the way, she is a good deal troubled by sickness, so they have reluctantly decided to abandon their plans for being in London for the Coronation. "The papers," she writes, "talk about nothing else. There are pages and pages about it, and endless photographs. I do hate to miss it, but Myron says I must put my health first. He promises me that when I am feeling better we will go direct to Paris. We would both like the baby—I am convinced it will be a girl—to be born there. I am sure she will enjoy, in years to come saying, 'I was born in Paris.'"

I wish I could convey the charm my parents had for us, the delight we took in being with them. Our whole world was created by them, and what was not within that world we cared nothing about. My father was one of the most likable of men, and in some ways, I suppose, one of the unwisest. He was always ready to amuse and be amused, and was almost always gently smiling. He was fair, of medium height and lightly built, like my Prentiss grandmother, and his mustache, until he was well on towards sixty, was golden. He spoke slowly, softly, almost with diffidence, and his voice was seldom raised above its normal level. To us he always looked very distinguished, and our pride in him was intense. He neither smoked nor drank spirits, but never sat down to lunch or dinner without wine. He was fastidious and orderly and liked us to be, and I never saw a room of his untidy. His skin was fresh and clear and always smelt pleasantly of lavender water.

My mother was only five feet three inches tall, and was a little inclined to put on weight, but we never at any time thought she put on too much, for she was light and quick in all her movements, and her plumpness seemed to us to accord perfectly with her warm, affectionate nature. And always, always, she was exceedingly pretty. Her large, nearly black eyes were immensely important in the even pallor of her face, and the photographs I like best of her are the ones that show them in all their dark expressiveness. She was a little vain of her hands and feet, would never wear her gloves more than a dozen times, and never had less than forty pairs of shoes and slippers in her possession. Her special shoe trunk always traveled with us.

One of the most vivid early memories I have of her is sitting on a cushion on the floor at my father's feet, her back supported by his knees, as he glanced through the evening paper, or perhaps the morning paper which he often did not trouble to read until evening or late afternoon.

"Read us any nice interesting bits you can find, darling," she would say to him. She disliked reading newspapers herself (the only ones I ever saw her spend any time on were the London *Times* and the *Christian Science Monitor*) for she liked to keep from her mind the knowledge of crimes, ugly scandals and disasters.

We never had pets as we were abroad so much, but I don't think we missed them except that Julian, as he grew older, began to long for a dog. The house in Sixty-sixth Street, which was large enough to house my father's growing collection, was closed for about half the year while we visited London, Paris, Rome or wherever my mother's whim or my father's picture buying happened to take us.

I remember feeling a little puzzled once as to why we lived so differently from some of the people we knew, and I asked my mother if we were very rich.

"No richer than other people," she said at once, and even then I knew that for some reason she felt she must say this. The wealthy, or at least the more refined wealthy like not only to minimize their wealth but to minimize to themselves the power and privileges that wealth brings and the gulf that exists between those who have far more than they need and those who have far less. They feel, I think, that their efforts and achievements are minimized by a commodity that most of the world has had to get along without. I once overheard her say to Miss Lola Hopkinson, who was an old friend of my Prentiss grandmother's and so poor that she was glad to come to the house to do occasional mending:

"Well, my dear Miss Hopkinson, we all have our troubles, you know. They may differ in kind, but troubles remain troubles however much or little you have in the bank."

I remember wondering what her own troubles could possibly be and supposed that she meant her occasional ferocious headaches which, when they came, kept her in her room with drawn curtains. But she gave Miss Hopkinson useful clothes and always remembered to send her a small check at Christmastime.

When I was eight, my mother's Aunt Sophy surprised us all by getting married—she married a well-to-do widower who had poor health—and the pair went out to Santa Barbara to live. To my parents it was as if they had gone to Siberia.

"I suppose we shall never see her again," my mother said sadly.

"She won't leave Mr. Mulroyd, and he'll never leave Santa Barbara, once he gets there." It never occurred to them that they might go to California themselves and in fact they never did. Their interests lay wholly in Europe. The four days' train journey across the American continent was something it never entered their minds to take. America, to all of us, was New York, though we had some awareness of Boston and Washington. As soon as spring came we were off across the Atlantic, and this seemed to us a part of normal procedure.

Our best friend and most constant visitor from the time I can remember anything at all was Sylvanus Dumont, my father's lawyer, adviser and, formerly, trustee. He called himself my godfather, but as my parents belonged to no church and disapproved of the doctrine of Original Sin, we were never baptized. Syl, or "Syllie dear," as my mother was fond of calling him, continued to take entire charge of my father's affairs, invested and reinvested his money, and was as clever, as my father used to say admiringly, as a barrel of monkeys. When, soon after old Gideon's death, my father wanted to sell Prentiss's General Stores to another big chain-store company which had long been interested in it, it was Sylvanus who brought the deal about to my parents' great satisfaction and enrichment. My father, as he had defiantly told old Gideon years before, had no head for business, and he knew he could trust Syl completely. "All I want to know, Syl," he would say to him, "is how much I can spend this year. Just keep me within bounds."

Syl belonged to the best clubs—he got my father into the only New York club he ever wanted to join, the Century Club—and in his younger days was a great leader of cotillions and very much in society. Syl would have liked to introduce my parents into this fashionable world and I am sure, being the influential man he was, could easily have done so, but they refused to be introduced. They said they cared nothing at all for New York society, that it was the most snobbish and the most money conscious in the world. Their friends were artists, art dealers—though only the very pick of the latter—or people in the literary and theatrical world. Sargent, who made several drawings of my mother, John Alexander, Barnard the sculptor, a few actors and at least one actress—my parents were a little unconventional in this, at least by New York standards—they counted among their intimates. Sylvanus was a devoted friend and admirer of Edith Wharton's, and brought her and my parents together, but my mother was not a great respecter of female celebrities, and somehow the acquaintance never ripened.

When my sister Clarisse was born we were living in Paris in an apartment my parents sometimes occupied near the Place St. Sulpice. It belonged to a wealthy French couple named Pichon who owned orange groves in Morocco and spent a good deal of their time there, and they would never let it to anyone else. It took up two floors in a lovely old house, had been comfortably modernized, and contained some paintings by Delacroix that my father longed for and repeatedly tried to buy. He had a great admiration for Delacroix both as a man and as a painter. "The father of the Impressionists," he used to call him, "and the first to break with the dull old school of classic art."

My mother went to the American Hospital at Neuilly and came back with a tiny, dark-eyed, flaxen-haired daughter. She and my father were as pleased that their second child was a girl as they were that the first was a boy, and it was to be expected that they should get what they wanted. I was little more than a baby myself, but we already had a good nurse, Françoise, and, of course, Louise, and I doubt if the presence of two young children incommoded my parents in the least. Françoise used to wheel us to the Luxembourg Gardens, and I have been told that we attracted a good deal of attention, I, gray-eyed, with thick brown hair, and Clarisse a tiny beauty with hair of silvery fairness and my mother's great dark eyes.

In 1914, my parents rented a villa in Florence on the hill leading up to Fiesole. It always seemed very strange to me that no one at that time appeared to have foreseen the calamity that was so soon upon us, the war which the world has been unable to end. I remember discussing this with my father—to whom it had come as a total surprise and shock—when I was about sixteen, and I can see him now, pacing up and down the library of our house in Sixty-sixth Street, as he tried to explain it to me.

"Surely," I had just said to him, "with all Germany's saber rattling and drinking toasts to *Der Tag*, and the building up of that huge army and navy—"

"My boy," he said, "you don't understand. After so many years of peace only broken by stupid, avoidable wars—I mean, for instance, our Spanish War, and then the Boer War—it was almost impossible to visualize a general war on that scale. No one could have imagined how such a war could come about; no one could imagine any great country wanting to go to war with any other great country, and other countries joining in. It was inconceivable. Things weren't settled that way—or so we thought—there were other, saner ways. Why, swarms of American tourists flooded Germany, England, France, Italy, even Austria, every year. Those countries seemed to us delightful playgrounds. War!" He shook his head. "It just wasn't possible. Germany made toys as well as battleships, remember; she built up trade as well as armies. I suppose the one hid the other from our eyes. We were so happy in that villa on the hillside above Florence when the war came. Julian was three months old. Your mother and I used to spend our time in the art galleries or in cool old churches, or sitting in the garden. There were ilex trees and a little fountain—I really think we must go back there someday." He paused, and I could see that it was all vivid in his mind. "We were so well occupied we hardly even glanced at newspapers. We weren't planning to come back here till late in the fall. War! It just didn't seem possible. I don't think I've ever been so completely stunned as I was when I realized we were really in for it."

We knew very well, of course, the story of the following months. We got to England, after some difficulties, and even then my parents were loath to go home. They had a good many friends in London, and I think too that the spectacle of a country they knew well casting off its peacetime occupations and turning to war (slowly, the unused, inadequate machinery creaking and laboring) fascinated them in spite of themselves. My mother records in her diary more than one meeting with Henry James; "I don't think," she writes, with a note of disappointment, "that he took to me quite as much as I took to him," and they made up their minds to settle down in London for the winter at Brown's Hotel. Spring came, and they were still there, a little bored and irritated by having to register as aliens and report their movements to the police. At last they booked passages for us all—except Françoise, who had decided to go back to France as a war nurse—on the *Lusitania*, which, as everyone knows, was torpedoed on its way over from New York. My father lost his best friend, Carl Frederickson, in that disaster—he was on his way to England on some war mission—and he was more indignant and wrathful about it all, my mother has told us, than she has ever known him to be before or since. He sent angry cables to President Wilson, whom he disliked, urging him to declare war, and for some time he talked of becoming a British subject, but in a few months' time, the submarine situation having temporarily improved, we were on our way back across the Atlantic, well convoyed, and we reached New York without incident.

I was eleven years old before we saw Europe again, in 1921. In the meantime I had not gone to school. In 1917 my parents had discovered Raymond de Vries, of Dutch descent, a graduate of the University of Pennsylvania, and more than willing to become my tutor. Owing to poor eyesight he had not been drafted, and I was proud to exchange him for the English governess, Miss Bewlay, an ex-Girton girl, who continued to come daily to the house to teach Clarisse and Julian. It was, I felt, a great promotion for me to have my own tutor. Raymond lived in the house. He soon became one of the family and fell completely under the spell of my parents.

My mother accepted Raymond's devotion as naturally as she accepted that of Miss Bewlay, of Sylvanus Dumont, of Louise, and of many others. Miss Bewlay, a neat, middle-aged spinster with an Eton crop, who was fiercely determined to establish herself in New York, had, I realize now, a sort of schoolgirlish adoration for her, and her narrow face with its beaky nose and thin lips would light up with sudden incandescence when my mother showed her some special kindness or approval. It did not take Raymond long to make his own place with us; my father liked him, we all liked him, and he was never in the way. I think he had hungered for years for just some such family life as ours, for his own childhood had been bare, pious and narrow. He was very blond with almost white hair and eyelashes, and so nearsighted that he could hardly recognize us across the street. He had been savaged as a child by a horse in a field and had a big half-moon scar on his forehead which greatly enhanced his importance in Julian's eyes. He was a first-rate Latin scholar and a good mathematician, and his knowledge of history was wide. I made satisfactory progress with him and he went with us wherever we went.

If my father had had any doubts about the rightness of my being taught at home he dismissed them as soon as Raymond came. He believed the education I was getting from him, plus what traveling and association with adults could teach me, was superior to anything I could get in an American school. Or so he easily persuaded himself. Sylvanus sometimes put in a plea that I be sent to Groton as soon as I was old enough—he had been to Groton himself—but my parents would not hear of it.

"We'd never see the boy," my mother would argue, "we're abroad so much. Besides, Syl, we've no wish to see him become a boisterous, commonplace American schoolboy, with no vocabulary at his disposal but the current slang: 'O.K., gee, swell, lousy'—no thank you."

"May I point out to you, my dear Ruth," Sylvanus said with a show of indignation, "that I am myself a product of the education you're decrying?"

"You, Syl dear," my mother answered, patting his hand, "are the exception to all rules. If we thought Halley would turn out like you, we'd plan to send him to Groton tomorrow."

I think Sylvanus was sometimes just a little hurt that my parents would so rarely be guided by him except in financial matters—in which, of course, they never disputed his judgments—and whenever he got the chance he would try to awaken in me a little of the ambition in which he considered I was sadly lacking.

"Don't you lose sight of the fact that you're an American boy, Halley," he sometimes said to me, "and that you'll grow up to be a citizen of the greatest country in the world. Everything is open to you, every possible career. Keep that in mind. Sometimes I don't think you know whether you're American, French or English. Well, you're American, and don't you forget it."

"I guess I'm American all right," I would reply, but I think I said this chiefly from a desire to please him.

If I were asked what plans my parents had for us, what hopes they cherished in regard to our futures I would have to answer, "They had none. None at all." They were passionately dedicated to the family idea and they hoped to keep us an integrated, happy little unit indefinitely. Why, in any case, need they look ahead? We would have enough to live on after their deaths and could then pursue our own interests. They agreed, I think, that someday we should marry, but it was a mistake to marry before full maturity. To this rule, they, of course, were the exception. I believe they could not contemplate the thought of our marrying—and so introducing strangers to the family circle or being ourselves drawn into other family circles—early or late, without anguish.

When we returned to Paris in 1921, we were all excited and happy. My memories of life abroad were few and dim, and founded on hearsay, and to Clarisse and Julian it was like going for the first time. The same flat was available to us, and though Monsieur and Madame Pichon were in Morocco, my father had arranged everything by cable. Paris, my parents said regretfully, was much changed, nevertheless it was Paris, and it was a good moment to buy pictures. To Raymond, it was almost a return to some spiritual home. He had steeped himself in the history of the French Revolution, it was "his" period, and his good fortune now seemed to him miraculous. Mirabeau—politically, and apart from his private life—was his hero, and he had hopes of someday writing his biography, to be followed later by a biography of Robespierre. We children shared our parents' distaste for horrors and bloodshed, and Raymond's enthusiasm did not communicate itself to us. But we indulged him and listened to him until we grew too bored, or Julian too tired—he was then sharing my lessons with me so far as he was able—and then went to play in the Bois, where we practiced throwing and catching a ball, almost the only fondness, it seems to me, that we shared with other American children. Sometimes we competed with the French children we met there in the long and the high jump, under Raymond's supervision, or ran races under the trees, but though Clarisse could run like a deer and jump almost as well as I could my mother put a stop to it on the grounds that she was growing fast and her heart was not strong. Clarisse took a good deal of pride in this actual or imagined disability, though if her heart was ever weak there was no sign of it in later life. She was never a tomboy, but she liked being in our company and being included in our games, and rarely made friends with other girls. She was at that time my ideal of girlhood, and if I thought about someday marrying, it was always to someone with long blond hair and dark eyes like Clarisse's. My mother usually dressed her in white and it gratified me to see how often she was stared at. When she was conscious of it herself—and I am sure she always was—she would swing her hair and turn away with pretended indifference.

The following year saw us once more in Paris. Mr. Harper Brandon was still living in his house just off the Champs Élysées where my parents had first met, and still giving parties, though he was approaching eighty and was nearly blind. My parents now considered his parties a little absurd. They never met anyone at his house, they said, but exiled Americans or foreign oddities, though they went now and again to avoid hurting his feelings. (I am sure that all really happy, well-matched couples are easily able to convince themselves that if they had not met at the time and place where they did meet, fate would have contrived their meeting at some other time and place.) Though he had lived in Paris for forty-five years, Mr. Brandon still spoke French with an atrocious accent and this greatly amused his few French visitors, who looked upon him as a "character." The French, so averse to keeping "open house" themselves, so shocked by promiscuous hospitality or any sort of purposeless spending, considered the old man so eccentric as to be not quite sane.

I was very happy working with Raymond and had no longing at

all for school. In fact, I did not want to go, because I did not see how I could live apart from the family. I could not bear to think that this warm, gently moving current in which we were all so secure and happy would flow on without me, for it gave to life all its sweetness and quality. When I observed the lives of other children, who lived in one place and went to school, I saw nothing to envy. On the contrary, I would not have changed places with them for the world. I was better taught in mathematics, literature, history and Latin than most boys of my age, and even chemistry—which my father said disgustedly only taught boys how to blow their fingers off —came within Raymond's scope. Clarisse was quite clever at drawing but none of us were interested in music, though we liked ragtime and waltzes. When, much later, I was, so to speak, exposed to good music for the first time, it was like falling in love. In fact it was a part of falling in love.

At first we preferred Paris to London—partly, I think, because we liked to show off our French—but later Julian and I decided we liked London best, though Clarisse remained loyal to the place of her birth. In both cities we felt perfectly at home, and we sometimes begged that we might spend the winter, too, in one or the other, but my father would remind us that our real home was New York, and we never failed to return there about the middle of October. We were always happy enough, after a few days, to be in our own house again, though New York itself did not greatly please us. There was nothing to look at, we agreed, but Grant's Tomb and some tall buildings, and as for the Metropolitan Museum, we had seen plenty of museums as good or better abroad.

"You mustn't become travel snobs," my mother said. "Make the most of New York. At least you've got Fred and Rosie and Helen here."

These were the children of Sylvanus's brother, Irving, and they were our best friends. Fred was three years older than I, while Rosie was Clarisse's age, and Helen about the same age as Julian. They were often at our house, and we were as often in their big duplex apartment in Park Avenue. Fred was soon to go to Harvard, but he good-humoredly tolerated and even seemed to like my company in spite of the difference in our ages. Rosie went to Miss Larne's, a small private school in Seventy-second Street, and my parents had sometimes talked of sending Clarisse there, but so far had done nothing about it. Miss Bewlay was always glad to come to the house during the winter months to give Clarisse lessons, and they saw no real reason to make other plans.

When we returned from a summer in Europe in 1925 my father bought a big Cadillac and engaged a chauffeur (he would never drive himself)—named Hicks. He came from Maine, and was a good-looking young fellow with nice manners. Clarisse used to pretend she was in love with him, and one day, in a moment of folly, I teased her about him in front of my parents. The result was that he was sent away and a fat, colored chauffeur named Johnson came in his place. If Clarisse grieved, it was for a day. She was soon saying that Johnson was a much better driver, and anyway she thought it was more "chic" to have a colored chauffeur than a white one. Whatever Clarisse did or said seemed to me to be due simply to the fact that she was a girl, and I accepted everything without criticism. I did not know any other girls well enough to make comparisons, and though I liked Rosie Dumont I did not think of her as on the same level with Clarisse. If Clarisse was a law unto herself, I believed she had a perfect right to be. Few children can ever have accepted one another as admiringly, as uncritically as we did. Julian's diffidence, his reserve, his lack of normal assertiveness, the difficulty he always had in deciding anything for himself, were all a part of the character I accepted and loved. We very rarely quarreled; in fact I cannot recall any disagreement worthy to be called a quarrel.

So my parents lived happily and idly. Idly, certainly, by American standards, for unless my father's picture buying could be called an occupation, he had none. He saw no reason why he should busy himself in other ways, nor did my mother, who loved to have him beside her and depended upon him—as he did upon her—for companionship. I know her one great dread and fear was that my father might die before her. And so long as they spent about half their time in New York, and so long as Syl Dumont was at hand to take complete charge of all my father's interests, they did not see that anything more was required. They were not, my mother used to point out, exiles, *déracinés*. They owned property and paid taxes in New York, my father was usually in America when the time came for him to vote—my mother always refused to vote herself—and their consciences, therefore, were perfectly clear. Sylvanus invariably got a scolding when he suggested that my father might go on the board of this company or that, or even interest himself actively in some charitable organization.

"It's all very well, Syl dear," my mother would say, "for you to work yourself to death if you want to—though God forbid that you should—you're a bachelor, at least. But you know what happens to American husbands—they nearly always die long before their wives. If I can help it, I'm not going to be a widow before my time—or ever, if it comes to that."

Sylvanus loved to leave his office early once or perhaps twice a week, and have afternoon tea with us in the library. I wish I could present Sylvanus just as he was, for even then I think he was a vanishing type. First of all, he was a New Yorker born and bred, and a fanatical lover of New York. Out of that vast, humming, multiracial "melting pot" (he would never have used the term himself) he knew only the hard center or core of the old city of the seventies and eighties. He knew and loved a New York which existed still, though pressed round and encroached upon by a great, pulsating jungle of "otherness" which he deplored and tried to exorcise by his refusal to recognize or accept it. A few clubs, a few families, a few houses, these he loved and clung to with devotion. Although constantly invited, he very rarely went away for weekends, much preferring to spend them in town, and his Sundays were jealously guarded. He was an Episcopalian, and never missed going to St. James's, where he was one of a little group of men who passed the plate and interested themselves in the financial affairs of the church. He was puritanical and at the same time extremely worldly, and I doubt if at any time in his life he gave much thought to spiritual matters. Existing quite apart from all this and never spoken of by him in "mixed" company, were his vast, his quite exceptional knowledge of Wall Street and its activities, and his small, exclusive, clearly defined law practice. Everyone liked and trusted him, and he was as much "in the know" as any man in New York. Besides being "in the know," his judgment and his prophetic sense were uncanny. As a trustee, he could not possibly have been bettered, nor as financial advisor, lawyer and friend. Unlike my parents, he cared nothing for Europe, and though he went to London occasionally, only Lombard Street and his Savile Row tailor took him there. He always dressed extremely well in a rather dapper way, was clean-shaven and wore pince-nez which drew up the bridge of his undistinguished nose. He was about as tall as my father, which was not very tall, and nearly bald, and besides being a great talker he had a playful sense of humor which endeared him to hostesses. When he smiled his teeth looked rather like the teeth of an old horse, but we loved everything about him, and our devotion had nothing to do with the fact that he gave us handsome presents. He carried on a sort of elderly flirtation with Clarisse, which added to her self-esteem, and flattered me by treating me like an adult. I realized even then what he meant to us, and my father rarely committed himself to buying a picture until Syl had told him it was all right, financially, to go ahead.

We were actually growing up in the period of "Flaming Youth," and we were scarcely aware of it. It was a period of drastically changing ways, of lost innocence, of old values going into the discard and nobody knowing what new ones, if any, would take their place. Millions of people were speculating wildly, confident that upward trends would continue indefinitely, the automobile was creating a restless new world, and yet, as far as we were concerned, we might almost have been living in old Gideon's day. Fifth Avenue, Central Park, Park Avenue, the residential streets between the East Thirties and the East Eighties, closed us in. We went occasionally to the movies, but only to see films approved of by my parents, and on the whole we preferred the theater. Prohibition had done its deadly work, it had made getting drunk an achievement, almost a new skill, and my parents spoke of it with loathing, but as my father had a pre-prohibition wine cellar, and as he and my mother never or very rarely touched spirits, they were personally unaffected by it.

There was a late afternoon in the winter of 1924 that I remember particularly vividly. Syl had come to have tea with my parents, but my father was out, and Clarisse and Julian were upstairs with colds. Raymond had gone home to see his parents, and was returning the next morning, so there were only Syl and my mother and me. I went upstairs for something, and as I came back into the room —Syl had been telling my mother some bit of gossip—I heard her say,

"I shall be glad when we can get back to London or Paris. I don't like the atmosphere of New York any more. There's too much of this drinking and disgusting behavior—it isn't only the young, Syl, it's their parents too. Prohibition! Oh, these do-good people, what a lot of harm they do!"

"It's only a phase," Syl said, in defense of his beloved city, and he patted the sofa beside him, so I took my teacup there and sat down. "It'll pass, Ruth. You'll see. In a short time, prohibition will be only a memory."

My mother looked at me and said,

"Just think, Halley—you don't mind if I tell Halley, do you, Syl?" At his sign of assent she went on, "Just think, Halley, Fred, who has always been so well behaved, was seen at a speakeasy the other night in the company of a young girl of good family, and they were both drunk. Syl has just been telling me. If they hear about it when he goes to Harvard—" and she shook her head.

"Fred!" I exclaimed. "Drunk! Goodness, he must be going the pace!"

"Well," Syl said, "I won't pretend not to be upset about it, and so is Irving, but don't let's take it too seriously. I suppose I must have drunk too much in my college days, though never in the company of a young lady."

"That's quite different," my mother pointed out. "A lot of young men together. But with a girl, and in a speakeasy—how could it have happened, Syl?"

"That," said Syl, "is what I mean to find out."

"Was the girl really drunk too?" I asked. I could not even picture such a thing.

"Both of them noisy drunk," Syl said. "The girl passed clean out. Of course Fred looks older than he is, still, it was a well-run place as such places go, and it ought not to have happened."

"I can drink quite a lot of wine," I boasted, "without it going to my head."

"That's because you've been brought up in the sensible, Continental fashion," my mother said, "and we've always had wine on the table. But this was some filthy gin, I suppose. Sheer poison. And these young girls," she went on, "parking their corsets at dances. No French girl would dream of doing such a thing."

"They dream about doing a lot of other things," Syl said, and my mother threw him a quick glance.

"Anyway," she said, "I don't want Fred coming here for a while, and you can tell him so with my love. This house is out of bounds till he's learnt how to behave."

"I can't guarantee when that'll be," said Syl, settling his pince-nez on his nose, "but I suppose it's as good a punishment as we can inflict on him. Rosie can still come, I presume, and Helen?"

"Of course, Syl dear," my mother said. "We all love Rosie and Helen. We love Fred too, but I really do think he'd better stay away for the present."

This did not distress me, as I saw very little of Fred except at holidays. We had all spent Christmas day together at our house.

Then I remembered something. "Oh, thanks, Syl, for sending me that Mauritius stamp. Raymond says they're quite rare."

"That one is," said Syl, "and don't you go swapping it for any-thing. It's for your collection."

"I expect Julian will be wanting one too," I told him.

"All right, I'll have to get him one then."

"Take another English muffin, Syl dear," my mother said, and took the lid off a covered dish. Then her sharp ears detected a slight sound. "Halley, your father's at the door. Run and open it for him."

My father came in with a light sprinkling of snow on the shoulders of his overcoat. Before letting me lay it down for Arnaud, the French butler, to hang up, he took some small parcels out of its pockets. One of these he handed to me.

"Just an un-birthday present for a good boy," he said, patting my shoulder. "Open it in the library. Is Syl here?"

"Yes," I said. "Oh, thanks, father!"

"See if you like it first," he said, and we went into the library together.

He couldn't resist giving us presents, in and out of season. I already had two knives, but this one was fitted with every imaginable small tool, sixteen of them in all. I have it still.

"Dearest, what on earth will Halley do with *ce machin là?*" my mother asked when I showed it to them. "We hope he'll never be cast away on a desert island."

"Well, I had a lot of fun buying it," my father said. "It's something I longed for when I was a boy and was never allowed to have." He went to my mother and dropped a small parcel in her lap. "Here's something for you, sweetheart," he said, and stooping, he kissed her forehead. Then he crossed to the sofa. "And I've got one for you, Syl."

Syl's present was a silver, Georgian skewer. He collected them, and always opened his letters with one. My mother made a little exclamation. She was holding up a gold bracelet for us all to see.

"What on earth have you got on your conscience, my darling?" she cried gaily. "This is awfully pretty and so unmistakably from Paris. I love it. Bless you!" And with a light movement she got up from behind the tea table and went and kissed him.

My father was standing with his back to the fire, holding a tea-cup.

"Well," he said, smiling round at us, "it was just one of those after-noons when the Avenue and everything on it looked lovely; the shops, the women in their furs, the lights just coming on, a deep yellow sunset glow under the edge of the clouds, a few snowflakes falling softly—you know how it is. I just had to go in and buy things."

Syl looked up at him shrewdly, his mouth pursed over those big teeth.

"Spill it, my boy," he said, wrapping up his skewer. "That isn't all. You've done something you didn't orter have done. I can read you like a child's ABC."

"Frankly," my father said, and even I could see how happy he was, how utterly content with everything, "frankly I suppose I have. I stepped into Blair & Fernando's—all right, Syl, keep calm—and, by golly, Ruth, they had something there I just couldn't say no to. I know I ought to have told you both about it first—especially you, Syl, as Ruth never scolds me—but it simply took my breath away. I knew I had to have it. I took the plunge then and there and bought it. Guess what it was. You can each of you have a guess."

"A Boudin," my mother said.

"No, not a Boudin."

"One of those great fat pink naked Renoirs you're so fond of," Syl said. My father shook his head, smiling.

"A Delacroix," I guessed, remembering the two in Paris that he coveted.

"All wrong. All wrong."

"Well, whatever it was," Syl said, delaying my father's moment of triumph, "why, at least, haven't you got the ordinary common sense to keep out of Blair & Fernando's? You know perfectly well they take the pants off you every time."

"I'm not such a fool as you think, Syl," my father said. "I beat them down a thousand." And then he made his announcement. "It's a Van Gogh. It's a marvel. Golly! Wait, just wait till you see those yellow fields fairly writhing under the sun. It's cheap at any price. I simply had to have it."

"You might just mention the price in passing," Syl suggested, "if you can force your lips to utter anything as outrageous as the sum those bandits have got out of you. Hold on to your hats, everybody. Here it comes!"

"I got it for nineteen thousand," my father announced, and looked defiantly at Syl.

"Is that all right, Syllie dear?" my mother asked with a little show of anxiety such as a bird might display over the disposal of a straw in a nest.

"No, it isn't, but we can sell some U.S. Steel," Syl said. "They've gone to a new high level, luckily for our spendthrift friend here."

"That's just what I thought," my father said. "If I can't buy one or two things during a boom period, when can I? I'm sorry, dearest, I hate buying a picture when you're not with me, but I couldn't wait. This is an absolute knockout." He looked at a picture on the wall opposite. "It had better go there, I think. The Bonnard can go upstairs somewhere. I'm just a little tired of Madame Chose at the breakfast table."

"Look out you don't get sent to the attic one of these days, Ruth," Syl said, getting up with a glance at my mother's portrait. He took the knife from my hands and looked at it. "Who can you show this off to, Halley," he asked, "now that Fred's debarred? Ask Ruth about that, Myron. No one but Clarisse and Julian and Raymond, I suppose."

I had been thinking that very thing. I had been picturing myself surrounded by a crowd of admiring boys, and without stopping to ask myself if I really meant it, I said, "Father, can I go to school next fall?"

There was a moment's surprised silence, then my father said, "Why, of course, Halley, if you want to. You know you can always do what you want to do. But it means saying good-by to Raymond, and no Europe, except during the summer holidays."

"Can't Raymond stay to teach Julian?" I asked.

"We could hardly expect Raymond to give his whole time to Julian," my mother said. "He ought to be tutoring boys for college. But if you really have a longing for school—"

"I haven't really," I said quickly. "It was only that—"

"I think myself the fall of next year will be plenty of time," my father said. "Plenty of time."

"Oh, let the boy go this year," Syl protested, giving me back the knife. "He's missing an awful lot."

"But Syl," my mother said, "of course Halley can go now if he wants to. As soon as they'll take him. Do you want to go, Halley? Never mind about being away from us all, I suppose it has to come sometime. And you needn't worry about losing Raymond. The point is, would you be happier at school?"

I was opening and shutting the little file in my knife.

"No," I said, "I wouldn't be happier. Of course I wouldn't. I'd much rather be with you. And I don't want Raymond to go."

"That would seem to settle it, then," my father said, smiling happily, "and in a way that pleases everybody. Syl, don't go away. Why don't you stay to dinner?"

[30]

"I would if I could," Syl said. "You know I'd rather be here than anywhere, but as it happens I'm dining out tonight."

"Tonight and tomorrow night and every night, I expect," my mother said. "Why don't you tell us where you're going, you old mystery box?"

Syl was longing to be asked this, and I expect she knew that he was. He steadied his pince-nez and said, "Oh, it's just one of Helen Vansittart's parties. She's giving it for Princess Vlasco, who's staying with her. There'll be about twenty of us. It's perfectly sweet of Helen to ask me, when she must have so many younger beaux she could ask."

"Rubbish," my mother said. "With all due respect, Syl dear, desirable single men are as hard to find as they always were."

"Well, I wish you and Myron were going to be there too," Syl said. "I simply can't understand why you always refuse to meet Helen. You act as though she had some sort of contagious disease."

"You know perfectly well why," my mother said, "and we're much too fond of you, Syl, to let you try to foist us on your friends. They'd find out that Myron was the son of that dreadful old Gideon Prentiss, and that I was the daughter of Mrs. Rudolf Denniker, and they'd remember all the scandal about her, and then, because they're fond of you they'd say, 'Still, I suppose we ought to ask them for Syl's sake.'"

"You're in Society with a big S," my father said, his arm about Syl's shoulders, "and we're not, and we don't want to be."

"All right, all right, you don't have to make speeches about it," Syl said, and it seemed very familiar to me, for I had heard it all before. He turned to me. "Look out for yourself, Halley, with that armory you've got there, and give my love to my little sweetheart. Tell her I'm sorry about that cold. A beautiful little nose like hers never ought to need blowing. Well, good night, my dears. Let me know as soon as that picture arrives. I want to see it."

"Of course," my mother said, turning her cheek to him to be kissed. "You're the one who has to find the money for it. Enjoy yourself, Syl, and pay your court to the Princess."

I went out into the hall with him, but Arnaud was already there. He helped Syl into his coat, and I saw Syl slip something into his hand. This, being a Continental custom, did not surprise me. Syl was there so much that he often gave Arnaud presents.

"You keep on about going to school this year, Halley," he said to me. "Just you nag at them till they let you go."

I nodded, but I knew I would do nothing of the sort. In the end it was Clarisse who brought the matter to a head, and in an unexpected way.

"Good night, Syl," I said. "Come again soon."

And then I showed Arnaud my knife.

III

I CANNOT REMEMBER MY PARENTS SPEAKING TO US AT ALL SERI-
ously about religion until I was in my fifteenth year. It was a subject
that, I imagine, rarely entered their minds. We sometimes spoke of
it amongst ourselves but as an idiosyncrasy of others that we neither
understood nor wished to understand. We would say of some contemporary, "Oh, he's churchy. He goes to church every Sunday," and
that meant that he and we could have little in common. This did
not apply to the young Dumonts because we knew that churchgoing
was insisted upon by their father and uncle. Our beloved Syl of
course went regularly to church and even helped to take up the
collections, but we looked on him as an old man with, we supposed,
an old man's fear of dying. Only people who were frightened of
death, we concluded, went to church voluntarily, and when death
was as remote and unimaginable as it was to us, churchgoing was
like going to hospital when one was perfectly well—silly, unnecessary
and even cowardly.

Both Miss Bewlay and Raymond, I learnt later, had been instructed not to allow religious matters to intrude into our studies. I
know now that my parents had a real horror of the Old Testament
and I remember hearing my father say that the New Testament
could only be understood by mystics. The whole subject of religion
was one in which they felt completely lost; a dark continent to which
they had neither map nor guide.

But one winter evening in New York my father surprised us by
saying, "Children, your mother and I have been talking about what
sort of religious teaching you ought to have, or if you need to have
any. Personally I think you can do very well without it if you've
been properly brought up, and I'm sure you have been." He was
speaking with the slight hesitation—it was not quite a stammer—that
was always a sign of embarrassment with him. "You've been taught
to speak the truth, honor your father and your mother, love one

another, be kind to animals and all the rest of it." He broke off and threw an appealing glance at my mother.

"It's Raymond who's been worrying us about it," she said. "He thinks you ought to know more about religion. He belongs to the Dutch Reform Church because his parents do. If your father and I belonged to a church we'd be Episcopalians and so would you. Well, I don't know how you feel about it. It's all very complicated and puzzling, but would you like to join a church and be confirmed? I'm afraid you'd have to be baptized first. You see, your father and I don't believe in the doctrine of Original Sin, but I won't go into all that now. Neither your father nor I have ever been confirmed, but that needn't influence you. Rosie and Helen and Fred have, and most other people, I suppose. How do you feel about it?"

She looked at us and waited, frowning a little and twisting one of her rings. I think she felt herself to be out of her depth and was not liking it. Clarisse was on the sofa beside my father and Julian was on the floor, where he always preferred to be, reading a book on the care of dogs. He had been carrying it about ostentatiously for some time. As the eldest I knew I was expected to speak first but for once Julian was ahead of me.

He lifted his head from his book. "I wouldn't mind being a Quaker," he said, and his face flushed.

"A Quaker?" my mother repeated, surprised, and my father asked, "Now what on earth makes you say that, Julian?"

Looking very self-conscious, Julian replied, "Because they don't have to listen to sermons and they don't believe in going to wars."

"We trust there'll never be another war," my father said. "And as for sermons, I don't think listening to a few would hurt you very much."

There was a brief silence and then Clarisse spoke.

"I'd rather be a Swedenborgian," she said. She pronounced it with a hard g and my mother corrected her and then asked, "What gave you that idea? I didn't know you'd ever heard of them."

"Rosie knows a girl who is," Clarisse answered. "She was telling me about it. I'd like to be one because there aren't many Swedenborgian churches to go to and because it's different."

My father laughed indulgently and patted Clarisse's cheek.

"Well, Clarry, that's honest anyway," he said.

"I don't think either you or Julian are being very helpful," my mother said. "What about you, Halley? You're the only one old enough to have a sensible opinion."

"I don't see why I should belong to any church," I said. "It seems to me that as soon as you belong to a church you have to disapprove of all the other churches. And look at all the wars of religion. No thanks, I'd rather keep out of it all, like you and father." And I felt I was washing my hands of Popish plots, the Inquisition and the persecutions of all the ages.

"The point is," my mother persisted, as if she wanted her conscience to be perfectly clear, "do any of you feel you're missing anything by not joining a church? Because if you do—"

We all assured her we weren't conscious of missing anything at all.

"At least," Julian corrected himself, "I only miss one thing and I guess everybody knows what that is. They ought to by now."

"Yes, we all know, darling, but your father and I feel we really can't have a dog here unless you'd be content with a very small one, and even a small dog would have to be left behind when we go abroad."

"You say we've been taught to be kind to animals," he argued, "but we haven't got any animals to be kind to."

What Julian wanted was a boxer. He'd seen one on Fifth Avenue and had fallen in love with it. Now nothing else would satisfy him.

"If such a powerful animal as this boxer you've taken a fancy to were to turn on any of you," my father said, "it would be disastrous. I'd never forgive myself. Now I don't want you to keep on worrying us about this, my boy."

So we passed from the subject of religion to the subject of dogs. After this my father told us that he and my mother had decided to take a furnished house in London for the spring and part of the summer and if we liked we could ask Fred or Rosie or both to stay with us. In August we'd go to some French seaside resort for the good of our healths. Clarisse and I expressed our pleasure at these prospects but Julian sulked and took no further part in the talk.

Not long after this Fred dropped in unexpectedly one snowy afternoon. The sounds of passing cars were muffled, and every now and then there was a fresh flurry of snow but the main fall was over and the clouds were breaking. I had a sore throat and was staying at home, my parents had gone to a matinee and Raymond had obligingly taken Clarisse and Julian to a party. Arnaud showed Fred into the library where I was sitting reading and I was surprised to see that he wore a black tie and looked unusually solemn. He even brought in with him a pair of black kid gloves.

He told me at once that he'd just been to the funeral of one of his best friends, like himself a sophomore at Harvard.

"Ever been to a funeral, Halley?" he asked me, sitting down and carefully pinching up the creases in his trousers. I told him I never had.

"Well, except for my mother's funeral when I was a kid, it was the first time for me," he said, "and gosh! it gave me the willies! Do you believe in another life? I know I ought to, especially after seeing Ed put in the ground, but I don't know. What do we do all day long if we live forever? It seems a heck of a long time."

"I guess if there is another life," I said, "time there would be different from our time. It wouldn't be divided up into hours and days, would it? There wouldn't be any clocks for one thing."

"Just a sort of timeless existence?" he asked, frowning. "Is that what you think? Ed wouldn't like it. He was a restless sort of guy, always wanting to be doing the next thing. I wouldn't like it either." He slapped his knee lightly with his black gloves. "Hell, it's no good thinking about it, I guess."

Arnaud came in then with a decanter of sherry and one glass—I was only supposed to drink with my meals—and he put it on a table beside Fred's chair.

"Thanks, Arnaud, I need it," Fred said. "I've just been to a funeral. I suppose you've been to a lot of funerals in your time. Is that right?"

Arnaud knew a good deal of English but he never spoke it if he could help it. A French butler is a French butler, and I think he would have felt he was letting us down if he did.

"Enough, Monsieur Fred, enough," he answered in French. "They are very sad, especially in winter."

"You've said it," Fred answered with fervor. It was his new way of agreeing with anybody. "*Triste!* I'll say it was *triste*." Arnaud went out and Fred poured himself a very full glass of sherry.

"Where's Clarisse?" he asked.

I told him she'd gone to a party with Julian.

"She'd go anywhere," he said, "just for the pleasure of being looked at. That girl's too easy on the eye for her own good, and I mean that."

"I don't see why," I answered. "I think it's pretty hard on a girl not to be pretty."

"A girl needn't be all that pretty," he said, and his expression was disapproving.

"Well, it isn't her fault," I retorted. "She was born that way."

"I never said it was, did I? All the same if she was my sister she wouldn't get away with a whole lot she gets away with here. You can bet Rosie doesn't." He took out a cigarette and lit it and then held out the case to me. "Smoke yet?" he asked.

"No, of course not," I said. "I'm not going to smoke till I'm eighteen and maybe not then."

"You will, brother, you will," he said. "So this time she's taken the kid along, has she? Seems to me she pretty near runs this family. Julian got anything to say for himself nowadays?"

I answered, feeling a little annoyed by his critical tone, "Julian's all right. He's the sort of boy who develops late, I expect."

"Late," he repeated with a hoot of laughter, "late! You said it, brother, not me. Oh, well. Going abroad this summer as usual?"

"Yes," I said. "Why don't you come with us? You and Rosie. I know mother's going to ask you. She said so."

"Well, we can't this year," he told me. "Dad's taken a fishing camp up in Maine, with a couple of guides and all that. It ought to be a lot of fun. Rosie's crazy to go and so am I. Maybe I'll shoot a moose. Why don't you come along for a while? I should think you'd be sick of Europe."

"Why should I be?" I asked. "Anyway, we've taken a house in London for four months, and in August we'll probably go to France. I do wish you'd come."

He shook his head.

"Too tame for me. Still, maybe I'll come next year, at that, just for a look around. When do Clarisse and the kid get back?"

I said I thought in half an hour or so.

"Guess I won't wait, then." But he did wait, as I knew he would, and he talked to me about Harvard and about what clubs had tried to get him—only lately, it appeared, the one he wanted to join. He drank two more glasses of sherry.

"When are they going to let you go to school like other people?" he asked me. "I think you're nuts to go on having a tutor. I don't know anybody else who does. It doesn't make sense to me."

I said it wasn't a case of their letting me. I didn't want to go till next year.

"Baloney," he said. "If you're thinking of going to Groton they won't like taking you so late. Still, I guess Uncle Syl can fix that, as he's one of the trustees. How's old Raymond these days? Think he can really get you into Groton all right?"

"Goodness yes," I told him. "I could go any time I liked. Passing exams doesn't worry me."

"Smart lad," he said. "Well, maybe you are pretty smart, at that."

There was the sound of a taxi coming to the house and stopping and then a key turned in the front door. Fred immediately straightened his tie and stood up. "I'll just say hello," he said to me, "and then I'll be off."

Clarisse came into the room first. I think she had smelt cigarette smoke—my father never smoked—and guessed who was there. She went straight to Fred and held up her face for a kiss. I was surprised to see that when Fred bent his head to her level she kissed him on the mouth, or anyway I thought she did. When I looked at Fred's face I was quite sure.

"I've been to a party," she announced, "and a good one. How are you, Fred?"

"Fine," he answered, looking at her. She took off the red cloth coat she was wearing and under it she had on her best party dress, black velvet with a white lace collar. The velvet made her skin and hair look lighter and her eyes darker.

"Why are you looking so funny?" she asked Fred. "Oh, I see, it's that horrible black tie. And black gloves, too!" she cried. "Have you been to a funeral or something?"

He told her he had and whose funeral it was and said he was feeling very depressed. As he was speaking, Julian and Raymond came in and Fred greeted them somberly. Then he sat down again and Clarisse sat on the arm of his chair.

"It's silly to be depressed," she said. "We've all got to die, haven't we? And when you're dead you don't know whether you've lived a long time or a short time."

"You might show Fred a little sympathy," Raymond protested mildly. "It's always sad to lose a good friend."

She reached for the decanter and held it up to the light.

"Well," she said, "he seems to have been consoling himself, anyway. It was nearly full at lunchtime. We had punch at our party."

"It was only fruit punch," Julian said.

"Well, anyway it was punch," she insisted. "I had a lovely time. Julian wouldn't dance and he wouldn't even talk, so I guess he didn't have much fun."

"You don't ever get me to a party again," said Julian. "I just despise them."

"It's a pretty poor prospect for me, then," Clarisse said, and she took a hair off Fred's collar. "One brother who's too old to go out with me and one who's too young. I need a boy friend. Will you take me out sometime, Fred?"

"Sometime," he answered and he got up and stood by the fireplace, I thought because he wanted to look at her.

"Halley often goes out with you," Raymond reminded her. "Don't be so ungrateful."

"Yes," she said, "Halley's pretty good, but I need a boy friend all the same. Where did you go, Raymond, while we were at the party? I forgot to ask you."

"I went to a movie," he said. "*Robin Hood*. Quite absurd but quite enjoyable."

Fred slapped his palm with his black gloves.

"I've seen it," he said. "It wasn't so hot. Too many acrobatics. Well, I guess I'll be getting along. Give my love to your mother and father."

"Tell Rosie I'll ring her up in the morning," Clarisse said. "I want her for something."

"Making dolls' clothes, I suppose," Fred remarked.

"Don't be so silly," she retorted. "I never did play with dolls, even when I was a child, and you know it perfectly well."

"Clarisse has no maternal instincts," Raymond said.

"Who wants to have maternal instincts at my age?" she demanded. "I'm only fourteen. Give me time!"

"You're a lot too old for your age in some ways, take it from me," said Fred, "and I mean that."

I guessed that he was scolding her for that kiss and that she knew it. They exchanged looks and then Fred went to the door.

"Well, good-by, all," he said. "I'll be seeing you."

"Good-by," Clarisse called after him, "you old prig."

He made no reply to this. I went to the door with him and helped him into his overcoat.

"Come again soon, Fred," I said.

"Sure," he answered, "if I can. I guess I'll be pretty busy from now on. So long, Halley."

Looking back it is easy for me to see that he had long ago fallen in love with Clarisse and that, child though she was, she was perfectly well aware of it. He always seemed to worry about her a good deal. He used to say to me sometimes, "Keep your eye on that sister of yours, Halley. You can never tell what she'll be up to. And I mean that."

[39]

"Oh," I would answer, "Clarisse is all right. She's full of life, that's all."

"Brother," he would reply, "you've said it. But just you remember to keep an eye on her. Now I'm telling you."

All this, I decided, was just Fred's way of talking. Older than we were, he liked to display superior knowledge and often hinted at mysterious sources of information denied to us. If we asked him how he knew he would reply, "I know, and that ought to be enough for you kids." In talking to me he sometimes referred to matters of which I understood nothing at all and being at that time both diffident and lacking in curiosity, I let them pass without asking him questions. But he never allowed the difference in our ages to affect our friendship. It was partly, I think, because as a family we fascinated him; the fact that our lives were so different from his drew him like a magnet. He was especially devoted to my mother and liked to tell people that when she forbade him the house after the speakeasy episode, "It knocked me right back on my heels," he would say, "and I'm telling you! Gosh! It took me pretty near a year to get back into her good graces again."

Whether being forbidden the house had any effect or not—and I thought it largely fanciful—Fred had early abandoned his wild ways. He drank rather less than the average young man, and never drank more than was seemly on social occasions. (The fact that he had had three sherries that afternoon only showed how the funeral had upset him.) When he was working hard or in training he never touched alcohol, and as he showed promise of becoming something of a football hero at Harvard, his health and fitness were of importance to him. When he took girls out they were nearly always the daughters of family friends, or school friends of Rosie's, and even my parents found nothing to cavil at, except that he was a "typical" young American who had never been abroad.

As for Syl, he was highly gratified at the way Fred was "shaping."

"Fred," he would say, "is as clean-living a young man as you could find in New York, and I'm mighty proud of him."

As I watched him walking away from our front door I envied him his good shoulders and athletic build. I had not yet reached my full height—five feet eleven inches—and I weighed only a hundred and thirteen pounds, but I said to myself that if I had to play football in order to look like Fred, I would just as soon stay as I was.

We went to London at the beginning of April, 1926, and the house in Sixty-sixth Street was closed, as usual, for the summer. My father used to pay Mrs. Schwarz, the cook, and Norah, the housemaid, retaining fees and they took temporary jobs while we were away. But Arnaud was considered irreplaceable and was paid his full wages whether we were there or not. He now owned a car but it did not accord with his ideas of propriety to drive himself to and from his work so he always came by bus from the West Side where he lived. The chauffeur, Johnson, was lent that summer to Syl, who, feeling wildly adventurous, was planning to spend a month or so touring Massachusetts and New Hampshire, visiting the country homes of his friends and later, still more adventurously, had promised to go to stay at his brother Irving's camp in Maine.

The Dumont family resembled ours in its closeness and clannishness. Syl would have done anything in the world for any of them and he was especially devoted to Fred, who was destined later on to join the firm of Dumont, Rowan and Dumont. Thanks to his brother's family and to his many good friends, Syl did not feel the lack of a family life of his own and he was never without the affection and intimacy that meant so much to him. It was impossible to think of Syl married, and if anyone teased him about his bachelorhood, he was deeply displeased. He was the perfect uncle, the perfect friend, the most dutiful of godfathers. My mother always took the greatest interest in his health and well-being and was quick to see when he was tired or out of sorts. None of us could imagine life without Syl. But one thing he would not do; he would never join us in Europe. European food, he would declare, disagreed with him, and though he had long been accustomed to our annual departures, he always grumbled when the time came to say good-by.

In London we occupied a big furnished house in Queen's Gate, close to Kensington Gardens. It had many stairs, was six stories high and had no elevator. The owners' four servants stayed on. Though I took it all for granted then it is a mystery to me now how my mother managed to run such houses with so little apparent effort. Her gift for getting on with people, for making everything go smoothly, was remarkable. Money was only part of the answer. It was rather that she had the wit and skill to extract the greatest possible ease and pleasure from it. She was so devoted to our comfort and happiness, of which her own happiness was the by-product, that to have failed to secure them would have seemed to her unforgivable.

The charm that the London of those days had for me is with me yet and I cannot look back on it without memories of happy expectation and fulfilled delight. My parents had useful friends who were always ready to get us tickets for anything we wanted to see: the Trooping of the Colour, Wimbledon on the best days, the Henley Regatta, the Tattoo at Aldershot. One of these friends was a middle-aged widower named Mr. Vivian Grantley, a tall, bearded man who wore a monocle, collected Chinese porcelains and had a place in Hertfordshire called "Wycks." He used to ask us all to stay with him there, Raymond too, and of course Louise, and it was a very comfortable house to be in. There was an old butler who used to come into Julian's and my bedrooms every morning after an equally old housemaid had drawn back our curtains and given us early tea, and he would put out our clothes for the day. This fascinated Julian.

"How *can* he know what we want to put on?" he would ask me as if seeking the answer to some profound mystery.

As I look back it seems nearly always to have been English summer at its best, though I well know this to have been one of the illusions of youth. The only bad period that stands out clearly in my memory is the time of the General Strike, in May of that year, when a cold wind blew week after week, and my parents, alarmed at what seemed to them a sudden instability in a country they had hitherto trusted, heartily wished themselves in Paris. Apart from this I seem best to remember London mornings that were colored by a faint, brownish haze through which the sun presently shone warm and golden, and flower sellers pushed their barrows through the streets with unintelligible cries and the trees in the squares and parks stood at ease after their green exertions.

We had lessons at nine every morning and Clarisse, that spring, decided to join us. She took to Latin in the most surprising way, and, thanks to Miss Bewlay, already knew nearly as much history as I did. Raymond said she had a remarkable facility for acquiring knowledge quickly and it was a great pity she was so bone lazy.

My parents made frequent visits to Paris, where they saw old friends (Mr. Harper Brandon died that summer in the way he would have wished to die—stricken suddenly at one of his own parties and dead in ten seconds) and busied themselves with art dealers and picture buying. My father's collection was becoming more and more important, both to him and to the few connoisseurs who were familiar with it. When he bought a new picture, items usually appeared in the newspapers, and he would cut them out and paste them into an album. As yet, the Prentiss Collection was hardly known at all to the public, but this did not trouble my father in the least. He was biding his time. The day would come when it would be accessible to art students and others, though he had not so far made up his mind how or where.

At the end of June something happened which greatly startled us all—or all except Julian who knew nothing about it, and Clarisse, who was the cause of it. I had no way of estimating its importance and to me it was unforgettable and disturbing. I can remember all the sensations that accompanied it: the sinking feeling in my stomach, the slight nausea—for when I was emotionally upset my stomach was immediately affected—and the fear that something dreadful and irrevocable had taken place.

We had just finished our lessons and Clarisse and I were washing our hands in the downstairs lavatory before lunch. Julian, for some reason, had gone upstairs. Clarisse was drying her hands as I was washing mine and she was unusually quiet. I remember perfectly the appearance of that little place; the green walls, the green linoleum on the floor, the small, barred, half-open window through which came the twittering of sparrows in the elm tree outside.

"Halley," Clarisse suddenly said, pushing back the cuticle at the base of her nails as we had been taught to do, "what would you say if I told you that I was madly in love with Raymond?"

A different boy, differently brought up, a boy who had lived with other boys, would probably have burst out laughing, or jeered, or been rudely scornful, but to me, bounded as I was by my family, this seemed indescribably shocking, catastrophic. I felt as if I and all of us had been overtaken by some disaster that we ought to have foreseen. For a moment I couldn't speak. The thought came to me that if I were going to be sick I could hardly have been in a better place.

"Clarisse!" I cried, after staring at her open-mouthed. "You can't possibly be in love with Raymond. What possesses you to say such a terrible thing?"

(How much was pure shock, how much anguished jealousy? Both, I am sure, were present.)

"Why can't I be in love with him?" she demanded. "I must be in love. Why else do you suppose I'm having lessons with you? I don't have to have lessons with you. I want to be with him the whole time, that's why. I don't ever want to be away from him. I'll tell you something else. I'd give anything I possess in this world if he'd kiss me just once. I'd give my new wrist watch, my seed pearls, anything."

She handed me the towel and I stood holding it inertly, unable to stop staring at her.

"Clarisse!" I cried again. "You mustn't say such dreadful things. I never could have believed—I don't believe it. It just isn't so."

She made an impatient little sound and swung her hair. Even that familiar gesture now seemed strange to me.

"Don't be so silly, Halley. I'm growing up and it's time I knew something about falling in love." (She was not yet fifteen.) "And now I do know. It's marvelous! Just you wait till it happens to you. When he touches me accidentally I could almost faint. I'd die for him, and oh, I hope he'd die for me. Do you think he would?"

I had just common sense enough to say, "Die for you? Why should he?"

"You'd die for me, wouldn't you?" she demanded, and her dark eyes, that were so like my mother's and yet so unlike, seemed to probe mine as if something of importance hung upon my answer.

I said quite seriously, "Yes, I suppose I would."

"Would you die for Julian?"

"I don't know," I said. "I'd rather not have to."

"Well, you see the difference," she said. "I make people feel that way about me, I know I do. Father would die for me and so would Syl I think, and I'm pretty sure Fred would. Do you want to know something?" She lowered her voice. "I put a note under Raymond's pillow last night."

What abomination, I wondered, was I to hear next?

"You're crazy, Clarisse," I cried outraged. "You must be crazy. What would father and mother say? They'd be furious, you know they would."

"Well, I felt awfully brave when I did it," she told me. "Go on and dry your hands, Halley. The gong will go in a minute. I told Raymond last night. I said, 'Feel under your pillow when you go to bed,' so he must have found it."

"What did you say in the note?"

"Oh," she said, with bravado, "I just told him I adored him and always would."

I could only repeat, aghast, "You must be crazy."

"I suppose people in love are a little crazy," she said. "It's one of the signs." We heard the luncheon gong booming from the hall. "You see," she went on, "I don't want to fall in love with anyone outside the family. It's so much cozier like this. Do you know what I mean?" And she hugged herself and smiled.

"I'm going to tell mother," I said, but I knew I wouldn't and she must have known it too. I foresaw the changes it might bring and dreaded them. My world already seemed to be in dissolution and I would do nothing to hasten it. And although at that moment I felt I hated Raymond and never wanted to see him again, I knew in my heart that he was without guilt or guile, and I believed he might know best how to deal with this.

As we went into the hall I asked, dreading her answer, "Has he said anything to you about it?"

"No," she answered, "he hasn't had a chance to yet. But he's bound to speak sooner or later."

Things did not turn out at all as Clarisse expected. The second housemaid, who did our rooms and Raymond's, found the note when she was making his bed and took it straight to my mother. Raymond, either not understanding or not hearing what Clarisse had said, had not looked under his pillow. It was plain to me as we sat at the table—my father was out that day—that my mother knew, though I couldn't guess how she knew, for she only once spoke to Clarisse, to reprove her for drinking too much water with her food, and hardly at all to Raymond, and there was a worried line between her eyebrows. As soon as lunch was over she called Raymond into the breakfast room where we had our lessons and they were shut up in there for about twenty minutes. When they came out, Raymond's fair skin had gone scarlet and the scar on his forehead showed up very white. Clarisse was sitting with her sketchbook on her knee doing a sketch of Julian and trying not to show that she was frightened, and Raymond threw her an icy glance and said sharply,

"Halley, Julian, get your caps. We're going for a walk. I need some air."

"Am I invited too?" Clarisse asked, her head on one side as she looked at her drawing.

"No, Clarisse, I want you," my mother said. "Put away your sketching things and come upstairs."

I dared not look at Clarisse, nor did she glance my way. Julian, who hated walking, said he wanted to stay at home too.

"I don't need any exercise," he said. "I guess I've climbed these old stairs fifty times today."

"Get your cap, darling," my mother said, "and go out with Raymond. At three you're going on with your lessons again. I've canceled the car for this afternoon. You can go to Hampton Court another day."

All the time we were out I was anxiously wondering what my mother was saying to Clarisse and how she would deal with this calamity. Would things ever be the same again? The elm trees along the Broad Walk in Kensington Gardens looked different to me that day, and the unclouded sky, the warm, embracing sun, even the soft green glory of the grass seemed to warn me of disaster. I remember how fast Raymond walked and how little he said and how angry and troubled his face was.

When we got home I went at once to look for Clarisse, for I felt I had to know the worst. I couldn't find her anywhere. No voices came from my mother's room. At last I went to the door of Louise's bedroom and there I heard muffled sobs and Louise's voice, angry, acrid, saying, "*Votre maman a raison. C'est une chose incroyable. Une jeune fille si bien elevée—*"

I then went to my mother's room and knocked, my thoughts in a ferment. My mother was sitting at her dressing table pinning on a little hat rather like an inverted flower pot, with two roses at one side. She seemed remarkably calm.

"Halley," she said turning to me, "how long have you known about this?"

I wanted to be quite sure what she meant, so I asked cautiously, "About what, mother?"

"About Clarisse, of course. About this nonsense of hers. She told me you knew. I don't expect you children to go telling tales on one another, but if you knew she fancied herself in love with Raymond, you should have told me at once. She put a note under Raymond's pillow last night and Jessie found it and brought it to me. So now the whole household knows. I never heard of anything sillier or more outrageous. I'm extremely annoyed."

"She only told me when we were washing our hands before lunch," I said. "It was the first I'd heard of it."

"In that case you're not to blame. Of course girls do sometimes get these fantastic notions, but I never thought Clarisse—well, there it is. I don't know what your father will say."

"Must you tell him?" I asked.

"There's no must about it," she answered. "You know we always tell each other everything. I'm sorry, Halley, but I'm afraid Raymond will have to go. I don't blame him for what happened. The poor boy hadn't an inkling. Still, it wouldn't do to keep him with us now. You'll have to go to school this fall instead of next, I'm sorry to say. Will you mind that very much?"

It had come at last, one whole year before it need have come, the separation I had always dreaded.

"I don't mind," I said. "At least I do mind, but I'll go just the same."

She held out an arm to me. I went to her and she grasped my hair, pulled my head down and kissed me.

"You're such a satisfactory boy, Halley," she said. "I'm so glad you are."

"What's that perfume you use?" I asked.

"It's Chanel No. 5. Do you like it?"

"Yes," I said. "It's lovely."

"Do you like my new hat, Halley? Your father hasn't seen it yet."

"Yes," I answered. "It just suits you. Where are you going? I'd like to come too. Please let me come."

"No, darling," she said. "You must go on with your lessons. You'll have to work very hard till Raymond goes, and I expect your father will want him to go at the end of July."

"What will he do," I asked unhappily, "when he leaves us?"

"He'll be all right, darling. Your father will do whatever is right. We're very fond of Raymond. But we must write or cable to Syl at once about your going to Groton this fall. Now I'm going to meet your father at Knoedler's. He's been lunching with two of the directors. Bring me my handbag, will you, darling?"

Thanks to my mother's healing touch, my world was righting itself again, but I knew even then that I would remember that day long after Clarisse herself had forgotten it.

IV

For some time my mother kept Clarisse with her as much as possible and she no longer had lessons with Julian and me. I still think Raymond might safely have stayed another year, for after a week or two Clarisse seemed to have put the whole thing out of her mind. But my parents had received a shock—the first that any of us had given them—and were taking no chances. Just before we left for our holiday in Dinard, Raymond returned to New York.

I dreaded the parting. I knew how happy he had been with us and I was deeply attached to him. To lose him was to lose a part of myself. I wondered, too, if Clarisse had been acting, and would perhaps show her real feelings when the time came, so I was amazed and even hurt when I heard her say that Raymond was really rather an old woman and she thought he had been with us quite long enough. It was different when Julian, who prided himself on having no attachments outside the immediate family, said, "I shan't miss him. I never really liked him and he never really liked me." All the same, when the time for Raymond's departure came I could see that he was sorry.

"Be sure to come and see us when we're back in New York," my mother said to Raymond when it was almost time for his taxi to come. "You must always keep in touch with us."

"Yes, don't forget us, Raymond, my boy," my father said, putting a hand on his shoulder. "We shall always look on you as one of the family."

"Forget you?" Raymond said, and though he tried hard to smile his lips were out of control and his voice broke. "Why, you're the best part of my life. When I think what I was like when I first came to you—just a poor, frozen Dutchman. I didn't know there was such warmth and kindness in the world." He took out his handkerchief and blew his nose. "If I try to thank you I shall probably burst into tears."

[48]

"Oh, do cry, Raymond, do!" Clarisse exclaimed, clapping her hands. "I've never seen you cry."

"I wouldn't cry in front of you, you hard-hearted little monster," Raymond said, putting his handkerchief away, and his words showed, I thought, how everything had been forgotten. "I hope when you go to school the other girls will bully the life out of you."

"I'd just like to see them try," Clarisse said, and added, "besides, I may not go to school at all, ever." She took my mother's arm and put it about her neck, snuggling closer to her. "I want to stay at home. I expect I know as much as the teachers do and a lot more than the girls."

"Well, heaven help them, if that's the case," Raymond said. "Julian is the only one of you three who hasn't got an exaggerated idea of his own cleverness."

"That's because I'm not clever," Julian said. "And anyway, I don't like myself. The others do like themselves."

"Don't you like yourself, my precious?" my mother asked, smiling at him. "Why? We like you."

"You may," Julian answered. "Nobody else does."

I knew then, with troubled certainty, that Julian felt himself to be different from the rest of us, and that although he was so deeply and closely a part of us, he yet felt isolated. I wondered if I were the only one to be aware of this.

My father threw him an impatient glance and said, "Don't talk such nonsense, Julian. I think your taxi ought to be here, Raymond. I don't want to hurry you but I don't want you to be late, either." He took out his thin pocket watch as he spoke. He was as concerned that other people should be in good time as that he himself should be. "Go and see if Briggs has found a taxi, Clarry."

Clarisse disengaged my mother's arm and went to the window.

"Here he is now," she said, "and he's got a nice new shiny one, not one of those old rattletraps."

Raymond began saying good-by. My mother took one of his hands in both hers.

"Good-by, dear Raymond. We shall miss you badly, but we always knew the parting had to come someday. I hope that wherever you are you'll be very, very happy."

"Good-by, my boy," my father said. "The best of luck. And if you think you'd like a job at the Smithsonian, just let me know and I'll get in touch with Dr. Ascher at once."

Raymond then shook hands with Clarisse and I marveled that

[49]

they showed no signs of awkwardness. Did she remember saying she would give her seed pearls for one kiss from him?

"Bye-bye," she said gaily. "Make lots of money and be sure to let us know when you get married."

"Good-by, Raymond," Julian said. "I guess you're glad you won't have to worry about my mathematics any more."

We all went to the door with him and saw him into the taxi. I shook hands with him again very hard but I couldn't speak and I was afraid the tears in my eyes would overflow. I stood waving until he was out of sight.

"Don't look so downcast, Halley," my mother said. "We're sure to see him from time to time in New York."

"I won't," I said, "if I'm away at school. I'll be out of everything."

"That reminds me," my father said, "that it's high time we heard from Syl. I cabled him over two weeks ago. I suppose he's moving about from one place to another."

Syl's cable in reply came two days later, and my father read it aloud to us.

"Commit any indiscretions you like over there," it said. "Wall Street booming and I sold a block of your C.P.R.s at handsome profit. Tell Halley everything fixed up for Groton in the fall and congratulate him for me. Hurrah. He's on his way at last. My love to you all, not forgetting my little sweetheart. Fine up here and Helen's farm a city man's paradise. Every possible comfort. Moving on next week to Cape Cod, care of Robert Price Llwellyn. Blessings, Syl."

I had heard so much about Groton from Syl that I knew what to expect, and I neither liked nor disliked it, though for the first three months I was cripplingly homesick. But I made a few friends and as I never craved popularity and couldn't understand the importance that the others, both at Groton and later at Harvard, attached to it, I didn't suffer from the lack of it. The world in which I most fully lived did not lie within the walls of either school or college. Apart from work, which I took seriously, all the rest was a kind of dream state from which I awoke thankfully at the end of each term. Unfortunately for me, I was at once nicknamed Halitosis, which was inevitable, I suppose, as the magazines of the time made so much use of the word in their toothpaste advertisements. I only hoped it wouldn't follow me to Harvard.

In 1927, my parents rented a furnished house on the Thames for the summer. They had seen it advertised in *Country Life* and after much cabling to and fro had decided to take it. They invited Fred to join us and he said he would, so he and I arranged to go to England on the same boat.

Julian now had his own tutor, Henry Burroughs, a thin young man with a bad complexion. My mother could hardly have found anyone less likely to attract Clarisse and I think that is partly why she chose him. We were all worried at that time about Julian's health. He was running temperatures for no apparent reason and had lately begun to have attacks of asthma, and my parents decided it was better to make no plans for sending him to school until he had outgrown these disabilities, as they were assured he would. I tried to find out how he felt about this, but he didn't seem to care much either way.

I had several letters from him after they were settled in the house on the river, and one came just before Fred and I left New York.

As of now [he wrote], I'm feeling pretty low. My health is poor, I don't really like Henry Burroughs and I'm wondering what I'm going to make of my life. Not much, I opine. [He had a fondness for using such words.] The rest of the family are enjoying themselves as usual and spend as much time as they can on the river, but it's been pretty cold so far most of the time. I keep wondering why I don't enjoy myself the way other people seem to do and how I'm going to fit myself into the scheme of things, if any. This place is all right, if the weather ever becomes more salubrious, though the house is sort of Edwardian, I guess, and it's full of the most awful pictures. Father keeps turning them to the wall but mother turns them back again. The gardens are pretty and go right down to the river, and there's a tennis court and an electric launch. Henry keeps trying to interest me in tennis but I can't say it appeals to me, and anyway the doctors say I oughtn't to take violent exercise. I'll tell you though what there is here. There's a thoroughbred red setter, a beauty, and he and I go for walks together, which helps. He likes me better than anybody now. Clarisse disports herself in a bathing suit a good deal, especially where people can look at her, but the water's too cold for me. Will you bring over my field glasses please? I've taken to watching birds. Henry was supposed to bring them, but he forgot and the ones here in the house are no good. This will be all for now.

> Your affectionate brother,
> Julian

Fred and I had a good trip across the Atlantic and he made a number of friends on the boat. When we reached Southampton and took the train to London his attitude towards everything he saw was condescending, which was more or less what I had expected, but I guessed, too, that it would pass. We spent a night in London at Brown's Hotel, ("Gosh! This is like something out of Dickens," was Fred's comment,) and went to a play.

My father sent the car to meet us at Abingdon and Clarisse was there waiting for us. She flung her arms about my neck and then about Fred's and said she had never been so thankful to see anybody.

"Oh, I'm so glad you're here!" she cried, walking arm-in-arm between us to the car. "Julian's such an old stick-in-the-mud he's no fun at all and now he's got this asthma which makes him worse. And I loathe Henry Burroughs. No, I don't really loathe him, but he's such a weed. Now you two are here we'll have a lovely time. I've learnt how to punt and I'll show you."

She kept looking at Fred in an appraising way and I could see that she was pleased with him. He was a very typical young American, I suppose, in most ways, and especially in appearance; he was the fair-haired, blue-eyed, Anglo-Saxon type and he seemed to me most enviably sure of himself. His thick, blond hair waved up from his forehead almost too luxuriantly, his teeth were perfect and he had a frank smile which came easily and always accompanied his too firm handshake. Tall and well built, he might have posed for one of those advertisements for Arrow Collars or Somebody-or-other's shirts. He was very fond of us all and my parents treated him almost like another son. He got an affectionate welcome from both of them when we arrived, and my mother kissed him and said she was only sorry Rosie hadn't come too, but she had promised to come over the following year. Julian, they said, was in his room resting, so presently I ran up to see him.

The house was as he'd described it—very Edwardian, with lots of glazed chintzes and mirrors everywhere and pieces of china in glass cases. There were dozens of photographs, too, mostly of ladies in Court gowns and feathers, and men in uniform. The paintings were awful and I could sympathize with my father for wanting to turn them to the wall. Julian's room—I knew it was his because he'd pinned a notice, "Private, keep out," on the door—was on the third floor and looked out on a paved courtyard and across to some brick stables where there was a big clock and a weathervane. He told me he'd chosen it himself. I thought he looked a bad color and I felt very sorry for him. He said the doctors were sure his asthma was caused by the state of his nerves, and besides he suspected that the

Thames Valley didn't suit him. It was too low and too damp. As we talked it didn't seem to me that his mind was on what we were saying, and soon I knew the reason. He presently snapped his fingers and a red setter came slowly out from under the bed looking shy, affectionate and embarrassed, as such dogs usually do. He sat thumping his tail on the carpet.

"Here's my best friend," said Julian with a sort of forlorn pride. "He understands pretty near everything I say to him. His name's Desmond. It's a funny name for a dog but of course he's Irish. He'll give you his paw if you ask him."

I did ask him, and he gave me his paw very nicely though I thought his embarrassment would be too much for him. Then he sat with his long muzzle on the bed and gazed into Julian's face with devoted eyes. I could see that this was a mutual love affair all right.

I asked Julian if he'd like Fred to come up but he said no, he'd rather see him when he went down. And then he asked, "How are you getting on at Groton?"

"Oh," I said, "it's not so bad. I'm getting on all right I guess."

"I suppose you're the most popular person there by now," he said.

This made me laugh.

"A very long way from it, I'm afraid, but I've got a couple of pretty good friends." And then, for the first time, I told him about the nickname they'd given me. I felt it might even things up between us a little if he knew. He only looked sadder.

"I guess no one will ever give me a nickname," he said, and I could see that he envied me.

"What sort of a trip did you have?" he wanted to know.

"Fine," I told him. "Good weather all the way."

He turned his head on the pillow and looked out of the window.

"Good weather all the way," he repeated. "I shouldn't wonder if that mightn't be your epitaph one of these days."

"You really do have the queerest notions," I said. "When are you coming downstairs?"

He glanced at the little traveling clock my mother had given him on his last birthday.

"I must rest for another three quarters of an hour," he answered, and he closed his eyes.

"See you later then," I said, and I went down and joined the others.

During a recent stay in Paris my father had bought another

Cézanne—a *"Nature Morte"* this time—two Signacs and a Seurat. I wasn't particularly enthusiastic about these last, but my father was widening his scope now and buying some of the Pointillistes, so I supposed he had to have them. My mother had been urging him to buy a Modigliani, too, but so far he had resisted. "When you do decide to buy him," my mother said, "he'll have gone up in price." But my father was convinced that Modigliani's paintings had a fictitious value that wouldn't last. "A creation of the dealers," he objected, "and anyway, he belongs to the twentieth century."

I found the new acquisitions placed on chairs in the drawing room, and my mother and father, Fred and Clarisse were looking at them. I got there just in time to hear Fred say, in answer to some gibe of Clarisse's, "Well, but look here, I don't get any time to play about with art. How do you expect me to know?"

My father and mother were looking amused. My father turned to me and said, "Just in time, Halley. I was about to give our friend Fred a little talk about Cézanne, whom he doesn't seem to have heard of. You haven't seen these yet, my boy. What do you think of them?"

The Cézanne was a beauty and became one of my prime favorites. It didn't matter where you hung it, it triumphed anywhere. The others I wasn't sure about yet.

My father then turned to Fred.

"Fred," he said, "you may take it from me, as you've no way of judging for yourself at present, that Cézanne is one of the great masters of painting and that you're looking now at one of his masterpieces. I don't think I put it too strongly when I say that I'm extraordinarily, oh, fantastically lucky to have it" (I learnt later that a rich German industrialist had also been in the market for it and only the French dealer's preference for my father had enabled him to get it) "and that you are very lucky indeed to be living with it for the next few weeks. Among the Impressionists and Post-Impressionists he belongs in the top four. The others are Manet, Monet and Renoir. Remember those names. Sometimes I place one at the top, sometimes another, according to my mood, but it doesn't matter. There they are, the top four. Strictly speaking, Manet is not, technically, one of the Impressionists, but it simplifies matters to include him.

"I won't give you dates, you wouldn't remember them. Cézanne was born; he died. I was even lucky enough to have met him once, in my second year in Paris, through my good friend Vollard. A year later, he was dead. He was short, squat, bearded; a man you couldn't forget; he was also an invincible genius. He saw more deeply into nature than other men; he was irresistible. He was valued only after his death. These men's tragedy was that they lived in a world that was artistically blind and stupid. Was it a tragedy? It may have made them. I don't know. I think it would have killed me. Well, my boy, look at it. But is it any good telling you to look at it? Your eyes aren't opened yet, and words fail me. A landscape, I suppose, would be easier for you, might perhaps appeal to you more directly. First of all, just look at that white cloth. It is more than a white cloth. It might have been the white cloth that was placed in the tomb of Christ. All right, Ruth, I'll stop now. I get carried away. Halley, help me to hang this, will you? We shall have to drive a nail in the wall, but there'll be the usual bill for dilapidations anyway, so we may as well have some fun."

"Well, thanks, Uncle Myron, for the little talk," Fred said. "Maybe I'll learn better someday, but right at this moment I wouldn't give any of them house room."

"Oh, Fred!" cried Clarisse, "don't be such a complete Rotarian! I wish you'd learn something about something. All you know so far is some law and about the insides of cars."

He turned on her, seized her by her long hair and wound it about her neck.

"Take that back!" he demanded. "Take it back. And how do you know what Rotarians are like? You're hardly out of the shell yet. My dad happens to be one, see?"

"All right," she said laughing, "I'll take it back. Now let me go, you bully."

"Children, children," my mother said mildly. "Behave yourselves."

Clarisse was now an inch or more taller than my mother, but she still wore her hair long, and it was as straight as water falling out of a flume. Fred was always twisting it or winding it around his fist, and I could see that it fascinated him. Clarisse writhed herself free and said,

"Come along out. It's too nice to stay indoors. Come out in the punt and I'll show you how good I am at punting."

I joined them later and she gave us both a lesson in punting. I don't know who had taught her; she had probably picked it up from watching people going up and down the river. There were two young Oxford undergraduates, she told us, camping near by and she said they kept coming past our place in their boat and trying to make her acquaintance, but she'd paid them no attention.

"Oh, yeah?" Fred said. "I know just how you pay no attention to young males. I've seen you paying no attention to them pretty often and it's quite an act."

"Oh, shut up, Fred!" she cried. "When they stare at me I just go into the boathouse and wait till they've passed."

Fred couldn't take his eyes off her as she stood there working the punt pole. As she swayed her long hair swayed with her. It was certainly an attractive picture that she made and she knew it. She wore a short, sleeveless white dress and her arms and legs were golden in the late sun. The glassy, greeny-brown Thames slid by beneath the willows' shade and I felt lazily happy and at peace and at the very center of everything I loved. And there was no one to call me Halitosis.

Wherever we were, no matter how briefly we occupied a place, my mother had the knack of always making it ours. She usually began at once to arrange things a little differently—"Halley dear," she would say, "just help me to move this table, will you? It doesn't make sense where it is—" and she would scatter books and magazines about (*Harper's*, the *Atlantic Monthly* and *Country Life* followed us everywhere) and arrange flowers so that they looked happy and natural. She disliked studied effects in the arrangement of flowers or anything else. She possessed a room or a house to such a degree that it couldn't fail to take on our family atmosphere, which, of course, was her own creation. I can't say just what this was, but I know that any family that is a family has its own.

When my father was in England he became quite English. I don't know if he was aware of it, but his vowels altered noticeably, he wore his hat at a slightly different angle, carried a stick or an umbrella and more often than not had a book of poems in his pocket. There are of course plenty of Englishmen who would never dream of carrying a book of poems about with them, but my father resembled the sort of Englishman who would. Just now, I found, he was reading James Flecker and Rupert Brooke, and before the end of my first day there, while I was unpacking in fact, he came into my bedroom, sat down and read me Rupert Brooke's poem about fish. He read poetry aloud very well and I liked hearing him, but for some reason it was a little embarrassing when I was the only listener.

I could see Fred's infatuation for Clarisse growing every day and it amazed me that my parents seemed quite unaware of it. They probably thought that, having known each other as they had from childhood, there was no danger of any romantic attachment, but I knew better. When we were out together, going for trips up and down the river in *Cygnet*, the electric launch, or having picnics, they teased and criticized each other as they had always done, but they showed a fondness for slipping away together too, and I was pretty sure I knew why.

One windy, rainy day when all the charm of the river seemed to have fled forever and we'd been halfheartedly playing ping-pong to pass the time, Julian went up to his room to rest and Fred and Clarisse vanished somewhere, I thought into the drawing room where there was a big picture puzzle spread out on a table. I was in charge of the boats and it suddenly struck me that I might not have tied up the launch properly when we came in, and the gale might be blowing it about, so I ran down to the boathouse to see. I ran straight into a love scene. There the two of them were, wearing raincoats and standing against the inside wall of the boathouse clasped in each other's arms.

When they heard me they sprang apart and I could see instant relief on their faces when they saw it was only I who had burst in upon them. I stood there not knowing whether I ought to go or stay, be angry and elder-brotherly, or treat it as a piece of foolishness to be laughed off. It was so silent in there that I could hear the loud beating of my heart. At last I said, as neither of them uttered a word,

"Well, so that's how things are, is it?"

"Yes," Fred managed to say in a voice unlike his own—and even in the dimness of the boathouse, tinged with moving green light, I could see how flushed his face was—"that's how things are and that's how they're going to stay. She's engaged to me."

Clarisse was cool and unflurried, and her hair, tied back with a black velvet ribbon, was perfectly smooth.

"Don't you dare to say anything to the others, Halley," she said. "We're going to keep it a secret for a long time, for two or three years, maybe. Fred and I are terribly, terribly in love, if you want to know. Aren't we, Fred?"

"You've said it," Fred answered, and it was almost a groan. He shook his head as if the pain and pleasure were more than he could bear. "Look, Halley-boy, we can trust you, can't we? You won't go and run to your mother and father about this, will you?"

Put as Fred put it I felt I had to say what I did say: "No, of course not. What do you think I am?"

"This is dead serious, you know," Fred went on. "I guess I oughtn't to have—she's so young—but, well, we just couldn't help ourselves. I didn't know this was going to happen. I didn't mean it to. It just happened."

I guessed that it had happened because Clarisse had intended it to happen, and had maneuvered Fred into the boathouse out of the wind and rain for no other purpose. Since I had been to school I had learnt a good deal about girls but it was all from hearsay and I was without experience myself. I had wanted to kiss one or two and had even planned it, but so far had not done so.

"Don't just stand there staring at us," Clarisse said. "Promise you won't say anything. Swear."

"I won't swear," I said, "and I have promised, but—"

"Oh, never mind any buts," Clarisse cried impatiently. Fred still had his arm about her and she was standing close against his side. "We know all about the buts. We know we can't be married for ages, but that doesn't prevent our being madly in love. Fred's the first boy I ever kissed—really kissed, I mean. Are you glad, Fred?"

"Oh, God!" he groaned. "Am I glad? Oh, Clarisse!"

It wasn't the same as when she'd told me she was in love with Raymond, though once again shock and jealousy were mingled. But this time the jealousy was because she was younger than I and yet seemed so much more adult in this business of love.

"If Mother knew," I began, but she broke in,

"Well, she mustn't know, that's all. Anyway, she was only a little older than me when she fell in love with Father, so she couldn't say much."

I knew the difference two years can make, but I couldn't argue with her, with Fred's arm tightly about her. I felt too deeply disturbed and embarrassed.

I turned away. "You know she sees everything," I said.

"If she does, she does. But we'll be very careful, won't we, Fred?"

As usual when emotionally upset, I had already begun to feel slightly sick and now I left the boathouse without any more words. I knew that the instant I was out of sight they would be in each other's arms tasting again this newly-found rapture. I went up to my room and sat down to think and to wait for the uncomfortable sensations in my stomach to pass. Was it my duty to tell my parents? But I had already promised Fred and Clarisse that I would not. I had learnt at school that telling tales was an unforgivable sin, a mean sin that put one almost on a level with a sneak thief or a pickpocket. On the other hand, my mother, at the time of the Raymond episode, had said to me that I must feel a responsibility towards Clarisse. Why had I been in such a hurry to promise to say nothing? I had been a fool. And yet, try as I might, I could not imagine myself going to my parents and telling them. I knew too well what the results would be if I did. Fred would be severely scolded, my father would suggest that he had perhaps stayed with us long enough, and he would go, cutting his visit in half. It would all be wretchedly uncomfortable for everybody. Questions would be asked, even Syl would be sure to hear of it.

And if I said nothing? I had caught Fred and my sister indulging in a pastime that was highly popular with the young and widely practiced. They had been "necking," or "petting." Was it so very bad? So bad that I ought to tell on them? In the end I decided that I couldn't possibly tell, and though this decision seemed to me then the only one I could make, I was by no means happy about it and it worried me a good deal. I did, however, speak to Fred in private. I asked him to please remember that Clarisse was my sister, that she was very young, and that he was doing something of which my parents would strongly disapprove. I even reminded him that he was a guest in my parents' house.

"For Pete's sake, Halley," he answered indignantly, "do you think you have to tell me all that stuff? What do you think I am, anyhow? Look, Halley-boy, I love that girl better than anything in this world. Do you think I'd do anything to harm her? I'll take good care of her, don't you worry. Why, my God! Clarisse is as pure as an angel. She's pure and she's going to stay that way. One day she's going to be my wife."

This embarrassed me but at the same time it undid me completely. The talk of purity and marriage took me right out of my depth. Here, I felt, was something almost too beautiful to be touched. I said no more.

But for some time I was troubled about this strange wildness in Clarisse. Though I couldn't have put it into words I guessed that there was a ferment in her blood, caused, or at least heightened, by her knowledge of her own beauty. I wondered if she ever looked in the glass without thinking, "What am I going to do with all this?" She wanted to love and be loved, and she wanted at the same time the shelter and safety of home. The comforting thought finally came to me that now that Fred was her devoted and avowed slave—had he sworn that he would die for her?—she would be content. She had everything that was necessary to her for the present.

But altogether it was a disturbing episode and left its mark. I wondered if I were unusual, in any way abnormal, perhaps, not to have felt as yet what Clarisse was feeling. Would I like to hold Rosie in my arms and kiss her as Fred had kissed Clarisse? I decided that I would, and I tried to build Rosie up in my imagination into the image of the girl I would sooner or later fall in love with and marry. But it did not come easily.

It was a week of surprises. A few days later my father astonished me by saying to me as I was quietly punting him up the river one afternoon, "I suppose, my boy, you're thoroughly instructed in matters relating to sex, aren't you? I'm referring, of course, to what are stupidly called the facts of life. I—well, it's just that I want to be quite sure."

I guessed that he had probably been meaning to put this question to me for years and had never been able to. It had been kept in cold storage long past its time, and now it could hardly have been more valueless, and he must have known it. He must have realized that it had absurdly missed its moment, but his conscience, at this late date, forced him to ask it. And now it was spoken, creating only an awkwardness between us.

I told him, wishing to help him as much as I could (far from being critical of him for being so much too late, I admired him for his courage), that I had known for years; I couldn't remember exactly how long. I did not add—and he did not ask for further information—that my instructor was a talkative French boy I had met in the Bois who found my ignorance at eleven years old hard to credit.

"I've been meaning to ask you for a long time," he told me, face averted and fingers drumming nervously on the sides of my punt, "but the truth is I always find the subject embarrassing."

I said I could understand that. There was a short silence and then he went on, "I hardly think it's necessary to say anything to Julian for a while yet. He's young for his age. Anyway, your mother understands him much better than I do. I'll let her speak to him when the time comes."

I merely nodded my head. I knew that Julian had acquired the basic facts some time ago, but I didn't like to say so. He had asked Henry Burroughs, in a sort of desperation, to tell him how babies were born, and Henry had been shocked to find how uninstructed he was. Julian, in one of his rare confidential moods, had told me all this.

"It's high time somebody told me something," he had complained to Henry. "Everybody else knows. Halley says father ought to tell me, but I know he never will. Clarisse knows, I'm positive she does. I'm always left out of everything. If you don't tell me nobody will."

Henry, it seemed, had painstakingly done his best, and after reporting the incident to me, Julian never spoke of it again. I think that we must have been unusually reticent, for we never laughed or made jokes about the things most children consider funny. I realize too that we were deplorably lacking in curiosity, about sex or about things in general. We accepted, we did not ask why; we took things for granted. I already knew that the visible universe was not what it seemed, that beneath any "simple" fact lay a whole world of mysteries and marvels, but these things, I believed, I could make my own by the expenditure of a small effort when I had the time and the inclination. I had no thirst for knowledge, I believed I would do very well as I was, and I was moving through an unclouded landscape which was everywhere pleasing.

I had been punting upstream for some time in silence, and then my father suddenly said, "I'm not altogether happy about Julian, Halley," and he was watching the small ripples his fingers made in the water. "It has struck me lately that he hardly seems one of us at all. Do you know what I mean? I've no complaints to make about him, he's a good boy and never wants to be anywhere but with us, but all the same he keeps himself too much to himself."

So I, I thought, was not the only one who had observed this.

"I don't think Julian's very happy," I said.

He looked up at me sharply. "Not happy? Why not? He has everything in the world he wants, hasn't he? At present he even has a dog."

"I think he's a lonely soul," I told him, and then I remembered that I had heard Raymond say that very thing.

"Lonely?" he repeated, looking at me now in a puzzled way. "How can he possibly be lonely with us? What do you mean?"

"Well," I said, hoping I didn't sound too foolish, "I think some people are born lonely. They feel they don't belong. They take their loneliness around with them wherever they go. I don't know why."

"Do you mean he needs friends outside the family? That we ought to have sent him away to school?"

"I don't believe it would have done much good," I answered. "I don't believe Julian would make friends."

"I admit I feel very impatient with him sometimes," my father said, "though I try not to show it. I suppose he's going through a phase. Do you think Henry is the right tutor for him?"

"I think he likes him much better than he did," I replied. "I think they get on quite well now. They talk together quite a lot."

"Well," he said, "there's really nothing much we can do till his health improves. I think I remember that my mother had attacks of asthma when she was young." He settled himself back on his cushions. "I'm enjoying this. I wish your mother had come too, but she'll only trust herself in the launch. There's something very soothing about a punt."

He took a book of poetry out of his pocket.

"I want to read you something," he said. "It's Flecker's 'The Old Ships.' I can't think how it is I didn't come upon Flecker sooner."

He read it to me, and when he came to the last lines:

It was so old a ship—who knows—who knows?
—And yet so beautiful, I watched in vain
To see the mast burst open with a rose
And the whole deck put on its leaves again.

his eyes filled with tears.

"I suppose you'll think I'm very sentimental," he said, smiling and taking out his handkerchief. "The truth is, Halley, I'm almost too happy, if it's possible to be too happy. I really wonder sometimes if anyone has a right to be as happy as your mother and I are. Though I'm pretty sure," he added, "that if there is a God He'd approve of our happiness. There isn't such a lot of it in the world. And at least we're grateful. Being happy and *knowing* you're happy and being grateful for it, that's the important thing. And I hope you'll never forget it."

The sunny, windless afternoon with the Thames flowing along so quietly with now and then a liquid chuckle in some eddy or about some root; the sallow, flickering shade under the willows; the quiet voices of people passing; the reedy smell of the water that ran down my punt pole—all these things are with me yet. And along with these is the picture of my father, his hair and mustache golden in the sun, his idle hands lying upon *The Golden Treasury of Modern Lyrics*, and the tears—tears that I knew sprang from some deeper

[62]

source than the lines he had just read to me—coming back into his eyes.

I could only smile at him without finding anything to say. We were passing a houseboat, gay with red and white paint and flower boxes filled with red geraniums and white daisies. It had little frilled curtains at the windows, and a young couple in deck chairs looked up from their books and watched us go by.

"How one relaxes here," my father said. "How peaceful it all is. I don't know why, but at home one's nerves are never soothed as they are here in England. Your mother feels it too. One is conscious here of something deathless and immemorial."

"Yes," I said, "I think I know what you mean. But maybe we could find peaceful places in America too if we tried. We've never tried."

"Maybe," he said, "maybe." Then he added with a note of finality, "No, it wouldn't be the same. Something would be missing. Here I feel the slow centuries; there I'm too conscious of today."

Instead of answering this I suddenly put a question to him that I hardly knew was in my mind. It slipped off my tongue almost before I realized I was going to ask it.

"Father," I said, "don't you think it's time I started thinking about what I'm going to do when I leave college?"

"Why, my dear boy," he said, much surprised, "that's years away, years away. Why worry about it now?"

"Oh," I answered, "I don't know. It's struck me lately that most other boys of my age have some idea of what they want to do and I haven't, that's all. I thought maybe I ought to have."

"Well," he said, smiling a little, "think about it by all means if you want to, but it's a long way off. I shan't try to influence you, of course. You can make what plans you like. But in my opinion it's too early for you to know what you want to do. You're not sufficiently mature. I was in my second year at Cornell before I decided that I wanted to paint. Do you feel drawn towards any particular career? Law? Medicine—no you'd never be a doctor—architecture, perhaps, or business?"

"No," I replied, "I can't say I feel drawn to any of them."

"Well," he said, "isn't that the answer? You're too young. It's too soon to know."

"Maybe," I rather doubtfully agreed, "but all the same—"

He broke in then with some reflections of his own.

"How I wish," he said, "that I'd been born a little earlier. Say twenty or thirty years earlier. What fun it would have been to have lived in the Paris of the seventies and eighties, when my good friend Ambroise Vollard had his shop in the Rue Laffitte—that famous number six. They all knew that shop, all the painters, and they all knew Vollard. That was the time when paintings by Renoir were selling for only a couple of hundred francs, and all those brilliant, unrecognized artists used to bring their work to Vollard and he would try to sell it for them. Van Gogh's famous 'Poppy Field' was going begging. Pissarro's smaller paintings used to sell for sixty francs, and about twenty years after his death one of them sold for nearly a million francs in America. Yes, they were thankful for what they could get, all of them—Monet, Manet, Renoir, poor Sisley, Cézanne. And what geniuses those men were! You know, Halley, we worry our heads sometimes about France as she is today—bled white by the war, tired, apt to take the cynical view of things, but, by golly! that was a great period, an astounding period. We must never lose sight of that fact. I only wish I could have been there in its heyday. Yes, by golly, France can look back on a recent era of originality and brilliant accomplishment unequaled anywhere in the world—except of course in Italy during the Renaissance. And just before the Impressionists, and a part of the breakaway, you get Delacroix, Corot, Courbet—magnificent painters, all of them. What a time it was! If only I'd been there!"

I listened as I punted him along. I had heard it all before but it wasn't often that he talked to me in this way, without other listeners, and I was pleased and flattered.

"Of course," he went on, "all of them owe something to Constable, and even to Bonington. Everybody owes something to somebody. But what a glorious rebellion it was—that break with Old Mother Classicism! You can almost hear the apron strings snapping. No more gods and goddesses, no more mythology, no more boring historical subjects, no more landscapes painted in stuffy studios. Just nature itself, with all its moods and changes; just men, women and children with the light playing on them, moving in a world of air and light and color. Living in God's good daylight. No more sentimentalized peasants, either, thank God! I tell you, Halley, it was a revolution. I doubt if there will ever again be such a time of artistic adventure and discovery. Yes, if I have any complaints to make against life, one of them is that I was born too late."

I was very literal-minded, I suppose, for all I could think of to say was, "But if you'd been born any earlier you wouldn't have met Mother, and then where would we have been?"

"Oh," he said, and he laughed, "she would have been there too, of course. We had to come together, that was inevitable. And I hope," he added, looking at me quite earnestly now, "that none of you will marry until you feel that in your very bones—that sense of rightness, of destiny, even. Do you know what I mean?"

I nodded. I thought of my seventeen years during which I had had no experience of love, or had loved only in daydreams.

"I expect I'll never marry at all," I said.

His only reply to this was a brief smile.

"But to go back," he said, "to what I was saying. Even when I was a young man in Paris I could have picked up treasures if only I'd had the money. I could have bought drawings by Constantin Guys and Toulouse-Lautrec for almost nothing along the *quais*. Yes, even then I could recognize what was first rate. But I never had a sou to spend. Not a sou! I can tell you, I suffered. I used to think, 'if only the old man would let me have a couple of thousand dollars I could pick up a fortune here.' I had the flair. You've got it or you haven't. I can't explain it. It's like water divining."

I got my punt pole stuck in the river bottom and had a little struggle to get it out. He watched me, and when it was free again he went on talking.

"Halley," he said, and he was looking at me differently now, "how do we know that you haven't got the flair too? Maybe you have. You take after me in a good many ways, and you've already got a better understanding and appreciation of painting than the average person twice your age. Why don't you begin now to take an interest in—well, let's say in modern drawings, for a start. You could spend part of your holidays going to the smaller galleries. You'd have to keep your ear close to the ground and find out what's going on and who's showing promise and beginning to be talked about and all that. You may never turn out to be a Vollard or a Durand or a Georges Petit, and it's pretty certain that you'll never find the rich mine of genius that they found, but still you may prove to have a discerning eye and begin what may someday be a fine collection."

I could see him warming to the idea. He fingered his mustache and looked past me into the distance and his eyes were bright.

"Of course," he went on, "this isn't a great period, but here and there it's produced some great men. A country that has so recently produced an Augustus John, a Sickert—men of real originality and power—must have younger men of talent coming along. I'd finance you—in a modest way, of course—and you'd have to back your own judgment and make your own mistakes. I've made mistakes myself. Not many—I've only got rid of three pictures in all the years I've been collecting, and I got rid of them at a profit. Personally I think you'd have a lot of fun. It might be just what you were talking about —something for you to take up when you leave Harvard. And meanwhile you can make a beginning during your summer holidays when you're over here."

There is a feeling I hardly know how to describe but most people I'm sure have experienced it. It is caused by the sharp, the almost painful recognition of the rightness of something for oneself. It is so sharp that it is a little anguish, except that it is intensely happy too, and to be complete it must resolve some doubt or inner discord. The pain and pleasure of it are partly physical—for it is a sort of bodily *crise* as well—and it can bring tears to the eyes and a lump to the throat. It is accompanied by a quickened heartbeat and a feeling of intense exhilaration; something heavy falls away. Religious conversion must be similar to it though of course greater and probably overwhelming.

All this in its minor though intensely pleasurable form I felt now. I looked down to hide the excitement and the moisture in my eyes. I was deeply grateful to my father, but I waited until I could control my voice and then asked, to avoid having to give expression to my feelings, "What about America? Wouldn't I find anything good there?"

"You might," my father said, "you might. But it's in Europe that you're more likely to find 'pay dirt,' to use a mining term. What do you think, Halley? The idea has possibilities, hasn't it?"

"Yes," I said, and I wondered if my voice sounded as odd to him as it did to me. "It certainly has."

"Are we going home now?" he asked. Without realizing it I had turned the punt around and was heading downstream.

"Well," I said, "I thought maybe we'd gone far enough. Unless you'd like to go further?"

"No, no," he answered, "it's probably time we got back home. Your mother will be expecting us. I've enjoyed this, Halley, and I think perhaps we've got somewhere, don't you?"

"Yes," I said, "I think we have." Presently I added from a full heart, "I expect I shall always remember this afternoon."

He smiled at me.

"Always," he repeated. "That's a word we use less and less as we grow older. Do you know, Halley, I'd like to live forever? I'd like life just to go flowing on and on and on, like this old river. Peacefully and quietly. That is, of course, as long as your mother is with me. Without her I wouldn't want to live another day."

I made no answer. I was longing to get home, longing to let it be known to the others in some not too abrupt or direct way that my future career was now decided on. It did not occur to me, so happy and elated was I, that what had been decided on was not a career but an agreeable hobby, and what is more I am quite sure it did not occur to my father.

V

THE GREAT DEPRESSION CAME WHILE I WAS IN MY SECOND YEAR
at Harvard, and as it played an important role in my life, I shall have
to speak of it often. Like the great influenza epidemic that followed
the First World War it is a still unburied monster that no one can
be sure will not take on life once more and tread us down again.
So it is spoken of with boredom, with weariness and disgust, but
never without fear and the respect due to a fearful thing.

For a long time before it struck, Syl had been saying, "We're
headed straight for the rocks, and I can't get any of these smart
Alecs in Wall Street to believe it." For the infallible Syl had seen it
coming long before anyone else; like some skilled old trapper he
could see signs in the forest that others missed. It didn't matter that
my father refused to believe him so long as he let Syl do whatever he
wanted to do in the way of managing our affairs, and my father, of
course, never interfered. He was only too happy to have everything
taken out of his hands. But as early as the spring of 1929, Syl was
advising him to "draw in his horns," and he absolutely refused to
let him buy two exorbitantly priced pictures that he had set his heart
on having. For my father had a number of rivals in the field now,
and there was one great collector not much more than a hundred
miles from New York who was sometimes able to outbid him. But
of course Syl prevailed; in the end my father always obeyed him,
however reluctant he might be to do so.

As for me, I was far too much occupied with myself, with my
few small and timid ventures into picture buying, with my family
life and with my day-to-day existence as a sophomore at Harvard
to listen to gloomy predictions. I had recently had, too, my first
amorous adventures. In the beginning these were transient and
wholly commonplace and left little impression. I had simply passed
a milestone that had to be passed, and such experiences seemed to
me those of youthful humanity rather than my own. Then, venturing

further in search of something more personal, more in the nature of an adult "affair," I got myself miserably entangled.

My father had just given me my first car, a Buick, and I was enjoying the privilege of being able to ask people, "Can I give you a lift?" "Can I drive you home?" One evening at a noisy undergraduate party I noticed a girl who was all too obviously not enjoying herself. Among all the "sweater girls" there, she looked, in her prim and unrevealing black dress, as if she'd strayed in by mistake. With her vacant gaze, her mournful eyes and her silence she was a dampening element, or she would have been if the evening had not reached a point where nothing could dampen it. I was feeling rather aloof from it all myself and I went and sat down beside her.

"You look as though you wanted to be taken home," I said. "Do you?"

"Oh yes, please!" she cried, with instant gratitude. "Would you really be so kind?"

"I think I've had about enough," I said. "Let's see if we can slip out without anybody noticing us."

No one made any great efforts to stop us and in a minute or two we were in my car.

"I don't know your name," I said.

"It's Anna Maria," she answered.

"Anna Maria what?"

"The rest is unpronounceable," she told me. "My father is Polish. Anyway, does it matter?"

I learnt that she lived in a one-room apartment on the outskirts of Cambridge and gave daily lessons in French and German at a language institute. I further learnt that her mother was Scotch and came from Glasgow, and she went on to tell me in a voice full of resigned melancholy, that her parents had been so unhappy together and had quarreled so continuously that she had decided to leave home and try her luck in the United States.

After that we spoke nothing but French, and I suppose this, and her Continental background, made me feel very much at my ease with her.

She asked me, after a moment's hesitation, to come up for a drink and though I didn't much want to go I thought she might be hurt if I refused. Her room was bare and tidy, and she had set up a small ikon in one corner of it. She invited me to sit down on the divan, which I knew would later serve as her bed, while she went to get something to drink. It turned out to be vodka, which she said she was able to get through her Polish friends, and she filled two very small glasses. We sat side by side on the divan, talking, and when she was happy and animated she was really very charming.

I felt sorry for her and I asked her to dine with me the next evening. Pity was much more apt to be a danger to me than any sexual attraction by itself could be, and in fact it was almost always a part of it. She told me the following night that she had had a lengthy love affair with a married man in Poland—another reason for her wanting to get away—and this admission, volunteered as I well knew for the purpose, made it almost inevitable that we should become lovers. Her hollow cheeks, her sad and sensual mouth, her tender, even glad acquiescence, all had their attraction for me, and in her fastidious, delicate and instructed way, she taught me much.

Lonely as she was she grew to depend on me and all too soon she became fanatically devoted. Whenever I went to New York I would find a pile of passionate letters from her on my return. From the beginning of the affair I told her I would never marry her, but I don't think she could make herself believe it. Although she was twenty-five and I was not yet nineteen she insisted that mentally there was no discrepancy in our ages. I knew she was convinced that the more often we were together in that little bare room, the stronger her hold over me would be.

I realized finally that I must break away. She was interfering with my work and I was fearful that it would all end in tragedy for her. I can never look back on my efforts to end that affair without remembering all too vividly the feeling that I was trapped—hopelessly and nightmarishly trapped by my own pity and the long-drawn-out pain of making her suffer.

Then one night we said good-by, and I wished with all my heart that the thing had never been begun. The next day she drank two bottles of vodka and was rushed to hospital. When I heard of it I sent flowers but resolutely kept away, and I answered only one of her imploring letters. In a week she was home again and whatever her sufferings may have been from that time on, she bore them alone and in silence. I don't know what became of her. I caught a glimpse of her some months later coming out of a drugstore and I was utterly thankful to see that, after all that had happened, she looked much the same.

It was after this that I tried to fix my affections on Rosie Dumont. I was grateful to Rosie for being what she was—a part of the familiar family scene, with no other aim than to be married to a nice boy as soon as possible after making her debut, which, unlike Clarisse, she did in the usual way, with an expensive dance, given by her father, and a round of parties. That by taking her out, kissing her in taxis and now and then making a foursome with her, Fred and Clarisse at film or theater on my brief trips to New York, I might be upsetting these innocent plans, never entered my head. Our behavior was in line with the behavior of other young people of our kind, or possibly rather better, and we were soon on the sort of footing that then, as now, seems inevitable between a young man and the girl or girls he takes out—half friendly, in the joking, teasing manner of the young, half emotional, with permitted intimacies to which there is an understood limit, though that limit is drawn generously far. Petting had become an accepted thing, and if a girl founded her hopes on these now conventionalized demonstrations, so much the worse for her. Rosie, alas, did. I didn't realize then that with the example of Fred and Clarisse before her eyes she thought it inevitable that we would someday marry, though the fact that my sister and her brother considered themselves engaged was as yet known only to the four of us.

Rosie had grown from a plain child into quite a pretty girl, though her prettiness was commonplace beside Clarisse's unusual beauty, and I used to wonder if it would last. There was a sharpness about it that I thought would probably increase with years. Her nose was small and pointed, her lips were thin, and her chin slightly too prominent. But her thick, dark brown hair had an attractive gloss and her figure was good. She had decided not to go to college but to stay at home and keep house for her father, who had long been a widower, and her younger sister Helen. Meanwhile she studied domestic science and "mothercraft" in New York.

My mother thought it a pity that Rosie had never spent a summer with us in Europe.

"It might have helped to rub off some of the sharp edges," she said. "I'm fond of Rosie, she's a dear, but she *is* just a little provincial."

In the spring of 1929, however, my mother asked her again and this time she joyfully accepted. Fred was still at Law School, and was going to spend his holiday time working with Dumont, Rowan and Dumont. In another two years he would be ready to enter the firm. That meant no more long holidays for him, in Europe or anywhere else, for Syl would keep him hard at work. Fred was sad about this, as it meant months of separation from Clarisse, but he

[71]

saw it as right and necessary. Clarisse was still greatly enjoying her secret engagement, but I had at last persuaded her to tell my parents about it. I said it was high time she did and that any parents but ours would have guessed it long ago. She promised me faithfully she would tell them while we were abroad that summer.

"I don't know why, Halley," she said to me, "but I simply hate the idea of telling them. It seems to make it all cut and dried and ordinary. It's like the difference between flowers that have just been picked, and flowers that have been pressed in a book. Don't you know what I mean? It's been so heavenly, being secretly engaged. I'd like to go on keeping it a secret forever."

"You ought to have told them ages ago," I told her. "They're bound to think you've been horribly deceitful, and they'll start off with a prejudice against the whole thing."

"Well, don't scold," she protested. She hated to be put in the wrong about anything. "Anyway, you made one big mistake; you thought mother would find out at once. Well, she still hasn't the faintest idea that we're in love. I suppose it's because she and father are so wrapped up in each other." She looked thoughtful. "I sometimes wonder if Fred and I will ever be like that. I'm still terribly fond of him of course, but somehow I don't believe we will. I suppose people aren't, nowadays."

I thought too that she would never be like my mother. Her attachment to her home and to my parents was as great as ever, but even I could see that she lacked my mother's singleness of purpose. It came into my mind that she was like one of those sea creatures that fasten themselves to a rock, yet are vulnerable and delicate, and depend for their subsistence on what chances to come their way. That I was exceedingly like that myself did not strike me at that time.

Julian had rebelled so strongly against any idea of going away to school that, as he was still liable to attacks of asthma if he was nervously upset, a compromise was reached and he now went daily to Browning's, in New York. Henry thought very highly of it, and my parents easily persuaded themselves that the course of least resistance was also the right and the best course. Although Henry no longer tutored him, Julian had developed a kind of dependence on him and he often came to the house, sometimes bringing his sister Vera with him. Vera was a thin, dark, serious girl, almost a caricature of a young "intellectual," and she was studying to be a social worker. As these two were Julian's only friends—he chose to look upon the Dumonts as our friends rather than his although Helen was just his age—my parents rather reluctantly encouraged them to come and they had Sunday-night supper at our house fairly frequently during the winter months. When my parents and Clarisse went abroad in the spring, Henry came and lived in the house to keep Julian company, going out daily to his tutoring. The rest of the time he and Vera shared an apartment in Greenwich Village. As soon as the summer holidays came, Julian and I would be off to join the others. This arrangement worked very well and did not interfere in any way with my parents' migrating habits.

The summer of 1929 Rosie crossed the Atlantic with Julian and me and we went on the *Europa*. This was Rosie's idea; we had always up to now traveled *White Star*.

"I knew Rosie would spoil everything," was Julian's comment. "She's too bossy."

My parents and Clarisse were in Paris at the time and they met us in Cherbourg with two cars. We were to spend part of the summer touring Italy and later were to return to France to revisit the château country, an arrangement my parents had made to please Rosie, who said it was what she most wanted to see. After that, we now learnt, we would spend the whole of September in a villa my father had rented in Antibes, and I thought this sounded like a pretty good ending to the holiday.

Now that I was obliged to admit to myself with a good deal of disquiet that Rosie believed herself to be in love with me, I made up my mind to go carefully. I knew that days and days of sitting side by side and even knee to knee with her in the car were not likely to help matters, so on the second day of our trip I had a talk with Julian in the garden of the hotel in Versailles, as the cars were being loaded up.

"Julian," I said, "are you quite sure you like sitting in front with the chauffeur all the time? Why don't you let me sit there for a change?"

He was on the defensive at once.

"Can't I even sit in the only place where I want to sit without someone interfering?" he asked, flushing with indignation. "If I have to sit in the back and listen to those girls I'd rather have stayed at home."

"Why do you always want to be by yourself?" I inquired. "You're getting to be a regular old misogynist."

"And you needn't start calling me names, either," he said. "You know perfectly well I never get my own way about anything" (it was nearly always impossible to find out what Julian's "way" was likely to be) "and you always do. Why shouldn't I sit in front with the chauffeur if I want to?"

"Well," I said, "because for once I'd like to sit there myself. Look, Julian, you say you're always short of pocket money. I'll give you fifty dollars if you'll let me have the front seat and go and sit in the back."

I had already planned to make this offer and I put my hand in my pocket and took out five ten-dollar bills. He looked from them to me with the deepest suspicion.

"You've got some motive for this," he said. "Well, you can't buy that seat for fifty dollars—you can't buy it for five hundred dollars. You know I just despise hearing those girls chatter chatter all the time."

"What about me?" I asked.

"You?" He stared at me. "But you're crazy about Rosie, aren't you?"

"I'm fond of Rosie," I said, "but I've got my own reasons for not wanting to be too near her all the time."

He still ignored the money in my outstretched hand.

"Why can't you tell me, right straight out?" he asked. "Can't you ever tell me anything?"

"Oh, for heaven's sake, Julian, wake up!" I cried, exasperated. "Can't you guess what I'm trying to say? Rosie's getting too fond of me, that's why."

As he took in my meaning he pushed my hand away.

"You can keep your money," he said, "but I'm not going to sit in the back either. You can have my seat and I'll go and sit in the other car with Louise."

"There's no room," I said, "with all the suitcases and things."

"I'll get the driver to make room," he said, "and nobody's going to stop me, either. Anyhow, I'm thankful you're not falling for a silly girl like Rosie."

"She isn't silly," I argued. "At least she's no sillier than most."

"Well," he said, "I don't only mean Rosie. I mean any girl, and that goes for Clarisse too."

No one did stop him. My mother smiled at him fondly and said, "Well, if you really prefer that, darling. It certainly gives us more room."

Julian was very fond of Louise and I often wondered what they talked about. She was a little difficult and short tempered nowadays, which was not surprising, for she suffered from rheumatism or arthritis, and her fingers were becoming stiff and knotted. But she would never be left at home. She had literally no private life of her own and wanted none. She could still iron and mend and pack, and she was fearful that the end of her time of usefulness to us was near. She knew my father would see that she never lacked for anything, but the thought of one day not being necessary to my mother and Clarisse must have haunted her.

We visited most of the lovely old towns of Tuscany and Umbria, and in Florence paid a visit to the house where Julian was born. American families are in some ways at an advantage in Europe; the unconventional thing is expected of them and we would have been surprised if the elderly Italian couple who now lived in the house and had never before heard of us had not immediately invited us in and offered us wine and cakes.

"It's all just the same," my father said with deep satisfaction, smiling and looking around at the garden. "Just the same. The fountain makes exactly the same sound falling into the basin, the ilex trees look just as they used to do." He and my mother glanced at each other and I could see how for them past and present happiness joined and became one. "You were born on a beautiful June morning, Julian," he went on. "I remember perfectly how the nightingales sang all through the night. Are you pleased with your birthplace?"

Julian had not wanted to come with us that afternoon. He dreaded being called upon for just some such answer as was now expected of him. And with everyone's attention focused on him he looked utterly miserable.

"Everyone's got to be born somewhere, I guess," he muttered and he fidgeted until we said good-by. But he looked slyly pleased when the old gentleman, accompanying us to the door, told my father that he thought his memories had played him false; that by June the nightingales had finished singing, as a rule, that it was in April and May that they were heard best.

"Well, I'm quite sure they sang the night my son was born," my father persisted, smiling, and we went on our way.

But in spite of Julian's odd, difficult nature we were all devoted to him and in a way proud of him. He seemed to make our family complete, to round it out as no one else could have done. Much that he said and did amused my parents when it did not irritate them, and I am sure my mother thought it original of him to be so unlike the rest of us. As long as his dependence on her and on the family generally was what it had always been, no one worried very much.

I think that all we saw and did passed before Rosie's eyes as a film passes. I got the impression that, to her, reality lay wholly within the boundaries of the United States, and that what she saw in Europe was a sort of illustrated travelogue. She called it a good day if she spent some part of it alone with me. She was a nice, honest, practical girl with one compelling idea which I couldn't share, and when she asked me, in Venice, looking across at San Giorgio which seemed to be floating on the pale blue water, "Halley, you *are* beginning to love me just a little, aren't you?" I wondered why schools didn't teach girls never, never to ask such questions instead of teaching them geometry or algebra. I answered, "I'm fond of you, Rosie, you know I am. Why don't we just leave it at that?" and though I knew it was a wretched sort of answer, I could do no better. She bit her lip and turned away.

Clarisse had made me promise to be there when she told my parents about Fred and herself, but she didn't want Rosie or Julian. She also wanted it to be out of doors somewhere, so that, as she put it, "things couldn't get too emotional." It was not easy to arrange things in just this way but she contrived it one day in Rome when we were standing looking down on the Forum from the Capitoline Hill. Julian, bored and tired out with sightseeing, was sitting by himself on the steps just under Castor and Pollux, and Rosie had been persuaded, not without difficulty, to go into the museum for a look at the "Dying Gladiator," which the rest of us of course had seen.

It was one of those late afternoons when Rome looks as if it had been washed in ochre and gold dust. There were swallows high in the air and shrill, and the four of us were standing at the edge of the Piazza where you can look down on Old Rome and Old Rome seems to open up its fabulous heart to you. Clarisse, I remember, was wearing a light blue summer dress and, as she was always careful not to get sunburned, a big straw hat with a blue scarf on it. She wore her hair twisted up now in a great shining coil and attracted a lot of attention everywhere we went. I was very conscious of the way people stared at her and took pride in it, though I tried not to let her see that I did.

She brought up the subject cleverly enough and my parents played nicely into her hands.

"I believe I'd like to come to Rome for my honeymoon," she said as we stood looking down on the Forum, and she took my mother's arm. "There's such lots to see and do here. You'd never be bored for a minute."

My father and mother exchanged looks at this. They were amused, I could see, at the idea that anyone could possibly be bored on a honeymoon.

"Well," my father said, with the look of amusement still on his face, "Rome will still be here when that great day comes, Clarry, about ten years from now, let's say."

"I'd like it to come a great deal sooner than that," Clarisse answered, and she spoke in a way that showed she meant what she said. I dreaded what was to come, but I knew she would never find a better moment than this.

Once more I saw my parents exchange looks, but this time there was no amusement in them; instead, the first symptoms of concern and alarm.

"Would you, darling? Would you really?" my mother cried, startled. "Why, you don't want to leave us, do you? Aren't we all happy as we are?"

"Of course," Clarisse answered, and then she said what for weeks past she had been planning to say, and the words came with a rush, "but you see—well, the truth is, Fred wants to marry me and I want to marry him."

There was a stricken silence during which the swallows' thin high twittering sounded louder in our ears, and I tried not to meet my parents' eyes. I thought the silence would never end, and at last Clarisse broke it herself by crying out, "Oh, don't look so awful, both of you! You surely don't mind if I marry Fred someday, do you? Why, he's one of the family."

I knew only too well what they were feeling and I was very sorry for them and wished I could have been as startled and shocked as they were, but I wasn't going to pretend I didn't know. My mother looked as though she had just heard of the death of someone she dearly loved and my father looked almost stupefied, as if he'd received a blow on the head.

"But my darling!" my mother cried at last, and she was pressing one hand against her heart. "How long have you felt this way about Fred?"

"Why didn't you *say* something to us, Clarry?" my father asked, and his voice was anguished.

"But I'm saying it now, I'm telling you now," Clarisse said, looking from one to the other. "It's been coming on—well, sort of gradually, I suppose, for a long time. I knew you'd be terribly upset or I would have told you sooner."

My mother turned to me then as I knew she was bound to do, as if I had betrayed her, and her great dark eyes were full of pain and reproach.

"You knew about this, Halley," she said. "How long have you known?"

Clarisse answered before I could. I saw that without deviating too far from the truth she both wanted to protect me and to conceal the fact that this had been going on for a year.

"Oh, Halley guessed," she said, quickly. "It isn't his fault. In fact he made me tell you. Oh, don't, please, look so miserable!" she cried, and her distress then was real enough. "You're fond of Fred, aren't you? You always seemed to be. It isn't as if I'd fallen in love with some stranger. After all, it's just Fred."

With all too obvious pain and bitterness my father repeated slowly, "Yes, it's just Fred."

She turned on him swiftly and indignantly.

"Well, who do you want me to marry? Some prince, I suppose?"

"Darling, don't speak to your father like that," my mother protested. "He doesn't mean at all what you think. We're fond of Fred, of course, we've always been fond of him, but we never, never thought of him as a possible son-in-law. And it's too soon, it's much, much too soon. That's what distresses us so."

"It's years too soon," my father said, wiping his face. "Years and years too soon, Clarry."

"Oh, darling!" my mother cried, her distress growing, "don't, don't make up your mind now. It's so foolish. Wait. Wait just a few years. You'll meet so many people—why, you're sure to meet dozens of young men who—" She couldn't go on.

My father turned pleading eyes on Clarisse, eyes reddened with painful tears.

"You're our precious, precious daughter," he said, "and we only want you to be happy. What else could we want? But your mother's right. You're much too young and Fred's much too young. And why hasn't he spoken to us? Five years from now would have been time enough. Haven't you told her so, Halley? Surely, you haven't let her think we'd approve of this?"

I shook my head unhappily, hating my own part in it all and wishing it were over.

"I didn't know what to think," I said. "After all, Fred's our best friend, and if Clarisse—"

"Just how long ago did you guess, Halley?" my mother asked me, and I knew she wanted to assuage one hurt by inflicting on herself the pain of another.

I lied to her for the first time in my life.

"Oh," I answered, "I suppose it was about the time you left New York. Fred was so miserable, and Clarisse—"

"Never mind about Halley," my father said, and he spoke more in his usual way. "Clarisse, at your age it's quite impossible for you to know what's best for you. For a few years more you must be guided by your mother and me."

"Mother knew what was best for her when she was only a little bit older than me," Clarisse argued. "Anyway, she didn't make a mistake."

"But what do you want, darling?" my mother asked. "You surely can't expect us to look on this as a real engagement. That's out of the question. Your father and I waited patiently for over two years."

"I just wanted you to know," Clarisse said, and she straightened her back, "that I consider myself engaged to Fred, that's all. Maybe we could announce it next year. I am engaged to Fred. I've told him I'd marry him—oh, dozens of times. And we're in love," she added, and it was like an afterthought.

I knew that my parents found themselves in difficulties. They were fond of Fred, they had nothing whatever against him except his youth; moreover, he was their beloved Syl's only nephew, and would one day be his heir. Such a marriage could only bring the two families closer, if possible. In a year, Clarisse would be eighteen, and my mother was engaged to my father at eighteen. There was little they could say, few reasons they could give for their dismay. They could only repeat, "Wait, wait," and hope to put off as long as possible a thing they hated and dreaded—a threat, the first threat, to the family's unity.

"Anyway," Clarisse said, "Syl will be pleased if nobody else is."

"Yes," my father answered, "of course Syl will be pleased. Why shouldn't he be? He loses nothing. You aren't his darling only daughter." Suddenly his voice broke and he buried his face in his lavender-scented handkerchief. Clarisse put her arm through his.

"Father," she pleaded, "don't take it so hard, please, please! I'm not going to run away. I won't be leaving you for ages. I'll never really leave you. I'll always be somewhere near."

[79]

A party of sightseers came and stood beside us and we moved away. As we crossed the Piazza we passed close to the great equestrian statue and I was too troubled to wonder, as I had wondered before, whether it was really Marcus Aurelius on the huge horse, or Constantine. (Raymond had been sure it was Constantine.) I was thankful that Clarisse had got her confession over, but I knew that however much my parents might try to comfort each other with the thought that perhaps it would all come to nothing, the summer was spoilt for them.

Just then Rosie came out onto the steps of the museum and my mother asked, quickly, "Does Rosie know?"

"Well," Clarisse said, "you know how it is. I just *had* to confide in somebody."

"So even Rosie knows," my father commented sadly.

"And Julian? Does he know too?" my mother asked.

"Oh, goodness no," Clarisse answered, glad, I could see, that in this she was blameless. "Julian doesn't know a thing about it." And then she did something that completely astonished me, for it seemed to me to show a callousness I could hardly credit. She called out to Rosie, "I've told them, Rosie, and it's all right. Isn't that marvelous?"

It was a moment of painfully clear vision for me. For the first time I saw my sister as if, out of the dark, a harsh light had been turned on her. It didn't decrease my love for her, but it altered it. It caused a shift in all my feelings about her, and accompanying this shift was a new sense of responsibility towards her. I could never again be sure that her feelings and responses would be right ones. As far as the feelings of others were concerned, I could never again count on her understanding. I hoped that my parents had not made a similar discovery, but to this, as I soon learnt, I need not have given a thought. If she had wounded them, and she had, she had wounded them, they believed, in all innocence, as a child might have done. They could not and did not, I am sure, expect her to be aware of it.

I heartily despised Rosie, at that moment, for being all smiles and arch pleasure.

"I'm so terribly glad!" she cried, and she kissed my mother, who almost drew back to avoid what must have seemed to her to put public approval on a thing she hated. "I felt awful," Rosie went on, "at having to keep such a big important secret, but I knew Clarisse would tell you very soon." She laughed happily and looked at me. "Now," she said, "we're just one big family, aren't we? Prentisses and Dumonts together."

"We could hardly be closer than we have always been, Rosie," my father said. "Now you young people must promise us faithfully not to say one word about this outside our two families. Nothing is to be said about it for one whole year. Is that fully understood?"

Both girls promised and I added my promises too. My mother looked at Rosie and did her best to smile.

"You know, Rosie," she said, "that we're devoted to Fred, or course, but all the same this has come as a great shock to us. It was totally unexpected, and we think it's far too soon. Much, much too soon."

"I didn't suppose you'd mind about that, Aunt Ruth," Rosie said. "You were so young when you got engaged to Uncle Myron. I hope I'll marry young. I'd like to have a baby before I'm twenty."

I had heard this before. Rosie frequently spoke of the family she meant to have with almost clinical candor, and when she did I felt as if a net were being drawn dangerously close, and some of my conviction that I was perfectly free to do as I liked about her went from me. I cannot explain this except by saying that the longing for fatherhood must have been stronger in me than I knew, and that Rosie was instinctively aware of it and was quick to grasp whatever power over me she could find.

When he was told the news later Julian's reaction was what I had expected it to be.

"I suppose everyone knew before I did," he said. "Well, I don't care. I'm never going to be surprised at anything any girl does. I think Clarisse must be crazy to want to marry Fred or anyone at all. That's all I've got to say."

"And it's quite enough," Clarisse retorted. "You can just mind your own business if you like, dear little brother. I shan't complain."

But she was not in the least angry and gave him a playful kiss.

That evening at about ten my mother called me into her room. We were staying at the Flora and her windows overlooked the Pincio Gardens. They were wide open and she had been standing looking out at the moonlit trees.

"Your father's gone for a little stroll," she said, drawing the curtains. "He's feeling very depressed. It's terrible for us, Halley. The first break! And we were all so happy before. I feel now that anything may happen." She looked at me closely. "Halley, you aren't falling in love with Rosie, are you? For heaven's sake tell me now if you think you are. I couldn't bear another shock like this one."

She put her handkerchief to her eyes and her shoulders began to shake a little.

"Don't you worry about that, Mother," I said, and I kissed her, and patted her back.

"Oh, Halley," she said, "are you sure? The way she looked at you this afternoon—I couldn't help noticing it. Are you sure she isn't getting too fond of you? If she is, I think I'd better advise her to go home."

"I guess the damage has been done," I said. "But anyway I can take care of that."

"Oh, then it's true?" she cried. "I ought to have guessed. I suppose your father and I haven't realized how you're growing up."

"I don't consider myself grown up yet," I told her. "Anyway, not grown up enough to think about marrying. I've told Rosie about a hundred times that I'm not going to marry till I'm thirty, and she knows it won't be to her when I do."

"Are you sure?" she asked anxiously. "Are you quite sure she understands that?"

"She ought to," I answered. "I tell her about once a week."

She reached up, pulled my head down to her level and kissed me.

"Oh, bless you!" she cried. "I'm so glad I asked. You're such a comfort to me, Halley. But you'll have to be careful. Now that there's this foolish, adolescent love affair between Clarisse and Fred, she'll want to follow suit. Why does Clarisse *want* to marry Fred, Halley? Can you understand it? She's so happy with us. One brings up the loveliest of girls, and watches over her and cherishes her, and then some perfectly ordinary, dull young man tries to take her away before she's learnt anything about life. How can she have given so much thought to him when she's seemed so perfectly content?"

"I guess it's human nature, isn't it?" I said.

"I don't know," she said mournfully. "It isn't like Clarisse to hide things and to be deceitful. I'm afraid Fred is a great deal to blame."

She sighed deeply.

"I don't think I've ever prayed in my life," she told me, "I suppose because I've always had everything I wanted. But now I shall pray that nothing comes of this, that we just go on happily, as we've always done, anyway for at least five or six more years."

While we were at the villa in Antibes, I had a bit of luck. I had been in Nice a lot, looking into second-hand shops in the back streets, and one day I picked up a water-color drawing by Dufy and a pen-and-ink drawing by Picasso. Both were signed. I let the old shop-keeper think I was really interested in some rather improper French prints, and when I offered him two hundred francs for the two drawings, he let me have them, looking rather surprised, I thought, at my wanting them at all. My father was very pleased with me when I told him that they were inside a big folio full of rubbish and that I'd chanced on them as I was glancing through.

"That old man," he said, "doesn't know his onions, luckily for you. Anyone can recognize a Dufy when he sees one, but you might easily have missed the Picasso. It's an early one and a good one. What wonderful economy of line! Brilliant! I shall begin to think you've got the flair, my boy."

Rosie said nothing at all when I was showing them to the family, but later when we were lying on the little breakwater in our bathing suits, sunbathing, she said to me,

"Halley, can those things you bought really be any good? It seems to me Clarisse could do a lot better. I thought that naked woman" (this was the Picasso) "was horrible."

"All right," I said indifferently, "you don't like them." And I refrained from adding, "So what?"

"Halley," she went on, "I know I'm a fool to worry about you so much, but what are you going to *do* when you leave Harvard?"

"What would you like me to do?" I asked.

She ignored this.

"You're an American after all. Anyway, you aren't anything else that I know of. Are you just going to play about Europe for the rest of your life? Aren't you going to think about earning your living like other people?"

"Are you telling me to find a job?" I asked.

"You know perfectly well what I mean," she persisted. "You'll have to earn your living sometime, won't you?"

"I think we might leave that to my father and me to decide," I answered.

"Even rich young men ought to do something," she went on. "Fred will be rich one day, and look at him. He's working hard. He's got some ambition."

"Fred's a marvel," I said.

"Well, at least he means to get somewhere," she told me angrily.

"At the moment," I said, "there isn't anywhere I particularly want to get."

Her anger changed to distress.

"Oh, Halley," she said, "I do wish you wouldn't talk like that. You'll be sorry someday. You don't seem a bit like an American boy to me."

"How perfectly terrible!" I answered. "Anyhow, if you disapprove of me so much, why do you pretend to be so fond of me?"

"I don't pretend," she cried. "If I weren't so fond of you I wouldn't care."

"Don't shout," I said. "People will hear you if you shout like that."

"I wasn't shouting," she protested indignantly, but she lowered her voice. "Just picking up silly drawings. Do you call that an occupation for a man?"

"Yes," I said, "and a very enjoyable one."

She quickly got up, stood for a moment on the edge of the breakwater and then made a neat dive. She had a pretty brown back, and looked her best in a bathing suit. I thought what a pity it was I wasn't fonder of her, for if it hadn't been for the fact that she could irritate me as no one else could, she would probably have been good for me.

"Are you going to lie there all day?" she called out, turning to look back at me. "Come and swim out to the raft with me."

"No thanks," I replied, "I'm all right where I am. I'll go in later."

She swam away without another word.

We kept pretty much to ourselves while we were at Antibes, and Clarisse shook off a number of young men as if to show us all that she was in earnest about Fred. My mother and father were quite happy to meet no one, my mother giving as a reason that the people there were mostly "Café Society," and the sort she couldn't endure. She went with my father to Paris a couple of times and they brought back a Berthe Morisot with which they were delighted. The very next day a letter came from Syl, and my father read it at the breakfast table with a very grave face. Then he coughed, drew in his chair a little closer to the table, leaned his elbows on it and said, looking round at our faces,

"Be quiet, everybody. Here's a letter from Syl, and I want you to listen carefully to every word. I'm going to read it aloud. It's typical of Syl, full of his salty humor, but it isn't funny and it isn't meant to be funny. In fact, it's got pretty bad news in it."

Having got our full attention he began to read.

My dear Myron:

As I've been warning these deaf adders in Wall Street for I don't know how long now, we're in for it. It's the Big Recession. Personally I think it's going to be the most God-awful slump this land of the free has ever known. You know how often I've predicted it, and how I've said all along that that man in the White House is about as much of an economist as the left hind leg of Balaam's ass. Well, events are proving that I was all too right and maybe understated things. Yes, sir, the big blow is on its way and you can thank the good Lord that I've seen to it that you and your family and I and my family have cyclone cellars to go to. Morgan's can't stop it, the Treasury can't stop it, in my opinion nothing and nobody on earth can stop it. Any minute now it'll be here. So if you're thinking of buying any more pictures, Myron my boy, just you sew up your pants' pockets good and tight, and if you're spending money to the tune of about four hundred dollars a day as I suspect you are, my advice to you is to close up that villa or whatever you call it and come right on home. If it helps any to send Rosie back right away, send her by all means. Anyhow, I'd rather you weathered the storm here, where I can keep an eye on you, than there. So get back as quick as you can and watch the bottom drop right plumb out of everything, because that's what it's going to do. Some of your friends and mine will probably be jumping out of the windows of tall buildings before it's over. It's going to be the Biggest Show on Earth, because that's the way we do things here, but it won't be any circus. Don't think I'm not scared. I am scared, because I don't see where the darn thing is going to stop. Anyhow, your family and the Dumont family are going to weather it all right and you can thank old Uncle Sylvanus for that.

Fred sends his love to you all, maybe to one person in particular, but I guess he attends to that privately. He's been here in the office with me right along and he's doing fine. He's put in a lot of good work this summer. Let me know as soon as you're headed this way.

My fond love to you all,

Syl

We all sat silent as my father put the letter back in its envelope and looked across at my mother.

"How soon do you think we can get out of here?" he asked her.

My mother could always be relied upon to give practical answers, and she said at once, "I should think in about a week. We'll have to get in touch with Monsieur Vatel" (he was the owner of the villa) "but as he's no further away than Cannes, that ought not to be difficult. The rent's paid up to the end of our tenancy, so he can't make a fuss if we leave earlier. But how soon can we all get on a boat? Isn't that the real problem?"

"It may be," my father agreed. "If what Syl says is beginning to be known, there'll be a big rush on the part of Americans to get home. I'd better ring up Cook's now."

Rosie offered to go immediately, saying that there was sure to be a single berth to be found, but my father, not seeing my mother's quick look at him, said, no, we'd all go back together.

"But what I want to impress upon you all," he added, "is that we must cut expenses right down to the bone. You'd better take your little Fiat back right away, Halley, and we can do without the motor launch for the rest of our stay. And no more dinners at Eden Roc. It looks," he remarked, smiling across at my mother, "as if we'd bought the Berthe Morisot just in time."

Cook's could do nothing for us under three weeks, so after some delay my father got through to a friend of his in London who was one of the directors of *White Star*. My father made it seem, on the telephone, that there would be a still worse financial crisis if he wasn't in New York to see to things, and in the end staterooms were booked for us on the *Mauretania* in eight days' time.

In the late afternoon my father hung the Berthe Morisot in the living room. It was a mother and child in an orchard in sun and shadow, and the woman was sitting sewing with bent head while the child played in the grass. Then my father gave us a little talk about it, addressing himself chiefly to Rosie, Clarisse and Julian. He didn't tell us how much he'd paid for it, he very seldom would, but he did tell us, by way of preamble, that he'd had quite a battle over it with a rich German who badly wanted it for his collection. It was the same powerful industrialist—his name was a household word— who had tried so hard to get the Cézanne, the *"Nature Morte,"* the year before, and my father was clearly delighted that he had won another victory over him.

"You're looking," he said, "at one of the best examples of the work of the best of all women painters. I don't think there can be any argument about that, and nobody needs to bring up the names of Madame Lebrun or Rosa Bonheur or Angelica Kauffman either. They're not in the same world with Berthe Morisot. Hers wasn't, perhaps, a wholly original genius—that's about the rarest thing there is—but it was genius all right. She and her sister met Manet sometime in 1865 when they were all copying pictures in the Louvre, and later Berthe Morisot married Manet's brother, Eugène. She's a remarkable phenomenon. A charming woman, a woman of the world living in society, living a normal, full, agreeable family life, happily married, and yet, by golly! she could paint like this! Don't tell me a woman has to be a freak in order to have a career." He shook his head in wonder. "I take off my hat to her. You've all seen—well, all but Rosie—that painting of hers in the Luxembourg, the '*Jeune Femme au Bal.*' Well, there it is. A triumph. I wish I owned it. Manet often asked her to sit for him, and greatly admired her. Mallarmé adored her. A gracious, lovely woman. With a little bit of luck, I might have met her, but she died too young. She died in 1895 at the age of fifty-four, while I was a schoolboy. I feel it almost as a personal loss. Halley, you might take it down now and we'll run it into Nice first thing tomorrow and get it packed up for the journey home."

"What about Mary Cassatt?" Rosie suddenly asked. "You hardly ever speak about any American painters."

"Mary Cassatt?" my father repeated, and he looked at Rosie in some surprise. "There's nothing wrong with Mary Cassatt. She had the good sense to live and work in Paris among the Impressionists. She can't be regarded as on the same level with Berthe Morisot, Rosie, though you were right to bring up her name. There is a touch of sentimentality about her work that I, personally, don't care for. When she paints a mother and child you feel she's trying to tell us more about Motherhood and Childhood in capital letters than is necessary. But she's a good painter, I admit it. Now then, Halley, take it down carefully. It may keep you from starvation one of these days."

It wasn't often that my father was in this semi-facetious mood and it struck me that he was perhaps stimulated and nervously excited by the news in Syl's letter, as well as by his victory over the German.

Then Julian spoke.

"We won't starve, of course," he said with that mixture of diffidence and defiance that was peculiarly his, "but I guess a whole lot of other people will."

My father gave him the sort of look he reserved for Julian when he had said something no one had expected him to say. There was annoyance in it, held in check, patience and a determination to answer reasonably and with care.

"I don't see why anyone should starve, Julian," he said. "That's just a morbid notion of yours. It simply means that a great many people will have to give up speculating in stocks and shares and stop buying expensive cars and radios and refrigerators. Things they couldn't afford anyway. There's been an orgy of spending in America of recent years and to my mind it's time it was stopped. Let's just keep our heads and look on whatever comes as inevitable and probably deserved. Well," he said, looking around at us and smiling now, "the rest of you can do as you like, your mother and I are going out now to look at the sunset."

They went out together, hand in hand.

"The lovers," said Rosie, and smiled and looked at me.

"I know," Clarisse said. "Isn't it wonderful? How do people stay like that year after year after year?"

"I guess you'll know all about that someday," Rosie said.

Julian, who never could bear listening to the girls' conversation, got up from his chair and hurried upstairs to his room. I went to the door. It was a lovely evening and the sun was going down in a sky of steady orange, shading far upwards to deepest blue.

"Where are you going?" Rosie called after me.

"Oh," I said, "just for a little stroll by myself."

I knew she wanted to come too but I was glad to get away alone. There was nothing much the matter, but I thought I would like to think about the news in Syl's letter. I wondered if we would ever again spend money as we had been spending it this summer and tried to guess what it must have cost my father to have taken seven of us for a tour through Italy and then France in two cars, stopping always at the best hotels, and then to take this expensive villa. Before that, of course, my mother and Clarisse had been in Paris buying clothes, and my father had added four pictures to his collection. I was interested rather than worried; in fact I was not worried at all. Nothing very much could go wrong as long as Syl was there to look after us, and it was inconceivable that a day would ever come when he would not be there.

VI

THERE IS NOT A GREAT DEAL TO SAY ABOUT MY TIME AT HAR-
vard, for there, as at Groton, my real interests lay outside. Apart from
work, which I enjoyed—though I took care not to say so—it was to
me an oddly unreal existence, and I never could and never did feel
part of it. I couldn't overcome a conviction that I was an interloper:
that I was there on sufferance and that sooner or later this was bound
to be found out. My life had been too different from the lives of the
others, too exclusive, and my family attachments were too strong
to enable me to feel that I "belonged." I never was able to associate
myself sufficiently closely with the other members of my house or
class to say "we." It was always "they." And from "them" I cautiously
selected—or was selected by—a few likeminded ones. One of these
was René Valmont, whose father had come to Boston six years ago
as French Consul and had decided to become an American citizen;
another was Dick Purbright from Denver, a city I had scarcely heard
of before I knew him. I found it hard to reconcile the fact that he
was "civilized" (as my father would say), bookish and intelligent,
with the fact that he lived so far from the Atlantic seaboard, for
though I had never been West and had no wish to go, I thought I
knew all about it. We three formed a close alliance. None of us spoke
the current *argot,* and none of us made any attempt to speak it. None
of us was able to bandy bawdy talk with ease or success, and none
of us greatly enjoyed rowdy parties either with or without girls.
(If I were interested in a girl I usually managed to keep the fact—
and the girl—to myself.) We took ourselves seriously and I have no
doubt that we were lacking in the rougher, more robust types of
humor. René had a pleasant Gallic wit, but he was so ugly that when
I asked him to Sixty-sixth Street for a weekend, Clarisse was repelled
by him and begged me never to bring him again.

"Why," she asked me, "do you have to make friends with a gargoyle? He looks as if he'd come straight off Notre Dame."

Dick Purbright's father was a partner in a Denver insurance firm which failed to weather the first onslaught of the Depression, and he was obliged to leave Harvard. He'd been to our house fairly often and he'd fallen in love with Clarisse, who liked him but who had eyes only for Fred. Dick was still in that stage of development in which a lovely face is irresistible, and I ought to have known what Clarisse would do to him. He combined this youthful, visual love with a lot of romantic notions, and he was so serious about it all as to be pitiable; indeed I pitied him sincerely. Clarisse might be my sister ten times over, but I could not help taking a sort of showman's pride in her unusual beauty, and I was perfectly well able to understand its effect on others.

I was sitting in Dick's room while he was packing his trunk, and I kept telling myself that it was I who ought to have been leaving, for I believed he would profit far more by the next two years than I would.

"What will you do, Dick?" I asked him.

"I'll find something," he said, "even if it's only a job in a filling station. My family have done a lot for me; it's time I did something for them. Anyway," he added, carefully folding a pair of trousers, "it settles things as far as Clarisse is concerned. As things are I couldn't hope to marry her in a hundred years. Not that I ever had a lot of reason for my hope."

I had been careful to keep the secret of her engagement, but now the need to comfort him took first place, and I told him about it.

He went on folding his clothes for a minute without speaking. Then he said, "Thanks for the cold shower. I guess it's just what I needed. You might tell her one day, if you happen to think of it, that I'll never love anyone else. Maybe I'll write to her when the engagement's announced; maybe I'd better not. But tell her what I said."

We were very solemn about it and I felt I was taking part in something pretty tragic.

"Perhaps you're well out of it," I said, still anxious to staunch his wounds. "Perhaps Clarisse is a sort of *femme fatale*."

"She's beautiful enough to be," he conceded. Then he added, with a wry smile, "Clarisse plus the Depression—what a combination of irresistible forces!"

I felt very sad when he left and altogether it was a gloomy winter, though the only change the Depression had so far made in my life was that my father put a ban on any further buying of drawings.

Actually I'd seen nothing I wanted or felt I could afford, and with failures and financial crashes on every hand I'd already decided to abstain. When spring came there was a general improvement in the whole situation and Wall Street announced a "Little Bull Market." Shares rose encouragingly and my parents began to make plans for their next trip to Europe; but Syl wouldn't hear of it.

"This isn't going to last," he warned my father. "It's just a flash in the pan. I'm willing to bet my bottom dollar that the worst is yet to come and when it does come, look out! This time it'll be the real thing. The whole banking system is shaky as hell."

He was right, of course, as he always was. Everyone knows how, after that brief improvement, things went from bad to worse; to unbelievable disaster. One hardly saw a smiling face, and though I hated leaving home I was almost glad, because of all the misery I saw, to leave New York and get back to Cambridge. Europe being out of the question, my parents decided to take a house on Cape Cod for the summer. It had six bedrooms, my mother wrote to me, only two baths and one large living room. As its owner had been badly hit financially he was glad to get it off his hands and the rent was low. My mother said they'd taken the house without even troubling to go up and look at it.

"If we can't go to Europe," she said, "I don't much care what we do except that I will not go to an American country hotel. My Aunt Sophy took me to one once, I can't remember why. It was in the White Mountains. We lived on tough mutton, sweet corn out of a tin, served in those little white dishes like the ones canaries take their baths in, and cold apple pie. The women gossiped all day long in rocking chairs on the porch and dinner was at six o'clock. Never again!"

Julian and I joined the family during the holidays and Fred came up as often as he could. It struck me that my parents' attitude towards Fred had changed; it was less cordial, less affectionate, more formal. They behaved with perfect correctness but they would not, by word or act, forward the affair or show themselves more acquiescent than need be. I doubt if Clarisse and Fred even noticed. Fred had his car and they were out most of the time. He was more in love than ever; in fact I thought his too obvious adoration quite fatuous, while Julian did his best to keep out of their way, cloyed by the very sight of the lovers. A neighbor's mongrel dog had attached itself to him and when he wasn't taking it for walks he would sit reading on the rocks within sight of the sea. One day I followed him, came up behind him noiselessly in my rubber-soled shoes and found to my surprise that he was in a state of deep dejection. For some time he wouldn't tell me what was wrong or explain his obvious misery, but at last I got him to talk.

"Will you do something for me?" he suddenly asked. "Will you tell Father that I don't want to go to Harvard?"

"Why don't you tell him yourself, if you don't want to go?" I asked. He hesitated and looked even more unhappy.

"I don't know," he said. "I just can't talk to him. You talk to him."

"If you don't want to go to Harvard," I said, "where do you want to go?"

"I don't really want to go anywhere," he answered, and he was digging moss out of the rock crannies with a small stick so that I couldn't see his face. "Maybe I could just read or study languages at home. I might even write poetry." Then he threw away the little stick and said, desperately, "It's no good, I just couldn't *take* Harvard, or any other university. I just couldn't take it. I'd rather die than go. I don't feel well enough for one thing about half the time. I've never felt well, not really well, since that asthma I had."

"Have you told Mother?" I asked him, but I knew he hadn't.

"It's no good worrying her," he said.

"Don't be an ass, Julian!" I said. "If you really don't feel well, you'll have to tell her and Father. You'll have to see Dr. Medlicott. You'll have to do something about it."

"It's my heart, I think," he told me. "I'm sure all those attacks of asthma have strained it."

"Dr. Medlicott has examined you often enough," I said. "He'd know if there was anything wrong. But if you won't tell Mother and Father how you feel, I'll have to."

"That's just what I despise most," he said, with an exaggerated shudder. "Talks, and being examined, and being discussed."

"Well, you'll have to put up with that," I told him. "I'll bring the whole thing up after dinner tonight. The sooner the better."

"If you'll promise to back me up," he said.

We had the talk, but nothing was settled, of course, except that my father said he'd ask Syl what could be done about putting Julian's name down for Amherst. He might decide later that he wanted to go there, and Syl had an old friend who was one of the trustees. As soon as we got back to New York, he'd get Medlicott to examine his heart again. My mother kept looking at Julian in the most anxious way.

"My darling," she said, "we had no idea you were feeling like this. Why do you keep everything to yourself? Don't you know that what matters most is your health and your happiness?"

And she made Julian promise to take no more long walks until he'd seen the doctor.

On the whole the summer was hardly a success, though to me the clean, salty air and the brusque, windswept landscape had great charm. My parents badly missed their sightseeing, their picture buying, and, to quote my mother, "the mental stimulus that only Europe can give." They would be glad, she said, to get back to New York, even though the painful moment had now arrived for the announcement of Clarisse's engagement. For Clarisse had shown no sign of changing her mind; in fact she repeatedly assured my parents that she not only had not but that she never would change her mind.

It puzzled me a good deal to understand why Clarisse was so determined to marry Fred, though I never doubted that she enjoyed sunning herself in his adoration. He was good-looking, vital, healthy; a fine tennis player, a first-rate swimmer. He could hardly have taken more care of his teeth, hair, skin, body generally if he had been a film star. (He was always trying new toothpastes and was a "pushover," as we used to say then, for the advertisements in the magazines.) His future was more than promising; it was assured. On the other hand I couldn't help noticing that he seemed almost perversely indifferent to the things that most of her life had claimed Clarisse's liking and attention. He was not at all susceptible to the charm of "foreignness," took no interest at all in art and was not much of a reader, though he did read some of the popular successes. (Clarisse, it was true, only read novels but at least her taste in novels was pretty good.) Whether this attitude of his was real or pretended I couldn't tell, but I sometimes suspected that he was out to "Americanize" Clarisse if he could. I knew he was fond of us all, but I guessed that if he could pry Clarisse loose from her close adherence to my mother and father, he would.

Syl, of course, had known about the love affair ever since my mother had written to him from Rome—a tactful letter saying how pleased we all were that it was Fred, but that we felt the two were far too young to marry. (He had replied by cable, saying "Hurrah. Let them wait a while, but not too long. It's never too soon to be happy.") Now, the public announcement simply delighted him. I doubt if anything in the world—not even an immediate end to the

Depression—could have given him more pleasure. That his "little sweetheart" was really going to marry his beloved and only nephew made him inordinately happy.

He came to see us on the day the announcement was in the papers and he was in a state of great excitement. He might almost, I thought, have been a prospective bridegroom himself. He said he particularly wanted to see Clarisse.

"She's up in her room, Syl," my mother said. "I'll ask Arnaud to tell her you're here."

"Any reason why I shouldn't go up myself?" Syl asked. "I want to see her privately." And he said this with a great air of mystery.

"Of course, Syl dear, if you like," my mother said. "Go right up."

I looked at my mother and saw that she was even more than usually pale, and that there were dark shadows under her eyes. She saw my glance and said, "Do I look very badly, Halley? All this has given me such a headache. And trying not to let Syl see how sad we feel about it isn't easy."

"He's as happy as a sandboy," my father said. "It makes it all very difficult. What do you suppose he wants to see Clarisse privately for?"

"Oh, darling," my mother said, "can't you guess? He's got an engagement present in his pocket for her."

"Good God!" my father exclaimed. "Presents, already? Has the horrible business actually begun? Are we going to have a whole year of this? It's intolerable."

"You'd better get your smiles ready," I said. "Everybody you meet will want to congratulate you."

"Good God!" he said again. "I don't think I'd visualized that part of it. I wish to heaven we could slip off abroad and take Clarisse with us till it blows over."

My mother gave a little laugh that was half a sob.

"Don't make it sound worse than it is," she said.

A few minutes later Syl and Clarisse came downstairs. Syl was blowing his nose and looking both moved and triumphant, and Clarisse was holding out her right arm dramatically.

"Look!" she cried, excitedly, "just look at what our darling Syl has just given me."

It was a sapphire-and-diamond bracelet, the biggest and bluest sapphires I ever saw linked together with diamonds in a very pretty design. My parents had never given Clarisse anything but simple jewelry and her eyes looked enormous with pleasure.

"Isn't it marvelous?" she demanded. "Isn't it simply gorgeous? Did you ever see anything so lovely?"

"By golly, Syl!" my father said. "You've got no right to preach to me about economy."

"Oh, Syl!" my mother cried. "You spoil our child. You always have spoilt her. It's beautiful. It's a gift for a queen."

"Well," said Syl beaming and showing those big teeth, "and that's exactly what it is. Let me tell you all, this is one of the happiest days of my whole life. When I read the announcement in the papers this morning for the whole world to see, I could have jumped over the moon."

"Oh, Syl," my mother said, and tears came into her eyes, "we do love you so and we're so grateful for everything, but all the same, Myron and I wish they were both a good deal older than they are. They're such children. Don't you think yourself they ought to wait till they're older?"

"Oh, Mother," Clarisse pleaded, "I'm as old as you were when you met Father. You knew what you wanted then and I know what I want now."

"No one's ever too young to be happy," Syl said, and he went to my mother and kissed her cheek. "Everything's going to be fine, Ruth. They're a lucky young couple, and Depression or no Depression, they can get married whenever they like. Fred will have enough to support a wife on and he'll take good care of Clarisse. He's a fine, responsible boy and he'll make a fine husband."

My father, I saw, was looking very worried and he now broke in. "Hold on a moment, Syl. The understanding was that the engagement would last a year, a whole year, and that there'd be no talk of their marrying till next fall. I don't see any reason to alter this plan."

"Oh, Father," said Clarisse, going to him and putting her arm through his, "if Syl says it would be all right for us to get married sooner, in the spring, perhaps, do let us! What's the good of waiting a whole solid year? We've waited a year already. We've been awfully good."

Syl was too well armored by his own satisfaction to see how disturbed and upset my parents were, for this was cutting the ground from under their feet. He turned to me.

"You agree with me, don't you, Halley?" he asked me. "Do you see any point in making them wait all that time?"

I took my parents' side.

"Well, Syl," I said, "if you really want me to tell you what I think,

I think they're pretty young. Fred's only twenty-three, and Clarisse could do with more experience than she's got."

She gave me a furious look.

"What sort of experience do you want me to have before I get married?" she demanded. "The sort you've had, I suppose? The sort all boys have."

Syl quickly intervened.

"I'm getting to be an old man," he said. "When you get near seventy, anything may happen. Maybe I'm selfish, Ruth, but I don't want to have to wait that long. Now you and Myron talk it over. If you can bear to part with her in the fall, I guess you can bear it just as well in the spring, and if you come around to my way of thinking, you'll be making me very happy. Now I've got to run along because I've got to go out to dinner. What I'd like to do would be to stay right here with you and eat a meal cooked by Mrs. Schwarz because she's the best cook in New York, but I've got to dine with an old client of mine. Bless you all!"

I started to go to the door with him but Clarisse gave me a quick frown and I stayed where I was and let her go. We could hear her in the hall thanking him again for the bracelet but we couldn't hear what he said because he kept his voice very low. I guessed he was urging her to stick to her guns, just as he used to urge me to be an American boy, and to ask my parents to let me go to school.

That night Clarisse came into my room after I was in bed and switched on the light. Then she sat down on the foot of my bed.

"Wake up," she said. "I want to talk to you."

She had on her pale pink negligée over her nightgown, and her silvery-blond hair was hanging down on either side of her face. I thought she looked like the Blessed Damozel in person except that I could see that she was angry.

"I wasn't asleep yet," I said, blinking in the sudden light.

"I think you're a mean beast," she said, keeping her voice low so as not to wake Julian in the next room. "What did you want to take sides against Fred and me for? You know perfectly well we don't want to wait another year."

"Why not?" I asked. "What's all the hurry about? Fred isn't going to run away."

"Oh, don't be so infuriating," she said. "A year's practically forever. It means I'll just be hanging about doing nothing all that time. If I were at Vassar or somewhere there'd be some sense in it. I sometimes wish I'd made up my mind to go to college."

"It isn't too late," I told her, but I knew it was too late; that she'd have had to take that decision long ago.

"Of course it's too late," she said, "and you ought to understand how I feel. You always say you're so wonderful at understanding people." (I had no recollection of having made this claim, though I may have done so.) "I didn't want a regular coming out like Rosie had, because we don't know enough people in New York to make it worth while, and I haven't a lot of friends here. It was different when I used to have Bewlay coming in every day. Girls don't just stay at home nowadays doing nothing. It would look silly. And it would be just as silly for me to try and get a job in a hat shop or something. But if Fred and I could find a nice apartment near by it would give me a *raison d'être,* and I can't see that it would make an awful lot of difference to Mother and Father. I could come in practically every day and be in anything that's going on. But if you're going to turn against me it's pretty hopeless."

"I haven't turned against you," I told her. "Syl asked me what I thought and I told him, that's all."

"Well, you might have thought of my side of it." She looked down at the bracelet which she hadn't taken off yet. "Halley," she said, and her lips and chin were quivering as if she were about to cry, "please help me. I wish I knew what I wanted. I don't, and that's the whole trouble. I want to get married and I want to stay at home. But now that the engagement's announced I feel I may as well go ahead and get married as soon as possible. Besides, you know how it is. Every man I meet starts the same old thing and Fred gets terribly jealous. It's really no fun for me. I think we ought to get married in June. Will you say you think so too? Please, Halley!"

"But if you aren't sure about it yourself—about getting married at all, I mean, why—?"

She didn't let me finish.

"Of course I'm sure, really," she said. "I suppose everyone has doubts sometimes. It means a big change in one's life. But I'm sure Syl's right, and it would be silly to wait for a whole year without any good reason. It isn't as though Fred couldn't afford to marry yet. Syl is going to see to all that."

"All right," I said. "If you really want me to say I think you might as well be married in June, I will."

She got up then.

"Don't you want to be tucked in?" she asked, and I knew this was her way of showing me she was grateful. "Your bedclothes are all out on this side."

"No thanks," I answered. "That's the way I like them."

She said good night, switched off the light and left me. I knew there wouldn't be time to say what she wanted me to say before I went back to Cambridge because I was driving up and starting early in the morning before my parents would be awake, so I decided to write it instead.

I did write it a few days later, and my mother replied in a long letter. She said that Clarisse wanted the wedding to be in June because Syl wanted it so much, but she and my father had now decided that, little though they liked the idea ("It gives them so much less time if they should want to change their minds") they ought to give in for Syl's sake. "We owe him so much, and after all he *is* getting on, and in this country men like Syl are apt to go off quite suddenly. He's never understood the meaning of leisure and so has never had any. June it must be, I suppose, and though our hearts will just about break, we must see it through. Speaking of hearts," she went on, "Dr. Medlicott has had Julian's carefully examined by a heart specialist, and while the specialist assures us there's nothing specifically wrong, he says it does show signs of fatigue. But he says this will soon pass, with reasonable care, and he thinks there's nothing at all to prevent his going to a university if that's what he wants to do. But I don't believe Julian himself is very keen about it. He spoke of taking up a course of studies at home, and your father thinks this is quite a good idea. How difficult it is to know, and how I wish you were all children again!"

I didn't look forward to Christmas that year as I usually did, though when it came it was—with us at least—much like other Christmases. But I was troubled and distressed by the misery I saw and heard about, and the threadbare young men selling apples at street corners had increased in number. It humiliated me that I could not feel as unhappy as I should; I didn't know how to adjust myself to the change, or if I should even try to, and I wished most earnestly for better times. Early in the spring I ordered a new suit, then despised myself for doing so. I canceled the order and gave the money it would have cost me to the Community Chest on one of its "drives," then, a couple of weeks later, I decided that I really would need the suit and was obliged to ask my father for the money. When I explained why I had to ask him he said:

"I think you've been a little foolish, Halley, though of course I believe in giving to charity now and again. It does the giver good and I've no doubt the Community Chest reaches many deserving cases. But the people of this country have got to learn their lesson once and for all. They don't understand the meaning of thrift. Here's a check, by boy, but please don't do it again."

The next time I saw Syl I asked him how I ought to feel and what I ought to do.

"It doesn't do any good," I said, "to go around with the corners of my mouth down crying 'Woe, woe, woe!' But I do feel too lucky and too selfish to live."

"It does you credit, my boy," Syl answered, "but all the advice I can give you is this; give what you can to charity and stop worrying. This won't last forever. In a couple of years—well, three at the outside—we'll be on the up grade. Don't you let anyone tell you this system isn't the best system in the world. I know it is. It's never broken down before and it probably never will again. We must all keep our heads and our confidence. We'll pull out of it. This country can pull out of anything if it's got the will, and it has."

I had gone to see him during the Christmas vacation in his apartment in Park Avenue, not far from his brother Irving's. Syl's was smaller but not much smaller, and he had a colored woman named Mimi and her daughter Pearl to look after him. No one could have been more comfortable. The only pictures he had were old American prints—Currier and Ives, and others—and some old maps. His bedroom furniture was in old-fashioned bird's-eye maple and he was very proud of it. He had one fondness that none of us could understand, and that was for playing classical music on his gramophone. He had a great many records, and he sometimes suggested that I sit down and listen to one or two while he played them through, but I always made some excuse, saying that I had an engagement or was expected back at home. On this occasion, however, feeling full of good will towards all men and towards Syl in particular, I agreed to stay, and he beamed with pleasure. He put on a Brahms symphony—I forget now which one it was—and played it right through. Before going to bed that evening I noted in my diary, "Went to see Syl after dinner. Talked about the Depression. Was persuaded to listen to a Brahms symphony. Didn't dislike it as much as I thought I would." In fact I scarcely listened; my mind kept straying away and I thought about a great many other things. In consequence I did not find it actually disagreeable or particularly boring, and it helped, too, to know that I was giving Syl a good deal of pleasure. He knew of course, none better, about my mother's early history and understood very well why we had never been encouraged to take an interest in music, but he had often predicted that someday I would.

"You'll come to it, my boy," he often said. "You'll come to it in your own time and in your own way."

Like most of his friends he was an ardent supporter of the Metropolitan Opera Company and during the season went regularly to the opera. We knew, too, that he went to a good many smart musical parties. For this reason I had always connected music in my mind with the "best" society, and I assumed that Syl did too, but looking at his face that evening I wondered if I hadn't perhaps been mistaken.

"Do this again, my boy," he said to me as I was leaving, and he patted my shoulder affectionately. "There's some music somewhere in your soul, and that's more than I can say for the other members of your dear family."

Clarisse and Fred had now begun to look for an apartment in earnest. My mother kept telling them not to hurry; they could take their time, she said, because if they failed to find what they exactly wanted before they were married they could stay in Sixty-sixth Street afterwards until they did. Then one day I had an anxious letter from Clarisse, and from the writing I judged it had been dashed off in haste.

Dear Halley [she wrote]:

I'm very worried. I don't know what's come over Fred and I want you to help me. He finds something wrong with every apartment we look at. The rooms are too small or the rent's too big, or it's too dark or it isn't in the right district. I admit that most of the time I agree with him though there was one in Sixty-eighth Street that I wouldn't have minded having. But now what do you think he wants to do? He wants to give up the idea of having an apartment in New York altogether and buy a house out in the suburbs. He's set his heart on Rye of all places! You know what it's like—neither town nor country—and I don't see myself as a little suburban wife. What on earth would I do in Rye? Can you imagine such a thing? He says I'll have a car of my own and can come in to New York whenever I like and that at least we'd have room to move about in. We've actually been to see a house there—I thought just one look at it would be enough for him so I agreed to go—and to my horror he says he thinks it would do perfectly! In fact he's quite crazy about it. It's near the golf club and it's got a garden and he points out that there'd be room for you or Rosie or even Father and Mother to come and stay with us sometimes. But Halley, I just can't bear the idea! What am I going to do? Of course I went straight to Syl because I thought he'd be on my side, but he says he thinks Fred's quite right. He says he thinks it's a fine idea at least while the Depression is still with us and that we won't spend nearly as much money as we would if we lived in New York. Well, I suppose that may be true, but how could I possibly bear that sort of life? I'd rather live in one room in New York near the family than in ten rooms in Rye. Halley, won't you please help me? You must help me. I've never known Fred as *entêté* as he is about this. He swears it would only be for a few years and that a house is a good investment anyway, but oh God! Halley, what would I do there all day long? Please talk to Fred next time you come down but you'll have to hurry because it's getting so late and he wants to buy the house right away. He might listen to you. Mother and Father entirely agree with me but they don't want to say anything because they're afraid of seeming to interfere. Really and truly, Halley, I'm feeling quite desperate.

Your loving but worried sister,
Clarisse

I did talk to Fred about it at the very first opportunity. I spoke to him privately, in his own bedroom, and as I had fully expected, he told me to mind my own business. But he was rarely angry for more than a minute or two and when his anger had cooled he sat down again and told me quite frankly that he thought it would be a good thing to get Clarisse away from the family for the first few years of their marriage.

"And I know I'm right, Halley," he said, "so don't you go putting your oar in. She'd be running in to be with your mother and father the whole time. Besides, there are other reasons. I want Clarisse to have a family, and quick, and if we live in a New York apartment she'd have a darn good excuse for not having one. And there's another thing. You know as well as I do that pretty near every man that looks at her begins to feel a proprietary interest in her, and I'm not taking unnecessary risks. Just let me tell you one thing more. You know I asked Jackson Harmer to be best man. Well, that's all off. I wanted them to sort of get to know each other and he took Clarisse out to dinner a couple of times—well, three times, to be exact—when I couldn't get away from the office. A few days ago he came and told me he'd have to beg off, and why. She's made me lose one of the best friends I ever had. Don't think I'm blaming her; I'm not. I was all kinds of a fool to think it might work. But that's how things are. So just keep your nose out of this, will you, Halley-boy? And while we're on the subject, I'd like you to be best man in

Jackson's place." He slapped me on the knee and got up. He and Clarisse and Rosie and I were going to have dinner together that evening and the two girls were downstairs in the drawing room of the big duplex apartment talking to Irving, Fred's father.

"Have a look at this," Fred said, without even waiting for me to answer, and I could see that he was now his old self again. "It's great stuff." He held out to me a tube of much advertised toothpaste. Then he smiled at me widely. "And have a look at this. My teeth are a whole lot whiter than they were, and it makes your breath sweeter, too. Try it, Halley. Take it home with you. I never believe these advertisements till I've tried them out, but this sure does what it says."

I put the tube in my pocket as he was so insistent and promised to try it.

"Do you really mean that you want me to be best man?" I asked.

"Who else would I want?" he said. "Of course I want you. It isn't going to be easy to explain the change of plan, but I'll think up something. Come on, the girls will want to be off. Now you get to work on Clarisse, she'll listen to you. Because we're going to buy that house in Rye, or else. See?"

I think that if the wedding hadn't been so near—it was the end of April and all the invitations were out—Clarisse might have put up a stronger fight, might even have broken off or threatened to break off the engagement, but things had gone very far and moral courage was scarcely one of my sister's attributes. She had had two fittings for the wedding dress, Irving Dumont had just given her a double string of pearls with a sapphire clasp to match the bracelet Syl had given her and her sapphire and diamond engagement ring, and presents, chiefly from the Dumonts' friends and relations, were already pouring in. My parents had bought all the young couple's silver and linen and it had been announced in the papers that my father was giving his daughter a famous Degas (her own choice) from his famous collection "for her very own." I am sure that Clarisse must have felt like a small, weak fly in the middle of an unbreakable web. As it was, she and Fred, she told me, had had one flaming row which had ended in tears and exhaustion on Clarisse's side— Clarisse sobbing out that she didn't care any more, let him buy his wretched little suburban house, they were only going to live wretched little suburban lives anyway—and alarm and some contrition on Fred's. But in the end the house was bought, Fred promising that they'd spend at least two nights every week in Sixty-sixth Street and take in all the best plays, and that as soon as the Depression was over she should have a couple of months abroad with my parents every year. I think that if he had not been so crazily in love he would surely have paused before making these promises to ask himself a few plain questions.

By fashionable New York standards it was not to be a big wedding, for concessions had to be made to the hard times we were going through. St. James's would only be about half full and Clarisse was to have only two bridesmaids, Rosie and Helen. Helen, now seventeen, was a little taller than Rosie and promised to have more brains. Sometimes, to tease Rosie more than anything else, I used to take her out, but I liked her very much and she was good company, and though I gave little thought to it at that time I knew that she was exceedingly fond of me.

I was spending a night in New York a couple of weeks before the wedding and it went to my heart to see how troubled and unhappy my parents were, especially my mother.

"Oh, Halley," she said, "how thankful I shall be when it's all over! I've always hated weddings and this is going to be a truly dreadful ordeal. Do you remember I said once that I was going to pray it would never happen?"

"Yes," I said, "I remember perfectly. It was at the Flora in Rome."

"Well, I have prayed," she said, and sighed deeply. Then she went on, "The sad thing is that my prayers were so nearly answered. Clarisse was utterly wretched about that house, poor child. She was almost desperate. If things hadn't already gone so far—" She broke off. "What I can't make up my mind about, Halley, is how much Clarisse really cares for Fred. I wish I knew. Do you know?"

"She's stuck to him pretty well," I said. "She's never really looked at anybody else."

"He's never given her a chance to," my mother said with bitterness. Then her eyes, full of mournful intensity, looked into mine. "Halley," she said, "I've always suspected that you knew about Clarisse and Fred long before you told me you did. If I'm right, and if you had told us then, at once, all this might have been prevented."

I knew she was right, and it had troubled me ever since that afternoon in the boathouse. If I had told them then it might have been just another Raymond episode. As it was, it had flourished on secrecy and on Clarisse's belief that she was doing something very grown-up and daring. I had been a fool and I was largely responsible for what had happened, and I was glad, now, to admit it.

[103]

"I think it's the only wrong thing you've ever done, Halley," my mother said, and let a few tears fall. "You've been such a good son and brother that I haven't the heart to reproach you. I never will reproach you, whatever happens, and we'll never speak of it again. But I must tell your father."

VII

F<small>RED</small> <small>GAVE</small> <small>A</small> <small>BACHELOR</small> <small>DINNER</small> <small>AND</small> <small>INVITED</small> <small>TWENTY</small> <small>OF</small> <small>HIS</small>
friends, and of course I had to be there. If he was at all worried he
certainly didn't show it, and I don't think he was. I think he felt
perfectly confident that as soon as he and Clarisse were married,
she would settle down quite happily and all would go well. He had
loved her ever since his twelfth birthday, as he was fond of telling
people, and he had never for a moment contemplated marrying anyone else. But I now fully shared my parents' apprehensions, and
this, combined with the nervousness I felt at the thought of being
best man, made it a joyless evening for me. I drank far too much
in the hope of bolstering up my spirits, and in the early morning
had to wake Louise and get her to bring me some mixture that would
soothe my outraged stomach and send me to sleep. I had no qualms
about waking her for she always enjoyed ministering to us and even
seemed grateful to me on that occasion for calling upon her, though
it was nearly three o'clock. As she left me she said that she would
give her right hand—no, both hands she assured me, holding them
out—if by doing so she could prevent the marriage.

"Stop worrying, Louise," I said. "Everything will turn out all right."

She gave me a look of scorn and pity and closed the door.

Weddings are pretty much alike, but Clarisse's was a painful ordeal for all of us, and I made up my mind then that if I ever married it would be in a registry office or in a small country church. I
would have given almost anything if Jackson Harmer could have
been in my place. On the day of the wedding my mother woke with
one of her worst headaches and my father said to me,

"If your mother wasn't one of the bravest women in the world
she could never go through with this."

"How are you feeling?" I asked him.

"About as gay," he answered, "as if I were going to be put up
against a wall and shot."

When I saw my father coming up the aisle with Clarisse on his arm, I thought he looked smaller and much older, but of course Clarisse seemed taller than she was in her long gown and veil with her hair done up on the top of her head, and she was holding herself very straight. In spite of the lovely dress and the lace and the pearls she didn't look to me as beautiful as she usually did. She was too pale, for one thing, and she'd refused to put on any rouge. Rosie, confident and happy, followed with Helen, who looked awed and nervous. They were dressed alike, in flowered chiffon dresses. Rosie kept catching my eye with a "We're next" look in it that I tried hard to avoid. My mother was sitting between Syl and Julian in the front pew, for Syl had said that he was going to be beside the mother of his little sweetheart and nowhere else. It was his great day and I don't think a single doubt clouded his happiness. It was not in his nature to take anything but a rosy view of marriage though he had been careful to avoid it himself and though the broken marriages of others must have occupied a large part of his time and attention. He clung to the Pollyanna view and wedding bells rang sweetly in his ears. No one in New York wore top hat, striped trousers, morning coat and carnation buttonhole more readily or oftener than Syl. Now he had got his heart's dearest wish and his eyes shone happily behind his pince-nez.

I knew of course that there would be about four times as many of the Dumonts' friends and relations at the wedding as there would be of ours. (In fact, our only known relation, my mother's Aunt Sophy Bligh, was unable to come.) Even so, I was hardly prepared for the great number of strange faces I saw. It all seemed to me like a part of someone else's dream into which I had wandered by mistake, and only Fred, my own family, Syl and Raymond—who was sitting on the aisle well toward the front—seemed real to me. Fred looked completely happy and serenely confident. His face shone, his blue eyes poured out his adoration upon Clarisse's bent head as they stood side by side, and he made me think of a muscular Angel Gabriel in modern dress.

Clarisse's responses must have been quite inaudible in the body of the church and even those of us who stood near could hardly hear her. I produced the ring without fumbling and thanked heaven that my duties were nearly over, for the heavy scent of lilies combined with the queasiness I always felt at times of emotional strain began to force themselves on my notice. I must have been as pale as Clarisse, for afterwards, when we were in the vestry, Irving Dumont came up to me, took me by the arm and drew me into a corner.

"My boy," he said, "you aren't looking too good. I've been watching you. I've got a little flask in my pocket—I always carry one. Here, nobody'll see us—take just a nip or two of brandy. It'll make all the difference."

I was grateful to him and did as he told me, though by that time I was feeling better.

"I don't think I would have fainted," I said, "but I certainly felt queer. Thanks, Mr. Dumont."

He looked a good deal like Syl, but he was bigger and heavier, and he reminded me sometimes of a *New Yorker* drawing of a powerful executive. Clarisse could draw a recognizable likeness of him in about five strokes.

"Call me Irving," he said. "I've always liked you, Halley, though I haven't seen as much of you as Syl has. Let's see more of each other from now on, shall we? Our place is home to you, my boy, and don't you forget it."

I felt pretty sure then that he knew about Rosie's feelings for me. I smiled at him and said I wouldn't forget, and then we joined the others who were signing the book. Rosie came and stood beside me.

"All right now?" she whispered. "You looked awful, Halley."

"I'm fine," I said. "What's all the fuss about?"

"You were so pale. I wish you'd seen yourself. You were as pale as Clarisse. But doesn't she look wonderful, Halley? There never was such a perfectly beautiful bride. She makes me want to cry. A lot of people were crying. I could see them mopping away at their eyes."

"Just wedding blues," I told her. "Nothing but wedding blues."

"Don't be so superior," she said. "You were all worked up yourself, and I don't wonder, as you've never been best man before. I'm so glad you were best man, you looked so much nicer standing there than Jackson Harmer would have done."

Fred came and put his arm across my shoulder.

"You were swell, Halley-boy," he said. "We couldn't have had a better best man. I'm glad now that Jackson ran out on us. Gosh! it's been wonderful, hasn't it? Take the girls along to the reception, will you, Halley? Dad's giving a lift to some of the cousins. See you later."

The reception was at the St. Regis, which was the hotel the Dumonts always patronized. My parents didn't much care where it took place, they simply longed for it all to be over as quickly as possible. Two friends of mine, Bob Lane and Harry Wilson, had come down from Harvard for the wedding, and I collected them and Rosie and Helen, and drove them all to the hotel ahead of the crowd.

The one person there I was really glad to see was Raymond. He had filled out quite a lot and seemed to have more self-confidence than he used to have. He told me that everything was going well with him.

"Clarisse looked wonderful, didn't she?" he said. "Born to be a bride. They ought to be happy, those two. There's something very touching about these boy-and-girl romances."

I wondered if he remembered the note Clarisse had put under his pillow, but if he did his face gave nothing away. I told him I wished I could see him oftener.

"I wish it too, Halley," he said, and he urged me to come and see him in Washington. For some time we stood talking in the midst of all the clamor, then he looked at his watch. "I'll just kiss the bride and say good-by to your father and mother, and then I'll have to get back to Washington," he told me. His face, which was rounder than it used to be, broadened into a happy if slightly embarrassed smile. "Halley," he said, "don't tell anyone else, but I'm getting married myself in a couple of months. She's a widow, a Mrs. Locksley. A most charming person, and I'm incredibly lucky. She wants me to write, so I'm giving up my job at the Smithsonian and we're going to live in France."

I shook his hand and congratulated him warmly. I knew that he had always wanted to write, and I guessed, of course, that his future wife had some money of her own. I felt as pleased as if some longed-for thing were about to happen to me.

"Mirabeau?" I asked, and he fairly beamed at me.

"Think of your remembering that all these years!" he said. "Yes, it will be Mirabeau. I can hardly believe my good fortune. And it all started when your father engaged me to come as your tutor. It all began then."

It was the only pleasant part of the whole day, seeing Raymond and hearing his good news, and I urged him to let me tell the family.

"All right," he said. "I'd like them to be the first people to know, of course. Tell them tomorrow, if you like."

He slipped away soon after that. As things turned out it was weeks before I remembered to say anything about it to anyone.

The crowd and the noise they made did nothing to raise my spirits, nor did the champagne I drank. I couldn't throw off the conviction that things had somehow got off on the wrong track, that this wasn't the way they should have gone. I suppose I had caught some of this feeling from my father and mother, but I simply couldn't make myself feel happy about Clarisse and Fred, however hard I tried. I had scarcely seen Clarisse during the last few weeks, and during the twenty-four hours I had spent in the house she had been busy with clothes or with directing Louise what to pack; or perhaps she had been deliberately keeping out of my way. When I had caught a glimpse of her she had seemed very subdued, so much so that I knew it couldn't wholly be put down to tiredness. "Well," I said to myself in the midst of the heat and the noise, the flashing of light bulbs and the clicking of cameras, "here we all are, and all because I made that promise to Fred in the boathouse." And my guilt seemed to me a monstrous burden that I would never shake off.

It was a blazing afternoon, more like July than early June, and I marveled that anyone should want to stay a minute longer than politeness required, but more and more people were coming in and nobody seemed to be leaving. I kept glancing at my mother, who was still standing in the receiving line and was glad to see that her face had not lost the determined smile she had bravely put on for the day. My father had already given up. He was standing in a corner talking to a friend of his, a Wall Street broker named Conrad Falke. He sometimes dined at our house and Syl and my father had many an argument about him because my father thought him very "civilized" and clever and Syl did not. I made my way through the crowd to speak to him but before I got there he had gone.

"How long will this have to go on, Halley?" my father asked me, passing a handkerchief over his forehead and about his neck. "Will it ever end? Can't we break away soon?"

"I should think there'd be another hour of it," I said. "Clarisse is just going to cut the wedding cake now."

"Good God!" my father said, following Clarisse with his eyes. "She doesn't look to me as if she could stand much more of it. What barbarous affairs these are! As for your poor mother—!"

"Well," I said, "I guess everything comes to an end sometime."

"I feel," my father said, "that there's little foundation for your optimism. By the way, Halley, I wouldn't drink too much of this champagne if I were you. Irving chose it and there'll be a lot of headaches tomorrow."

I went away presently to see how Bob and Harry were getting on. I'd left them with Rosie and Helen and they appeared to be getting on very well. I couldn't find Julian anywhere and I learnt later that he'd gone to a drugstore near by and had sat drinking lemonades for over an hour.

Presently my father came to me and took me by the arm.

"I had a word with Clarisse," he told me. "She says she and Fred are leaving here in ten minutes. Halley, are you planning to go out anywhere tonight?"

"Well," I said, "I was thinking of going out somewhere with the two girls and Bob and Harry, but I'm quite ready to call it a day. I'm not particularly keen on going out."

"Why don't you tell them so?" he asked. "Your mother and I are both feeling pretty miserable, and it would help a lot if you were going to be in this evening. Do you think you could arrange it that way?"

"I could think up some excuse, I guess," I answered. "I don't feel particularly like making whoopee, to tell the truth."

"I should think not," he said. He lowered his voice. "I'm convinced the whole thing has been a horrible mistake, from beginning to end. Do you think Clarisse is going to be completely absorbed by Dumonts? I must have been introduced to fifty of them today. Thank heaven we're a family and not a clan."

Rosie and Helen, with Bob Lane and Harry Wilson, came back to the house with me. Fred changed in my room, and Rosie and Helen went up with Clarisse while she changed. Bob and Harry sat with us in the library, having a drink or two, and my mother sat on the sofa with her feet up, resting. Fred came down first, dressed in a light Palm Beach suit, and presently Clarisse came down followed by the two girls. She had on a blue linen outfit and a little white hat and white shoes. She and Fred were going to Bar Harbor the next day for a two-week honeymoon, and now the time had come to say good-by. Bob and Harry went out into the hall and talked to Arnaud while the good-bys were said, and Rosie and Helen took the hint and followed them. Clarisse, without speaking, put her arms about my mother and tears were running down her cheeks. My mother couldn't speak either; they embraced each other wordlessly and then Clarisse turned to my father, her face quivering.

"Oh, Clarry, Clarry," was all he could say, "oh, Clarry!"

"Make it snappy, sweetheart," said Fred, smiling at her. "Don't prolong the agony."

She broke away from my father and threw Fred a most unbride-like look. Then she turned to me.

"Halley," she managed to say, brokenly, "thank you for all you did."

I kissed her and my face was wet with her tears and my own too. Then she turned to Julian.

"Don't you cry over me," Julian said, backing away, but she ran to him and threw her arms about him, grateful to him, I could see, for having broken the emotional tension.

"I don't care if I never see you again, you little beast," she cried, hugging him and half laughing, half crying, and Julian drew the back of his hand across his eyes.

"Please don't say 'good-by,'" she pleaded, looking round at us all. "Please don't use that word. I can't bear it if you do."

"It's only for two weeks, sweetheart," Fred cheerfully reminded her. Then he kissed my mother fondly and shook hands with my father, Julian and me.

"Write and tell us what it's like there," I said. "We might go some-day."

We all went to the door with them. Louise, who had been seen to cry steadily throughout the ceremony, Arnaud and Mrs. Schwarz were all there. The Cadillac—a new one—with Johnson at the wheel, was waiting to take the bride and groom to the Plaza. We waved till they were out of sight.

"Aren't they just the luckiest pair ever?" Rosie asked. It was the sort of remark I might have guessed she would make. I was still very fond of Rosie; I had always known her and the familiar was dear to me, but her power to irritate me had not lessened with the years. I said I wasn't coming out with them after all, that I was too tired, and Rosie's face at once took on that hurt look I knew so well.

"We don't want him anyway," Bob Lane said. "He only makes an odd number. Come on, girls. Where do we go from here?"

"If I know Rosie," I said, "you'll discuss it for about an hour and then end up at the Stork Club."

"If you aren't even coming with us," Rosie said tartly, "you might at least allow us to make our own plans without suggestions from you."

"Why should Halley come," Helen asked, "if he doesn't feel like it? Good-by, Halley dear. I've drunk so much champagne that I feel at peace with all the world."

She put her arms around me and kissed me and I remember think-ing as I felt her cheek against mine that if she had been the elder sister instead of Rosie, things might have been very different. I wished at that moment that I could have taken her out to dinner, just the two of us, alone, because I was sure that, young though she was, I could have talked everything over with her, and that we would have been in complete accord. I think she was wishing it too, for she gave me a wistful and loving look before she turned away.

They walked down the street to find a taxi, and I stood at the front door till after they had rounded the corner out of sight. It was a lovely evening. The sun hadn't yet gone down and was still gilding the house fronts and setting fire to windows, and the sky was deeply, benevolently blue. It was a moment of peace, the first one that day, and I was glad I had got out of going with them. When I went back to the library my mother was standing on tiptoe to look into a little Italian mirror, powdering her nose and at the same time stopping to wipe her eyes. She looked round as I came in.

"I hope I didn't behave too badly, Halley," she said, "but I simply couldn't pretend to be glad."

"Well, dearest," my father said walking up and down the room with his hands behind his back, "it's only for two weeks, remember. Just think, in two weeks she'll be back with us again."

"As Mrs. Fred Dumont," my mother said with a little sob. "She's never been away from us for two weeks in the whole of her life before, and now she'll come back as Mrs. Fred Dumont."

It was no good my saying that these things were bound to come and that they wouldn't have wanted her not to marry. They hadn't wanted her to marry now and they hadn't wanted her to marry Fred, and nothing was going to console them.

Mrs. Schwarz gave us a delicious little dinner and Arnaud served it with mournful sympathy, putting down the plates as if someone in the house were lying dead. He kept looking at my mother, whose eyes were still red, and I could see he longed to say something comforting.

At about half past nine Julian said he was going up to bed. He announced at the same time that he hoped never to have to go to another wedding as long as he lived.

"Don't imagine you're the only one who feels like that, my boy," my father told him, and my mother kissed him and said tenderly, "Don't sit up late reading, darling. You look very, very tired."

"I'm not really tired," Julian said. "I'm only disgusted, and I don't think I like the human race much anyway."

The three of us sat there talking for about an hour, and we tried not to speak of Clarisse and Fred. My father told me that he was getting a Miss Halpern who sometimes acted as his secretary to help him make some alterations and additions to the catalogue of the collection.

"It really wants reprinting," he said, "and bringing up to date. I want to get out an illustrated catalogue sometime, with short biographies of the artists. You might help me with that, Halley."

"I'd like to if I could," I said.

He went on, "I've got a plan in my mind that I'd like to tell you about. So far I've only discussed it with your mother and with Syl. For some years, as you know, I've been wishing I could buy old Barnard Richter's house next door. Well, now that the old man's died at last it's going to come up for sale. It's the same as this, more or less, and what I'd like to do would be to open up the drawing-room floor and this floor and put the two houses together. Then I could hang all the pictures instead of having to keep about half of them in the basement. Someday of course I mean to form a trust, and then I'd turn the collection, with the two houses containing it, over to the nation. If Syl would let me do as I liked I'd buy that house tomorrow. I mentioned it to Conrad Falke this afternoon and he said he thought I'd be making a perfectly safe investment even if I wanted to sell the house again later."

"Syl would be furious with you," my mother told him, "if he knew you'd been talking to Mr. Falke about it."

"Well, we just won't tell him," my father said.

I knew of course that my father intended to give his collection to the nation someday (there had been a time when he had wanted to house it in Paris and give it to the French, but Syl had talked him out of it) though I hadn't supposed it would come in the foreseeable future. I asked him where we would live.

"Do you mean before the trust is formed? We'd live here, of course, just as we do now. If Syl would let me buy that house, Clarisse and Fred—" he hesitated before he spoke their names—"could live on the two top floors of it. After the trust is formed we could go and live abroad and just keep an apartment somewhere here. Your mother and I feel that life on this side of the Atlantic hasn't a great deal to offer us."

"Especially now," my mother said with a deep sigh.

"What would you call it?" I asked. "The trust, I mean."

"It would be called the Prentiss Foundation," he said, and there was a tremor of pride in his voice. "There would be classes for art students, lectures, all that sort of thing." And he went on to outline the whole plan which, I could see, had lately taken a much clearer shape in his mind. I knew then as well as if he had said so plainly that this was the dearest ambition of his life.

"I really don't think I ought to miss this opportunity," he said. "It's what I've always dreamed of. It means a very great deal to me. Syl forgets that other well-to-do men buy steam yachts, or squander money on mistresses—"

"Sweetheart!" my mother murmured in soft protest.

"Well, isn't that true? We haven't even got a place in the country. And we don't entertain—or only in a small way. Quiet little dinner parties now and again. My collection—and I need hardly add, my family—have been my whole life. Literally, my whole life. Depression or no Depression, I think I ought to go right ahead and buy that house."

I thought so too, though I wasn't asked for my opinion, and I am quite sure my mother did, for she hardly ever opposed my father in anything he wanted to do. I only wondered how Syl's objections could be overcome.

And then in the little silence that followed my father's statement the front doorbell began to ring and went on ringing, and at the same time there was a loud, impatient knocking. I can hear the sound yet, shocking the quiet of the house; I can call it back whenever I like, and sometimes I still do, playing it over to myself like a record on a gramophone because it marked the moment in our lives from which everything began to be different.

Arnaud had already gone home, after locking up the house for the night, and as I jumped up my father said, a little nervously, "I suppose it's just another of those telegrams," and I caught a look of real alarm in my mother's eyes. Could her Aunt Sophy Bligh have died suddenly in Santa Barbara, I wondered. The knocking became frantic, outrageous. I ran the last few steps, shot back the bolts as quickly as I could and opened the door.

It was Clarisse. She was alone, and I saw a taxi just driving away.

She looked like a pale messenger of disaster. She looked as if she had come to tell us of flood or war or pestilence. Her eyes were wild and bright with terror.

"For God's sake, couldn't you be quicker?" she almost screamed at me, and I can hear her yet. She turned around like a mad creature, slammed the door shut again and rebolted it with crazy haste. At the sound of her voice my mother and father came running into the hall and their faces were stiff with fear.

"Clarry!" my father cried out in a voice loud with amazement—was there a note of triumph in it too, I wondered later—and my mother opened her arms wide.

"Clarisse! Oh, my precious darling! What's happened?"

Clarisse at once broke into wild, hysterical sobs and cries and flung herself into my mother's arms. She tried to speak, she tried to tell us something, but the only words we could catch in the midst of her sobbing and shuddering and the frightening intervals when she couldn't get her breath were, "Don't—don't—" or "Keep—keep—" and the rest was noise and terror. Between them my parents got her into the library and onto the sofa, and they sat on either side of her, trying to calm and reassure her. At last we knew that what she was trying to say was, "Don't let him in!" and "Keep him out!" My mother looked at me over Clarisse's head and said,

"Get Louise, quick! Tell her to bring sal volatile, anything she thinks may help. Tell her to hurry."

Glad of something to do I raced up the stairs to the top floor, for the slow little elevator which I rarely used would have taken twice the time. I knocked softly on Louise's door, as I didn't want to wake up Mrs. Schwarz in the next room. Louise was at her dressing table, combing out her thin gray hair and wearing the old red woolen dressing gown that I had known for most of my life.

"Louise," I said, "she's come home. Clarisse—she's come home. She's got hysterics. It's terrible. Mother says bring sal volatile—anything. And hurry."

I was sure I saw a look of triumph on Louise's face as she ran to a cupboard and took out bottles and powders. She never uttered a word. It was almost as if she had been expecting it. I turned and hurried down the stairs again. Clarisse was still crying and sobbing in the same alarming way, shuddering and twisting herself about, and holding her breath, and even my father couldn't control her frantic hands. My mother was terrified, I could see, by every sound she heard in the street, more, I thought, than she was by Clarisse's hysterics. In a minute Louise was there, kneeling at Clarisse's feet, and saying to her in French, "Look, *chérie*, it's your own Louise who loves you and who has something good for you. Drink this, my little one, my little child. It will do you good. Drink it to please Louise."

I saw a look pass between my mother and Louise; it was the sort of look that women must have exchanged over the centuries. It was an old, old look and it wasn't hard to interpret, but I knew that they were wrong, quite wrong. It wasn't what they thought. Things had never, I was certain, got so far. Clarisse had panicked and run long before that. She had panicked. I could have told them. To begin with, she was wearing one of her trousseau dresses—the sort of dress girls like Clarisse wear to dine in a good restaurant—simple and smart. And she hadn't put it on in a hurry. She was wearing the necklace that Irving Dumont had given her, Syl's bracelet and of course her wedding and engagement rings. When she came in her hair had been done in a big coil, not on top of her head as she had worn it at the wedding, but low on her neck, showing that she had spent some time at her mirror. (Now it had come down and was all about her shoulders, and her face was blurred and swollen and pitiful with tears.) She had tricked Fred in some shocking way to get here, I was sure of it, but if she had asked me to die for her then I would have willingly done so. Never in all our lives, whatever deplorable thing she had done, had she been more wholly and unalterably my sister.

She was at last sipping from the glass Louise had been holding for her and she was a little quieter, though there were still occasional paroxysms of sobbing. I knew that my parents were anxious to get her out of the room and up to her bedroom as soon as we could possibly manage it, and now that she was no longer twisting and struggling, my father and I between us lifted her up and with some difficulty got her into the elevator. Louise had rushed up ahead of us and was making the bed, and my father sat down in an armchair till it was ready, holding Clarisse in his arms.

She had been in the house about twenty minutes, and I knew it was time for the next thing to happen. There would be a knock on the front door or the telephone would ring, so I decided I had better go downstairs, and I hadn't been in the library more than two minutes before the phone rang. I picked up the receiver and of course it was Fred, and my stomach felt ready to turn over.

"That you, Halley?"

"Yes," I said. "Hello, Fred."

"Is she there?"

"Yes," I said. "She's here."

"I was sure she would be," he answered. "I'm coming around right away. Thank goodness you didn't go out somewhere."

"Look, Fred," I said, "hadn't it better wait till morning? She's in a terrible state. We've got her to bed. She's ill."

"Don't be a damned fool," he said. "Do you think I'm going to stay here alone? I'm coming to fetch her. I'll be right there." And he hung up.

I hurried upstairs again and opening the door of Clarisse's room a few inches, beckoned my father outside. He closed the door and came halfway down the stairs with me so that we shouldn't be heard.

"Fred's rung up," I said. "He's coming right away."

He was biting his lips and his face was white with anxiety.

"You mustn't let him in," he said.

"Suppose he just keeps on ringing and knocking?" I asked. "If I know Fred he'll keep it up till he rouses the whole street."

"This is a terrible situation," my father said. "Terrible! Fred must have behaved—good God! The whole thing is horrifying! He certainly can't see her tonight, that's out of the question. If he makes a nuisance of himself, I suppose you must let him in and try to reason with him. We don't want a lot of noise over this." He passed a nervous hand over his forehead. "But understand, Halley, your mother and I will on no account allow him to see Clarisse tonight. Make that quite clear. He is not to come upstairs."

"No," I agreed, "I won't let him come upstairs."

He looked at me with eyes like small blue flames.

"My God, Halley! Have we all been horribly mistaken about Fred?"

"No," I said. "No, of course not. Not in the way you mean. I think she just got into a panic and ran."

And then we heard Fred's loud, determined knocking and I went down and opened the door.

He was standing there smoking a cigarette and he was wearing his new double-breasted dinner jacket and black tie. At first glance he looked as though nothing had happened, but his eyes were narrow and stony.

"Come in, Fred," I said, and I led the way into the library.

"Can you get us some drinks?" he asked. "I could do with a good stiff Scotch and soda. You look as if you could too."

I went to get them and he sat down on the sofa where Clarisse had been a few minutes before. When I came back with a tray he was picking up from a corner of the sofa a handkerchief of my mother's with which she had been trying to staunch Clarisse's tears. It was a little wet ball, and he tossed it on the table.

"So she put on a good act, did she?" he said.

I poured out two drinks without replying, and gave one to him. Then I sat down in a chair opposite to him.

"You'd better tell me, Fred," I said. "I may as well hear the worst."

"That's just what you're going to hear," he answered, and he held out his cigarette case, for he never could remember that I didn't smoke. Then he said, "Where's your father?"

I said that both he and my mother were upstairs with Clarisse.

"She's in a terrible state, Fred," I told him. "I've never seen anything like it. In fact I never saw anyone with hysterics before. It scared me to death, nearly."

"Did it?" he said. "Well, I think your father had better come down here."

I didn't like the way he said it.

"I can't make him come down," I told him, "if he doesn't want to, and I know he doesn't. Look, Fred, they're Clarisse's parents, and they're terribly worried about all this. They don't know what happened and neither do I, but Clarisse is nearly out of her mind and they're doing the best they can for her."

"Have they sent for Dr. Medlicott?" he asked.

"No," I answered. "They'll send for him in the morning. Now they've got her to bed and given her sedatives."

"I'd like you to go up," he said, more reasonably, "and ask your father if he'll please come down. I want him to hear what happened. I guess your mother and Louise can cope with Clarisse."

"Well," I said, "I'll try, Fred, if you insist."

I went up and spoke to my father again but he absolutely refused to come.

"I don't want to speak to Fred," he said, "until I've heard what Clarisse has to say tomorrow. It may be that I'll never want to speak to him again. Until this thing has been cleared up it's best that we shouldn't meet."

I tried to persuade him that in fairness to Fred he ought to come down, but it was no good. I went back to the library. I told Fred that my father was willing to speak to him tomorrow, but not before. He narrowed his eyes.

"So they're going to gang up on me, are they? All right. I'll tell you, and you'd better get it straight and pass it on the way I've told it. No smoothing it down to please the family. Just you listen carefully and get it straight."

He took a long drink and sat back.

"She walked out on me," he said. "She walked out on me while we were having dinner downstairs in the Persian Room at the Plaza. I didn't want to have dinner downstairs, I wanted to have it upstairs in our sitting room, but she wanted it downstairs so we compromised and had it downstairs. She'd given in about the house in Rye, and I was perfectly willing that everything else should be the way she wanted it to be. Well, I'll go back to the beginning now.

"As soon as we got to the hotel after leaving here, we started unpacking our things for the night. She was just as she usually is and we talked about the wedding and the reception and some of the people and she said she thought it had all gone very well but that she was pretty tired. I said I was tired too and I suggested that we order a little dinner upstairs and have it in our dressing gowns and relax. But that didn't appeal to her. She said she wanted our first meal as married people to be downstairs in the room where we'd so often dined before. It was the place she liked best in New York. So I opened a flask of cocktails I'd brought with me and we made a little ceremony of it and drank to each other and to happy times and I kissed her and she was just as she always was. Part of the time she was sitting in my lap. I don't know what started things off unless it was the arrangement of the beds. They were the usual twin beds except that they had something I hadn't seen before. There was no space between them and they had shelves and little cupboards sort of attached—part of the outfit—where you could put books and things, and I said I thought it would be a good idea for us to have the same sort of arrangement in our bedroom at Rye. She didn't say anything and I let the subject drop. Then we dressed, taking our time, and went down to dinner at about a quarter of nine. She seemed perfectly all right and took the sort of interest she always does take in ordering the dinner. You know the way she always says I don't know how to order a meal. We finally ordered caviar, a clear soup and chicken *sous cloche*. We ate the caviar and drank the soup, and then she said she wanted to go to the Ladies. I was a little surprised at that because she'd been just before we came down, but I put it down to nerves. I told her to run along, and asked her if she had any money. She looked in the new evening bag that Rosie had given her and said she had plenty. So off she went, and I sat there waiting. As soon as she'd gone an old friend of Uncle Syl's who'd been at the wedding came over and spoke to me. He said I'd married the most beautiful girl in New York and I said I knew that, and we chatted for a minute. Then he went out. I suppose I didn't realize how time was passing. The chicken came and I told the waiter to take it away and keep it hot, and then I began to get worried. Clarisse can take as much time over doing her face as any other girl, but she'd done all that before we came down. So I went along to the Ladies to see if she was feeling sick or something. I spoke to the attendant and described Clarisse, and she said she hadn't been there and certainly wasn't there now because nobody was.

"Well, then I knew that something had gone wrong, and I took the elevator up to our suite. She wasn't there and she hadn't been there. Halley, I've never been so fighting mad in all my life. If I could have laid my hands on her I'd have turned her over my knee and half beaten the life out of her. Chivalry? I didn't know the meaning of the word just then. I lit a cigarette to calm myself down, and when I could trust myself to speak, I rang you up. That's what happened and it's all that happened. And don't get me wrong. When I say all I mean all."

He got up and began to pace up and down the room.

"Yes," I said, "I see."

He stopped in front of me.

"Well? You'll oblige me by telling me what you see."

"It's just what I thought," I told him. "She panicked."

"She panicked all right," he said, "and she'll panic back again pretty quick. God! To think that Clarisse would do that to me! Clarisse! Do you remember that day in the boathouse, Halley? Neither she nor I have ever looked at anybody else since then. My God!" He picked up a paperweight from the writing table and weighed it in his hand and put it down again. It was a glass one with glass flowers inside, and I remembered that ever since he was a boy he had been fond of it. "Well," he said, "you'd better go up and find out how she is because I'm going to stay right here till she comes down."

"Fred," I pleaded, "can't you leave it till tomorrow? It's no good trying to get her back tonight. She's absolutely all in. If you could just have seen her and heard her—"

"I don't need to see her and hear her," he said, "to know she put on a good act. I can picture the whole thing and I'm not impressed. She knew how to get you all rallying round. Look, Halley, I don't want to get tough with you, but just you go on up and say I'm waiting, will you? The sooner she makes up her mind to stop this nonsense, the better for everybody." And he added more gently, "Give your mother my love and tell her I know how to handle this. She can leave it to me."

He was manly and sensible, and he may have been perfectly right. Perhaps he could have handled it, for I guessed that Clarisse had made the same sort of scene over the house in Rye. But I knew that now that she was safely here she wouldn't go back unless my parents forced her to, and I knew that they wouldn't be able to force her to. They simply couldn't. They would never be able to say, "You must go." My heart was very heavy as I went upstairs.

They had given her some sort of sleeping draught and she'd just dropped off to sleep. When I opened the door very softly my mother put her finger to her lips and Louise frowned at me and shook her head. I beckoned my father outside and we talked in low voices on the landing below. I told him the story and I could see that he was disappointed and baffled by it. He had expected to hear of something that would explain, or go some way towards explaining, what Clarisse had done.

"Do you believe him, Halley?" he asked me. "Do you believe Fred's story? It doesn't sound probable to me."

"I believe every word of it," I told him. "I'm certain Fred's telling the truth."

He stood grasping the stair rail with both hands and biting his lips.

"By golly!" he said. "If it's true it makes the whole thing even more difficult. She won't go back to him, I know she won't. She says she'd rather die than go back to him. She even said she'd—" he passed a hand over his forehead— "she'd kill herself if we tried to make her go back." And his shoulders shook with a dry sob.

"She wouldn't," I said. "She would never do that."

"She might," he said, "if she got into a state like this again. She might do anything. Your mother will never force her to go back, and I won't either. We couldn't. It would be utterly cruel. Poor child, she's made a terrible mistake and she knows it now. If only she'd listened to us." He took out his handkerchief.

"Maybe we ought to look at it from Fred's side too," I suggested. "We ought to, oughtn't we?"

"Fred's a man. He can take it."

"Can he?" I asked. "And will he? I don't know. I don't believe he will."

"There's nothing to be done tonight in any case," he said nervously. "Nothing, and you must tell him so, Halley. Make it perfectly clear. Tell him to come tomorrow and we'll talk the whole thing over quietly. I'm perfectly willing to see him tomorrow, but not tonight. We'll see how Clarisse is in the morning and hear her version of what happened. I'm sure she'll tell your mother."

Fred, I could see, was now the enemy at the gates, and I went slowly downstairs again hating to have to tell him what I must tell him. He had a fresh drink in his hand and was sitting on the sofa again. He gave me a narrow look as I came in.

"No good?"

"No good," I said. "He's perfectly willing to see you tomorrow but he says Clarisse can't possibly be disturbed tonight. She's only just dropped off to sleep."

"Fine," he said. "Fine. Can you lend me a pair of pajamas, and a toothbrush, maybe? Because I'm going to stay right here. I'll sleep on this sofa."

"Fred!" I cried. "You can't do that. Why don't you just go back to the hotel and I'll ring you first thing in the morning?"

He swore then, and I'd never heard him swear before. He wasn't the swearing sort. Then he said, "O.K. I'll do without the pajamas or the toothbrush. Do you feel strong enough to throw me out? Because that's what you'd have to do. I'm staying right here." And then he burst out, "My God, Halley, don't be a fool! Do you suppose I'm going back to that damned bridal suite alone?"

I think I fully realized Fred's position then for the first time and the implications of the whole thing. I felt terribly sorry for him.

"All right," I said. "You do what you think best. I'll get you everything you'll need and some blankets. It's all pretty ghastly, Fred. I guess I needn't tell you how I feel about it."

"All right," he said, "so long as you don't try to interfere. So long as nobody tries to interfere."

I did what I could for him and then went upstairs. I told my father that Fred was going to sleep on the sofa in the library and he looked more harassed than ever.

"This is going to upset your mother terribly," he said. "What a coil it all is! What a coil! You'd better get to bed, Halley. You look all in. Did you give him a blanket?"

"I gave him the one off my bed," I said. "It's a hot night, I shan't need one."

"I don't see at present," he told me, "any decent way out of this at all."

Neither could I, unless Clarisse would go back to Fred of her own accord, and I thought the odds against that about a thousand to one. If I knew my sister, she would stay where she was. Before I dropped off to sleep I wondered about the chicken they'd ordered, and how long the waiter had kept it hot for them.

VIII

I GOT UP EARLY AND WENT DOWN TO SEE FRED. HE HAD WASHED and shaved in the downstairs lavatory and he was fully dressed and his black tie neatly tied, but his face was pale and some of the blue seemed to have gone from his eyes.

"I've seen Arnaud," he told me, "and I thought he was going to faint when he saw me. I told him Clarisse was taken ill last night and I guess that's what we'd all better say. He's going to bring me some breakfast. Have you seen your father?"

"No," I said, "he isn't awake yet. They were up half the night with Clarisse."

He let this pass.

"Well," he said, "I'm staying right here till Clarisse comes to her senses and is ready to go to Bar Harbor with me, and she'd better not waste any time. And now here's what I'd like you to do. I'd like you to go around to the Plaza, tell them Mrs. Dumont was suddenly taken ill last night, pay the hotel bill and get the maid and the valet to pack up our things. Maybe you'd better wait right there while they do it and then bring our stuff here. I'll make you out a blank check."

I was grateful to him for giving me something to do, and I went at once. When I got back to the house over an hour later, Fred told me that Dr. Medlicott had been and gone and that he'd had a short talk with him. Dr. Medlicott had tried to persuade him to go home and wait patiently for a few days. When Fred asked him how many days, the answer had been, "For ten days at least." Clarisse, he had said, needed care and medical attention. She was in no fit state to travel.

"He looked at me," Fred said, "as though I'd suddenly grown horns and a tail. They're all ganging up on me. Look, Halley, you'd better tell your father that if I can't see Clarisse today I've got to see him.

I'm pretty sick of this. And if I can't see him I'll see Clarisse if I have to use force to do it."

"I'm sure he'll see you today," I said. "He promised he would. If he does, will you go home and wait there?"

He gave me a look.

"I'm not stirring from this house," he said, "till I've seen Clarisse." He hurled a half-smoked cigarette into the grate. "My God! Has anybody in this family thought what it's going to be like," he demanded, "when the papers get hold of this? If not, they'd better start thinking. And they may get wind of it any minute. When they do there'll be hell to pay and that's an understatement. You'd better just pass that thought along to your father in case it hasn't occurred to him yet, because if it does happen he isn't going to like it."

He sat down and dropped his head in his hands. I went over to him and put my hand on his shoulder.

"I've got an idea, Fred," I said. "I'll get Arnaud to put up a bed for you in the study. Your suitcases and things can go in there and it'll be more comfortable for you and for everybody."

"O.K.," he said wearily. "There's some sense in that I guess. But go up and see your father first and tell him I've got to talk to him. And tell him I'm staying right here."

None of us had spoken of Syl. His name had not once been mentioned either by Fred or ourselves, and yet he was inevitably in all our minds. He must have been in Clarisse's thoughts as she lay in bed, to outward appearances utterly exhausted but with her determination not to go back to Fred coiled up inside her like a steel spring. I knew as well as if she had told me herself that she was capable of throwing everything into the discard if by doing so she might stay where she was. As I went upstairs to find my father and urge him to come down I could see not a single ray of light anywhere in all this unless—and I found myself almost praying for it— he would at least be fair to Fred. For the first time in my life I had become his critic. The same shift had taken place in my mind in regard to him as had taken place in Rome in regard to Clarisse. The bond of love was no less strong—indeed it was painfully strong—but my youthful adoration of my father and my complete trust in him were tempered now, and from this time on he would live and move in a harsher light. The only sufferer, as I knew even then, would be myself.

Just outside the door of my parents' bedroom I met Julian. He had been in to see them as he always did before going down to breakfast

—they breakfasted, Continental fashion, in their room—and they had told him the news.

"I overslept," he said nervously. "If I go down now I won't have to see Fred, will I?"

"Not if you go straight into the dining room," I told him. "I haven't had any breakfast myself yet."

"I'll just have a bite," he said, "and then I think I'll clear out for the day."

The elevator was there on the landing and he went down in it. I didn't see him again that day. I heard later that he'd gone up to the Bronx Zoo and had then taken in two different movies, getting home after eleven that night.

My parents were in their dressing gowns and their breakfast trays were still there. My mother looked ill with worry.

"I suppose you've seen Fred," my father said. "Medlicott promised to tell him that the best thing he could do was to go home."

"He won't until he's seen you," I said, and I added, "and Clarisse."

"That's out of the question," he told me. "Medlicott's orders are that she is to see only the family."

I started to say, "Isn't Fred—?" but he was too quick for me.

"We've just been talking it all over, your mother and I," he said, "and we think that it would be best for your mother to see Fred and tell him, quietly, what we've decided. If I talk to him I may lose my temper and I want to avoid that if possible. Your mother can be counted on not to lose hers."

I looked at my mother, but her eyes met mine defensively. I saw that she would be with my father every step of the way.

"I've talked to Clarisse," she told me, "and she has repeated substantially what Fred told you last night. Poor child, she's utterly disillusioned and 'out of love' with him. She says she'd rather die than go back to him. She keeps repeating that she'll jump out of the window rather than go back. It's frightening, Halley. Feeling as she does, how can we possibly try to make her go back?"

"I don't know," I said, "but we ought to try, oughtn't we?"

"It would be unspeakably cruel," my mother said. "It's out of the question and I think your father's quite right, Halley; if he and Fred got into an argument either or both would lose their tempers, and we don't want that to happen. It seems wisest for me to talk to him, but I'd like you to be there if you will."

"I still think father ought to be the one," I said.

"We've explained our reasons, Halley," my father said with some sharpness, "and I know we're right. He'll behave better with your mother. She can persuade him to go home and wait. In ten days or so we'll see what's to be done."

I said what Fred had asked me to say.

"Is there any reason why the papers should get hold of it?" my father asked, but I could see that he had thought of it and that he dreaded it. "Surely Fred won't talk, and naturally we won't. If we all behave decently, perhaps the newspapers will behave decently too. If they don't—" he threw up his hands—"well, I suppose we must try to bear it. But I would take your mother and Clarisse abroad as quickly as possible."

I had one last try.

"I do wish you'd come down yourself, Father," I said. "After all, Fred hasn't done anything wrong."

"Not done anything wrong?" he cried. "I entirely disagree. He made love to Clarisse when she was nothing but a child, and behind our backs. He persuaded her that what was really a childish affection was an adult love. In my opinion he has behaved abominably."

"He's certainly not blameless," my mother said with a sigh, and I could almost hear her say, "Nor are you either," but she did not utter the words. "Tell him, Halley, that I'll be down in twenty minutes."

I had a cup of coffee and then got Fred and his suitcases into the study. In twenty minutes exactly my mother came down.

"My mother's in the library, Fred," I said. "She wants to speak to you."

"Your mother?" he said, and he threw me a look that was full of comprehension. It had told him, better than anything else, how things were going.

She was waiting on the sofa, dressed in one of her simple little black dresses. She never wore make-up and her paleness today would have shown through it if she had.

"Come in, Fred dear," she said, but she didn't of course offer him her cheek as she usually did. "Come in and sit down. This is a dreadful business, and I can't tell you how grieved and unhappy we are."

Fred's face softened at this gentle approach and he sat down beside her on the sofa.

"Could I talk to you alone?" he asked, and he glanced at me.

"I'd like Halley to be here, if you don't mind, Fred," she said. "After all, he's your good friend." And she gave me a quick look which plainly said, "Don't go."

"Aunt Ruth," Fred said, "if anybody had told me that such a thing as this could happen to Clarisse and me—"

He shook his head and broke off with a great painful sob. My mother put a hand on his sleeve.

"I know, Fred, I know," she said. "Well, it has happened, as sad things often will, and we must try to deal with it sensibly and wisely. I know the story of what happened last night, I have heard Clarisse's account and Halley has told us yours, and they agree. Now we know better where we are." She clasped her hands tightly and turned to look Fred directly in the face. "Fred, Myron and I must stand by our daughter, however foolish and mistaken she has been. She needs our protection and support. I'm afraid I have only bad news for you. She is absolutely determined not to go back to you. That being the case, we cannot force her to go back. That would be too cruel. Her home is with us, if that is what she wants and needs, and it is. I am deeply sorry. It's a tragedy for us all, but those are the facts."

Fred said quietly, "Has it occurred to anybody in this house that Clarisse is my wife? That no longer ago than yesterday she made certain vows in the sight of God?"

"Fred," my mother said, "rightly or wrongly—wrongly, as I think —such vows are broken every day. I don't have to tell you that. Clarisse realizes now—rather late, unfortunately for us all—that she made a tragic mistake. She knew it yesterday, she knew it most of all last night. What that poor child has gone through mentally I can hardly bear to think. She ran here in an extremity of fear and despair. It seemed almost as if she might go out of her mind. The truth is," she went on, and she was still looking straight into Fred's eyes, "Clarisse and all of us have been wrong. She is not ready for marriage. She is far too immature. That is Dr. Medlicott's opinion and it's ours too. We are greatly to blame for ever having permitted it."

Fred was sitting very straight, his hands gripping his knees.

"All right," he said, "I can wait. When do you think she'll get over being immature?"

My mother bit her lip.

"It's foolish to speak to me like that, Fred," she said. "I'm desperately serious."

"So am I, Aunt Ruth."

She went on, "Clarisse doesn't love you in the way a wife should love her husband, and she never has. She's too young and undeveloped to be capable of feeling that sort of love for anyone at present, but what is more, I am convinced she will never, never feel it for you. It's a hard thing to say, but I must say it. She mistook childish affection for love. We are all very fond of you, Fred, you know that—"

"Would you mind leaving all that out please, Aunt Ruth?" Fred said, but he didn't say it rudely; it was as if he couldn't bear to hear it. "Let's stick to facts. Clarisse is my wife. I love her and I've always loved her. I always will love her. And till dinner time last night she loved me. I know what happened. She got scared. Lots of young brides feel like that I guess, but they don't all scuttle back to their families. If we'd had dinner upstairs instead of downstairs, or if you hadn't been so near at hand, none of this would have happened. It couldn't have happened. I understand Clarisse better than you think and I was prepared to be patient—to be very patient. If she'd stayed with me everything would have been fine."

"I'm afraid, Fred," my mother said, "that you're mistaken in saying that. The tragedy would simply have been postponed for a little while."

He looked hard at my mother for a moment.

"Nothing you've said," he told her, "not one single thing alters the fact that Clarisse is my wife, that I have a right to see her, that I'm going to see her and that I'm not leaving this house until I have seen her. You aren't even trying to help, neither you nor Uncle Myron. You're determined to come between us. Well, I'm just not going to have it."

It went backwards and forwards like this for some time and I scarcely put in a word. When my mother told Fred that Clarisse threatened to kill herself rather than go back to him he said it was the way a petted and spoilt girl like Clarisse would be sure to talk at first, and that it meant nothing. Then, as my mother was not yielding an inch, Fred suddenly sprang up and went to the telephone.

"There's only one thing to do," he said. "I'm going to ring up Uncle Syl."

At once my mother sprang up too and she caught his arm.

"No, Fred," she cried. "No. I forbid you to do that!"

"Mother," I said, and I got up too, "Fred's right. Syl's got to know. He'll be ringing up pretty soon anyway, or dropping in. What are you going to say when he does?"

"Oh," she cried, and all her calm had gone now, "I don't know, I don't know." And she pressed both hands to her forehead. "But, Fred, you mustn't try to force our hands like this. You've no right to. If you knew the state of mind Clarisse was in, how frightened and desperate she is, you'd have pity on her. Pity on us all."

"O.K., Aunt Ruth," Fred said, but his hand was still on the telephone. "I know just how Clarisse feels. Will you let me see her? I can handle this. Just you let me see her, that's all I ask."

"But, Fred, I can't, I can't," she cried. "I've promised her we wouldn't make her see you. I've promised. I had to promise."

"O.K.," he said again and this time he lifted the receiver and dialed a number. My mother threw me a look of poignant appeal.

"You speak to Syl, Halley," she implored me. "Don't let Fred tell him. Please, Halley, please!"

I went to Fred and took the receiver out of his hand.

"I don't care who tells him," Fred said, "as long as somebody does. It's your own house, so you tell him."

It was Syl's office number and his secretary answered. I told her who I was and she said Syl had just come in. In a minute I was speaking to him.

"Syl," I said, "it's Halley. We're in some trouble here. Clarisse was taken ill last night. She's here at the house and Fred's here too. Yes, the doctor's been. It isn't anything serious—her illness, I mean—but we think you'd better come along if you can. Yes, right now. Fine. Good-by."

"He'll be here in about twenty minutes, or as soon as the traffic will let him," I said.

My mother broke down then and sobbed into her handkerchief. Then she hurried out of the room without looking at Fred again.

Syl got the bare facts from Fred and me before my father and mother came down. For this time of course my father did come down. Syl had stood the first shock of the news better than I had thought he would, but of course he was counting on my parents' help to put things right. When the help he expected was not forthcoming he looked from one to the other of them as if they'd suddenly been changed from people he devotedly loved into hostile strangers. He couldn't believe they meant what they said, however sorrowfully they were compelled to say it.

"But Ruth, but Myron," he said, outraged and bewildered, "you can't do this to Fred, you can't. Don't you realize the position he's in? He's Clarisse's husband, and he loves her. You must make Clarisse see reason. You can if you will. My little sweetheart would never do such a thing to Fred and to me. She's overtired, that's all. She was worn out with all the excitement of the wedding. She ran home without thinking what she was doing. Another day in bed and she'll be herself again."

"She says she will not on any account see Fred again," my mother repeated wearily. "She says she would rather kill herself. Are we to force her to see him? Are we to beat her, or starve her into submission? What would you have us do, Syl? She's on the very edge of a serious nervous breakdown. We cannot force her."

"Before things go any further," said Fred, who had been walking up and down the room (keeping his distance from my father, who had not yet spoken directly to him), "I want you to tell Clarisse this. I want you to tell her, please, that I'm putting that damned house in Rye into the estate agents' hands right away. I'm going to sell it. Tell Clarisse that, and tell her I'm sorry I insisted on buying it. I see now I was wrong. So she needn't have that on her mind. And tell her I love her better than anything in the world, and that everything's going to be all right. It is; I know it is."

"I'm afraid it's too late, Fred," my mother said gently. "I'm afraid things have gone far, far beyond that now. I can only repeat what I've already said many times; she will never again see you of her own accord. Never."

"But, God!" Fred cried, pausing in his walk. "She loved me until a quarter of nine last night. She couldn't have stopped loving me fifteen minutes later. She couldn't!" He flung himself into a chair, covered his face with his hands and sobbed.

Syl was growing desperate. He went to my father and grasped both his arms.

"Myron," he said, "look at me! Listen to me! What's going on here? Don't you realize the position Fred's in? Don't you realize his whole happiness is at stake? Don't you realize what people are going to say, the construction that will be put on this? Are you going to condemn Fred to that shame for the rest of his life? All because you refuse to tell your own daughter where her plain duty lies? A little persuasion from you, a little fatherly advice, a little motherly counsel from Ruth, and she'd see reason. What Fred says is right. She couldn't have stopped loving him all of a sudden like that. It doesn't make sense."

"She never did love him," my father said. "Ruth and I always suspected it, Syl. We are all of us to blame. She was too young. They should never have been allowed to marry."

Syl gave my father a look, then he went over to Fred and put a hand on his heaving shoulders.

"Fred," he said gently, "Fred, my boy, I think you'd better come home with me. The spare room's always ready. We'll take your suitcases along with us and go home. In a day or two, Clarisse will have come to her senses." He turned to my father again. "We'll give her a week, Myron," he said, "a whole week. Everyone will think they're up in Bar Harbor. So far, no harm's been done. But as soon as the doctor will let anybody see her I want you to promise me I can. For the sake of our old friendship, Ruth, I want you and Myron to promise me I can see her. If you ever loved me, as I've always loved you both—"

He turned away from them and took out his handkerchief. Holding it to his eyes we heard him say, in a breaking voice, "Tell her she needn't be afraid to see her old Syl. She's my little sweetheart and that's what she's always going to be. Everything's going to be all right. Tell her Fred's as fine a boy as there is and he can make her happy. Come, Fred, we'll get along now."

It was the worst part of all this miserable business. Syl suddenly seemed years older, pitifully older, and I had never loved him so much. I went with Fred to collect the suitcases and we carried them out and put them into a taxi. Syl pressed my hand before they drove away, but they didn't speak again, either of them. I went back into the library. My father had his arms about my mother and was patting her back gently. She was crying.

"Halley," he said, "must you go back to Cambridge tonight? Can't you stay a few more days, till we're clear of this wretched business?"

"I'm afraid I've got to go," I said. "I'll keep in touch, though."

My mother released herself from my father's arms and turned to me wiping her eyes.

"Of course he must go, Myron," she said. "But Halley, do you think it would help if you talked to Clarisse before you leave? Quietly, of course, and without exciting her?"

"I will if you like," I said. "You mean you don't want me to say anything about her going back to Fred?"

"I wouldn't do that if I were you," my father said. "It would only delay her recovery. It would be better if you just spoke to her affectionately and asked her how she feels. You'll see for yourself how exhausted she is after last night."

She was propped up on her pillows when I went in and she was wearing a bedjacket she'd bought in Paris, not one of her new ones. Her face was very white and her eyes were still red-rimmed. Her hair was smoothly brushed and hung down on her shoulders, framing her face. She looked pathetically young. Louise was with her, and as I came in she got up and left us alone.

"I suppose you hate me, don't you?" Clarisse asked.

"No," I answered, "of course not."

"I expect Fred hates me, and Syl, and later on Rosie and Helen will. Has Syl gone yet?"

I told her he had gone and that Fred had gone with him. She gave a great sigh of relief and said, "Thank heaven! It was awful, knowing he was still in the house. Does he hate me, Halley? I suppose he must, mustn't he?"

"No," I told her, "he certainly doesn't hate you. He loves you, poor devil. I'm not supposed to say anything to excite you, but why didn't you just stab him in the back or put poison in his wine instead of doing this to him? It would have been a whole lot kinder."

"Don't say things like that, Halley," she pleaded, and her lips trembled. "I'd rather have killed myself than do what I had to do to Fred, but I'm too much of a coward. I keep saying I'd rather jump out of the window than have to go back to him and it's true, but I'd never have the courage to do that either. I wish I were dead."

She turned away her face. I had seen enough tears that day.

"There's no need to cry," I said. "You know you ought to go back to him, don't you?"

"I can't, Halley," she whispered. "I can't. I've come home. I'm safe now. It's like reaching a fortress and pulling up the drawbridge in the nick of time. I'm safe. All that horror is behind me. It's such a wonderful feeling—even though what I had to do to Fred makes me wretched."

"Have you really thought about anybody else's feelings?" I asked. "*Really* thought about them?"

"If you mean Fred's and Syl's, I think about them all the time." She looked at me with her great dark eyes. "Do you think Syl will ever forgive me?"

"No," I said, "I don't think he'll ever forgive any of us. Now don't cry. I guess I'd better go."

"If you only knew what a nightmare it all is," she whispered, and her lips quivered again.

"I've got a pretty good idea," I told her.

"I know what you think I ought to do," she said, "but if I went back to Fred I'd be offering myself up as a human sacrifice to spare other people's feelings. Do you want me to do that?"

"I guess I'd better go," I said again.

[132]

"Where's Julian?" she asked.

"Gone out for the day."

"I might have known he would," she said, and she smiled a little.

I kissed her and went out and closed the door, and then I remembered what Fred had said, and opened it again.

"Fred wants you to know," I said, "that he's selling the house in Rye. He said you don't have to have that on your mind, and he doesn't ever want to see it again."

Once more I saw a flicker of a smile.

"All that," she said, "seems a hundred years ago. I can't even believe it was me he had all those rows with about it. It just doesn't matter now."

"Well," I said to her, "don't worry. A hundred years from now none of this will matter. Are you seeing the doctor again?"

"Oh yes," she said, more brightly, "he's coming at six. If anyone asks you, Halley, I've had a nervous breakdown."

"Nobody's going to ask," I told her. "Everyone thinks you're at Bar Harbor. I'll keep in touch," I added, and then I closed the door again.

I rang up the house every day or so to see if there was any change in the situation, but there was none. Then I had a letter from my mother. Her handwriting was as neat and pretty as it always was. Her letters were always a pleasure to look at.

I couldn't talk about this on the telephone [she said], so I'm writing it instead. A shocking thing happened yesterday. Arnaud let Fred into the house about two o'clock and he raced upstairs before anyone could stop him and went straight into Clarisse's bedroom. He fell on his knees and took the poor, terrified child into his arms and tried to stifle her screams with kisses. But luckily Louise heard her cries for help and ran and got Arnaud and Mrs. Schwarz. Your father and I had gone out for a while and Julian just shut himself up in the library. You know how nervous he is. Clarisse implored Fred to go away, and kept her eyes shut and her hands over her ears, and finally Arnaud managed to persuade him to go because Clarisse was on the verge of hysterics again. It was a dreadful thing for Fred to have done, and now Arnaud says he'll keep the chain on the door and won't open it till he sees who it is. If you write to Fred, Halley, please tell him that we will see him by appointment, preferably with Syl, at any time, but he must never try to force himself in again. Rosie, of course, has been to see Clarisse two or three times. She doesn't know yet what the situation is and thinks that Clarisse simply had a nervous breakdown. So do Helen and Irving. Syl has held me to my promise and he's coming tomorrow to see Clarisse. I dread it for both of them, but it's no good putting it off any longer, I suppose. I'm afraid this is going to cause us all a great deal of suffering and sadness.

Two days later she wrote to me again.

It's over [she wrote], it's all over, and I hardly believe anything could have been more painful except a death. I am worn out, and last night I hardly slept, but I want you to know as soon as possible what happened. Clarisse of course was dreading her talk with Syl, but she realized that it couldn't be put off any longer. He arrived, poor dear Syl, with a great box of long-stemmed American beauty roses and he took them up to her room. At first he was as tender and kind as could be. He said if only she'd give Fred a chance, everything would be all right. They could have their honeymoon at the house of a friend of his on Lake Placid so there'd be no publicity. Marriages that got off to a bad start, he said, often became brilliant successes. He just couldn't believe Clarisse meant what she said when she told him she would never go back to Fred. At last, hoping to convince him, she opened a drawer and took out his bracelet, and the pearls Irving gave her, and Fred's engagement ring and put them all into his pocket. He took them out again and flung them into a corner of the room. Then, with a white face he got up, trembling, she said, and told her that it was the end, that he never wanted to see any of us again. After today he would never willingly see any member of the Prentiss family as long as he lived.

Then he came down to where we were in the library, your father and I. It was a dreadful moment for us. He came into the room, looking so terribly old, and told us we were largely to blame for what had happened. We had brought up Clarisse abominably. She was utterly spoilt and selfish. As for us, we were hardly less selfish. We could have persuaded her to go back to Fred but we had chosen not to. We had ruined Fred's life and brought upon him (Syl) the heaviest sorrow he had ever known. It was the end, he said, of twenty-three years of affection and devotion. He washed his hands of us. It was the end.

He wouldn't listen to us. I pleaded with him, I begged him not to allow this unhappy affair to come between us. He simply repeated, "It's the end." I never saw your father so shaken by anything. And even after Syl had said, twenty times, that it was the end, he seemed not to be able to go. He kept looking at the room, at the pictures, at the furniture, as if he wanted to be sure to remember all of it, and yet hated it. It was painful beyond words. Your father tried to reason with him. He said that when all the anger and bitterness had gone, the friendship would remain. He tried to take Syl's hand, but Syl wouldn't let him. Then he gave me one last look and cried, "Ruth!" It was a *cri de coeur* if I ever heard one. Then he turned and almost ran out of the room and the front door slammed behind him. I think it really is the end, Halley. I'm afraid we shall never see our dear Syl again. But given all the circumstances, could we have acted differently? I don't think we could. It is the first tragedy in our lives and we must feel that we are closer together than ever because of it. I wish you could come home if only for a few hours. It would help.

But I couldn't get away just then. My father wrote to me to say that Clarisse was up and about, but had not yet been out of the house. She was nervous about going out; someone might see her; for the present she preferred to remain indoors. It was clear that he was bitterly angry with Syl for being unable to see things from his and my mother's point of view. I don't think he quite believed, yet, that that chapter of our lives was over. He said he kept thinking of things he might have said and wanted to say to Syl.

What did he expect me to do? [he wrote]. Sacrifice my daughter to the Dumont family pride? Preach down a daughter's heart? If he had ever had a daughter himself, how differently he would have seen it all. I'd have felt like a murderer if I'd forced her to go back. And what hope could there have been for such a marriage? None.

Rosie had written to me three times, imploring me to do something to bring Clarisse and Fred together again.

It's all so tragic [she wrote]. Fred is quite changed, and although I don't know about hearts breaking, if they can I think his has. Can't you and I meet, Halley? Must we go all Montague and Capulet? It seems so silly. Can't we at least go on being friends? I can't ask you here and I can't go to your house now unless I'm invited, but couldn't we meet somewhere else, on neutral ground? It seems almost like the end of the world to me.

But I knew it would be foolish to see Rosie. I could only have done so now if I'd been in love with her. In fact I missed Helen more than I missed Rosie. I would of course miss Fred; but I would miss Syl most of all.

Two weeks after the wedding and while I was up at Cambridge, the news broke; the newspapers got the story somehow and from that time on it was sheer misery for all of us. My father couldn't bear it. I hurried down to spend a night and he was like a caged animal that was being infuriated and tormented by small boys. He didn't know how to get back at his tormentors. He raged helplessly, bought all the newspapers including the tabloids and worked himself into a nervous frenzy. He felt that the whole family had been insulted, soiled, degraded. That Fred must have felt all that he was feeling and more ("Beautiful, blond society bride, daughter of wealthy picture collector Myron S. Prentiss, flees from scion of prominent New York family on wedding night") did not, I think, occur to him. It was in his flesh that every arrow found its mark. My mother, surprisingly, took it all rather more philosophically, but then she read few of the papers. She was fortified of course by the satisfaction of having Clarisse under the family roof, unattached, wholly ours. Any unpleasantness, she must have felt, could be borne, no price was too high to pay. I was at home long enough to see some reporters and give the papers a story that was fit to print. The bride's return to her family had been necessitated by a nervous breakdown. For the present she was allowed to see no one. Future plans would be announced later, and so on. It was unconvincing, but it was the best we could do. We had to look at pictures of the bridal couple, of our house, of Irving Dumont, of the bridesmaids, of myself as best man. One paper even gave a reproduction of the Degas that my father had given to Clarisse as a wedding present.

"In no other country in the world," my father raged, "would decent, law-abiding citizens have to put up with such outrageous and offensive treatment."

My mother wrote to me that he had gone to see Conrad Falke, the stockbroker, about taking charge of his investments. He went to a new firm of lawyers, Dimlock and Wineberg, and asked them to proceed with the dissolution of the marriage. He tidied up his affairs and, having done what he could, booked passages on the next *White Star* liner for Southampton for Julian, Clarisse, Louise, himself and my mother. I was to follow later. My father said he wouldn't have a happy moment until he had reached the shores of Europe.

Three days after they had sailed, and items to that effect had appeared in all the papers, Fred went to a second-rate hotel on the West Side, booked a room for a night and shot himself.

IX

Up to that time i had never experienced even the smallest grief. When I saw in the papers the news of Fred's suicide it was pure shock at first, the shock that numbs, that goes fumbling through the mind without reaching the seat of the intelligence. Sorrow was such a novelty to me that I felt it belonged to someone else; someone near, perhaps, but not me, not me! And when that someone and I were slowly merged, it was more than I could bear alone.

I wirelessed the news to my father on the ship, flinging myself on the bosom of the family in the blind desire to lessen or share my guilt and my anguish. I tried to imagine what my father's reply would be. When it came it was:

"Terribly shocked. Send newspapers Brown's Hotel."

Reluctantly, forcing myself to read them first, I did so, hoping at the same time that my father would keep them from the eyes of Clarisse and my mother. The story of the wedding night had been revived with many added details. This time the fact that the "Runaway bride" was the granddaughter of Mrs. Rudolf Denniker—"About whom there have been many curious stories"—was frequently referred to. Again there were photographs. There was one of Clarisse as a little girl bracketed with one of Fred as a schoolboy, the two set in a heart-shaped frame surmounted by a lover's knot, with the caption, "He had always adored her." In two of the tabloids there were ghastly photographs of Fred stretched on a bed, behind him a hideously spattered wall. I sent these to my father along with the rest, with the idea, I suppose, of transferring some of my horror to him. Then for three days I "went sick," physically and mentally, and kept to my room, admitting only René Valmont, and the elderly woman who did the cleaning, made the bed and brought me an occasional cup of coffee. I suppose it was René's extreme ugliness that made me feel that he—with his long gargoyle face and prominent ears—more than anyone I knew, would have some acquaintance with tragedy. He talked to me in French, sitting beside me smoking cigarette after cigarette, and he made me talk and it helped.

I told myself again and again that there was nothing I could have done. I had written to Fred—a difficult letter to write—telling him how sorry I was about everything, and he had not replied. I had not tried to see Syl, but it would have done no good even if he had been willing to see me, which I doubt. But I could not free myself from blame—the blame I shared with the family. It stretched its dead weight upon me, half paralyzing me. I lay awake, hunted by a baying, close-following pack of memories. Now I loved Fred as I had never loved him before; his virtues grew in my anguished sight, his prospects seemed more than ever dazzling, and his trustful blue eyes, his bonhomie, his simple, uncomplicated attitude to life pervaded my thoughts and my dreams. We, my parents, Clarisse and I, had killed him. Clarisse, my sister, going into his arms in the boathouse that day had held a dagger for him in her hand. Because of us Rosie and Helen had no brother, Irving Dumont no son, Syl—better not think about Syl! No, but I thought of him constantly. I was as anxious now to sail for England and leave it all behind me as my father had been. Fred was so well remembered at Harvard that every other face I saw seemed to accuse me, and some of the faculty looked at me sorrowfully, I was sure, and then hastily looked away. Bob Lane and Harry Wilson were inarticulate in their sympathy, but even if they could have expressed what they felt, what was there they could say?

Dick Purbright wrote to me from a Colorado mountain resort where he taught skiing in winter, tennis in summer ("though only while the Depression lasts").

"The papers here," he wrote, "have printed plenty about that awful business. To say I'm sorry seems so inadequate as to be almost worse than saying nothing at all. Do you remember what you said to me the day before I left Harvard, when I was packing up? I guess you were a prophet without knowing it." (I had said, hoping to comfort him, that perhaps Clarisse was a "femme fatale." I had not meant it; now it stayed in my mind.) "I wonder," he said, "how all this will affect you? Knowing as I do that things like affection and loyalty mean a great deal to you, I expect it will hit you very hard. You must try not to let it. I never knew Fred Dumont, but I think that what he did was pretty cowardly."

Fred cowardly? I was shocked and hurt. I repudiated the charge indignantly in my reply. He answered briefly, "Have it your own way, but neither you nor I would do such a terrible thing to a girl we were fond of. And why didn't he think of his sisters, and his father?"

"A girl we were fond of!" How inadequately this described the situation in which Fred had found himself, or his lifelong devotion to Clarisse! I remembered her saying to me once, years ago, that she believed Fred would die for her. Had he in fact died for love of her? Or had he died of the injury she had done him? I didn't know. I only knew that I was bitterly angry with Dick for calling him a coward.

And so I packed my trunk and thankfully departed, leaving Arnaud and his wife Angèle in charge of the house. Mrs. Schwarz was "retiring" and going to live with a sister in Brooklyn, and in future Angèle was to cook for us. My father felt it was necessary to have someone living in the house, and I am sure the insurance company with whom he insured the pictures took the same view. It was a mournful leave-taking. The whole house seemed to share in the tragedy, and whenever I went into the library it was as if Fred had actually killed himself there, so vividly did he haunt the room. I saw him sitting with his head in his hands; heard him tell my mother, "I can handle this, Aunt Ruth." It was good to get away.

I thought a great deal about the coming reunion at Brown's Hotel. Would we see guilt in each other's eyes? Would we look at one another and look away? Would there be awkward silences? I saw that the days on the ship would be hard to get through. I had learnt to play bridge at Harvard, and when I discovered that a married couple named Parkman and a Philadelphian named Brodie were in search of a fourth, I gladly joined them. I lost thirty-eight dollars, but I decided that it had been well worth it.

I needn't have worried. There were to be no displays of sorrow or remorse. My mother contrived to appear precisely as usual, busy, alert as always to serve the interests of the family, warmly welcoming, warmly loving. We were to be as we had always been. If my father smiled less readily, perhaps, and had acquired a trick of nervously jingling the coins in his trouser pocket, I saw no other alteration in him. Julian was inclined to be silent, but that was his way, and when he wasn't being directly spoken to his mind always seemed to be following some private train of thought, and it was almost as if he wasn't there at all. Clarisse was in her room when I arrived, but she came into the sitting room a few minutes later and she was all in black, as became a widow. But that meant nothing; like my mother she loved to wear black, and with her blond pallor, her honey-colored hair and dark eyes, it became her perfectly. In her first glance at me, before I kissed her, it seemed to me that she signaled a warning; what I guessed it to be, was, "Not a word, for pity's sake, about you-know-what."

I asked Julian, to recall him from one of his absences, what he had been doing, and my father answered for him, a note of pride in his voice, "He's been going every day to the British Museum."

I looked inquiringly at Julian and he said, "Oh, it's just something to do. I rather like it there."

I tried not to look surprised and merely said, "Good for you!" but I was puzzled.

When I asked my father if they'd made any plans for the future, he said, "We must have a talk about all that, Halley. Why don't you go and unpack now—your room's just along the corridor. Julian will show you—and then we'll have a little family conclave? I want to tell you what we've been discussing. I won't say what we've decided, because naturally we wouldn't decide anything until you came."

Julian took me to my room and sat down on the bed, his delicate-looking hands clasped in front of him. A lock of his fair hair hung over his forehead and he kept tossing it back.

"Why don't you get your hair cut?" I asked.

"I've been too busy," he answered. "I've been spending all my time in the Reading Room of the British Museum."

"The Reading Room?" I repeated, surprised. "Doing what?"

"Reading, of course," he said, and tossed his hair back.

"How would I know?" I said. "You might just have been sitting on your fanny."

"If I told you what I was reading," he said, and I heard a slightly defiant note in his voice, "you'd be surprised."

"All right. Go ahead and tell me."

"Not now," he answered. "Later on perhaps." Then he added, as if fearing that the subject might be dropped, "I may be going to write a book."

"Sounds as if you were thinking of laying an egg," I said, unlocking my trunk. "Well, that's fine. Get on with it. And perhaps the less you cackle about it in advance, the better."

"That's just what I thought," he replied. He never resented anything I said to him. "That's why I haven't told anybody. And don't tell the others if I do tell you." Then he broke off to say something quite different. "Halley, don't let them talk about you-know-what while I'm there, will you? I just can't take it."

"Has there been much talk about it?" I asked.

"At first there was. I just went out of the room. I couldn't listen. But I don't mind if you and I talk about it."

"I don't want to," I said. "There's nothing to say. It's happened. It never ought to have happened. We're all guilty as hell. Not you; the rest of us. Now let's shut up about it."

"But what do you think Clarisse is feeling?" he asked. "I can't quite make out."

"You'd know better than I would," I told him.

"I don't think she gives a damn," he said.

"Now shut up, Julian," I protested. "You needn't start saying catty things about your sister. Besides, it isn't true."

"I'm pretty sure it's true," he said, "and I wasn't being catty. I admire her for it. Most girls would have wallowed in tears and faked-up remorse and all that sort of thing. She kept her head up and took it as if it was the normal thing."

"She doesn't choose to show her feelings, that's all."

"Feelings?" he repeated, but he caught a look from me and stopped. Then he asked, "What I want to know is, is she really a widow? Can a girl be a widow without—you know what I mean?"

"Naturally she's a widow," I said. "She was married wasn't she? Anyhow, I'd rather talk about something else."

"There was a little in the papers here," he went on, "but not much. Just a paragraph or two, and one or two photographs. Father's cabled to a press-cutting agency in New York. He wants to find out what's said about the inquest. I know, because he tore up the first one he wrote out and I saw the pieces."

"Here," I said, handing him a suit. "You might as well help me as you're here. Hang this up, will you?"

When he had hung up my suits he sat on the bed again.

"I'll tell you what I'm doing," he said, "if you promise not to say a word about it to the others."

"All right," I agreed, forgetful of the past. "Provided it isn't something criminal, I promise."

"Well," he said, "then I'll tell you. I said to Henry before I left that I wanted to find something to do, just to sort of pass the time, and he said, 'Why not have a try at doing something that really needs doing?' I said I didn't suppose I could, but he said I really could do something that needed doing if I really wanted to."

He paused and I said, amused by his "reallys," "Go on. What was it he really thought you could really do?"

"Don't be sarcastic. Henry said he didn't know a single good book written for children and young people about Karl Marx. So I'm reading up his life and making notes and I'm reading about Communism too. What Henry wants me to do is to put the whole thing into simple words. He and Vera both think I could do it very well."

I gave a whistle.

"So those two are Communists, are they?"

He shifted his position and looked at me a little nervously.

"Didn't you know? Vera was first and then Henry became one."

"How would I know, and why didn't you tell us?"

"How could I?" he asked scornfully. "Can't you imagine what Father'd say? He'd never have had them in the house again and they're the only real friends I've got. You know how he is about any new ideas."

"They're not all that new," I said.

"Well, they'd be new to him. He'd consider the whole thing the invention of the devil. He'd think Karl Marx *was* the devil."

"Just a clever, industrious but badly mistaken old gentleman," I said.

"That's what you think," he retorted. "I don't suppose you've ever thought about it either."

"Don't you?" I asked. "You may recall that I go to a place called Harvard where Marxism is not unknown and where it's discussed about as much as any other subject."

"Well, don't be sarcastic," he said. "I knew you couldn't help being."

"Never mind. Go on talking. Are you reading *Das Kapital?* I should think you'd find it pretty tough going."

"Henry said I needn't if I didn't want to. He said I'd get on better by reading books about it. He gave me a list. But I've read a life of Karl Marx, and I agree with Henry and Vera that he's probably the greatest man who ever lived."

" 'Probably,' " I repeated. "Well, let it pass. Do you call yourself a Communist now?"

"I'm not anything really, but I think I'd like to be one. Henry said I could join here. He told me who to get in touch with but I haven't done anything about it yet. He says that only Communism can end wars."

"It can probably end pretty well everything," I said, "including itself. Look, Julian, I don't want to be elder-brotherly, but isn't Henry persuading you to do this just so you'll get yourself indoctrinated?"

"If I'm converted by what I learn," he argued, "what's wrong with that? If it appeals to my conscience and my reason, oughtn't I to accept it?"

I could always tell when he was quoting.

"Well," I said, "it seems to me a pretty silly idea and I think I know what Henry's motives were in urging you to do it. There must be lots of books on Communism for young people and children. The Communists would see to that."

"Henry says there aren't any good ones," he said, and I could see that, for him, that settled the matter.

"Are you fond of Vera?" I asked him.

"Yes," he answered, "but not in the way I suppose you mean. She isn't like other girls. She's an intellectual."

"You mean, no sex at all?" I asked.

"Oh, I don't know," he answered, coloring. "I don't care either. I'm just not interested in all that."

"Well, it's about time you were," I told him. He became uncommunicative then and said no more. When I had finished putting things away we went back and joined the others.

I was seeing more clearly now what I had long suspected, that we knew very little about Julian, and I blamed myself for not talking to him more. But never talking about anything but day-to-day matters was a family trait. My parents almost never did (the great exception, of course, was my father's half-hearted and belated attempt to instruct me in the facts of life). It was a part of their tremendous hold over us: that it was always highly agreeable and never uncomfortable to be with them. There were no questions, no awkwardnesses, no show of parental authority. They asked nothing of us except love, and that was theirs without asking—a spontaneous growth of almost tropical luxuriance. There was in fact something tropical about the whole climate in which we lived; we swam without directives, without guidance, in a degree of warmth which perfectly suited us; primitive, unicellular creatures, our every need supplied. I was beginning to perceive this but without any urge towards change. I was, as always, immensely content that we were together. The proximity of my mother was a delight to me. Where else could I possibly be so happy? And my criticisms of my father's behavior towards Fred, the deep shame I felt at Clarisse's shocking act (though I understood it and could feel under my own skin, her terror of the trap she had herself made)—these things only bound me closer to them, only deepened my sense of responsibility; just as what Julian had now told me increased my sense of responsibility towards him.

My mother was sitting with some embroidery in her hands, and as we came in she looked up with contented love and satisfaction shining in her eyes. My father, who had been reading what I later saw was yesterday's *Times,* tossed it aside and Clarisse closed the novel she was reading. I saw that it was one of D. H. Lawrence's.

"Now," my father said, smiling at us, "here we are, and thank heaven we're all together again. When one of us is missing it's like having to do without an arm or a leg. Now let's talk about our plans for the future. Sit down, Julian, I can't talk if you're going to fidget about. This concerns you, my boy, just as much as any of us." Julian tossed back his hair and went and sat down beside my mother, his face expressionless. Then my father went on, "We're an American family, even though two of us were born in Europe, but we're an American family with deep roots over here. Your mother had a European education, the most formative years of my young manhood were spent in Paris, as you know; we've lived in Europe just about as much as we've lived in America, and I don't think any of us feels any deep allegiance to the U.S.A." He gave a little cough and added, "Whatever our feelings may have been earlier. I don't like bringing up the past, but I must just say that I don't think many families can have been subjected to what we have been subjected to. The vulgar, prurient publicity, the shameful notoriety, the whole shocking, scandalous treatment we've received at the hands of the American press over an unfortunate, purely domestic matter. I haven't the words to say what I feel about it all. Well, I think you know. Anyway, as a result, your mother and I feel—but only, of course, if you all agree—that we'd like to make our home over here. Here, or perhaps in Paris. That's something we must work out together. But neither your mother nor I—and I'm sure Clarisse feels as we do—you do, don't you, Clarry?—neither your mother nor I feel we ever want to make our home in America again."

"You mean we'd live here altogether?" I asked, astonished.

"Altogether," he said. "Personally, apart from everything else, I'm pretty sick of prohibition and rum-running and bootlegging and all the disgraceful things that accompany it. I think we've had about enough of it."

My mother, who must have felt that I was looking at her, glanced up from her embroidery and met my eyes.

"Naturally," she said, "I want to do whatever your father wants to do, provided, of course, that you children want it too. Or are willing to acquiesce in it."

There was a little silence. Then Julian said, with that toss of the head, "I don't much care, one way or the other—it makes no difference to me."

Clarisse said with quiet and deadly certainty, "I never want to see New York again as long as I live. For us, New York *is* America. I hope we'll live in Paris."

"This is pretty sudden," I said. "I suppose the rest of you have had time to think about it. Aren't there a lot of difficulties? Won't you have to pay income tax in both countries, Father?"

My mother glanced at me quickly and her eyes lit up with amusement.

"Does anyone ever have to pay income tax in France?" she asked.

"Even if we did have to," my father said, "it would be worth it, in my opinion. But I believe adjustments can be made. I'll have to go into all that, of course, with Dimlock and Wineberg."

"What about the house?" I asked. "What about the pictures?"

"We would sell the house," my father said. "The pictures can be packed up and sent over here. Blair & Fernando could see to that. And we could bring over as much of the furniture as we needed."

"The last time we talked about it," I said, and I remembered that it was just before we heard Clarisse's wild knocking on the door, "you spoke of giving the pictures to the nation—forming a Prentiss Foundation or something."

"Yes," he said. "That was what I had hoped and meant to do, but not now, not any longer. And anyway, isn't it more fair and right that I should give them one day to the French nation? So many of the best works of the Impressionists have gone to America, I don't see why these shouldn't be given back to France. And if I did decide to give them to the French in my lifetime, at least I should be made an *Officier* of the *Légion d'Honneur*. In America, I'd get no recognition at all."

"I've always wanted to live in Paris," Clarisse said. "After all, I was born there. Mother, if we do, I promise I'll do all the housekeeping. I like dealing with French servants, and ordering French meals."

"I'll gladly take you at your word, darling," my mother said, smiling at her.

"We could come over here whenever we wanted to," my father went on, "though I don't feel the same confidence in England since she went off the gold standard, and we'd have Italy and all the other countries of Europe at our doors without that tedious crossing and recrossing of the Atlantic. But what about you, Halley? Do you feel you must finish at Harvard? That's what we want to find out."

There was a silence and they were all looking at me. I didn't know then that it was one of the crucial moments of my life though perhaps I knew it subconsciously, for my heart began to pound as though I were faced with some sudden danger. I felt I had to say something and I looked over at my mother, whose great dark eyes were fixed on mine with anxiety and yearning. If I had not met that look of hers it is possible that I might have answered differently, but so deep was my love for her, so strong was the pull of the family that before I had come to any real decision I heard myself saying,

"I don't really mind leaving. I don't know that I was getting so much out of it."

And not only was there the pull of the family. I thought, as soon as I had spoken, of the looks of sympathy or of curiosity I had had to meet, I thought of all the hastily averted eyes, I thought of New York, where any day I might run into Rosie or Helen, might meet and be cold-shouldered by Syl. What had been dear and familiar was now wholly to be dreaded.

"No," I added, and I was trying to convince myself now, "I don't really care if I never go back. I could take a year or two at the Sorbonne instead, or maybe go to London University."

"Oh!" my mother said, putting down her embroidery, and I could see her whole body relax. "How I was praying you'd say that, Halley!"

She got up and ran to me to give me a kiss, and her movements were as light and quick as ever.

"Are you sure, darling?" she asked, looking into my face, an arm about my shoulders. "Are you sure you're not making a sacrifice?"

"Quite sure," I said, but my heart hadn't yet stopped its pounding.

My father got up and began walking about the room, and I could see that he was deeply gratified. It was one of those hotel sitting rooms, similar to many others we had occupied in the past, that had taken on so much of the family atmosphere that there was nothing alien about it.

"Well," my father said, and his voice was a little unsteady, "I must say, that makes everything just perfect. One reason we weren't absolutely happy about the idea was that we hated the thought of the long separations from you, my boy. Also the thought that you'd have no home to go to in New York. We're very, very grateful to you for what you've said. Your mother and I are grateful to all three of you. Now we can really go ahead and make plans, but not just at this moment." He took out his thin pocket watch. "We all ought to think about dressing for an early dinner now. We've got seats for the theater. I hope you're not too tired, Halley."

"Goodness no," I said. "How's Louise?"

My mother folded up her embroidery. "Darling," she said, "would you just go in and see her for a few minutes? She isn't at all well. In fact we're very much worried about her. I know she'd love to see you."

She told me the number of Louise's room. It was on the top floor and I went up there and knocked on the door. Very faintly I heard Louise's voice telling me to come in. She was propped up in bed and she had a French Bible in her hands. (She was a Protestant, a fact my parents had ascertained before they engaged her.) I saw that she had altered very much for the worse. Her prominent nose sharply divided her sallow face and her lips had fallen in. She held out her hand to me and with pity and a feeling of dread I bent down and kissed her forehead. Her hand tightened on mine and she seemed to look at me from a great distance.

"Now," she said in French, "we are all together, and that miserable affair that should never have been begun can be forgotten. God forgive him his sin."

"Don't try to talk about it, Louise," I said. "It will only upset us both. I'm sorry to find you in bed. When will you be up again?"

"The doctor says in a week," she answered. "I say never. We will see who is right." She closed her eyes, opened them again and said, "Clarisse. *Elle est plus belle que jamais. Ma petite fleur pâle.*"

It was years since I'd heard her call Clarisse her little pale flower. To please her I said, "Yes, she's more beautiful than ever."

"And now she belongs to us," she said, and she smiled. It was a smile of triumph. I wondered, not for the first time, what part Louise had played in undermining Clarisse's wavering courage. I thought I could guess that she had done what she could.

Two days later she had a stroke. She couldn't speak, but she wrote, her hand supported by my mother's, that she wanted to be buried where her family were buried, near the Port St. Denis. The wishes of a dying woman are sacred, and when she died, twelve hours later, my father made all the necessary preparations. It was a disagreeable task but Louise was a member of the family and he undertook it bravely. I offered to go to Paris with him.

"Thank you, Halley," he said, "but I think this is something your mother and I must do together. You know we engaged Louise together when we were on our honeymoon. Perhaps when it's over we might look at one or two apartments. It would cheer your mother up."

My mother shed tears at Louise's death, but I don't think Clarisse did. She said Louise had been very lucky to have gone so painlessly.

"What worries me," Julian said to me privately, "is who's going to be next. First Fred and now Louise. These things go in threes, don't they?"

"If they did," I said, "world population would be going down instead of up. Think of something else to worry about."

I went to Victoria with them and saw the coffin, which had arrived the night before, put into the van. Not everybody, I thought, would be doing what my parents were doing.

"It's queer," my father remarked when it was almost time for the train to start, "how things seem to come round in a sort of circle. Though of course they aren't quite the same when they do."

"I know what you're thinking," my mother said, and she put her small black-gloved hand on my father's arm. "You're thinking of that time when Halley and Clarisse were babies and we were on our way to Paris and Louise discovered she'd left her handbag and all her money at the house in Hyde Park Square."

"Yes," he said. "I can see her now, coming back almost in hysterics escorted by that big solemn policeman. You know, Ruth, it seems like yesterday."

They must have been standing within a few feet of where we were standing now, and I wished I could catch a glimpse of a brown-haired, gray-eyed child named Halley Prentiss. Then the whistle blew and they took their seats and the train moved smoothly off as the best English trains do, without the smallest jerk, and I had always wondered how it was done. Victoria Station was far more familiar to me than either Grand Central or Pennsylvania, in both of which I felt a stranger. The ugly, old-fashioned place with its smoky smell had its own charm for me, perhaps because it not only meant arriving in London in the spring but because it also meant leaving London for France, Switzerland, Italy. But all the same I walked back to the hotel feeling sad and unsettled. I tried to make up my mind once and for all if I had any regrets about our leaving America. I couldn't throw off a feeling that we were burning a pretty important bridge behind us, and yet when I came to analyze it the bridge was Syl, and for us he wasn't there any more. But was it altogether true that I was making no sacrifice? Certain places in Boston, Cambridge, New York were dear to me. There were winter evenings, yes, and summer evenings—and there were mornings too—when Fifth Avenue was surpassingly lovely. (Does any other city, I wondered, lean so heavily for its claim to beauty and distinction upon a single great street?) There were brisk, cold days that I loved, days on which I seemed to feel most vividly that I was an American in America, when the breath steamed from my lips, and little wisps of steam fluttered up from the gratings in the streets and the blue sky was cut with scissor sharpness by unique towers that seemed to lean against it, and snow shovelers were at work. But suppose that instead of being cut off from America I was about to be cut off from Europe? Then how would I feel? My experience of Europe was large, my experience of America very limited. It was not surprising that I made the choice I did.

I think that if I had said I wanted to finish at Harvard, my father might have made it possible; he might even have let me take a room or a small apartment in New York. But now that I had spoken, now that I had made them all happy and relieved my mother's mind it would have been hard to go back on what I had said. All the same, on that walk from Victoria Station to the hotel, I was in a miserable state of uncertainty, and I felt that I had taken, all too hastily, a step I might later regret. And yet, whenever I tried to imagine myself removed from that warm current that was life to me, I knew that I could not have spoken differently. I couldn't, I couldn't cut myself off from them all. I was a long way from becoming the creature that someday would be equipped to leave that ambient, enveloping sea, creep onto the land and make its final home there.

When I got back Clarisse was at the telephone. I had been wondering if now that we were alone she would make any reference to the topic we were all so carefully avoiding, but she had other things in mind.

"That was Flavia Grantley," she said as she hung up. "I rang her up to tell her we were here. She was very friendly and said she'd love to see us, so I said we'd all go out somewhere tomorrow night. Do you think you could get seats for a play?"

Flavia was the daughter of Mr. Vivian Grantley, the rich, somewhat eccentric but kindly widower who used to invite us all to stay at Wycks. She was only there once when we were there, for as a child she'd had a weak lung and she'd been educated in Switzerland. Until she was grown up and quite cured she was seldom in England. I'd seen her picture in one of the illustrated papers and she'd been described as a handsome heiress who had been one of the most popular debutantes of 1929. I managed to get seats for a musical show and we arranged to meet at the Berkeley for dinner.

Just before it was time to go I went to Clarisse's room. She was ready, and she had on a white dress and a black velvet wrap. She'd done her hair in a new way, drawn back from her forehead and coiled around the back of her head, and it suited her.

"I felt I wanted to look different," she said, turning her head for me to see. Then she looked at me nervously. "Halley, you don't want to talk to me about anything that's happened, do you? Because I don't want to, please. I'll let you know when I do."

"I want to know what you're going to say, or have already said, to Flavia," I told her. "We'd all better say the same thing, hadn't we?"

"Oh," she said, "that. Well, she knows I'm Clarisse Dumont because I sent her a wedding invitation, and she knows I'm a widow. Isn't that enough?"

"All right," I said. "I'd better have a word with Julian about it, hadn't I?"

"You can if you like," she answered, "but you know he never talks anyway and he'd certainly never talk about that."

Flavia was about as tall as I was and looked like a gypsy except that she was well dressed and neat. I knew as soon as I'd spent half an hour with her that she wasn't a girl I could ever fall in love with, but I liked her and she was as easy as an old shoe. She even got on well with Julian and I thought she'd never stop laughing when he told her he didn't like women under forty.

"You're out of date, Julian," she said. "Women of forty are hardly more than girls nowadays. You'd better raise your age limit to fifty or sixty and even then you might not be safe."

She was doing research work in biochemistry at London University. She'd had so much to do with doctors in her youth, she told us, that she'd got interested in the whole subject of medicine. She thought that later on she'd specialize in cancer research. To us this seemed a fantastically unnatural type of work for a girl to take up. We told her we thought she was crazy. Neither could we understand her fondness for music. I told her that I'd only once listened to classical music and that was on a gramophone.

"You're just a lot of barbarians," she said. "You don't know what you're missing. That reminds me, I've got two tickets for a concert at Queen's Hall for Friday night. Which of you wants to come with me?"

"You'd better take Halley," Clarisse said, "as he's been exposed to classical music at least once in his life."

"Will you come?" she asked me.

I had no desire to go but it was hard to refuse so I said I would.

"Good," she said. "Don't bother to pick me up. I'll come in the family car and meet you by the ticket window a little before eight."

She invited us all to Wycks for Saturday and Sunday, but we said we might be going to Paris.

"Why don't you settle down in England?" she asked. "It's a much better country to live in than France. It's a shame for you to go off just as we've got to know each other again."

"We'll be here a good deal," Clarisse said. "But I'd rather live in France. You see, I was born there. Paris is my spiritual home."

"Where's yours?" she asked me.

"I haven't any idea," I said. "Heaven, I guess."

"That sounds awfully conceited," she said. Then she turned to Julian.

"It's no good your asking me," he said. "I don't believe in spirits and I don't really feel at home anywhere."

"You always were a funny boy," she told him, amused. "I remember that we kept losing you when you were at Wycks and then we discovered that wherever Todd, the old butler was, there you were too. You followed him about like a little dog." Then she added, in her frank way, "I'm really awfully glad you've turned up again. I always thought you were a fascinating family, you were so different from any other family I'd ever known. I liked the way you just drifted aimlessly about without seeming to belong anywhere."

I thought it an unflattering description of us.

X

THAT FRIDAY EVENING AT QUEEN'S HALL, LIKE THE NIGHT OF Clarisse's panic return, is one that I can always go back to and every detail remains clear and in place. They are like records that I can play over and over, one giving me nothing but pain, the other nothing but pleasure.

At about five that afternoon Flavia sent a note to the hotel enclosing the two tickets.

"I'm afraid you'll have to find someone else to go with," she wrote, "or face it alone. Poor Daddy crushed two fingers in the door of the car today and he's in such pain I haven't the heart to leave him. But do go, please, and you can tell me how you enjoyed it next time we meet."

I was disappointed for I knew she would have been a good guide for me on my first adventure into music. Clarisse and Julian had got seats for a play, so I pocketed the two tickets and went alone. When I got there I found there was a queue at the box office and they were beginning to turn people away. I was about to hand in the extra ticket when I had a better thought and decided I'd give it to someone myself. At the very end of the queue there was a young girl waiting; she seemed to be alone and she looked like the sort of girl to whom a free ticket might mean something. Also she had a face that happened to please me. I waited until she got to the window in her turn and I saw her look of disappointment when she was told there wasn't a seat left. She couldn't, I thought, be more than seventeen. She wasn't wearing a hat and her short hair was smoothly brushed and fitted her head like a brown cap. She had a dark coat on and her handbag was shabby. I went up to her and said:

"I heard you couldn't get a seat. I've got an extra ticket here and I wondered if you'd care to have it." And I held it out to her.

Her eyes fairly sparkled with pleasure and surprise.

"Oh, what luck!" she cried. "Of course I'll take it. I was so disappointed because usually I can get a seat at the last minute. Please tell me what I owe you." And she hurriedly took a little change purse out of her bag.

"You don't owe me a thing," I told her. "The ticket was given to me."

"This *is* my lucky night!" she exclaimed. "Is the seat next to yours?"

I said it was.

"Oh, good!" she said. "Let's get in quick, it's nearly time. I'm ever so grateful. I did want to hear Sir Henry Wood conducting the *Haffner*, and the Tchaikovsky Sixth."

I got a couple of programs and we slipped into our seats just as the orchestra took their places. Then they started tuning up, and whenever I've heard an orchestra tuning up since then I'm taken straight back to that evening in late July, 1931, with the nameless girl sitting beside me. I glanced at her face and I saw that she could barely contain her joy at simply being there. I took several more looks before the lights were dimmed and I was suddenly taken back about eight years, and I remembered standing beside my father at a famous private collection he sometimes took me to, looking at Renoir's *"Portrait au Bord de la Mer,"* the little woman sitting in a wicker chair against a background of cliffs. I could hear my father say,

"If you ever marry, Halley, marry a woman of that type. That is what a woman's face should be like: full of sweetness, good temper and fun."

Then the music began. I had looked quickly at the program but it had meant very little to me. The first thing was Strauss's *Don Juan.* Then came a symphony by Mozart to be followed by a symphony by the same man who had written *The Nutcracker Suite.* I knew that much because we had it among our dance records.

I'm not going to describe in detail what I felt that night. All that the music did for me was to release a thousand inconsequential thoughts and images. My mind went agreeably straying to an accompaniment of music. It was pleasant enough and I was glad I was there. I could feel the intensity of the girl's enjoyment; she was lost to everything but sound, raptly absorbed. She might, as far as I was concerned, have been alone. She had made herself small, her arms were close to her sides and her hands clasped in her lap.

When the lights went up during the interval she got up and said, "Please excuse me, I've got to go out. I came here straight from the office."

I was amused at this and at the same time astonished to hear that she worked in an office. Surely, I thought, she was too young to do anything but lick stamps. When she came back she said, "Excuse me," again and got into her seat. Then she turned to me and said, "Excuse me, you're American, aren't you, if you don't mind my asking?"

When I told her I was, she said, "You're not nearly as American as some. I mean, you don't really speak American, do you? You know, with a funny accent I mean."

She was too young to be snubbed. I only said, "Well, you see, I've lived here and in France a good deal."

"Do you speak French?" she asked next and when I nodded she went on, "Oh, I wish I was good at French! I'm trying ever so hard. You can't learn it properly at school."

I asked her how long she'd been out of school and she made a little grimace.

"Everyone asks me that. I'm older than I look. I'm twenty-two actually. I've worked in an office ever since I left business school. I wish I didn't look so young, it's ever so hampering."

"You'll outgrow it," I said. "All the same, I thought you were about seventeen. Do you go to concerts a lot?"

"Whenever I've saved up a bit of money. That's why it was such luck your giving me the ticket. Now I can come again next week."

"I've never been to a concert before in my life," I told her.

She stared at me in amazement.

"Don't you know anything about music, then?"

"Not a thing."

"What made you come to this one?"

I told her how it had happened.

"Fancy," she said wonderingly, "just because that poor Mr. Somebody caught his fingers in a door, here I am instead of your girl friend."

"She isn't my girl friend," I replied.

"Well, anyway," she said, "here I am." After a minute's silence she asked, "Where do you live?"

"Mostly in New York, but now I shall be living over here. At the moment I'm at Brown's Hotel."

"Is that very posh?" she wanted to know. I told her it was a nice family hotel. Then she said, "Shall I tell you my name? It's Selma Roberta Jackson. Selma's what they call me. Roberta's for an aunt but she's dead now. I wish you'd tell me your name." I did tell her and she approved. She said it was a very nice name. She then asked if I thought I would like concerts.

"So far," I said, "I'm enjoying this one."

"The next thing's lovely," she told me. "It's called the *Pathetic Symphony*, I don't know why. I hope you'll like it. It's one of my favorites. I wanted to study music," she went on, "but girls like me have to earn their living. I do take piano lessons though from a friend of mine who plays in a theater orchestra. He gives them to me free. It's ever so good of him."

"Ever so good of him," I thought. "He's in love with you, that's why he gives them to you free."

"How often does he give you lessons?" I asked. She surprised me by saying, "I can guess what you're thinking but it isn't a bit romantic. He's married, and his wife is my mother's cousin. I haven't had any romances in my life, not real ones. Oh, you know, there are people who like me but I only like them enough to go to the pictures with them sometimes. My mother has a saying—shall I tell you?"

"Yes," I said. "Tell me."

"She has a saying, 'Two hot meals and it has to be one thing or the other.' Did you ever hear that before?"

I laughed. I couldn't help it. "No, never," I said, "but I think it's very funny."

"My mother doesn't think it's funny. She's quite serious. If I ever do accept a proper meal from anybody she says, 'Here we go.' As a matter of fact, I very seldom get asked."

Her mother, I thought, sounded unusual.

"What would she say," I inquired, "if I asked you to have supper with me after the concert?"

Her eyes—clear brown eyes the color of good after-dinner coffee —seemed to search mine.

"Are you asking me?"

"I'd like to," I said. "I want supper somewhere and I'd be glad if you'd come with me."

She looked a little worried. "I wonder if I dare?" she said.

"Dare?" I repeated. "There's nothing very daring about having supper with me."

"It isn't that," she said. "I can see you're all right, but you see we aren't on the telephone and they always expect me back about eleven when I stay for a concert. My mother always has hot cocoa on the stove for me. She'd worry."

I could see the picture more and more clearly, but I still wanted her to come with me.

"Couldn't someone take a message?"

"Mrs. Fulton could but she goes to bed early. She lives next door but one and she's got a telephone because her daughter Mrs. Jevons is a midwife."

"Better ring her up quick if you're going to," I said. And I added, "It can be a cold meal if you like."

She saw the joke all right and when she laughed her face seemed to broaden and her thick lashes almost hid her eyes. Her teeth, I noticed, were healthy and regular. As a family we were quick to notice teeth and were proud of our own. Altogether I liked the girl; she amused me and she had charm.

"Hurry along," I said. "You'd better do the telephoning yourself but I'll come with you. Here are some pennies."

She said, "Thanks," and took them, and when we got outside she disappeared into a telephone booth. She emerged looking crestfallen.

"What's the matter?" I asked.

"Mrs. Fulton was in bed. She has to get up and go and tell them. Mrs. Jevons was out on a case. I do feel ashamed. She's quite an old lady."

"Never mind," I said. "She'll survive. It's a nice warm evening."

She cheered up as soon as we were back in our seats and she applauded Sir Henry Wood's return with enthusiasm. "Now for my favorite," she said. "I do hope you'll like it as much as I do."

I found it was easy to like, much easier than the Mozart, and I could understand why she liked it so much. Again she sat with her arms at her sides, not even sharing the armrest with me; in fact I thought she carefully refrained from doing so. I liked her for that.

I decided to take her to the Carlton Grill for supper, and I could see that she was a little nervous. As we went down the stairs she said, "I do wish I'd known; I'd have put on my blue silk. I've only got an old office dress under this coat. Does it matter?"

"Not a bit," I said. "That's the best of a grill, you don't have to dress. Besides, a girl with nice hair and a face like yours needn't worry much about clothes."

She paused at the bottom of the stairs and looked at me with curiosity but without any coyness.

"Do you like it?" she asked. "My face?"

"Yes," I said. "It amuses me."

"Oh," she said, and then added, "Well, I don't mind."

There was a fatherly headwaiter in the grill who'd known us for a long time. As he showed us to a table he said my father and mother and brother and sister had been in twice within the last week, and he'd wondered when he was going to see me.

"I haven't been back long," I told him. I tried to avoid the girl's eyes because I could see she was impressed and it embarrassed me. When he'd gone to speak to someone else I said, "That welcome was for my father, not for me."

"Think of this happening to Selma Jackson," she marveled. "I think I must be dreaming."

She decided after some hesitation not to take off her coat. I began to study the menu.

"Well," I said, "what's it to be? Hot or cold?"

She laughed again; I could see she liked my teasing her.

"That's for you to say," she told me. Then she said she wished I'd do the ordering. "If you leave it to me I'm sure to say scrambled eggs and cocoa."

When we'd decided what to have she wanted to know how old I was.

"You do things as if you were about forty," she told me.

"I'm younger than you are," I said. "I'm twenty-one."

"Oh, but you're much older than I am in everything but years," she said. "I'm terribly inexperienced. Do you mind?"

I told her I preferred her that way.

She hadn't exactly a Cockney accent, but she very nearly had. I thought she had been quite carefully brought up and had been to a fairly good school. Like most girls of very limited experience she brought her friends and acquaintances freely into her conversation. She had a "girl friend" named Edna Shelbridge and I soon knew what Edna liked to eat, where she lived and worked and who her "boy friend" was. Selma didn't approve of him.

"I mean to say, he oughtn't to treat Edna so offhand."

I stopped the artless flow by asking her why she was so anxious to learn French.

"Because I'd get better pay if I did. I'm working for a firm of exporters and my boss keeps saying he wishes I could write letters in French."

"Let's hear how good you are," I said, hoping it would keep her from talking about Edna. "Let's speak French for the rest of the evening. Don't be shy, you'll never get on if you are." And I asked her in French if she'd come to another concert with me soon.

She understood all right and her eyes shone, but she played fair and answered me in French, speaking very slowly, "If you ask me I will accept, but are you serious?"

I said we'd go the following week if she liked, there was a concert on Thursday. It was amusing helping her and correcting her accent and she entered into it with zest. At twelve she looked at the big, serviceable wrist watch she wore and said she really must go.

"I'll drive you home," I said.

"What? All the way to Battersea? Oh, no, it's much too far. I can still get a bus."

"Nonsense," I answered. "We'll take a taxi."

As I paid the bill she said, "What a thrilling evening! Wait till I see Edna. Won't I have something to tell her?"

The thought of being described to Edna didn't please me at all.

"Would you mind," I said, "not telling Edna?"

She looked like a child whose doll has been snatched from her.

"Just to please me," I insisted. "Do you mind?"

"I was terribly looking forward to it," she said, crestfallen. Then she brightened. "Oh, well, it'll be fun having a secret from her too. But I can tell my mother and father, can't I?"

"Of course," I said. "I just didn't want to be talked over with the 'girl friend.'"

Then she launched a well-placed little dart that I hadn't expected.

"You think 'girl friend' is common, don't you?"

"Well," I said, "it's all right to say 'girl friend' and 'boy friend' in fun."

"Your sister wouldn't have said it."

"No," I said, "she wouldn't, except perhaps in fun."

"Oh," she said. Then she looked at me sadly. "There'll be a million things you won't like about me and about my home and about my parents," she said. "I think we'd better not see each other any more."

"Why?" I said. "Can't we be frank with each other? I expect there'll be lots of things about me you won't like."

She picked up her handbag, avoiding my eyes.

"That's just the trouble," she said. "There won't be."

I took her home and we sat as far apart as the limits of the taxi would allow. We stopped at the door of a small ugly house in a row of small ugly houses in a part of London I didn't know at all. I said it was late and I wouldn't come in but perhaps she'd let me come in some other time. She looked at me very doubtfully in the light of a street lamp.

"I'd better give you the telephone number of where I work," she said, "so if you change your mind about the concert you can ring me up."

I wrote it down, though I said I wouldn't change my mind, and she opened the door. There was a light on the landing above and I could see a narrow hall, a hatrack, a hideous umbrella stand and stairs that went steeply up. She said "Good night," and quickly went in and shut the door.

As I drove home I had to make up my mind what I'd say to the others about my evening. Should I keep my little "girl friend" to myself? I decided that for the present I would, and they could think I'd spent the evening alone. I wasn't even sure, ten minutes after leaving Selma, that I really wanted to see her again. But I knew how much, in spite of some small reverses, she'd enjoyed the evening. I had known little until now of the pleasure of giving pleasure. I was to find it irresistible.

On Tuesday evening my father rang me up from Paris and we had quite a long talk. It was an understood thing in our family that if one had occasion to make a long-distance call one did not skimp the conversation in order to save a little money. He said he and my mother had seen an attractive and roomy apartment just off the Champs Élysées that would be vacant in the autumn and he thought we'd all better come over and look at it. After consulting with Clarisse and Julian I told him that they would come but that I'd like to stay in London if he didn't mind. Anything that pleased them would please me, and there was a sale at Sotheby's I rather wanted to go to. I thought I might pick up a drawing or two.

"That's all right," he said. "We'll be back Friday or Saturday anyway. There's just one thing though, Halley. I wouldn't buy anything too expensive if I were you. I've had a bit of bad luck lately. I cabled Conrad Falke to buy a block of International Electric Equipment shares for me, thinking they'd reached bottom and were due for a rise, but, by golly! they hadn't. There doesn't seem to be a bottom any more, and I've lost the last bit of faith I had in Hoover. The fact is, I've taken quite a knock. So just go slow, will you? I'm not worried, but I've just got to watch things a little. I've got a lot of money tied up in one way and another."

"All right," I said. "Maybe I won't buy anything, but I'd like to go along and see what turns up."

"Fine," he said heartily. "I'll be interested to hear. Everything went off very well—the funeral, I mean—but it was a depressing business. I'm taking your mother to the play this evening to cheer her up. You might see that Clarisse and Julian get off all right tomorrow, will you? They're not used to doing things by themselves."

I said I'd see them off at Victoria and he hung up, leaving me with something to think about. I'd wondered often enough how he was going to get along without Syl. I knew that he had sold a lot of government bonds and "blue chip" shares before leaving New York and had recently bought some more potentially rewarding but more speculative shares instead, though I didn't know how many. Syl had always been, of course, on the conservative side and my father had often complained of this in the past. Now he felt free to follow his own "hunches," and I wondered where these would lead him. It was no business of mine and I knew even less about it than he did, but for a man who had always boasted of his total indifference to financial matters, it struck me that he was perhaps being somewhat rash.

By Thursday evening I was beginning to have regrets and second thoughts. Did I really want to sit through another whole evening of music? Did I really care whether or not I ever saw Selma Roberta Jackson again? The impulse came to me as I waited in the foyer to leave a ticket in her name and go, but I couldn't bear to spoil so much pleasure. She arrived breathless but in good time. She'd gone home, she said, to put on her blue silk and she'd had to hurry. She was wearing the same dark coat, her brown cap of hair was glossy with brushing, and she smelt of eau de cologne. After she'd got into her seat she slipped off her coat and for the first time I saw her without it. I couldn't help noticing how well rounded she was and she must have seen me looking down at her for at once she was on the defensive.

"I know I'm too fat," she said. "You see, I don't get enough exercise. Edna and I used to play tennis in Battersea Park every weekend, but now I spend the time practicing instead."

"Don't worry," I said. "It suits you. Go ahead and practice, you can lose weight any time."

She gave me a happy smile then and I thought that she had the sort of face my father would approve of, though I doubted if he would approve of anything else about her. I wondered, at the same time, about her parents. She hadn't said anything to suggest that her mother was not English and certainly her name was English enough, but there was a look about her that was decidedly not English. She might have had Russian blood, I thought, or perhaps Hungarian, for what else could account for that faintly Slav or Tartar look? When I'd said her face amused me I was telling the truth. There were moments when I even felt an inclination to pat one of those smooth, round cheeks.

It was going to be an evening of Brahms, and she asked me if I knew anything about him. I said I didn't, that the only composer I knew anything about was George Gershwin, so she did her best for me in the few minutes before the concert began. She had a book on the lives of the great composers at home, she said, and she'd even memorized the dates. Then she settled herself into her seat with that same look of blissful absorption on her face that I'd seen before and appeared to forget that I was there.

This time I found I did more listening and less dreaming, but I realized I had a long way to go before I knew what it was all about. In the interval I asked her what time she'd said she'd be home.

"You didn't actually invite me to supper," she answered, "but I told them not to expect me home early, so it will be all right if you do invite me."

"Good," I said. "I was going to anyway. Shall we do as we did before, or would you rather go somewhere where we can dance?"

"Oh, could we really?" she asked. "I dance quite well, though maybe you won't think so. Edna says—" She broke off with a guilty look.

"Go on," I said, "tell me what Edna says just this once."

"No," she said, "I'm going to learn. I can see now how silly I was, but after this I wish you'd tell me, straight out. I'd rather it was that way."

She was a quick learner and very little escaped her notice. When we were dancing, and she danced, as she had told me, quite well, I wondered if I weren't in some danger of liking her too much. There was the danger, as well, of her liking me too much, and I decided I'd be frank with her from the start. I told her that evening that I didn't intend to marry till I was thirty, and if she was at all disappointed she was careful not to show it.

"I'm ready to get married," she said, "whenever I meet anyone I like well enough. Then perhaps I'd get time to work at the piano. I don't really like being a business girl."

Later in the evening she said, "I do wish you'd tell me what your father does. From the way you all travel about I suppose he's some sort of a diplomatist, isn't he?"

"No," I said, "he isn't a diplomat."

"Then is he just a rich man who doesn't do anything at all?"

"Well," I said, "he collects pictures."

"What for?"

"What for? Because he likes having them. It's hard to explain about my family, but I'll try to one day."

"Are you really going to see me again?" she asked.

I said I hoped so.

"Then perhaps you'd better come and meet my parents," she suggested. "They're very curious about you. My mother says she nearly married an American once."

"Well," I said, "think of that. All right. Whenever you like. You choose a time."

"Could you come and have tea with us on Saturday?"

I said the family were coming home on Saturday.

"Sunday, then?"

"No," I said, "Sunday isn't much good." The truth was I couldn't bear the thought of that house and that street on a Sunday. "What time do you leave the office as a rule?"

"About half past five," she said, "unless my boss wants me to stay to take down some letters."

I said I'd pick her up at half past five on Monday and take her home, if that was all right. She said it would be.

"Are you going to tell your parents about me?" she asked.

It was a question I'd hoped she wouldn't ask, for I had decided I wouldn't tell them. For some reason it pleased me to keep this child—and I thought of her as a child—to myself.

"Someday," I said. "Not just yet."

"I don't mind," she said, "but if you don't soon you never will. It'll get harder all the time." Then before I could speak again she said, "Please don't think I want you to do anything you don't want to do. I'm very lucky to have you for a boy—for a friend, I mean. You are my friend, aren't you?"

I said certainly I was.

"Well," she said, smiling, "don't forget, it's only for as long as you like."

XI

I USED TO WONDER AT THAT TIME IF CLARISSE WAS SUFFERING from a guilt complex. She avoided being alone with me, as if she wasn't sure she could trust me not to allude to things she couldn't endure to hear talked about, and she kept closer than ever to my mother. I don't think she was precisely unhappy but she seemed unsure of herself. It was as if she were feeling her way out of a dark place.

Then one night after we'd all been to a theater she knocked softly on the door of my room and came in. I was already in bed and she turned on my reading light and sat down on the foot of my bed. Her honey-colored hair was hanging down on her shoulders and there was a troubled look in her eyes. I remembered that long ago I used to think she must spend a good deal of time wondering what she was going to do with so much beauty. Now it was I who wondered.

"Halley," she said, "are you avoiding me? It seems to me you hardly ever talk to me any more. What's the matter?"

"It's funny you should ask me that," I told her. "I thought you were making it pretty plain you didn't want to talk to me."

"I don't know why you should think so. You're the only one, except Mother, that I ever do talk to."

"You don't have to wait for me," I said. "Go ahead."

"Well, don't make it difficult for me," she protested, frowning a little. "Can't you understand that I feel on edge all the time for fear someone will say something I don't want them to say?"

"Yes," I answered. "I guessed that, of course."

"You've been so aloof lately," she went on. "I think you must have some private interest in your life. Have you?"

"Think again," I said. "What have you got in your life that you want to talk to me about?"

"I haven't got anything," she replied. "The trouble is I don't know what I want, nor what I want to do. Everything seems to have come to a stop." She played with a pearl ring my father had given her. Then she said, "I suppose you know that I refused to benefit in any way under Fred's will?"

"Yes," I answered. "Father spoke about it."

"Do you think I was foolish?" she asked. "I just felt I couldn't touch any of it. And I suppose you know that I sent all that jewelry back by registered post before we left New York."

"I think you were quite right," I said. "Anyway, it's what I would have done if I'd been in your place."

"You really would?"

"Of course I would."

"The worst of it is," she went on, "I think Father's lost a lot of money lately. We're an expensive family, I suppose, and the Depression isn't making things any easier. Mother and I have decided to do without a maid from now on. Do you think you could find out if Father's lost a very great deal?"

"I don't think he'd tell me," I answered. "He's warned me to go slow, though."

"He's warned me too. I suppose in a way everything is my fault."

I didn't see for a second what she meant.

"Your fault?" I repeated.

She looked away and then said in a low voice, "Syl and all that, I mean."

"Well," I said, "it's no good worrying about it. Everybody's less well off than they were, and plenty of people are having a tough time."

"I never can see that that helps matters," she remarked.

"I didn't say it did. I suppose things will right themselves one of these days."

"I don't want to be a burden," she said. "I suppose I ought to marry again someday if this Depression goes on, but the trouble is I just don't want to marry. I don't want to have to live somebody else's life. I thought I could marry Fred because he was—well, just one of us, but when it came to the point—"

"Yes," I said quickly, "but need we talk about it?"

"I don't want to talk about it any more than you do. But if Father did lose his money, I suppose I'd have to marry again."

"Worry about it when the time comes," I said. As a matter of fact I was worried about it myself. What could any of us do?

"Anyway," she went on, "it's too soon even to think about it yet as

I've only been a widow such a short time. What I'd like to do would be to stay just as I am."

"You wouldn't have much fun," I told her.

"But don't you see," she said, "I could have, whenever I was ready to. As a widow I could do pretty well what I wanted to do."

"What do you want to do?" I asked.

She didn't seem to know that any better than I did.

"Couldn't you suggest something for me to do?" she inquired. Before I could answer she went on, "I've often thought that what I'd really like would be to have a sort of salon in Paris. I'd like to know a lot of artists and writers and poets and provide a meeting place for interesting people, but you can't do that without a good deal of money. Father makes me a pretty generous dress allowance, of course, and I have enough money for theaters and taxis and that sort of thing, but it wouldn't go much further than that."

"Have you talked to him about it?" I asked.

"Well, I did ask him how much more he could let me have," she said, "but I don't like worrying him. He's always so good to us all."

I thought I understood better now what my father was trying to do.

"You'd better not push him," I said. "You know he'd do anything on earth for you. Maybe that's why he's been losing money lately; he's trying too hard to make it."

"Well, perhaps I won't say anything more," she agreed. "I don't think Mother's worried, though. I did ask her if she was and she simply said that as long as the Depression lasted everyone had something to worry about." She got up. "I suppose everything must be all right really or Father wouldn't have agreed to take that expensive apartment. You'll like it when you see it, Halley. It might almost have been planned for us. There's even a spare bedroom, and I told Flavia she could come and stay with us sometimes. You like her, don't you?"

"Yes," I said, "I do."

"It's a pity you're not a few years older. She'll be very rich when her father dies."

"She's too keen on dissecting," I said. "She frightens me."

Clarisse laughed and turned to the door. Before opening it she said, "What's Julian been spending so much time at the British Museum for, do you know? I asked him but he wouldn't tell me. It isn't a bit like him to take so much interest in a museum."

"He's doing a little work for Henry Burroughs, that's all," I told her. "Looking things up for him. It makes him feel he's doing something."

"Why on earth couldn't he say so, instead of making a mystery of it? What a funny boy he is! You know, I sometimes think Julian may surprise us all one day."

"He may," I agreed, "but I can't help hoping he won't."

She said good night then, and it was a long time before we had another talk.

When I asked Julian how the book was getting on he replied evasively and I gathered it wasn't making much progress.

Mr. and Mrs. Jackson were something entirely new in my experience.

Selma had told me that her father was a retired post office official, now living on his pension and on what he had been able to save during forty years of employment. I don't know what the words "retired post office official" invoke in other minds but to me they could never invoke anyone now but Mr. Jackson. He seemed to me to fit the job he had held for so many years as the government officials in Chekhov's stories fit theirs.

He was a slight, medium-sized man of sixty-three. (He and Mrs. Jackson had married fairly young but they had had to wait fourteen years, Selma told me, for their first and only child.) His thin hair was brushed with precise care across a nearly bald head, his thin skin was stretched tightly across his angular nose and the veins at his temples showed plainly all their visceral convolutions. He had a thin, almost lipless mouth. He seemed a man without blood; passionless, slow and precise of speech; all that was once consumable in him long ago consumed. He collected stamps, he played lengthy games of chess with a neighbor, he liked going for slow walks to nowhere in particular and back again. Having acquired his pension he seemed to have achieved his total ambition, to have come to a state of complete rest, complete equilibrium. He once told me that he had not a single wish. His manner was pleasant enough in a negative way and he had no small talk at all. I soon learnt that he regarded all nations other than the British as mad, incomprehensible to a man of sense, and not worth comprehending. I learnt, too, that he would rather have owned that ugly little house in Battersea with its bit of front garden about nine feet by six than a palace anywhere else. He was so dull as to be fascinating, so limited, by his own will and choice, as to be impressive.

Mrs. Jackson was his very opposite. She was voluble, over-warm in her welcome, romantic, and likable. Rather self-consciously, I think, she was something of a character. If she had been well off she might have developed strong eccentricities. I had already learnt that limited incomes often limit personalities, keeping them within narrow boundaries and inhibiting their growth, and if Mrs. Jackson's had been given full scope it is anybody's guess what she might have become. In most ways she had conformed, as she would have had to do in order to lead the life she did lead, but it was pretty obvious that in one respect at least she was a badly frustrated woman. She craved romance, and she had never had it. Never having had it she wanted it both for herself and vicariously, through Selma, and so a pit was dug for the feet of Halley Prentiss. But I couldn't help liking her, she was so like a fire on a chilly day. She had handsome and rather full blue eyes and her graying hair had a good deal of red in it. I could see she had been a good-looking woman and in fact, I suppose, she still was. She had a kind of lively archness that I didn't dislike because I could see that it came from high spirits and a quick response to anything that touched upon pleasure, gaiety or "romance."

After introducing us, Selma went upstairs to "tidy" and I sat down at a table spread with what I guessed was a high tea, though it was my first experience of one. There was a covered dish of scones in front of the gas fire (the summer was just then taking a backward—or perhaps forward—look at winter), plates of sandwiches on paper doilies, boiled eggs in egg cups with little "cozies" on them, bread and butter and a pot of jam that, I was told, Selma had made, and a solid-looking fruitcake. Mr. Jackson offered me a cigarette from a battered silver case that had an inscription on it and seemed surprised when I said I didn't smoke. His fingers, I noticed, were yellow with nicotine. He took a cigarette himself and from that time on, whenever I was in his company, I wished that tobacco had never been discovered.

First, the cigarette was portentously tap-tap-tapped on the back of his left hand before being placed in his mouth. Then he lit it, putting out the match by waving it about with exaggerated gestures. Then, in the process of smoking he didn't inhale or exhale in the ordinary way, he opened his mouth extremely wide and simply let the smoke drift out as it would. It wasn't propelled by any breath, it merely emerged from that cavernous opening (I saw that he wore upper and lower dentures); and he watched it as it came as if he could read in it some message for the world.

I have described all this because of the effect it had on me. I suppose he must have acquired these habits a very long time ago because Mrs. Jackson appeared to be perfectly "conditioned" to them. Indeed she would have to be, otherwise she would either have cured him of them or hit him over the head once and for all. I watched Selma to see if she were conscious of them and I felt pretty sure she was for she saw me looking at her father—his head tilted back and his mouth wide open—with I don't know what expression on my face, and when I looked at her she quickly lowered her eyes.

All the same it was plain that she was fond of both her parents, that she took pride in the lavish tea and in the oh-so-cozy, ugly little room, and that my being there with them made her happy. Seeing her with her father and mother, I knew her, if I had had any doubts before, which I hadn't, for a good little character. She laughed and talked, quite at her ease, or anyway, appearing to be, and told them how I had picked her out from a whole queue of people to give the ticket to, and that I had never been to a concert before in my life until that first evening. But though she seemed so happy and at home in her environment I had the feeling that she didn't belong there and I could see not the faintest resemblance to either her father or her mother. These two middle-class (were they lower-middle? middle-middle?) people made her seem foreign, almost exotic, and I thought she must have got her attractive, faintly Slav look, her wide-apart eyes and cheek-bones from some grandparent. I observed again that her feet and legs were shapely and pretty but that her hands were not; they were broad in the palm with short, strong fingers. This did not matter to me for I have never thought soft, pretty hands of any importance.

Mrs. Jackson was eager to let me know what a good daughter she was. She turned over to her, she told me, half her earnings and was always buying her little presents.

"Oh, Mummie," Selma protested, "as if anybody wouldn't do the same."

"Ever since she was a kiddie," Mrs. Jackson went on, "she's always wanted to give me things. She gave me this cameo brooch for my last birthday."

"Why shouldn't she give you presents?" Mr. Jackson asked, but he asked it without expecting an answer and passed his cup for more tea.

[168]

"Daddy!" Selma exclaimed, almost with pride. "That's your fourth. What a thirst you've got!"

Mr. Jackson turned to me.

"I gather you are not tea drinkers in your country," he observed. "It's a pity. There's no better drink. Coffee makes people nervy, liverish and bad-tempered."

He spoke with oracular finality. I wasn't going to start a tea-versus-coffee argument or even complain of English coffee, so I only said, "We drink a good deal of tea in my family," and let Mrs. Jackson fill up my cup.

This unfortunately encouraged Mrs. Jackson to ask me a good many questions about my family life and try as I would I couldn't avoid letting the fact emerge that we were well off. When she asked me how many times I'd crossed the ocean and I had answered, "Twenty-seven times, that is, thirteen double crossings and one single one," they all looked at me as if I couldn't possibly be telling the truth.

Then Mr. Jackson said: "Well, it's satisfactory to know that you appreciate the advantages of living in this country."

I could see that Mr. Jackson and I were not likely to become boon companions, but apart from his atrocious way of smoking I didn't dislike him. He presently asked me if chess was played in America.

"It's quite popular," I replied, "but I've never learnt it."

"If you come again," he said, "I'll give you a lesson."

I said it was very good of him but I doubted if I'd be a good pupil.

"Collect stamps?" he then asked.

"No, sir," I said, "I'm afraid I don't."

"You should think of your old age," he told me.

"Oh, Oswald!" cried Mrs. Jackson. "Fancy saying a thing like that to Mr. Prentiss! Why, he's hardly more than a boy! Collect stamps for his old age indeed! I wish I'd been born a man. There'd have been no collecting stamps for me. The things I would have done! I'd have seen life, I can tell you."

"I dare say," said Mr. Jackson dryly, and lit another cigarette.

"I've got quite a weak spot for Americans," Mrs. Jackson then told me. "I nearly married an American once." She glanced archly at her husband but he was not even looking her way. He had his eyes fixed on the smoke that was slowly exuding from his open mouth. "He was ever such a nice boy," she went on. "He came from Tex-ass. He said his father was something or other in the oil business, a driller, would that be it? It nearly broke my heart to say no to him, but it would have killed my poor old mother if I'd gone away to a foreign country. She'd lost her only son and I was all she had. Then, quite soon after that I met Mr. Jackson. Do the right thing, I always say, and Providence is sure to reward you."

"Thank you, Polly," Mr. Jackson said, "for the kind words." He glanced out of the window. "Is it raining yet, Selma?"

She went to look.

"No, Daddy, but it looks as if it might, any minute now."

"If it does," he said, "I shan't have to water the dahlias."

I had been there an hour and I now got up to go. Mr. Jackson stayed where he was but he politely urged me to come again, adding the usual invitation to take pot luck with them, preferably on a Sunday.

"As if Mr. Prentiss," Mrs. Jackson said, her eyes sending me one of their flashing blue signals, "hadn't better things to do! I'm sure he's a very gay young man indeed, out at wonderful parties half the time. I would be if I were him, that much I know. All the same, Mr. Prentiss, if you ever found yourself with an idle hour, we'd be happy to see you. Selma dear, see Mr. Prentiss to the front door. Maybe he'd like a private word with you."

When, both somewhat embarrassed, Selma and I were at the front door, I said, "I was hoping I was going to hear you play."

"We haven't a piano," she said. "I have to go to my friends' to practice."

"Well," I answered, "I must hear you someday."

"Someday," she echoed. Then she added in a low voice, "It was ever so kind of you to come, but please don't feel you have to come again unless you really want to. I just wanted them to see what you were like. You know, that you were all right."

"I'm so glad I've met them," I told her, and in a way it was quite true. "I've had a lovely time."

She suddenly raised her eyes and gave me a beautiful, clear, altogether understanding look.

"Good-by," she said, and the way she said it, it sounded almost final.

"Don't be in such a hurry to get rid of me," I protested, for I could see she doubted that she would ever see me again. "Look, I'll ring up one day soon and we'll fix up something."

"Don't ring me up at the office," she said, "unless it's terribly important. My boss doesn't like it."

She looked down at her father's dahlias. There were about a dozen green clumps with quite large flower buds on them. I had a painful feeling that she was seeing everything as if for the first time, and I didn't want her to.

"O.K.," I said. "I'll write. I can do that, I suppose?"

She smiled at me.

"Yes," she said. "I'd like a letter." And then she added, "Good-by," again and turned back into the house.

I did write, but it was to tell her that I was going with my family to Scotland for a couple of weeks. When I got back I wrote again, this time to tell her that I was sailing to New York with my father as we had business to attend to there. It was over three months before I saw her again.

Clarisse would not set foot in New York and my mother did not want to leave her, so in the end it was decided that my father and I should go, and my mother said she would be quite content to let us decide what was to be shipped over and what left behind and sold.

Arnaud and Angèle, who had been told to expect us, were not at all surprised, it appeared, when they heard we were going to make our home in Paris. They said that they had always planned to return themselves one day, and if we wanted them, they would join us as soon as they could make their arrangements. My father was extremely touched and, I thought, a trifle embarrassed. He could hardly pay them less than the wages he had always paid them, and I think he had counted on getting servants in Paris for a good deal less money, but, as he said to me, Arnaud and Angèle were practically members of the family, and if they chose to stay with us, stay they must.

We selected the furniture we wanted to keep, and for days the packers were busy in the house. Blair & Fernando took away and packed up the pictures and my father saw to their insurance while in transit. He said that everything seemed unconscionably dear and he wondered where the rise in prices was going to end. To my surprise he asked me to come with him when he went to see Conrad Falke.

"I'd like you to be there to hear what he says," he told me, "and afterwards you might give me your impressions. I don't think I could have made a better choice, but so far you've only met him socially, and I'd like you to see him in his office too."

I went with him and was duly impressed with the office and everything in it, but less impressed with Mr. Falke, now that I saw him again. He summoned his secretary, who seemed to me unnecessarily good-looking, and told her he was not to be disturbed for twenty minutes. I didn't care for this much and I could see that my father didn't. I thought he needn't have troubled to let us know quite so precisely how much time he thought we rated. Also, he had a sort of bedside manner I thought inappropriate to a stockbroker's office. He seemed to want to convince my father that there was nothing whatever to worry about, although he admitted that stocks were worth about half what they had been a year ago. The bottom having been reached, he said, it was inevitable that an upward tendency was to be looked for, and for his part he was quite convinced that it had already begun. This was so much what my father longed to hear that I could see he was more than ready to believe it. Mr. Falke told him he would never have advised him to buy International Electrical Equipments, there were fifty things he would have recommended first, and he thought that in future my father had better leave such decisions to the people who were on the spot. He was "Casey at the Bat" all the time, he told us, that was what he was there for, and if my father wanted a home run he'd see that he got it, and soon.

"Trust the man on the spot," he said again, and I could see that he was getting ready to say good-by to us though he had made only the smallest movement in his chair. It was just the right sort of movement to suggest that it was time we were on our way. My father took the hint and got up, saying he knew what a busy man he must be. As we neared the door Mr. Falke's manner became very much friendlier and he showed us to the elevator himself, giving us a wave of the hand as we shot down out of sight. Without his having to say a word I knew that my father thought Mr. Falke a good deal less "civilized" than he had seemed when he came to dine with us in Sixty-sixth Street with his good-looking wife, but I think he had been impressed, in spite of his first feeling of annoyance, by his somewhat casual treatment of us.

"Frankly," my father said as we looked for a taxi (the Cadillac had been sold, far from profitably, two days before and we had said a regretful good-by to fat old Johnson), "frankly I'm afraid Falke hasn't got the *nous* that Syl had, though I suppose he knows what he's about. Anyway, I'm going to let him have a freer hand from now on. I suppose it would have been wiser to have consulted him before instructing him to buy those Electric Equipment shares, but I didn't want to wait."

"Who advised you to buy them?" I asked, though I felt he didn't want me to ask it and didn't propose to answer it.

"Someone who ought to have been in the know," was all he said, and I only learnt long afterwards that it was the man who used to cut his hair in London.

He didn't ask me what my impressions of Conrad Falke were. I don't think he wanted to hear.

While we were in New York my father gave a farewell dinner to eight of his old friends. There were two art critics, a famous art dealer, a theatrical producer who said, gloomily, that he was about ready to jump off the nearest tall building, Mr. Frisbee, my father's banker, a painter who had originally come from Russia and whose work my father thought highly of, though not highly enough to buy, and Dr. Medlicott. No one connected in any way with Syl. It wasn't a great success and it was the first men's dinner my father had ever given.

"I shouldn't have done it," he told me afterwards. "They all knew it was a farewell party, which made it a little depressing from the start, and it needed your mother and some of the wives to pull it together. God forbid that I should ever have to live without your mother. I want to get back to her as quick as we can. Now that the house is up for sale I feel that the last link with the old life here is broken."

Several times before leaving New York I sat by the telephone wondering if I had the courage to ring up Rosie or Helen. Would they have spoken to me? Helen, I thought, might have spoken to me; Rosie would almost certainly have broken down, either in anger or unhappy tears. She must hate Clarisse, she might well hate my father and mother. I didn't think she would have hated me, but I couldn't, in the end, put it to the test. I did, however, ring up Syl's apartment, not from the house, I couldn't bring myself to do that, but from a call box. If he had been at home I would have given my name and asked to speak to him. He wasn't in and I hung up without giving my name. I came out of the call box with my heart thumping wildly. If he had been in, if he had come and spoken to me, what would I have said? I thought I would have said,

"Syl, it's Halley. Syl, I just wanted to hear your voice once more. Just tell me how you are."

XII

WE WENT STRAIGHT TO PARIS, WHERE THE OTHERS NOW WERE AND we found a surprise had been prepared for us. Knowing that it might be many weeks before the furniture arrived from New York, my mother had bought beds, bed linen, a few chairs and tables and some kitchenware and had moved into the apartment, so there the three of them were, installed. "It was so much cheaper," my mother explained, "than all of us living in a hotel." She may have been right, and my father and I found everything running smoothly. My mother's skill had already made the place seem homelike and my father, after his first astonishment, told her she had done wonders. We all felt, I think, that as a family we were beginning a new life, and the one to feel it most, was, I am sure, Clarisse.

The weather was brisk but not yet cold and from the windows of the big drawing room we could see the last of the scorched brown leaves being whisked from the trees along the Champs Élysées. We could see, too, the top of the Arc de Triomphe, and on clear days, far beyond. It was a beautiful apartment with polished parquet floors and not a dark corner anywhere, and I never asked my father in all the time we lived there how much it was costing him. It was one of those things I felt I would rather not know.

I decided to take up three subjects at the Sorbonne: philosophy, French history and French literature. René Valmont had suggested philosophy to me as a worth-while study, French history was in memory of Raymond, and French literature I knew very little about, except that I had lately discovered Proust. I thought I would enjoy all three and without taxing myself overmuch, for I wanted time for my favorite pursuit, which was looking for drawings at moderate prices. I asked my father one day, feeling suddenly worried about my future, if instead of attending the Sorbonne I ought not to be fitting myself for a wage-earning job, but he scoffed at the idea.

"Why, you haven't finished your education yet, my boy," he said.

"Besides, there's no reason why you should worry. Let me do the worrying. We've only got to ride out the Depression and everything will be all right, and then you can have double the allowance I'm giving you now. I hate keeping you short, but it's only temporary."

We were going to pick up my mother, who was trying on a hat at the place she and Clarisse always went to, close to the Madeleine, and as we walked we passed an art dealer's window and my father saw a Utrillo and pulled up short.

"I regret now," he said to me, "that I only have one Utrillo. That one's first rate. I wonder where he got it. I fancy it's from that sale I ought to have gone to at Picard's the other day. It'll be a fancy price now, I'm afraid. I promised your mother, though, that I wouldn't do any more buying at present. What poetry there can be in walls and village streets and the flat faces of houses, all keeping their secrets! And that single, bony tree. By golly! I'd like to have painted that picture myself. Well, come along, we'll be late."

I assured him, going back to what I had been saying, that I thought he was treating me very generously but that I didn't want to be a burden on him forever. He cut me short.

"As soon as the pictures arrive," he said, "do you know what I want to do? I've told your mother of course, and she's enthusiastic about the idea. I want to exhibit them. I think it would make quite a stir. I'd thought of the Orangerie, but my old friend Aristide Bloch wants me to have it at his gallery. He says a private gallery would suit the pictures better. Perhaps he's right. I'd like you to help me with it when the time comes."

I said there was nothing I'd like more.

"Couldn't Julian help too?" I asked. "He ought to be occupied in some way. I don't know what he does with himself all day long."

"I don't know either," my father said, "but I don't think we need to worry about him. He's a good boy, and he helped your mother a lot when they moved in. He's as devoted to her as ever in his odd way. He said the other day that he'd like to take up fencing, but I think it would cost a good deal. It might be better to let him have that dog he's always wanted. However, we'll see."

"I don't like his sitting in cafés so much," I said. "He's taken to going and sitting in the Cupôle and the Dôme, all by himself. He told me so."

"Has he?" my father asked, surprised. "I don't think he drinks anything, except a glass of vermouth occasionally. I suppose he just likes watching the people. Perhaps he'll write one day." And then he asked, "How do you think Clarry seems? Don't you think she's much happier now?"

I said I did, that it was quite noticeable.

"It's curious," my father said, "that however black things may look to us at the time they happen, they have a way of working out for the best. Leaving out what happened to Fred—and more and more I'm convinced that he did what he did after a bout of drinking, when he wasn't responsible for his actions—leaving that out of it, I don't think any of us will need to have any regrets, or want to return to the past."

I looked at him, and I saw that he believed what he said and that he was confident and happy, so I let it pass. When he was in Paris he discarded the stick or umbrella he carried in London, and without any particular alteration in his dress he contrived to look like a Frenchman. His hat was at a slightly different angle now, and it seemed to me that he walked differently, more like a Boulevardier. He had let his hair grow a little longer, too. Yes, I thought, he might easily be taken for a Frenchman, and then I understood the reason. It was because, now that he was in Paris again, he was feeling like a Frenchman. It was as simple as that.

When we'd been in Paris about a month I decided to go to London for a weekend, and I wrote to Flavia to ask her if she could find me a room somewhere, as I didn't want to go to a hotel. At the same time I wrote to Selma, asking her to meet me at the Hungaria for dinner on Saturday night. And now my divided life began. I didn't give her our address in Paris because I didn't want her to write to me there. I simply said I hoped she'd be at the Hungaria at eight o'clock, and I was pretty sure she would be. When I spoke to my family about going to London I told them I'd be seeing Flavia, which was true, and I added that I didn't like being away from London for too long, for if I did I'd lose contact with such people as I knew there. My mother said I ought to get in touch with one or two old friends of my father's and hers, but I wouldn't make any promises.

I never knew a more obliging girl than Flavia; she'd do anything any of us asked her to do and do it well. When I rang her up on Friday she told me she'd booked a small room for me in Chapel Street, Knightsbridge, at ten shillings a night, bed and breakfast. "I think you'll be moderately comfortable," she told me. "Make a friend of your landlady and perhaps she'll let you have a room whenever you want it."

I asked her if I could see her at her flat that evening.

"Come if you like," she said, "but I don't mind telling you that you'll be rather *de trop*."

I guessed it was that red-haired young surgeon she was interested in. He didn't often get down from Edinburgh and when he did she had little time for anyone else. She suggested, however, taking me down to Wycks for lunch on Sunday, so I supposed that by that time he'd have gone back. I asked her when she was coming to stay with us in Paris.

"I might fly over for a night or two during the Christmas holidays," she said.

"Why fly?" I asked. "What's wrong with the normal method of travel?"

"Oh," she said, "haven't you flown yet? I often do. I love it."

"I guess I'll be content to wait a while," I said. But it was like her. She had plenty of enterprise and courage.

My room was small and at the top of the house, and I had to go down two floors to the bathroom, but I grew quite fond of the room in time and fond of my landlady, Mrs. Holness, and she soon said that whenever I wanted that room it was mine, and it was. I always let her know as far in advance as I could and she never once let me down.

I hadn't any doubt at all that Selma would be at the Hungaria. Nothing but illness would keep her away and I couldn't somehow imagine her ill. She was there ahead of me and she sprang up joyfully when she saw me, her delight plain to see. She looked very well, and so did the blue silk. It was a nice dress, simple and becoming, but whatever she'd had on, I thought, I would have been glad to see her.

"You look fine," I said. "You've grown or something. What is it?"

"I've grown thinner," she said. "Ever since I saw you looking at me that night I've stopped eating potatoes."

"Well, don't overdo it," I told her. "I'm old-fashioned. I like girls with figures."

I was the only one in my family who liked dancing. My parents had never danced—my father had never even learnt—Julian despised it and Clarisse was indifferent. This was unusual, for the early thirties were almost as much the dancing years as the twenties. We had dinner and danced between courses and after, and Selma was in a state of complete bliss and made no effort to seem otherwise. That was one of the things I liked best about her; pleasure and affection were not to be hidden, and I never knew anyone in whom happiness was such a real, almost palpable thing. It seemed to be a property of her own, and even when she was not happy—and had good reason not to be—I didn't feel it was far away. At a touch it would spring to life. She made me think of a good little lamp that, once lighted, burns with a steady, unaltering flame.

I decided that night that I had to go on seeing her. She filled a need that I had hardly been conscious of before I knew her though perhaps it was always there. It was the need for something entirely my own. For the first time I understood why Julian had so longed for a dog. He had everything, but he had nothing that was "all his own." Nor had I. Selma contained within herself all the qualities of a rewarding pupil, an affectionate and responsive pet and a private hobby. I was greatly pleased with her and greatly pleased with myself for having discovered her.

At dinner she showed me, laughing as she did so, a list of things she was trying to learn not to say.

"Girl friend, boy friend."

"Ever so." (I had teased her about this just once, mimicking her, and she'd dropped it, though I knew she had to watch herself.)

"Smashing."

"Ripping."

"Posh."

"Gentlemanly."

"I expect I'll have to add a lot more," she said.

Suddenly I felt ashamed. I had seen a revival of Shaw's *Pygmalion* not long before and had greatly disliked it. I thought it by far his worst play. It seemed to me to be pure snobbery overlaid with something I couldn't put a name to, but something utterly bogus. When the word "bloody" came and the audience shrieked with delighted laughter I felt like getting up and walking out. Now I felt myself to be guilty of the same sort of tasteless priggishness, which was as near as I could come to what I felt about the whole play from start to finish.

"Selma," I said, and I reached out and took one of her hands, "just go on, please, being yourself. That's good enough for me. Never think about all that nonsense again." And I screwed the paper into a little ball and flung it under the table. Why, I thought angrily, was I trying to alter her to suit myself, simply because it amused me to

[178]

take her out to dinner? Just as she was, just as she had been, she was worth ten of me and I knew it.

She knew what I meant but she wasn't going to have it that way.

"Please," she said, "I want to go on improving myself. Can't I, just for my own satisfaction? If you don't help me, who will?"

"Help you?" I asked. "What help do you need from me, for heaven's sake?"

"But I need a lot of help from you," she insisted, and I could see that she meant it. "You're like a big window, to me. I don't even know anybody else who's ever been to New York. And now you even live in Paris. Paris! Think of it! If you won't be the window I can look through into another sort of world, where am I going to find one?"

"I'll be anything you like," I said, deeply touched by this plea.

"Oh," she said, "now I'm happy again! You don't know how long and dull the months have been without you. Only one thing comforted me; that I knew you were away and couldn't come."

I wanted to keep her, I was determined to keep her as my secret pet and hobby. The problem would be to keep her from wanting to be anything more.

"Look, Selma," I said, "I like you an awful lot. I like you so much that I'm going to be absolutely frank with you. Do you mind? Now listen. I'm not thinking of marrying you. I'm probably never going to marry you. I told you that I wasn't going to marry until I'm thirty or so, and even when I do, it'll be to somebody else because you'll be married already. Now, can we just go on being friends and having dinners like this and dancing and going to concerts? Can we? Is it all right with you? If it isn't, tell me so now."

She gave me one of those clear, comprehending looks and said, "It's all right. I understand and I'm quite content."

"You're a darling," I said. "And one thing more. I think you'd better tell your mother just what I've said, don't you?"

"All right," she agreed. "I'll tell her." Then her eyes lit up with amusement. "She'll be terribly disappointed," she said.

"I know she will," I answered. "I know she took a sort of liking to me. But isn't it better to have everything plain and straightforward?"

"Of course it is," she said, "and I see things I didn't see before."

"What things?" I asked.

"For one thing I can see you're too young for me, or rather I'm too old for you. And we belong to a different class. It wouldn't do at all. And besides, you aren't in love with me. Perhaps," she added with a smile, "that's all that matters and I needn't have bothered about the rest."

"I'm very nearly in love with you," I told her, "but it isn't going to lead to anything because neither of us wants it to, and we're going to enjoy things the way they are. O.K.?"

"O.K.," she repeated.

"All right," I said. "Come on and dance."

It was after this that I began giving her presents. They were trifles at first and then, intoxicated by the pleasure of giving and by the pleasure the gifts gave her, I gave her better and better things. I brought her scent from Paris, gloves, costume jewelry, handbags, a good colorprint of Pissaro's "Approach to the Village" (that lovely moment of spring with the thin bare trees casting their delicate shadows across the road) to hang up in her room. I began to give her books too, but these I got in London. Her mother owned a whole set of George Eliot and Selma had read them all. *Middlemarch* was her favorite. I gave her a set of Jane Austen and she said to me next time we met with an air of being completely vindicated,

"You don't like me to say 'gentlemanly,' but Jane Austen says 'gentlemanlike' all the time. I suppose you think it's out of date."

I nearly always managed to see Flavia but I couldn't take her out because I couldn't afford to take out both girls, so, afraid that she would think me mean, I told her something about Selma, knowing that she was completely to be trusted. She scolded me like an elder sister.

"You know how this will end, Halley," she said. "You're terribly foolish. You're too honorable to have an affair with her and too class conscious to marry her, even if you weren't too young. I can find you lots of nice girls to go about with. You'll only make her unhappy."

"No I won't," I said. "She understands perfectly. I don't want other girls, I just happen to like that one."

"You're storing up trouble for yourself," she insisted. "And what about her parents? Mightn't they try to put the screws on?"

"Oh, no," I answered. "They're nice people. Anyway, I'm going to make the whole position perfectly clear to them."

After this talk with Flavia I sat down and wrote a letter to Mrs. Jackson. I wrote it in my cold little bedroom in Chapel Street with its one window looking out over the chimney pots, and when it was written I felt happier.

Dear Mrs. Jackson:

I know you must think I'm an odd sort of person to see so much of Selma and to give her so many presents—though they're only trifles—without explaining to you and Mr. Jackson what my feelings for her are. I just happen to like Selma a very great deal, but I'm not going to fall in love with her and she isn't going to fall in love with me. I'll take good care of her and if you don't mind my taking her out and giving her things, then everything's all right. I'm too young to marry—I'm not twenty-two yet—and I'm in no position to support a wife. Selma has promised to tell me if anyone with serious intentions comes along because when he does I mean to clear out as I would hate to spoil anything for her. I thought it was best to be perfectly frank, both with her and with you and Mr. Jackson. And thank you for all the confidence you have shown in me.

With kind regards,

Yours sincerely,
Halley Prentiss

On my next visit to London two weeks later—I now traveled second class on the train, first class on the boat, to save money—Selma handed me her mother's reply. We were having dinner, and I didn't know whether to put it in my pocket and open it when I got home or read it then and there.

"Please read it now," Selma said, seeing my hesitation. "I'm longing to know what she says."

So I opened it, and Selma sat watching my face. It was an untidy letter and the writing was scratchy and hard to read.

Dear Mr. Prentiss:

Thanks ever so for yours. Mr. Jackson and I are both well and hope you are the same. I must say, I think Selma's a lucky girl! All the nice things you've given her and all the times you take her out to posh places. Well, I must say I only wish I was in her shoes. Now don't you worry, Mr. Prentiss, I'm not worrying and if Mr. Jackson chooses to that's his lookout. Don't you be so sure you aren't in love, you two. Mr. Prentiss, you're young and as someone has said we're only young once. Live and let love, that's my motto. I'd like Selma to have all the romance that never came my way, so go your ways rejoicing and make the most of every fleeting moment. I say this from the heart, Mr. Prentiss. Selma's a good girl, none better but maybe nobody will ever come along who she could give her little heart to the way she could to a nice boy like you. So think over what I've said and don't spoil the ship for a ha'porth of tar.

Yours truly,
Polly M. Jackson

"What does she say?" Selma asked when I had read it.

"She says everything's all right," I told her, putting the letter quickly into its envelope and then into my pocket.

"Really and truly? So we can go on as we are and they won't mind?"

"Well," I said, "everything seems to be fine as far as your mother is concerned."

"That's all right, then," Selma said. "Whatever Daddy thought I don't think he'd say anything. He hardly ever does."

I longed to show the letter to someone but of course there would never be anyone I could show it to. Mrs. Jackson had certainly given me the green light, but so help me God, I thought, I was never going to take advantage of it or behave any differently to Selma because of it.

My father and mother were now deeply engrossed in preparing for the exhibition and at the same time in doing what they could to provide Clarisse with a suitable circle of friends. Never gregarious themselves, their interests did not lie in the social world, and for the first time in her life I think my mother really regretted this. She urged me to bring home some young men from the Sorbonne but I told her that the ones I'd become friendly with weren't likely to please Clarisse.

"Your father and I are very much to blame," she said, "but you know how it is. We've always been so completely absorbed in each other, the family and the collection. We must really make a great effort now and provide Clarisse with some gaiety."

It wasn't long after the furniture came that the apartment began to fill up with young men. Clarisse's beauty and her widowhood were both powerful attractions and soon she was once more practicing the art of shaking off those she was not interested in without giving offense. She said she liked my mother's parties, at home, far better than the ones she went to outside, which were too stiff and formal. I hardly ever came back to the apartment nowadays without finding somebody there, and usually quite a gathering. Then one day my father told me that he had taken four tickets for a charity ball and that he thought I ought to come.

"Clarisse doesn't want to dance with me," I said. "Why not ask one of her young men?"

But he said he thought it would look better if I came. After all, he explained, she had been so very recently widowed.

The ball was held at the Opera House, in January, and it was quite an affair. I remember that the tickets cost the equivalent of thirty dollars each, or about two thousand five hundred francs as the rate of exchange was then, but as it was in aid of tubercular children my father said he supposed it was in a good cause. It was an evening I shall always remember because it was the evening that Clarisse met Bastien de l'Orchat, and we are none of us likely to forget it.

We knew enough people there to make our little party not quite the family affair I was afraid it was going to be, and the way Clarisse was looking that night it was inevitable that others should be drawn in. With her pale gold hair, white skin and the dark eyes that made them both so striking, set off by the cloudy gray tulle dress that had come from Lanvin, she couldn't fail to attract a lot of attention. Even I could see that she was the loveliest girl there, or perhaps to do justice to the others, the most noticeably lovely, and my parents could scarcely look at anyone else. Neither, I noticed, could a tall, rather good-looking man with a white streak in his dark hair who kept hovering near quite obviously trying to find someone who could introduce him. He succeeded at last and he at once began to make himself agreeable to my parents as if that had been his prime object all along. He took plenty of time about asking Clarisse for a dance, letting her go away to dance with two or three other men first while he sat talking to my father and mother, so that she must have wondered if he was ever going to ask her. But when at last they did take the floor they made a fine-looking couple, and I was pretty sure that having contrived to arouse Clarisse's interest by his somewhat unusual behavior, he was off to a good start. I asked my father who he was as I hadn't caught his name.

"Oh, one of these innumerable counts," my father said, but I could see that he was enjoying everything, Clarisse's success most of all. "They seem to be thick on the ground tonight. The name sounded something like de l'Orchat."

"It is de l'Orchat," my mother said smiling, "and I thought he was perfectly charming, but then I'm always charmed by people who treat me as if I were twenty-five."

"You don't look a day more," my father said, gazing at her proudly, and it was true that my mother was looking wonderful. She was wearing a color that few women can wear, an orchid shade that suited her dark hair and eyes and her paleness.

"Come and dance with me," I said.

[183]

"Oh, Halley," she protested, "you know I'm no dancer. Your father and I never dance. You ought to be dancing with some nice girl."

But I made her dance and she did well, for she was always light on her feet, even though she had lately been putting on a little weight.

"Your father's so happy," she said to me. "He's happy to see Clarisse happy again, with all that misery far behind us, and he's happy to be living in Paris again and having us all under one roof. We used to miss you so when you went away to Groton and then to Harvard. Do you ever have regrets? I mean do you ever wish we hadn't cut ourselves off from America?"

"Not particularly," I answered. "Anyhow, there's no law to prevent us going back there any time we want to."

"No," she said, "that's true and I'm glad you said it. I've been so afraid you might feel we'd put pressure on you. We always want you children to do just what you want to do. I'm very proud of you, Halley, and you're so good-looking in your dress suit."

"I don't know why you should be proud of me," I said, "I haven't done anything yet."

"You will," she answered. "Even Julian seems more alert and more interested in things since we've been in Paris. I'm proud of you all, and I still think that your father is the most perfect of men. In fact at this moment I'm completely happy."

I pulled her up so short that a couple bumped into us hard.

"Don't say that, Mother," I said. "Please!"

"Why, Halley, what's the matter? I never dreamt you were superstitious."

"Well, I am, about making statements like that," I said, and we went on dancing. It was true that a shiver had gone down my spine.

"I've heard your father say he was perfectly happy a thousand times, and nothing dire has happened."

"You don't know," I said. "Maybe he brought on the Depression."

She looked up at me and laughed, and just then we nearly bumped into Clarisse and her partner. They didn't even see us; they were too busy looking at each other.

After that night the Count de l'Orchat was a regular visitor. He was nearly always there when I got back from the Sorbonne, or if he wasn't he was expected shortly. He knew how to make himself at home and it wasn't long before he seemed like a member of the family. I heard my father remark one day, half jokingly, that when other people were there he hardly knew which of them was the

[184]

host, he or de l'Orchat. His mother had been half Irish and he was bilingual, but she had died a good many years ago and he'd only once in his life crossed the Channel. That was to pay a visit to London, which he had heartily disliked. His father was still living and he had two unmarried older sisters, but they very rarely, he told us, left the family château, which was about fifteen miles from Orléans. He was advertising manager for a firm of silk manufacturers, not, he took the trouble to explain, because he was obliged to take a job but because he didn't care to be idle. Eight years earlier—he was now thirty-two—he had been a racing motorist, but after a bad smash which cut his head open and caused the white streak in his dark hair, he had given it up. Now he was learning to fly.

My mother thought it surprising that he had not married and she once hinted delicately, when she and I were alone, at the probable existence of a *chère amie*.

"Though I'm sure he hasn't time for anyone except Clarisse now," she said, "whoever there may have been in the past."

He was companionable, talkative, charmed with my parents—sometimes I wondered a little jealously if he knew for certain whom he was in love with, Clarisse or my mother—and extremely friendly to Julian and me, even, at times, assuming the role of elder brother. The way he tunneled his way into our family circle showed that he knew what he was about and that he understood the sort of family we were. What I very much wanted to find out was how much Clarisse liked him. I thought she had lately been more thoughtful for others than was usual with her, and I wondered if the events of the past had not at least taught her something. She had kept her promise and had taken over the housekeeping from my mother, but as Arnaud and Angèle had recently arrived from New York, a cause of much rejoicing, she did not find this task very exacting.

Clarisse and I usually breakfasted alone, for Julian was hard to rouse in the morning and my parents always breakfasted in their room. Clarisse was one of those rare people who are at their best when they are first out of bed: fresh, relaxed and unpreoccupied, happy to be starting a new day. It was the time when she always seemed most my sister and when she charmed me most; and when it was easiest for me not to remember Fred. It was pleasant, too, to breakfast in the sunny room with its walls of French gray and its curtains gaily striped in red. The furniture, which was Empire, had been bought by my parents in Paris before the war and shipped to

New York. Now it was back again after all those years in Sixty-sixth Street, looking none the worse for its travels.

I asked Clarisse one morning, encouraged by a good-morning kiss which was by no means habitual, if she liked seeing de l'Orchat there so often. I said it seemed to me he spent most of his time there.

"If I didn't he wouldn't," she said, smiling, and she picked up a letter from him that was lying beside her plate. I remembered that he had gone to the château for a few days.

"Is it serious?" I asked her. "You might just tell me if it is."

"You're longing to know, aren't you?" she answered, and I saw she was eager to open the letter. "All I can tell you is that I like him better than any man I ever met. Will that do?"

"It'll do for me," I said. "I don't know if it'll do for your friend Bastien."

"He's nice to have around and to go out with," she said, and she decided to open the letter without further delay, "and I like the way he's made himself one of the family." She read a little and then looked up. "He's going to give Julian a boxer, did you know? He's got a friend who breeds them. He says he's going to bring the dog here one day next week."

"What will Mother and Father say?"

"They don't mind, now that we're settled here, provided Julian will take full responsibility."

"That'll be something, if he does."

"I wish you'd call him Chico," she said.

"Why? He isn't going to be my dog."

"Don't be absurd, Halley," she said, but she laughed. "You know very well it's Bastien's nickname. Everyone calls him Chico. It seems unfriendly not to when he likes you so much."

"He's got a warm heart," I said. "Perhaps I'll get around to it in a year or so. Is that all you've got to tell me?"

"Absolutely all," she said. "What have you got to tell me?" And she looked at me with suspicious eyes.

"Not a thing," I said.

"I suppose you'll be spending the weekend in London all the same. I'd love to know what you do there. I don't believe you see as much of Flavia as you'd like us to think. I know about that young surgeon she's so fond of and I'm sure that would put you off."

"I just happen to like that town," I said. "I always did." And I wondered if a time would ever come when I could speak about Selma.

I hoped with all my heart that if Clarisse married Bastien she'd be happy and that she'd behave well, but I was afraid for her too because I didn't like him as much as she and my parents did. It never did any good to oppose her, it only stiffened her resistance and I decided I'd better keep out of it. In any case, he'd said nothing about his intentions yet, no doubt out of respect for Clarisse's recent widowhood. Such things, I knew, were very correctly timed in France. I wondered what he'd been told about her marriage, or if he'd been told anything at all. I thought that in all probability he hadn't.

My father was gratified by the enthusiasm shown by Chico—the rest of the family now called him this, so I had to follow suit—when he saw the pictures for the first time, and he took a great interest in the coming exhibition, which was timed for the first week in May.

"Chico says," my father told me one day, "that it's the best private collection of Impressionist paintings he's ever seen. He made a guess as to what it might be worth today."

"How would he know?" I asked.

"Chico? Oh, he knows a great deal about pictures, really a surprising amount. It seemed an incredible figure, though." And with a gratified look on his face he told me. I agreed that it was pretty high.

"All the same, he may very well be right," my father said. "If he is, and they've increased a hundred per cent in value, I won't have done so badly. He thinks I'd be wise to buy that Utrillo we saw, too. It's still there. It would be safer than buying Wall Street shares."

He bought it a few days later, and for once I don't think my mother altogether approved. She liked the picture but she said she wished my father had someone to tell him it was all right to go ahead. Syl's name wasn't mentioned—it was never mentioned now —but I could almost hear him telling my father to button up his pants' pockets, and I'm sure she could too.

I'd arranged to take Selma to the Savoy the next time I went to London, and knowing that she would be wearing an evening dress I went all the way to Battersea to pick her up. I didn't go in because she was waiting on the doorstep for me. She told me her mother was out and that her father was playing chess with his friend Mr. Boyson. She had her dark coat on and all I could see of what was underneath it was a glimpse of pink silk. Of all the colors in the world, bright pink is the one I cannot endure, and I feared the worst but I didn't say anything.

When we got to the Savoy she went straight to the cloakroom and I waited for her in the lobby where people sit drinking cocktails. Then I saw her come out. She looked like a dressed-up German doll off a Christmas tree. It was a terrible dress. The color itself was atrocious and it had bows here and there and bits of lace and I could feel myself growing cold towards her; cold and bored with the whole thing. Suddenly it all seemed flat and pointless and I wondered why I was there. Even her face had lost its charm for me. I wanted to say, "I don't feel well, I'd better take you home. We'll go out some other night," but irritated and put off though I was I couldn't quite do it like that. Her eyes had met mine with eager expectancy, but her perceptions were very quick and it didn't take her more than a fraction of a second to know what I was feeling.

"Is it awful?" she asked as she came up to mé, and I felt I was about to kill some small, trusting animal.

"I suppose Edna chose it for you," I said.

"No, my mother came with me. She thought it was pretty. Oh, Halley, I'm so sorry. I never bought an evening dress before."

She was distressed, biting her lips to keep back the tears. I knew I was behaving outrageously but my affection for her had been temporarily wiped out by that terrible dress.

"Come on," I said, turning towards the restaurant, though in no haste, "it can't be helped I suppose."

"No," she said, and she made no move to follow me. "I'm not coming. I'm not going to disgrace you. I want to go home, please."

"All right," I said indifferently. "Just as you like. I don't mind."

We looked at each other and all the pleasure we had felt in being together again was dead; it seemed to lie like an obscene bundle at our feet. I couldn't help what I felt; it was something beyond my control. She turned, went back to the cloakroom, put on her coat and came out again. She was looking in her purse.

"I've got enough money to pay for a taxi home," she said and she kept her eyes lowered to hide the tears. "You needn't come with me. I expect you'll want to go and cancel the table. Good night. I'm very sorry, and I expect this is good-by."

I was wishing she hadn't said she was sorry. I didn't want the hardness I felt towards her and was even enjoying, to go—at any rate, not yet.

"I'll take you home," I said.

"No," she protested. "Please, I'd rather go alone."

I knew that if I went to the restaurant she'd slip off without me so I told her to come with me while I spoke to the headwaiter. She hesitated and then followed me a few paces in the rear. She could keep her coat on, I argued with myself as we went, we needn't dance, but it was no good. The evening couldn't be saved now; I couldn't go through with it. I canceled the table.

We got into a taxi and I gave the driver the address. She sat as far away from me as she could, gathered tightly and miserably in her corner and I knew that she was quietly weeping. We drove in silence and I watched the streets and the lights and hated myself and all but hated her.

And then without rhyme or reason, unless it was caused by some faint sound she made, my hardness went. It happened in an instant and I knew there was only one way to comfort her and to make amends. I pulled her to me and took her in my arms and I rocked her as if she had been a child, without saying one word, and she broke down completely and sobbed aloud, and she said nothing either. It was a wonderful feeling, forgiving myself and being forgiven. It was good, too, that she didn't say anything apologetic or stupid or reproachful, but simply entered into the silence, and I knew that our closeness and forgiveness were enough for her.

I took out my handkerchief and put it into her hands, and I wanted to go on driving in the dark taxi forever with that hurt but now so happy child in my arms. After we'd crossed Albert Bridge and were on the other side of the river I put my face down against her round wet cheek, and then we kissed for the first time.

We didn't speak till we were nearly at her door. She freed herself and sat up with a long sigh.

"What shall I say to them?" she whispered.

It was certainly a problem and I had to think. I told the driver to wait, that I'd be going back with him, and we sat there in the half dark.

"I know," I said. I took out of my pocket a tiny knife that Syl had once given me and that I kept on my key ring. I made two cuts in the skirt of the pink dress and then ripped it down the front in two places.

"You caught your dress on something and it tore," I said. "That'll explain the tears and everything else."

"Cut it once more," she whispered. "I loved hearing it tear," and so I did cut it once more, to please her.

[189]

"If it's the worst white lie you'll ever have to tell," I said, taking her into my arms again, "you'll be a lucky girl."

The driver seemed content to wait, sitting there beyond the glass with his broad back to us, and we were content too. I was completely purged of all my irritation and distaste and she was purged of her anguish. We had taken a long step forward, and I dared not ask myself towards what end.

Chico brought the dog one evening and presented it to Julian. For Julian it was the end of a long period of frustration and longing. He was red with pride and embarrassment at being—next to the dog—the center of attention. It was a fine young boxer five months old, housebroken and over distemper and full of intelligence and play.

"He's just what I've always wanted," Julian said, stammering in his excitement and gratification. "Thank you, Chico. He's the best present I ever had in all my life. Can I name him whatever I like?"

"But surely," Chico said, pleased and amused. "Why not? He is yours."

"What would you like to call him, darling?" my mother asked.

Carefully not looking my way Julian said, "I'd thought of calling him Karl."

So he was called Karl and Julian took him out about five times a day, or kept him out for long periods. If the dog showed signs of restlessness in the early morning—he slept on the foot of Julian's bed—Julian would get up, put on trousers and a coat, and take him into the Champs Élysées. I think he was consciously and positively happy for the first time in his life. As first we could see that he suffered for fear the dog would show no more affection for him than for the rest of us, for he watched him with jealous eyes, but it wasn't long before he was unmistakably Julian's dog, and no one else was allowed to feed him. This was good and everyone was pleased.

Then about a month later when we were walking with Karl under the budding trees of the Bois, Julian said to me in the nervous, abrupt way in which he usually started to say something confidential, "I've made a lot of acquaintances since I've had Karl. Everybody admires him."

"What sort of acquaintances?" I asked.

"Oh," he said, "various sorts."

"Charming ladies?"

"Well, no," he answered. "Oh, one or two girls have spoken to me but I don't pay any attention."

"Who then?" I was sure he had something to tell me.

He hesitated, tossed back his hair which he would never have cut often enough and said, "Well anyway, I've got a friend of my own now. He's about fifty and I like him better than anyone I ever met. He talks to me as if I were somebody who mattered."

"That's interesting," I said. "Where did you meet him?" For some reason I hardly understood myself, my heart missed a beat or two, and then I realized that I was afraid of what his diffidence, his feeling of inferiority and ineffectualness might lead him into, and I suppose I had always been afraid. He named a well-known café.

"It was just luck," he said, "my meeting him like that. It's the best thing that's happened to me, next to being given Karl."

"What is he? What does he do?" I asked.

"Well, for one thing he's one of the editors of *Après Demain*."

"I never heard of it," I said.

"Neither did I until I met him, but now I buy it every week." Then he altered this to, "At least I've bought it twice. I've only known him a little over two weeks."

"What sort of a paper is it?" I asked.

"Well," he said, "it has what people like Father would think very advanced views."

This wasn't what I'd feared, and I felt relieved because it was better than I'd feared.

"It's Communist, is it?" I asked.

"I suppose so," he agreed.

"You mean you know so," I said. "How often have you seen this man?"

"Six times," he said. "The first time he came over to where I was sitting to admire Karl."

"And you told him what his name was."

"Yes," he said, "and who I'd named him after, too."

"So after that," I suggested, "things went along pretty fast. Did you tell him what you'd been doing in London?"

"Yes," he said, "of course I did. He said that if I really wanted to be of some use in the world there were better ways."

"Did he suggest some?" I asked him.

Julian was casting his mind back. He never found it easy to recall conversations, but I could see that he was trying hard to recall this one.

"He asked me if I knew what the Maginot Line was," he said.

"What did he take you for? A moron or a two-year-old?"

"He had a reason for asking. When I said, 'Of course, everyone knows about the Maginot Line,' he said, 'What everyone doesn't know is that it's just a vast booby trap designed to destroy millions of young Frenchmen.' He asked if I wanted to see the bodies of my friends rotting on the barbed wire again. I told him I was too young to remember the war but I knew it was horrible, and then he said that if the capitalists had their way there'd be another one within the next ten years, perhaps quite soon."

"Workers of the world unite," I said. "Nothing to lose but your chains and all the rest of it, I suppose."

He ignored this. "Actually," he said, "the thing that made him come over and speak to me wasn't entirely because of Karl. He mistook me for Louis Seguy."

"Well, that was odd," I remarked. "I saw a picture of him in the *Monde Illustré* just the other day and he has a small dark mustache."

"He thought I might have shaved it off."

"I suppose he didn't even notice that you had fair hair," I said.

I could see that he had been greatly flattered by being mistaken for a well-known and very *avant-garde* young writer.

"So," I said, "one thing led to another. What does he want you to do?"

"Well, naturally," he answered, "he thinks I ought to join the Party."

"Naturally," I repeated. "Does he imagine you're rich?"

"We never even talk about money," he said indignantly. "I think he's just taken a liking to me, strange though that may seem to you."

"I think it's very far from strange," I said. "Do you want to join the Party?"

I had a feeling that he would never go all the way in anything, but it was possible that I might be wrong.

"I don't know," he answered. "I have to find out first just what I'd have to do if I did join."

"I can tell you one thing you'd have to do," I said. "You'd have to leave home and go your own way."

He stared at me.

"I don't see why," he said.

"I'll tell you why," I answered. "You aren't going to live at home and accept everything from Father and Mother and at the same time give your whole allegiance to something they'd loathe." (As I said this I was feeling righteously indignant, and I don't believe that any thought of Selma and myself entered my mind, so entirely did I separate Selma in my thoughts from my family and my life in Paris.) "You just can't do this, Julian," I said, my wrath increasing, "and what's more, you'd better be careful, my boy. You may get yourself involved in things you wouldn't like getting involved in."

"I don't see why," he said again, and he seemed surprised at my anger. "I like him and I trust him. We call each other by our first names."

What a child he is, I thought, and my anger cooled.

"What's his name?" I asked.

"His friends call him Peter."

"Why Peter? Why not Pierre? Isn't he French?"

"I suppose so. I don't know why he's called Peter. He just is."

"But Peter what?"

"Just Peter. His other name doesn't matter."

I could see that if Julian knew what his other name was he wasn't going to tell me, and anyway, it didn't matter. I asked him when he was going to see his friend again.

"Tomorrow," he said, "at the same time and place. We usually meet about half past five."

"Who pays for the drinks?" I asked.

"He does," he said. "He'll never let me pay. He has a Pernod or two and I just have a vermouth."

"Shall I walk by tomorrow and have a look at him?" I suggested, for I guessed that he was anxious for me to participate to that extent at least, and he agreed at once. "All right," I said. "If you see me just ignore me."

I think he liked the slightly conspiratorial sound of this, and I guessed too that he was a little nervous about the whole thing and didn't want to be obliged to make his own decisions. He didn't want to feel quite unprotected, and I was glad. So the next day I went along and there they were, sitting outside in the late afternoon sun. I decided there could be no harm in my sitting down too, so I chose a table well out of earshot and ordered a beer.

Julian's new friend wasn't at all a bad-looking chap. There were plenty of worse types to be seen and there were a few better ones. He was the sedentary type, running to fat and heavy-jowled, but he had a look of authority and dignity, and when he took off his soft hat I saw that he had a big head and sandy-colored hair. His eyes were light blue and he looked to me more like a German than a Frenchman except that his head wasn't flattened at the back as so many German heads are. He and Julian were deep in talk and Julian seemed to have more to say to him than he usually did to most people. I wondered if I ought to tell my father, but the idea was repugnant to me. I wanted to deal with this myself if I could, otherwise Julian would never give me his confidence again as long as he lived. He looked over his shoulder now and again at the people walking by, but he hadn't seen me, as I was sitting directly behind him.

I'd been there about ten minutes when a couple came and joined them, drawing up chairs and sitting down at their table. Merely by looking at Julian's back I could see his discomfiture. He didn't like the look of the two newcomers and I couldn't blame him. The woman had very short hair cut like a man's, and was smoking a cigarette in the longest holder I ever saw. She was wearing a rough sort of tweed suit with the skirt to the knees, and around her neck she had on a black stock such as men used to wear in the early 1800's. The man had a black beard and a long, pendulous nose and wore a red carnation in his buttonhole. The woman talked entirely to Julian, who kept tossing back his hair nervously, and he finally bent down to stroke Karl, who was lying beside his chair. The woman bent down and stroked him too, so that their heads were very near together and Julian quickly sat upright again, pushing back his chair a little to put more space between them. The little episode amused and rather pleased me. When I'd paid for my beer I got up and went past their table so that Julian couldn't help seeing me, and started to walk home. I went very slowly, stopping to look in shop windows, and before long he overtook me, as I'd hoped he would.

"I don't know who those other people were," he said crossly. "I wish they hadn't come."

"You'll meet plenty like them when you join the Party," I said, "and anyway you shouldn't be put off by appearances. They may be charming when you know them."

"You needn't be sarcastic," he said. "I thought that woman was awful and she kept blowing her smoke right in my face. It wasn't Peter's fault. I don't think he was even expecting them."

Suddenly I felt I'd had more than enough of the whole business and now was the moment to let him know it.

"Look, Julian," I said, "this has just got to stop. You're not going to spend your time sitting around in cafés getting picked up by anyone who chooses to pick you up. You can stop being so damned idle and useless. You must be sick of it yourself. You're going to start taking a course in typing and shorthand as a beginning and you're going to start now. It'll come in useful someday and it's high time you had something to do. Either you agree to do this or I tell Father the whole thing. And I mean just what I say."

We'd often discussed this project before but he had always made objections. He wasn't feeling well enough, or it was just no good his trying to apply his mind to anything. Now he had another excuse ready.

"I can't, now that I've got Karl," he protested. "I can't leave him alone all day. I promised I'd look after him myself."

"You'd better do what I say," I told him, "otherwise I'll go straight to Father and Mother and tell them the whole story beginning with Henry and Vera. You can take your choice."

Just then Karl brought us to a halt by a tree, and Julian said miserably, "Because I'm not as well and strong as the rest of you, you all think you can bully me. Supposing I did go and take this course, would they let me bring Karl?"

"Start the course first," I said, "and then see."

He knew I meant business and he couldn't face my father's certain anger. He could visualize, too, as well as I could, my mother's shocked and startled incredulity.

"Well, all right," he said. "I suppose I'll have to try it, but it won't work. I won't be able to keep it up. I'll only get ill."

"I'll have a bet with you about that," I said, but he was too dispirited to take me up.

My father was delighted when he heard what Julian was proposing to do. He went with him to the secretarial college and paid for the first six months' tuition in advance. After three weeks of daily attendance, during which time the rest of us took turns at exercising Karl—dogs not being admitted—Julian had a bad attack of asthma in the middle of the night, the first in a year and a half. My mother was terrified and a doctor was hurriedly sent for. The strange thing was that there was absolutely no fake about it; it was one of the worst attacks he had ever had. A few days later eczema broke out on the backs of his hands and then on his face, especially the eyelids, and it didn't disappear for some weeks. He never went back to the secretarial college and I don't think the money my father paid was ever refunded.

I once asked a psychoanalyst I met crossing the Atlantic how people in his profession accounted for asthma, with its unpredictable tricks. He said that more often than not it was caused by unhappy relations with one parent, or possibly both, and I used to wonder if there was any truth in this. Certainly Julian in his undemonstrative way adored my mother and never wanted to be away from her for long, but it was equally certain that there was a repressed enmity towards my father dating from many years back.

Anyway, the attack of asthma plus the eczema worried my parents a great deal, so much so that they even discussed it with Chico. Chico's solution to the problem was for my father to give Julian a car. It would do him good, he said, to learn to drive it. My father thought this over and then bought a small Renault, and Chico— who held that no member of a family should ever teach another member of it to drive a car—taught Julian how to drive it. Quite soon, Julian was driving out into the Bois by himself with Karl sitting beside him, and when he was more sure of himself and we were more sure of him, he frequently acted as family chauffeur. He certainly seemed happier and it gave him a feeling of importance. The car was regarded as his and before making use of it or of his services as driver, his consent always had to be obtained. He knew nothing at all about mechanical things and couldn't even jack up the car to change a tire, but my father had it well serviced so that he was unlikely to get into any trouble.

I knew that my father had hoped to do without a car in Paris, preferring to hire one when necessary. There seemed no limit to the amount of money he felt himself obliged to spend and I sometimes wondered how long it could go on, and if I shouldn't try to get myself a job, now that I was nearly twenty-two, but he would never hear of this. I hadn't finished my education and there was nothing to worry about. The Depression wasn't over yet, but it soon would be and then everything would be all right.

XIII

When, some two weeks later, I was getting ready for another trip to London, my father came into my bedroom and sat down.

"I wish I could go with you, Halley," he said, "but your mother doesn't like leaving Clarry and I don't like leaving your mother." He took a gold pencil out of his pocket and began playing with it. "Do you ever go to the Tate Gallery?" he asked.

I said I did now and again. (In fact I had taken Selma there one Saturday afternoon quite recently.)

"I'd like to look at some things there I'm fond of," he said. "That Manet portrait of the lawyer, M. de Jouy. I remember telling you once that it was one of the very great portraits and I haven't changed my opinion. It's curious how some pictures take hold of you and become part of your life." And then he said what he had come in to say: "Try not to spend too much money, Halley. I don't know why it is but I find it very hard not to live like a millionaire, and I'm not a millionaire, though I suppose I was one before the Depression. I don't want to cut down your allowance, but I'm giving you more than I really ought to give you."

"All right, Father," I said. "You spoke just in time. I was going to ask you if I might have a little extra this week."

"You mean you've seen something you want to buy?" he asked.

"I expect I shall see something," I answered, "but it doesn't matter." (I wondered what he would have said if I'd told him I wanted to buy a dress for a girl.) "And I'll try to make my allowance last longer after this."

"I wish I could let you have more," he said regretfully. "I hate not to give you children everything you want."

I was afraid he might ask me to give up my trips to London but he didn't. He presently said, "It seems queer for England to be off the Gold Standard; I can't seem to get used to the idea. Well, I suppose nothing is what it was, and I haven't much faith in the U.S.A. any more either. I wonder how that man Roosevelt is going to turn out? He doesn't seem to have done anything much in the past."

"I expect he's all right," I said. "Anyway, he seems to have a lot of confidence in himself."

"We can only wait and see, I suppose." He got up and went over to my table where some books were lying. "You seem to like Proust very much," he said. "Isn't he a very unwholesome sort of writer?"

"I don't know," I answered. "He's fun to read."

"Your mother and I have gone back to Victor Hugo," he told me. "He gives you a sense of timelessness. Halley, do you realize that I shall be fifty next birthday?"

"Yes," I said. "Do you mind?"

"Terribly," he said. "Terribly. It's a terrible thing to know that the inevitable decline is about to set in. The only answer to it that I can see is to live every day to the full. That's why I can't bear to be separated from your mother, or see you children go away. When will you get back, Halley?"

"I'm coming back on the night ferry, Sunday night," I told him.

"Well, take care of yourself, my boy," he said, and he patted my shoulder. "You know how infinitely precious you are to us." And he left me to finish my packing.

I had asked Selma to meet me at Victoria Station. Her boss, Mr. Vining, was going to the races that Friday and she'd asked for the afternoon off. She was there, waiting as close to the gates as she could get, and when she saw me she threw me one of her joyful looks. I didn't kiss her, but she put her face against the sleeve of my overcoat for a second and said,

"I believe I can smell Paris."

"I'll take you there one day," I said. "I promise I will."

She only smiled at me as if I'd promised to take her to the moon and asked where we were going now. I told her I wanted to do a couple of errands and afterwards I was going to take her shopping. We went first to a small art gallery just off Baker Street kept by a man named Oakenshaw whom I'd known for some years. I left Selma in the taxi and I showed Mr. Oakenshaw three drawings I'd brought with me and hoped he'd buy. They were the Picasso and the Raoul Dufy I'd picked up so cheaply in Nice and had nearly quarreled with Rosie about, and a sketch by Forain. He gave me a check for thirty pounds—it was the Picasso he wanted most—and I thought I hadn't done badly. We went to Barclay's Bank, where I cashed the check and afterwards I took Selma to a shop where my mother had sometimes bought dresses for Clarisse.

It was almost as much fun as buying a picture and in a way I was buying one. And buying a picture never gave me the godlike feeling that this did. Selma came out of the cubicle four times before I saw her in a dress I really liked. It was black lace and I thought she looked like a painting by Goya in it. It brought out all her odd and unusual charm. For the hundredth time I wondered where she'd got her looks from, and I rejoiced that she wasn't merely pretty, for it was a face I knew I would never find banal or grow too accustomed to. I think I realized then that I must be in love with her, for this wasn't merely making amends; it gave me a new and acute pleasure. She had no hesitation whatever about accepting the dress; she only wanted what would please me, but she was a little troubled because she thought the price too high.

"I was bursting with pride," she said as we went out with the dress, which needed no alteration, in a box. "It was lovely seeing you sitting there wanting me to look as you wanted me to look. I felt as if I belonged to you."

"Maybe you do," I said. "Maybe you do," and she smiled at me joyfully.

That night she wore the dress. We went first of all to a Beethoven concert at Queen's Hall. It was the first concert I remember listening to with ears and mind, and I knew I'd reached a point in my enjoyment of music when I would quite willingly have gone to a concert by myself, though I liked better to go with Selma. Afterwards we went to the Savoy and had supper and danced, and by now the episode of the pink dress had had all the sting taken out of it and had become one of those things that lovers like to remember and to laugh about. It was a happy evening and I made up my mind not to worry about the future. It wasn't till we were nearly ready to go, and Selma had opened her bag to be sure she had a shilling for the cloakroom attendant, that she saw what she had meant to give me earlier: a letter from her mother. She was full of self-reproach.

"How could I have forgotten? She wrote it in my room while I was dressing. I don't know what's in it. I expect it's just to thank you for the dress."

"I'll read it later on," I said, but she wanted me to read it right away.

"You needn't tell me what's in it if you don't want to," she said, "it's just that you might want to send her a message."

The writing was hurried and not easy to read.

Dear Mr. Prentiss:

Never have I seen such a beautiful dress. Selma looks lovely in it, quite the society girl, but it's a pity all the same that she tore that nice pink one, it was such a lovely color. She's a lucky girl to have a friend like you and it's nice to see her so happy. Mr. Prentiss, I know you've got better things to do of a Sunday, but just this once couldn't you come to see us at three o'clock? Selma will be out practicing and there's something I want to say to you that I don't want to say in front of her. Do come, it will be a pleasure to see you and there'll be a nice cup of tea for you when you want it.

Yours truly,
Polly M. Jackson

"Well," I said, putting the letter into my pocket, "she certainly liked the dress. Tell her I'm glad."

"Even Daddy thought I looked nice in it," Selma said, "and it isn't often he pays me a compliment. He keeps asking me when we're going to be engaged." And she gave me a shy, apologetic little smile.

"What do you say?" I asked.

"Oh, what can I say, except that I'm twenty-three and able to look after myself and that everything's all right? I do wish he wouldn't worry."

"Fathers will be fathers," I said, but I wasn't as confident as I sounded. I wondered if Mrs. Jackson had written that letter because Mr. Jackson had asked her to on the ground that it was time they had a frank talk with me. But whatever the reason for it and however it turned out I knew I had to go there on Sunday, and I wasn't looking forward to it. I didn't think they were going to "put the screws on," as Flavia had suggested they might, because I couldn't see what screws they could very well put on. It was unlikely that they would try to stop our seeing each other, but all the same some sort of plea, I was sure, was going to be made. If things had been different I knew I would have wanted to marry Selma, but as things were I didn't see how I possibly could. She was my private treasure, my own discovery, my charming, accommodating, chosen companion, but I did not see how I could make her anything more. I had only to consider the problem presented by my situation as a young man totally dependent on his father, plus the problem of bringing

Selma's parents and mine together (and could I myself contemplate a father-in-law who smoked like that?), for the whole thing to turn nightmarish. It was unthinkable; it just couldn't happen. But equally unthinkable was the idea of giving up Selma, who was now, I felt, partially my own creation, and these two unthinkables, so closely linked together, did not make for peace of mind. All the same, I was not unhappy. I must have inherited from my father his capacity for drifting with the stream and making the most of present joys, and first love brings with it its own solaces and reassurances. I was easily able to persuade myself that if we were only allowed to go on as we were, without outside interference of any sort, everything, sooner or later, would be all right. Selma was wholly and undemandingly happy, and that happiness of hers seemed to me to justify everything. I only wanted to keep her happy as long as I possibly could.

The blank feeling of everything having come to a Sunday stop, of post-Sunday-dinner inertness and heaviness, seemed to lie in wait for me and to fall upon me with sluggish strength as I went to the door of 47 Windelsham Street, Battersea, at three o'clock. Lucky Selma, I thought, happily working away at her practicing elsewhere. She was never at a loss on Sundays whether I was there or not. She devoted the morning to church and the afternoon to the piano, usually stopping for a chat with Edna on the way home. In the evening, she told me, she washed her hair or mended her clothes in preparation for a busy week. She was like a bird in a perpetual springtime, and there was never an idle moment. Now her absence seemed to make the ugly little house desolate, and I had an impression, not for the first time, that when she was not there, Mr. and Mrs. Jackson had little to say to each other, and that there were long and arid silences.

The sitting room faced north and there was a chill even on that mild and sunny April afternoon. Whenever I had been there before the table had always been lavishly spread, but today it was covered only with a red woolen cloth. Mr. Jackson always sat in an armchair facing the window—I say "always," but counting back I remembered that I had been there just four times—and he was sitting there now, his ashtray, mounted on three legs, beside him. Mrs. Jackson opened the door to me and she was looking very festive. She had on a red satin blouse, a string of pearls the size of pigeons' eggs around her neck and some fancy combs in her hair, but it was right for her and I liked her and was glad to see her, in spite of my apprehensions.

I had liked her from the first and her warmth and romanticism and zest for life partially explained Selma, whereas Mr. Jackson, so far as I could see, offered no explanation for her at all. He didn't get up from his chair—there was no reason why he should have done—but he offered me a limp hand and a brief and wintry smile. He wasn't glad to see me and at least he wasn't going to pretend he was, and I respected him for it. I was aware of no reason why he should have been glad to see me.

For a few minutes we talked about the weather and the spring flowers in Battersea Park—which Mr. Jackson asserted was the finest park in the world—and presently I had to watch him go tap-tap-tap with his cigarette, light it, wave the match about as if he were signaling for help from a sinking raft and then, settling himself well back in his chair, open his mouth wide and permit the first slow cloud of smoke to emerge. If I ever did marry Selma, I thought, I'd have to take her away, anywhere at all but away, so that I'd never again have to see Mr. Jackson smoking a cigarette. I wondered when I was going to be told why they had wanted to see me, but there seemed to be some reluctance on their part to begin and I was going to let them take their own time. Mrs. Jackson asked me some questions about Paris and Mr. Jackson said he wondered how anyone could go and live among foreigners when they could perfectly well stay in their own country. I said that we had lived in France so much that it didn't seem like a foreign country at all, but as soon as I had spoken the words they sounded foolish to my own ears and I wished I hadn't said them.

"Must be queer, all the same," he said, "to have to listen to that jabbering all the time."

"Well," Mrs. Jackson said, "all I can say is that if ever I got a chance to go to a foreign country, off I'd go and I wouldn't be in a hurry to come back, either."

"I dare say," he replied.

Then she rested her elbows on the table, glanced at Mr. Jackson and asked, as if the right moment had come at last for the afternoon's business, "Well, Oswald, shall I tell him now?"

"When you like," he said. "It was your idea to tell him, not mine."

"All right," she said, and she faced me squarely. "Now, Mr. Prentiss," she began, and I thought it was time I asked her to call me Halley as she didn't seem inclined to do so of her own accord, "I'm going to ask you first of all not to say a word to Selma about what I'm going to tell you until we've talked it all over. I'll make it as short as I can. Selma isn't our own daughter. I took her out of a home. Mr. Jackson and I had been married fourteen years and never a sign of a child of our own, so after a good deal of persuasion Mr. Jackson gave in and said I could take one but it had to be a girl, so take one I did. All anybody knows about her is that she was found on a seat in Liverpool Street Station just over twenty-three years ago fast asleep. I named her Selma Roberta after my sister who died when she was six. We were moving here just about that time from out Putney way where I'd always lived, and as nobody here knew us it was easy just to let people think she was our own. Only a few old friends know differently. Well, there it is and I hope you're not too upset. Maybe we ought to have told Selma as soon as she was old enough to understand but we thought it was better for her to think she had real parents like other children."

I wasn't upset; it was a common enough thing for people to adopt children, and I wondered why on earth I hadn't guessed it. What was more uncommon was for people who have been married for fourteen years to produce a first child, and it explained much; it explained why I had always marveled that Mr. Jackson, so thin and dry and cold, could possibly be Selma's father, and it at least helped to explain her oddly foreign looks. I felt an absurd regret that she hadn't been found in Victoria Station instead of Liverpool Street Station with which I had no associations, and I was sorry, liking Mrs. Jackson as I did, that she wasn't Selma's mother. But at the same time I thought I understood pretty well why she had wanted me to know.

I said, "Thank you very much, Mrs. Jackson, for telling me. I'm glad you felt that you could, and I appreciate it."

Mr. Jackson was now putting out his cigarette and it was obvious, as he turned towards me with a little cough, that he was about to say something.

"Mrs. Jackson's quite right about one thing," he announced. "I never wanted to take the child. If people don't have children they're not meant to have children, but she'd made up her mind and so take her we did. That's the way things go in this house. But all the same, Selma's been a good girl and she's paid her way since she was seventeen." He got up, buttoning his coat as he did so. "Now, if the palaver's over, I'll go out and take my walk. I'll just say this, in case you want my opinion. She's thought she was our child all along, and I'm in favor of letting her go on thinking so, but if Mrs. Jackson thinks differently, she thinks differently." He was at the door now, and he paused there for a moment without turning his head to look back, and said what I guessed he had been waiting to say: "And there's one thing more. I don't want to see her go the way her mother probably did."

With that, he made his exit, and a silence followed. I don't think I was actually blushing though I felt as if I was, and I didn't look at Mrs. Jackson till the front door had closed. Then she pushed back her chair and got up.

"Now, Mr. Prentiss," she said briskly, "what about a nice cup of tea? I'm ready for one if you are."

"Fine," I said. "I'd like one too," and I was grateful to her.

"The kettle's on," she told me. "I won't be long."

In a couple of minutes she was back with a tray and she put it on the table between us. We were both more at our ease now with Mr. Jackson out of the way. He seemed to freeze everything by his mere presence, but now the thaw had set in and I could see that Mrs. Jackson was beginning to feel relaxed and comfortable. I felt I could say anything I wanted to say to her and I hoped she felt the same about me.

"Mrs. Jackson," I said, "I wish you'd explain to me quite frankly why you've told me about Selma. I'm sure you had a good reason, and I'd like you to tell me what it was." And I added, "And I wish you'd call me Halley."

"I'd be pleased to, I'm sure," she said. "It's a nice name, and Selma told me you were named after some sort of a star. A falling star, was that it?"

"Yes," I said, feeling rather foolish, "a comet. It appeared when I was born."

"I've always liked a fanciful name myself," she said. "Well, you've asked me a question and I'm going to answer it. I had more than one reason for telling you about Selma, and you may as well prepare yourself for another surprise. I'm leaving here, Mr. Prentiss. I'm leaving Mr. Jackson for good."

I said, "That certainly is a surprise. Even more than the other."

"You see," she went on, "I've waited a long time, and now that Selma's got you and she's happy, I'm going away to keep house for another gentleman." A deep blush spread over her face and even down onto her neck. "I've known him for six years, and he thinks the world of me. He often stays with his daughter, Mrs. Telford, who's a good friend of mine, and when Mr. Jackson is playing his game of chess with Mr. Boyson, I slip away and go and see them. The fact is, and maybe you've noticed it and maybe you haven't, Mr. Jackson and I don't get on any too well, and what I feel is that I'd like a little happiness before I die. Do you blame me, Mr. Prentiss?" Her warm voice trembled a little and she took a handkerchief out of her sleeve, and put it to her eyes.

"I've no right to blame you," I said. "Your life and your happiness are your own, Mrs. Jackson. I'm only sorry for Selma."

"Well," she said, and she put her handkerchief away, "young people have to live their own lives sooner or later, but now you see why I had to tell you. Selma's going to miss me, Mr. Prentiss, especially at first. She isn't as fond of Mr. Jackson as she is of me, and anyway, as soon as I've gone his sister Maud will move in and keep house for him. She's always wanted me out of the way and she'll be ever so pleased. The trouble is that Selma can't bear her Aunt Maud, and she won't want to go on living here after she comes. She's a fault-finding old maid but she thinks Mr. Jackson's perfect, and they used to keep house together before I married him. Really and truly, I don't know why Mr. Jackson ever did marry, though of course I was considered very good-looking in those days. He's not the marrying sort and I should have known it, but there it is, we all make mistakes and I'm not the one to grumble and complain. This gentleman I'm telling you about is what you'd call a man of the world. You know, he likes a race meeting now and again and doesn't think it's a crime to have a little something on the Derby. He owns a bus company and he's got a car, and now that he's ready to retire he's bought a nice little house in Torquay and that's where I'm going to live, and I hope I can make him happy and comfortable. If you ask me, I've waited long enough."

I didn't know what to say. I only knew that I felt sorry for her and it was easy to understand how she felt. She had missed so much in her life, and now she was going to try to win something back, and I only hoped she'd succeed. She had waited until Selma's happiness seemed to her assured and I respected her for that and for being the warm-hearted, romantic woman she was. She had been starved for love, and if she were now, in her craving for it, shifting her responsibilities towards Selma onto me, I understood that too. What she didn't see and what I seemed unable to make her see was what a broken reed she was depending on; or if not a broken reed, one that was too young to bear any weight. She was determined to see in me the solution to all her anxieties concerning Selma, and nothing I could say would convince her that I was quite unfitted for the role of Selma's husband. To her I was a rich and independent young man and she felt certain that my affection for Selma was sufficiently strong for me to be willing and anxious to make her happiness my concern. The trouble was to know how to bring it about.

"Does Selma know anything of this?" I presently asked, for it was something I had to find out.

"No, but I'll tell her as soon as I get the chance," she said. "I want to do everything the right way, and I don't want her to feel unhappy about my going. So there's two things she'll have to know, Mr. Prentiss. One is that I'm leaving here, and the other is that Mr. Jackson isn't her real father, and she doesn't owe him very much if the truth were known, except that he did agree to my taking her in the end, and a hard time I had persuading him. Everything that's been spent on her I've spent, out of the money my father left to me. And that's how things are. I'm leaving here tomorrow week, while Mr. Jackson is out taking his walk. I'll leave a letter for him, telling him I won't be back, and he'll go straight off to Putney to see his sister Maud. He won't feel bad about my going, Mr. Prentiss, and it's no good pretending he will."

"I'm very much worried about Selma, though," I said. "You see, Mrs. Jackson, I'm in no position to marry her or anybody."

She looked at me with those warm blue eyes and smiled.

"Now, Mr. Prentiss," she said, "don't you worry. Selma's had a good training and she need never be without a job. She can go on working and she won't have to give me half what she earns any more. She'd be happy in one room somewhere if it was with you. Love will find out a way, Mr. Prentiss, that I'm sure of, and it was a very lucky thing you came along when you did. I don't think I could have waited another day."

"I remember telling you," I said, "that I wasn't going to marry till I was thirty."

"Yes, you did," she agreed, "and you wrote ever such a nice letter, too. But plan as we may, Mr. Prentiss, things have a way of turning out otherwise. We all know that."

I had to get away. I had to think. I got up and I felt as though instead of drinking tea I'd been drinking pure alcohol. My knees would hardly let me walk upright.

"Well, thanks for the confidence you've shown in me, Mrs. Jackson," I said. "And in case I don't see you again, I hope you'll be very happy. I promise I'll do the best I can for Selma, although at the moment I'm afraid I don't know what that will be."

"Selma trusts you and I trust you," she said as we went to the front door, "and that's good enough for me." And she gave me her hand.

I took it and held it for a moment. I felt moved and uncertain and unhappy and yet at the same time there was excitement and wonder in the thought that Selma belonged to no one but me. She seemed now to exist in a vacuum, and I could see all around her. She was a person without a single tie and it made her, in my eyes, still more of a person than she had been before. I wanted terribly to see her and I wished I didn't have to go back to Paris that night.

"Well, good-by," I said, "and thanks again."

"If you and Selma are ever near Torquay," she told me, "we'll be ever so glad to see you, Mr. Selby and I. The house is called 'The Willows.' Selma will have the address. Good-by and good luck."

The last thing I saw of her she was standing in the doorway of the ugly little house with its fancy trimmings of yellow brick and its "Gothic" windows, waving at me.

I walked all the way back to Chapel Street.

That night I had supper with Flavia in her flat, and the young surgeon was there too. His name was Alexander Moray, pronounced Murray. He had lively blue eyes, red hair and a sense of humor that I appreciated but wasn't in the right mood for that evening. I liked him though, I couldn't help liking him, and they told me they were going to get married in the autumn, so I congratulated them and Flavia opened a bottle of her father's champagne. If she had been alone I might have told her about the jam I was in, but I was glad afterwards that I hadn't. It was probably better that I shouldn't know, in case the family asked her any questions afterwards, but at the same time it would have helped me a lot to have talked it over with her. When I got up to go, she went to the door of the flat with me.

"You've got something on your mind, Halley," she said, looking at me with probing eyes.

"Yes," I said, "I have."

"Is it about that girl?"

"Yes," I answered, "but don't worry. It isn't what you probably imagine."

"Well," she said, "if it isn't, it probably will be, and I think you're a perfect little dolt. Unless, of course, you're thinking of marrying her. And if you do that, God help you."

"You're a wonderful comforter," I said. "So whatever I do will be wrong."

"I know a little about the Prentiss family," she told me. "Don't go and do anything silly, Halley, will you? You might be terribly unhappy."

"All right," I said, "I won't."

"But if you want any help," she said, "I'm always here, and you know I'm fond of you. I'm fond of you all, but I like you much the best."

I never knew a franker girl than Flavia, but for some reason her saying she liked me much the best hurt me and made me feel she intended some criticism of the others. If she hadn't said that I probably would have confided in her the next time I saw her. As it was, I decided to keep my own counsel.

I was in a jam, but it wasn't like that other jam I had got into in Cambridge in my Harvard days. There was no doubt in my mind at all that I was in love with Selma and would do the very best I could for her and I had no impulse to give up my trips to London and slip out of it all. I didn't worry my head, even, about who her parents might have been. Whoever they were, Selma was Selma and it didn't seem to make a lot of difference. Ever since I had known her I had teased her by giving her nicknames like "Little Russky" or "Little Polack," or even sometimes "Little Chink," according to my mood or the way she happened to be looking, for though she certainly didn't look Chinese she did sometimes look as if she might have some Tartar blood in her. Whatever blood she had, the result was highly pleasing and that was good enough for me. I didn't get to sleep on the train ferry for a long time, but what was worrying me most was the fact that I didn't see how I could conceivably tell the family about her. It was a hurdle that was too high for me. I could not imagine myself speaking the words that would acquaint them with the facts; of bringing myself to the point of confession. My mind balked at the whole thing. For the present, it seemed to me, I had no choice but to continue living my double life, and I presently began to think over what Mrs. Jackson had said. As long as I had to live a double life I might as well go the whole way and marry Selma. As Mrs. Jackson had said, she could go on working. She had lately had a raise and there was no reason, even if I did marry her, why she should give up her job—at any rate, until I could find some way to stay in London and find a job myself. I didn't trouble my head much about what sort of a job I might be able to get. I was sure I could always get taken on in some art gallery if everything else failed, for at least, I thought, I could sell pictures.

But the family—there lay my real problem. I knew very well that I was not yet weaned from them; I knew I was far from ready to break out of that charmed circle. The very thought brought with it a feeling of paralysis. I told myself that I could, in any case, do nothing yet. There was the exhibition coming on quite soon now, and I wanted very much to have a hand in it. I wanted to wait, too, till Clarisse had made up her mind whether or not she was going to marry Chico; and there were my responsibilities towards Julian. Moreover, I knew that, fond though I was of Selma, I was not yet ready to begin married life. My home was with my parents and my brother and sister, and a total breakaway was something I found I couldn't yet contemplate.

But I had to consider Selma too. What would she do? It was true that she was sturdy and self-reliant, but she loved me devotedly and now she had no one else to turn to; and I greatly liked myself in the role of her protector and benefactor. She had once said that if she had neither home nor parents she would probably share a room with Edna, and that I did not want her to do. She was still very friendly with Edna, and there was no reason why she should not have been. I had met Edna once and she was a nice girl, but I didn't want to share Selma with her. Selma was now too much a part of myself to be shared with anyone. No, Selma must find a room of her own, somewhere not too inaccessible; and then, following up this train of thought, it dawned on me—and it was very like a dawn, bringing with it its own reassuring light—that what I really wanted was to marry Selma and share the room with her whenever I could. Our present intimacy, our recently-found delight in kisses and embraces, could not go on forever. She was my girl and I wanted her wholly, and she had kept in step with me from the first. I saw now what I must do, as an interim measure, and having decided that it was the only possible course I turned over and went to sleep comforted, and the waves that the wind had beaten up in the Channel rocked me in my berth.

XIV

THE OPENING OF THE EXHIBITION AT THE BLOCH GALLERY WAS, I know, a red-letter day in my father's life. It had been a good deal written up in the papers in advance and it was arousing a lot of interest. A great many invitations to the private view had been sent out and when the day came there was no doubt that "all Paris" was there. The Minister of Fine Arts opened it and made a speech, and during it he made the announcement—by previous arrangement, of course, with my father—that the majority of paintings on view that day were being presented to the French nation. He thanked and extolled my father for the generous "and indeed princely" gift, and said he could only compare it to Caillebotte's magnificent gift to the Louvre. He said that for this wonderful gesture to be made by an American would surprise no one, for American generosity was proverbial, but it was especially significant and moving that it should have been made during the giver's lifetime and by one who, when a young man, had himself aspired to be a painter, and had lived, as a poor student, much the same sort of life as had been lived by the great men here represented. And so on and so on. He spoke for a good fifteen minutes and while he was speaking I saw my mother sway a little and put a hand over her heart. I moved nearer to her and took her arm and I could feel that she was trembling.

"All right?" I whispered, and she whispered back, "I'll be all right in a minute. Don't say anything to anyone."

I had never seen her like that before and it would have surprised me less to see my father turn faint. As it was, the usually fresh color had gone from his face and it was obvious that he was deeply moved and excited. It was natural that he should be. This was the summit of everything for him; his whole life had been leading up to just this, and when the Minister, at the end of his speech, went forward and shook his hand and then kissed him on both cheeks amid loud and enthusiastic applause, it was a big moment for all of us. Even

Julian, standing as far back in the crowd as he could get, used his handkerchief once or twice, and Clarisse, standing out in front with Chico beside her, looked on and listened with shining eyes. I thought I could guess what she was thinking; she was thinking how narrowly she had escaped being a suburban wife and living in Rye and how everything now seemed to be justified and for the best. I looked away from her and watched Chico's face instead, and I thought that from his expression he might have been presenting the collection himself. I was pretty sure Clarisse had made up her mind to marry him and their standing side by side on this important public occasion almost proclaimed it. Chico was now practically one of us. He had taken his time; he had carefully and in many ingenious ways made himself a part of the family and there was no doubt that he had showed shrewdness and foresight. My parents had repeatedly said of late how much they had grown to depend on him and my mother had even gone so far as to say that if Clarisse must marry it would be difficult to find anyone who seemed less like an "outsider." She would merely be adding one more to the family circle and would hardly be taking a step beyond it. Or at least, she had added, this would certainly have been the case if it hadn't been for the Duchesse de Marboeuf, Chico's aunt (his father's sister), and her husband.

Chico had often spoken of these two, saying that they had more or less brought him up, but it was typical of his astute and cautious way of conducting his affairs that he had not arranged a meeting between them and my parents until things were pretty far advanced and he was practically certain of Clarisse's feelings for him. I could see well enough why my mother and father now regarded them as a possible source of difficulties. The Duchesse was a very striking-looking woman of about sixty, tall, with fiercely aquiline features and an air of terrific authority which was heightened, if anything, by her frumpy and old-fashioned clothes. Her husband was still taller but as stout as she was thin. His large white beard was parted in the middle and he wore eyeglasses with a broad black ribbon. They were an imposing couple and they must have carried a great deal of weight socially, judging by the attention they received. Aristide Bloch, my father's old friend and the owner of the gallery, had received them as if they were visiting royalties. They were standing beside my father now and they had listened to the Minister's talk with what seemed to me a gratified air. If anything could have made them well disposed towards Chico's matrimonial hopes, this, I thought, would be it. I had only met them once but when, at a meaning look from Clarisse, I went up to speak to them later, and I stood in a queue to do it, they remembered me and were very gracious. But I couldn't help feeling that if ever two people knew what they wanted and exactly how much it was worth to them, they did.

The exhibition, as the Minister had pointed out in his talk, had been well timed and the art world had certainly moved a long way since the exhibitions of 1874 and '75 when some of the very pictures that were on the walls today had roused such hostility and derision. And as I followed the crowd through the gallery afterwards, I wondered, as I had so often wondered before, just why it had taken people so long to see in the work of these painters what anyone not suffering from prejudice or blindness now saw in them so easily. Perhaps never again, I thought, looking at a boating scene by Renoir with all the feeling it gave of life lived gaily and amicably on a day of soft sunlight and watery reflections, perhaps never again would there be paintings that were so unflawed by any sentimentality and were yet so *lovable*, for I could think of no better word for what I felt about them. I marveled, too, that my father could have brought himself to part with them, and as I made a pilgrimage from picture to picture I was remembering how they were bought and when, and the occasional tussles my father had had with Syl over the sums he had paid for them. I knew that the impulse to make this gesture and make it now must have been irresistible, and I knew that it was a sacrifice he had been proud to make. And perhaps it was not all sacrifice. He was sure now of a place in the art world of France; his name would be forever connected with the gift; and he was certain, too, of his little red rosette. This last, I knew, mattered to him greatly. Clarisse, whether she decided to marry Chico or not, was almost certain to marry in France, and it gave him a standing he had always coveted. A more cautious man would perhaps have held his hand and waited for better times before parting with an asset of such value, but all the same I felt I understood why he had wanted to make his gesture now.

Afterwards he told me that while the Minister was speaking he had taken a backward glance at that morning so many years ago when he had told my grandfather at the breakfast table what he meant to do. He said he could see his father as plainly as if it were yesterday, buttoned tightly into his business suit, as angry and dangerous as a wounded boar, telling him he could get out of that house in double-quick time, while his mother sat crying and trembling in her chair.

"What a lot depended," my father said, with a wondering shake of the head, "on that morning, and on the decision I took then. By golly! What a lot!"

Yes, what a lot I thought, but I asked myself what he would do now that his occupation was gone, for it was doubtful if he would ever buy another picture. Values were soaring, his resources dwindling, though he still believed in an eventual comeback, and while he said little of his losses to me, feeling it was something to be hidden, like a gross disfigurement, my mother had told me that he was worrying and not sleeping very well.

"Do you realize, Halley," she had said to me only a few days earlier, "that your father's income is now less than a quarter of what it used to be?"

"Is it really as bad as that?" I asked. "I haven't been following the stock market, I'm afraid."

"Perhaps you ought to," she said, "and perhaps you ought to talk things over with your father more. He says the value of his investments is only about half what it was when you and he were in New York last fall."

"That's pretty serious," I agreed, "but when I try to talk to him he just changes the subject. Well, by this fall I'll have done my two years at the Sorbonne and I'll look for a job."

"I wish you could get a diplomatic post, darling," she said. (She hated the word "job.") "I think you'd do so well as a diplomat."

I answered without thinking, "I'd need a university degree for that."

She threw me a quick look and cried, "Oh, I'd always hoped that your not going back to Harvard wasn't going to be a handicap to you!"

"It doesn't matter," I said, and actually it didn't matter now because whatever happened I knew that I was going to marry Selma and that I would take any job I could get. And I was wishing at that moment that I could have made a clean breast of everything, but as things were this did not seem to me even remotely possible.

At home that night, after the exhibition—and the presence of Chico hardly made it less a family gathering—my father once more went through the list of pictures to be included in the gift. When he came to Cézanne's *Nature Morte* that he had bought that summer five years ago, he hesitated.

"You know," he said, "I hate to part with that. I love it for itself, of course, but it reminds me of that happy summer by the Thames as well."

Then he caught Clarisse's eye and they looked at each other, and I knew that they were both remembering, as I was, the day the picture was shown to Fred and his saying he wouldn't give it house room, and then, at some gibe of Clarisse's, seizing her and winding her long hair about her neck.

"I think the collection needs it, don't you, Father?" Clarisse said. "You know there aren't many still lifes in it."

He included it of course without another word. He would have given the whole lot—with the exception of my mother's portrait—to please her. He was keeping the Berthe Morisot he and my mother had bought just before Syl's letter arrived warning him of the coming crash, and of course the Manet that Madame Druet had given him (she had died, my father had lately told me, in the influenza epidemic of 1918) and there were seven more, including a Sisley, and the Van Gogh he had bought that snowy afternoon on Fifth Avenue. All the rest would now go to the Luxembourg, perhaps to be hung, later on, at a new art gallery that was at present in the blue-print stage. He could see them as often as he liked, and there were still the ten that he would live with and see every day. I don't think he had any regrets and I am sure he believed he never would have any.

Chico was taking Clarisse to a night club later, where they were meeting some American friends of Clarisse's, but before they went Chico took me by the arm and drawing me to one side said he'd like a few words with me. We went out into the hall, which was large for an apartment and furnished like a living room, and sat down on a small sofa there. I thought I could guess pretty well what he was going to say.

"My good friend Halley," he began, lighting a cigarette, "and you are certainly well named for you appear and disappear like the comet, though luckily at shorter intervals, there is something I would like to ask you."

He then told me that he hoped to become my brother-in-law, which I already knew, and that my father had expressed his willingness to consider him as a son-in-law as soon as Clarisse was sure of her feelings for him. He asked me if I would welcome him into the family.

"Sometimes," he told me, smiling, "you look at me as if you were not quite sure about me; or do I imagine it? About Julian—well, I think he doesn't disapprove of me, though I would hardly put it higher than that, and he is grateful to me for Karl. But I would like you to tell me how *you* feel, because if Clarisse consents to marry me, and I have reason to think she will, I should like to feel that we were good friends."

"Well, why not?" I said. "I certainly hope so too."

"For my own part," he went on, "nothing could be easier. But this is a very united family, and frankly, in wooing Clarisse I find it necessary to woo each one of you, beginning with your parents, to whom, naturally, I am devoted. So, at least you don't dislike me?"

"Of course not," I said, feeling awkward and embarrassed, "and all that matters anyway is that Clarisse should be happy."

I wished he hadn't asked me these questions. I couldn't say straight out that I liked him and was glad he would be marrying into the family and I doubt if he would have believed me if I had. I looked at his cold, too handsome face and his sleek black hair with the white streak in it and I suddenly remembered a blackbird with a white feather in its wing that I'd picked up in Kensington Gardens years ago near the bridge over the Serpentine. I think it had flown into the windshield of a car and was momentarily stunned. I held it in my hands for a while and suddenly it gave me a ferocious peck and flew away. I hadn't thought of that bird for years, oddly enough.

I hoped we'd finished the conversation, but he next said, looking at his cigarette, "Clarisse had told me something about her marriage. My God, what an incredible story! What a barbarian that chap must have been!"

Even though he wasn't to blame, and I knew very well where the blame lay, I wanted to hit him. I sat perfectly still for a moment and I could almost imagine that Fred was standing at my elbow saying, "I can rely on you, can't I, Halley-boy, to put this right?" because if he could have materialized just then that's what he would probably have said. I took my time, and then I answered, "I'd rather not talk about it, if you don't mind. Fred was a pretty good friend of mine, and anyway the whole thing was a tragedy from start to finish."

"A tragedy, yes," he agreed quickly, "and I'm sorry I spoke of it. Well, we are to be good friends, then?" And he held out his hand.

"I certainly hope so," I said, and we shook hands on it, and I didn't like him any better.

Just before he and Clarisse left, my father said, "Don't be late,

Clarry. It's been quite a day, and you must be tired too. Bring her back well before one, won't you, Chico?"

"Yes," my mother said. "She's been going out such a lot, and we like her to get her beauty sleep."

"I too want her to get her beauty sleep," Chico said, smiling at her.

"We're meeting Phoebe there you know," Clarisse said, "and Ben Marshall."

"Well, please don't stay late," my father said again. "Phoebe would sit up all night if you let her."

When they had gone, Julian said in the overvehement way in which he always spoke of anything or anyone he disliked,

"I can't *stand* Phoebe Hurling! I just loathe *déracinés* Americans."

I didn't like her much either. She had spent most of her life in Paris and her father represented one of the big American oil companies. I thought her hard and rather malicious, but Clarisse had become quite friendly with her, or as friendly as she ever became with any girl, Rosie excepted.

"What about us?" I asked Julian. "Aren't we *déracinés* Americans?"

"We aren't like that," he said. "We don't try to be more French than the French. We're just cosmopolitans."

"Julian's quite right," my father said, and it wasn't often he agreed with any opinion of Julian's. "There's a great difference, as he points out. All the same, if we continue to live here as I hope we will, I might decide to become a French citizen."

"You'd better not," Julian said. "They say there's bound to be another war with Germany."

"Nonsense," my father said. "Who's 'they'? Who says so?"

"A lot of people," Julian answered, a little defiantly. "I keep my ears open. I often listen to what people are saying in cafés."

"I wish you wouldn't go to cafés quite so much, darling," my mother said. "It can't be a good thing to do."

"Where else can I go?" Julian demanded. "I don't belong to any club and I haven't got friends. I have to go somewhere."

"Didn't I hear Chico offering to put you up for the Travelers Club in a year or so?" my father asked him.

"'In a year or so,'" Julian repeated. "I may be dead by then."

I made up my mind to ask him, at the first opportunity, if he were still seeing "Peter," but in the events which so soon followed I forgot all about it.

Before going to London again I had a brief talk with my mother about her health, for her faintness at the opening of the exhibition worried me. She said she'd been to a doctor and he'd given her something for her heart. He said she had been overdoing things and must rest more.

"I'll be all right soon," she said. "Don't say anything to your father. It's the only thing I've every kept from him, but he'd worry so terribly."

It seemed that I was always promising some member of the family not to tell something to the others.

"I think you ought to tell him," I said, "and Clarisse too, and then she wouldn't drag you out to so many parties."

"I promise to tell him," she said, "if it gets any worse or if it doesn't clear up quite soon. I do get a little out of breath, but I really am resting now, every afternoon. Must you go to London so soon, darling? I wish you weren't so fond of London."

"I only go about every two weeks," I said, "and I'll be back first thing Monday morning, by the night ferry."

The truth was that I could hardly wait to see Selma now. I'd written her a letter, addressing it to the office where she worked, and I'd told her that I loved her very much and that I didn't care who her parents were, I was only grateful to them for what they'd produced. And I begged her not to make any plans or leave home until I'd seen her, for whatever plans were made I wanted to have a hand in. Sturdy little character though she was, she'd had two pretty severe shocks, both coming at once, and I was anxious that she shouldn't feel alone.

We met at a small restaurant in Soho. I was trying to spend as little as possible, and anyway, Selma preferred not to go to expensive places. She had a way of always looking first at the prices and then announcing that she wasn't hungry. I got there first and was at the table when she arrived. The happiness that showed in her face when she saw me made me think of a lamp suddenly put in a window at night, and I knew then that nothing could really hurt her if I went on loving her. For a moment we just sat holding each other's hands tightly under the table and I was so glad to see her that I knew I had made no mistake in telling her I loved her. This was, this must be, the real thing, even though its realness made it no less of a problem.

She presently told me that her aunt had arrived and that she and her father had now settled down quite happily together.

"He was furious with Mummie for a few days," she said, "then he got over it and said it was all for the best. Ever since Aunt Maud has been there they've done nothing but talk over the good old days before Daddy was married. Aunt Maud has my room now and I sleep on the sofa in the sitting room. I'd have left by now if you hadn't asked me not to, but I must find a room of my own somewhere, before very long."

I said we'd find one together and as soon as possible, and I asked her if she'd heard from Mrs. Jackson.

"Oh, yes," she said, more happily. "I've had two letters from her. She loves being in Torquay. She says Mr. Selby's so good to her she feels like a queen, and he gives her four times as much housekeeping money as Daddy gave her. They go out a lot in his car, and she's been to a race meeting. There's a garden, and a man comes in twice a week to keep it nice, and his wife helps in the house. She said the only worry she had was about me."

"She won't have that worry long," I told her.

She threw me a glad look, then she said, her face clouding over, "I see now that I was one of the reasons why things went wrong between her and Daddy. He never wanted me, and I think even Mummie sometimes regretted taking me because of all the trouble it made." She added, "Well, now they'll both be happier."

"And so will you, my darling," I said.

I couldn't suggest her taking a room in Chapel Street because Flavia often sent people there and she'd have been sure to find out. I wanted to keep Selma wholly to myself, so I knew we'd have to look elsewhere.

We got a list of furnished rooms early the next day and we decided on one in Ebury Street during the morning. It was very convenient for me, as it was so near Victoria Station, and I liked the landlady, Mrs. Reese-Crampton, who was a big, kindly blond of about fifty. She owned the house and she'd seen better days, but she didn't tell us so more than once. The room that was vacant was furnished as a bed-sitting-room and it had a double bed in it, so I knew it was the room for us. Mrs. Reese-Crampton was obviously a little worried about our relationship, and as I didn't want her to think anything uncomplimentary to Selma, I spoke the words which settled our joint future. I didn't know I was going to until they were said, and when I heard myself say them it was almost as though they were being spoken by someone else.

"I'll be living here too, Mrs. Reese-Crampton," I said, "at least part of the time. Miss Jackson and I are getting married very soon, but at present I can't leave Paris, except now and again, and she wants to go on with her job here. Later I hope to arrange things so that I can be here all the time."

She gave us a great big smile then and congratulated us, and I could see how relieved she was, but what really interested and delighted me was the way Selma took it. Her expression never even altered, it was just as if she hadn't heard me and I was greatly pleased with her. Whatever happened after that, I thought, I could rely on her to keep her head. We settled everything; Selma was to move in on Monday, and I paid a week's rent, in advance, just to clinch matters. We said good-by and went out of the house and down the shallow steps. I took Selma's hand and we walked along Ebury Street without speaking. Then I looked at her and saw that her eyes were brimming with happy tears, but her lips were trembling so that she couldn't speak.

"That's the way things are going to be, sweetheart," I said. "Anyway, for the time being. Can you bear it?"

Two or three tears flashed down her cheeks and then she said, and I knew it was true, "It can be forever if that's best for you, and if you go on loving me." And then she wiped her eyes and smiled. "Oh, Halley, I'll be so happy there! I'll never want anything better. Did you see the petunias in the window box? And the gas ring? Did you? I could cook things on it. And the bathroom was almost next door."

"As soon as we can," I told her, "we'll get a little flat with a bathroom of our own, even if it's just one room and a bath."

"Don't go too fast," she begged. "What we have now is so wonderful. I still can't take in what you said. Is it really true that we're going to be married? Could you please say it again?"

I did say it again and that was all she asked me to do. She didn't even ask if I meant to tell my family. She was happy to leave everything to me. She trusted me so completely that it almost frightened me, or it would have frightened me if I hadn't been so sure I was never going to let her down.

"It's going to be you and me always, little Chink," I said.

She was used to my calling her that, or "Little Russky" or something of the sort; she hadn't minded before, in fact she'd liked my teasing her, but now she looked at me a little anxiously.

"Oh, Halley!" she said. "Do you think it could be that?"

"No," I said, and I laughed. "No, of course I don't, but let me tell you once and for all that I don't care what it is that makes you look the way you do, because whatever it is I love it and I always will."

That made it all right, and afterwards she didn't care what I called her. Because of me, and because I had picked her out in that queue at Queen's Hall, she could accept the whole thing and even find a sort of happiness in it. And once we made a sentimental pilgrimage to Liverpool Street Station, that grim terminus, and selected the bench we liked to think was the one she had been found on. That helped too. I don't know how it would have been with her if I hadn't been there to love her, but as things were, it was all right. Otherwise, I felt, it might have been like taking a parachute jump for the first time, but knowing Selma I think she would have taken it bravely and landed on her feet. She was that sort of a person.

It was always hard for me to understand, looking back, where I had got the courage, or the reckless foolhardiness, to do what I did, and it's hard, even now, to provide an explanation, most of all for the shameful way I deceived and lied to my father and mother. I *had* to do what I did, or so I believed and wanted to believe, and I loved them too much to shatter their confidence in me, and their trusting love, by telling them about it. My burden of guilt was now too great to be got rid of by confession. I had put myself so much in the wrong that I was totally unable to right matters. I was acting like a bigamist who is obliged to divide his life into two halves and forever keep them separate, and although I foresaw the dangers and difficulties of it I accepted them because this private happiness that I had found was necessary to me.

Just seventeen days after taking the room in Ebury Street, Selma and I were married by special license at Caxton Hall, with Mrs. Reese-Crampton, who assumed that my parents were in America, and Edna, who had promised to tell no one, as witnesses. We didn't want people to know, I said, until I could arrange things so that I could be in London all the time. Selma wasn't even telling her boss, Mr. Vining, for he had frequently expressed the view that to keep a secretary who was married was like buying a typewriter with half the keys missing. She was determined to prove, first, that she was as good a secretary married as unmarried.

I sold some more drawings, got a drive-yourself car and took Selma to an inn at Midhurst, in Sussex, for a week, from Monday to Monday. It was the first half of her two weeks' holiday, and we hoped to spend the other half together in October. The country was looking beautiful as we drove down, with everything still fresh and vividly green, and they were just beginning to cut the hay. I was remembering the vow I had made at Clarisse's wedding: that if I ever married it would be like this. I was so happy that I managed to put all thought of the future out of my mind. Somehow or other, everything was going to be all right; I was going to contrive to be a good husband, and a good son and brother too, and I had made Selma so happy that it was a delight just to watch her face. If she had any doubts at all about what we had done she certainly never expressed them. She simply made me feel that whatever I chose to do must be right, and she seemed to have found a satisfactory explanation for everything in her own mind. If I didn't want my family to know, that was my affair, and I had my own good reasons. If she wanted anything to be different, she gave me no hint of it.

As for me, it was like the pleasure I had felt when I gave her little presents, but enormously magnified. I suppose that all my life I had taken and never given, and no one had ever told me what an agreeable thing giving could be. I had had to find it out for myself. The engagement ring I had bought for her—a very small sapphire surrounded by little rose diamonds and costing twenty pounds—might have been the Koh-i-noor. She kept looking at it and putting it to her lips, and when I said I'd give her a fine, square-cut sapphire one day she looked at me as if I'd said something derogatory about our first-born.

I told her, as we drove down, about Clarisse and her engagement, and about the rest of the family spending the next few days at the de l'Orchats' château, making the acquaintance of Chico's father and sisters. I might have been telling her about gods and goddesses out of mythology, and I doubt if they were much more real to her, except, I think, that my mother seemed real to her because she was my mother. She knew of course that Clarisse was a widow, and I had even told her about Fred although it was a thing I always found it difficult to talk about.

The inn at Midhurst was peaceful and comfortable and just what I hoped it would be. When I wrote in the book, Mr. and Mrs. H. S. Prentiss (there could be other H. S. Prentisses, but there wasn't likely to be another Halley Prentiss) and gave the address in Ebury Street, Selma was standing beside me watching and looking as she might have looked if she'd been seeing magic writing appear on a wall. Nobody who had seen us could have mistaken us for anything but what we were, a very newly married pair very much in love.

It was hard for us to believe in our own good fortune, in this bliss we had snatched out of its most unlikely context and which had now reached what seemed to us a flawless fulfillment. The secrecy and anonymity with which we were surrounded heightened it. Nothing had been planned by anyone but ourselves; we were the sole authors and begetters of the event, and we would have, forever after, only ourselves to praise or blame. It was strange and wonderful to feel so alone, so cut off from everything that was not ourselves.

I had been thinking of Selma as partly my own creation, but she surpassed all that I knew of her so far, and I came to the conclusion whenever I thought back to Mr. Jackson that in her case heredity had certainly triumphed over environment. From whatever country or countries her forebears had come—and that was something I would never know—I felt certain they were old countries because it seemed to me that her knowledge of everything pertaining to love was a surer and older knowledge than mine even though no man had ever been her lover. She knew very little of the world but she had wisdom and combined with this was a charming innocence peculiar to herself. Together they gave me a happiness I hadn't dreamed of.

I stroked her cheek as we lay on the bed in the light of a warm morning and said, "You realize you were born to be my wife, don't you?" and she smiled up at me in joyful assent, too happy to speak, and held me closer.

She was so utterly content there in our big, low-ceilinged bedroom that she was reluctant to go outside it. The mere fact that here in our private universe clothes were not needed charmed her, and she took a simple pride in her firm young body. Once I saw her sitting in front of the glass like a small wise goddess meeting her reflection for the first time.

"How strange it is," she said, staring into her own eyes, "to feel so different and yet to look just the same!"

It was a wonderful week, though it rained for three days with hardly a letup. I felt sorry for the haymakers, but as far as we were concerned it was all right. I only wondered now how I was going to endure the time I would have to spend away from her. If there is anything sweeter or more magical than the total happiness of two healthy young creatures who love and who have never loved before, I have not found out what it is. I don't need anyone to tell me that there are other kinds of happiness to be found only in maturity, because I've learnt that too, but I'm thankful and grateful that we had what we had, and that it was unalloyed, even though I could see into the future no further than I could have thrown the oak four-poster that was in our room. Perhaps it even made it all more perfect.

XV

Just over a week later I was home and the familiar atmosphere of home closed over my head. We were all together again and when we were together we seemed to make up a sort of total, a sum that was somehow indivisible. I could slip out of it from time to time but I had to get back to make the sum come out right. Past and present merged and my mother, powerful catalyst that she was and unchanging through the years, made everything as it had always been. My father played the part he had always played: the giver, the provider, yet wholly dependent upon those who depended upon him. Was it possible that I was married, had a wife elsewhere, had a room that was home to her as this was home to me? Yes, but it all belonged to another place and time. I even had to remind myself of the cause of the pleasant weariness I felt, of the sleepiness that almost overcame me as I listened to accounts of the visit to Chico's family.

My father's comment was, "Well, it was just about what I expected. The old Count and the two sisters are buried alive but luckily for them they don't know it. The château is just as it was when the Count was first married, in about 1900."

"I do wish, darling," my mother said, "that you'd been with us. We missed you badly, and you'd have been so interested. How utterly different French country life is from English country life! Here, when people live in the country, they seem to be living in exile. In England they seem to belong to the country, to be as well rooted as their trees. But the old Count had beautiful manners and they were all three quite charming."

"I couldn't see so much charm," Julian told me. "I think they're worse than buried alive; they're just dead on their feet. I'm thankful I'll never have to live with them."

"I imagine they're equally thankful," Clarisse said, "and that's hardly the way to speak of my future in-laws, dear little brother."

But she smiled at him as she spoke and it struck me that she more than half agreed with him. Then she said to me, "If you want to know what the old Count is like I'll tell you. He's a nice old fuddy-duddy with a big white mustache and black eyes, and he's only interested in one thing, and that's the genealogy of the de l'Orchat family. You know, don't you, that they're descended from Henri Quatre?"

"Well, he's an ancestor to be proud of, anyway," I said. "Which mistress was it?"

"Oh, Gabrielle de l'Estrées, of course," she said. "Chico told me that a long time ago. And then down through her eldest son, Caesar of Vendôme."

"I can't see that that's anything to boast about," Julian said. "I should think they'd want to keep it dark."

"Darling," my mother said, smiling, "surely you know that people are always proud of being descended from a great king, whether it's the legitimate or an illegitimate branch."

"Well, I can't see why," Julian said.

"What are the sisters like?" I asked.

"The younger one's a little simple, I think," Clarisse answered. "She keeps a lot of birds in cages and the whole place smells of them. The older one is about to become a *religieuse*."

"What?" cried Julian. "Do you mean to say she's going to become a nun? Nobody told me that."

"Well, she is," Clarisse answered. "She told me so herself, when she was showing me her room. I don't suppose she tells everybody."

"It would be better than rusting away there, anyway," Julian said.

I asked what the château was like, and they told me that it needed a good deal done to it to make it habitable, that the plumbing was terribly out of date and the garden neglected.

"No one ever cuts the grass," Clarisse said, "and the flower beds only have begonias in them. In fact it's like most French châteaux where the owners aren't very rich and I don't suppose the de l'Orchats are."

My father gave a little cough and said,

"I think that's probably an understatement, Clarry."

"Well, anyway," Clarisse said, "I don't propose to live there and neither does Chico. We might spend a few weeks there in the summer, and we might give a house party from time to time. The old Count and Madeleine, the younger sister, are going to live in a small house close to the village when Chico and I marry," she added. And

[225]

then she asked, as if she were tired of the whole subject, "Tell us what you did in London, Halley. I know you didn't see Flavia, because she's in Scotland. What did you find to do with yourself all that time?"

"Oh," I said, "I didn't stay in London the whole time. I decided I'd like to have a look at Sussex so I went down there for a few days and stayed at an inn."

"But all by yourself, darling?" my mother asked.

I wished that it might have been possible to tell them then, but it was not possible. My whole world would have fallen apart. I answered, "I don't mind being alone, now and then. I had plenty of books with me and I walked a good deal. I enjoyed it." And then seeing my father looking at me with a rather worried look I added, "I sold some drawings that I didn't particularly want to keep, and that paid for the trip."

"I wish you wouldn't do that, my boy," my father said. "I wish you'd hold on to what you have. Now promise me you won't sell any more without consulting me."

"I guess I'd better not promise that," I answered. "I might have to sell one or two."

"Well, I don't like it," he told me. "You have a very nice little collection and they'll increase in value all the time. You hold on to them. If you need more money for anything, come to me and I'll see what I can do." He looked at my mother. "Was there any change today?"

It worried him so to read the daily stock market reports that my mother was now doing this for him.

"I'm afraid not, dearest," she answered. "I'd have told you at once if there'd been a change for the better, and you made me promise to tell you if there was a change for the worse. Prices are just where they were."

Clarisse got up then, announcing that she was going to bed. She went to my father, kissed the top of his head and said to him,

"You mustn't worry so much, *papa chéri*. Remember, I'll be off your hands soon."

"That's the very last thing I want, Clarry," he said. "I don't know what your mother and I are going to do without you."

"I won't be far away," she said, and I remembered her saying the same thing on another occasion. She kissed my mother, passed a light hand over Julian's hair and then, to my surprise, kissed me. At the same time she whispered in my ear, "Come and see me·

later." I was longing for my bed, but I knew she had something she wanted to say to me, so when the others had gone to their rooms, I went along to her room and made a faint sound on her door. She opened it and then jumped back into bed.

"You'd better keep your voice low," she said. "I don't want anybody to hear us." I sat on the foot of her bed and she went on, "And for heaven's sake don't let the others know I've talked to you, will you?" She smoothed her hair back from her forehead and asked, "Halley, do you think it's all right for me to marry Chico? I think he's terribly attractive and I don't want to lose him, but I'm not sure I'm really in love with him. I don't think I know what it feels like to be really in love."

She looked at me appealingly, and there was just the trace of a frown on that smooth forehead. She could always charm me, and she charmed me now, so that I could almost forget the past. She seemed really troubled and in doubt, and I only wanted to help her if I could.

"Well, don't marry him then," I begged her, "if that's all you feel for him. Don't, Clarisse. Why do you want to marry him if you don't love him? It isn't as if it was your last chance. You'll have dozens of men after you, you're bound to have. You could wait ten years if you wanted to. Twenty years. You won't have to worry."

She was twisting a long strand of hair about her finger and still looking at me.

"But what would I do," she asked, "if I didn't marry? Have love affairs? Phoebe does, but the men she has them with aren't very attractive. They're the sort of men I wouldn't have in the house."

"There are other alternatives," I said. "Aren't there?"

"Well, tell me one or two." But she didn't wait for me to name them. "Oh, I suppose I'd better go through with it," she said. "Plenty of other girls and even married women and a famous actress have been in love with Chico; I don't know why I'm not. Or, anyway, not in the way I suppose I ought to be. And yet I'd miss him terribly if I didn't have him to go out with, or if he didn't come here any more. And of course I could go anywhere, socially, as Chico's wife and the de Marboeufs' niece. But do I want to? Do I care about any of it?"

"I give it up," I said. "You asked me a question and I answered it. I can't do any more. Perhaps you'll get fonder of Chico after you're married to him."

"I'm fond of him now," she said. "Very. But that isn't the same thing as being really in love."

Then I said to her, "You're afraid of something, aren't you?"

She lowered her eyes.

"All right," she said. "Yes, I am."

"I suppose you wouldn't be, if you were in love," I said.

"Perhaps I'd be in love if it wasn't that I was afraid," she answered, and I thought that was very probably true.

"Don't you want children?" I asked, and I was surprised that I could ask her, for it was something we never spoke about.

"No," she said. She didn't look at me, and I felt certain that she was speaking the truth. "I simply can't imagine myself having children. I can't imagine it."

"Chico will want children," I told her. "You can be pretty sure of that. Anyway, he'll want a son."

She gave her head a shake as if it were something she couldn't bear to think about.

"Raymond always said I lacked the maternal instinct," she said, "and he was right. Well, I suppose I'll have to go through with it now, and anyway if I marry Chico I'll never have to go back to America. Sometimes I dream we're on our way back. Several times lately I've dreamt we were actually on the boat and then I've waked up and realized that it was only a nightmare and felt happy again."

"Well," I said, "we don't seem to be getting anywhere and I want to go to bed."

"All right," she said, "go to bed. Anyway, I've made up my mind now and I'll go through with it." And it seemed to me that I could almost hear the unspoken words, "This time."

I got up to go, but I hadn't taken two steps before I remembered that there was something I had to say. I said it, keeping my voice low.

"Listen, Clarisse. I don't know what you told Chico about Fred and I don't want to know, but whatever it was, it wasn't the truth."

Her eyes had an angry light in them now, like lightning flashing just below the horizon on a dark night.

"How do you know it wasn't the truth?" she demanded. "There are plenty of things I haven't told you about that; things I never will tell you."

"If you felt you couldn't tell the truth," I said, ignoring this, "you might have told a kinder lie, for Fred's sake."

Tears suddenly and surprisingly gushed out of her eyes.

[228]

"Go away," she sobbed. "Don't go on standing there like a bad conscience. Leave me alone. When I want comfort and help from you, this is what I get."

She had slipped down further in the bed and her shoulders were shaking. I wanted to tell her not to cry and give her a good-night kiss, but somehow I couldn't. I only said, "Well, good night," and went out. But now I was all pity for her and I wished I had said nothing, because I understood that this was something she couldn't cope with. Anyhow, I had no right to be a stickler for truth. My whole life was now a lie, but at least, I told myself, it was to make someone happy. I wasn't harming anybody alive or dead.

Clarisse's engagement was announced just before the family left for a holiday in Biarritz. It was like my father that he couldn't bring himself to suggest a holiday in some less expensive place—and Biarritz was Chico's choice—or even contemplate not going away for a holiday at all. We had always had expensive holidays and would do so now. Julian was driving them down in his car, but Chico had taught Clarisse to drive too and they would take turns. Chico was following with some of the luggage that couldn't go into Julian's car, and I had given a half promise to join them for a week in August, a half promise I didn't keep. I had told my father that I was determined to find a job for myself in London.

"But what sort of a job?" he asked.

"Well, anything I can get," I answered. "I haven't got any particular qualifications, you know."

We were walking along the Champs Élysées together, keeping in the shade as much as we could as it was a blistering hot day. We had Karl with us because Julian had had a mild attack of asthma the night before and was staying in bed.

"Don't talk like that, Halley, please," my father protested. "You've had the best possible education, you speak perfect French, you've traveled, you're a gentleman."

"Fine," I said. "What sort of salary would I draw for being a gentleman?"

"My dear boy," he said, "all those things are assets. But let me see if I can't get you a position of some sort here through the Ministry of Fine Arts. By golly, they ought to do something for me and it isn't much to ask."

"But I want a job in London," I said.

He looked quickly at me and I could see that he was hurt and puzzled. Then he switched to another subject.

"There's just one thing I don't like about the French," he said. "I can't reconcile myself to this business of being expected to give away a large *dot* when you give away your daughter. Of course I always meant to settle a considerable sum on Clarry, but what I dislike is the feeling that if I didn't there'd be no marriage. The African tribes do things better. With them the prospective bridegroom has to put up the money—or at least the cows and goats."

"Well," I said, "I suppose that's how things have always been here." And what he had said seemed to me like an echo of something I had heard many times before.

He went on,

"I've had a meeting with the de Marboeufs' lawyer—he's the old Count's lawyer too—and he managed to give me the impression that what I proposed to settle on Clarry was hardly enough. By golly, they ought to give it to me, on their knees, for handing over the loveliest girl in the world. I'm no eagle-screaming American, but thank God we look at these things differently over there."

"I suppose it could hardly have come at a worse time for you," I said.

"That's just the point," he agreed. "I'm having to sell a lot of shares at rock-bottom prices. Still, it's for Clarry, and there's nothing I wouldn't do for her. I did just ask her if she couldn't hold Chico off for a few months, when things may be better, but she said he was very impatient, and that if he wasn't impatient she wouldn't want to marry him at all."

I said I could see her point of view.

"I'm thankful," he told me, "for one thing, and that is that Chico isn't a Catholic. If he had been I don't believe I'd have given my consent."

He was understating things, as I well knew. Chico not only was not a Catholic, he was even anti-Catholic and anti-clerical. This suited Clarisse very well, as she would have disliked having to take any decision about joining a church, especially the Catholic Church.

Karl had been trotting at my father's heels but now we looked round and he wasn't there. He had stopped to exchange a few words with another boxer and for a moment I couldn't see him anywhere. My father said anxiously, "If anything happened to that dog, Julian would go out of his mind. Whistle to him, Halley, for heaven's sake."

I whistled and presently he came bounding after us.

"Frankly," my father said as we walked on, "I don't quite know what to do about Julian. I'd give any of you children the shirt off my back, but giving money to Julian is like pouring it into the gutter. I don't know what he does with it and he doesn't seem to know either, but at the end of the month he never has a sou left. The worst of it is, I think I'll have to cut his allowance down."

"Cut mine down instead," I said. "I'm bound to get a job soon." I told him then that Oakenshaw might be willing to take me into his gallery, but I didn't tell him that it would probably be on a commission basis only, and he didn't ask.

"In this family," he said, "we buy pictures, we don't sell them. Still, I suppose it might do just for the present, though I hate your being away from us most of the time."

A few minutes later he said he'd walked far enough and he called Karl and turned towards home. I wanted to buy a little present for Selma in the Rue de Rivoli, so I went on down to the Place de la Concorde. While I was waiting to cross with a group of other people I heard an American voice close beside me and it was a voice I knew well. I looked and sure enough it was Raymond. He was standing there with his wife—they were arm in arm—and I have seldom been so glad to see anybody. He looked pretty much the same except that he'd put on weight, and he was as pleased at the meeting as I was. We crossed the Place together and walked along the Rue de Rivoli, talking. His wife was a pleasant, quiet sort of woman with a gentle face that I liked at once. I could see that Raymond felt a little shy with me—it was the first time we'd met since Clarisse's wedding—but at last, after asking about the others, he asked about her.

"And Clarisse? How is she?"

"Fine," I said. "She's going to be married in October. To a Frenchman, the Comte de l'Orchat."

He nodded as if this were just what he'd expected.

"I hope she'll be very happy," he said.

They were staying in a *pension* on the Left Bank and they asked me to have dinner with them that night. I said they must come and have dinner with us instead, and that I'd telephone home to arrange it.

"Arnaud is still with us," I told him, "and his wife, Angèle, cooks for us. They've been back here more than a year."

"How very pleasant!" he said. "I never knew a family where there was such continuity. It'll be grand to see you all."

"How are you getting on with Mirabeau?" I asked.

He looked at his wife and they smiled at each other.

"With Lucille's help," he said, "splendidly. I could never have done it without her."

"Nonsense, Ray," she protested, tenderly. "You can do anything you put your mind to. But it's such fun," she went on, turning to me, "doing it together. It's one long treasure hunt with something coming to light every single day."

"Yesterday," Raymond said, "we found a contemporary word picture that delighted us. I memorized it. 'His features seem to agree with his character—a bold and hideous countenance, a daring and threatening look, a sallow complexion, an ungracious form and a bad manner.'"

We all laughed and I felt happy with them and part of my happiness was in their happiness.

Raymond said they were coming to London soon to do some work at the British Museum. He wanted to become better acquainted, he said, with Mirabeau's friends, Lord Shelburne and Sir Samuel Romilly, and with Mirabeau's time in London. He asked me how they could find furnished rooms and I gave him the name of the agent through whom I'd found the room in Ebury Street. Perhaps this was rash, but it seemed unfriendly not to give him any help I could. I said that I was in London a good deal myself (I knew he would be sure to hear this from the family) and that when they were there they must be sure to let me have their address.

I left them soon and telephoned home, and my mother was delighted.

"Perhaps they'll be good for Julian," she said. "He seems to find it so hard to make new friends."

All the time the family were in Biarritz I was in London with Selma trying to find a job. She now understood how I was situated at least as well as I understood it myself. Anyway, she was in possession of all the facts, and with her I felt I stood on firm ground. It was wonderful to me the way our relationship altered and deepened. She saw, in the strangeness and incompleteness of our marriage, a challenge and a mission. If there had been anyone to point out to us the folly of it and the dangers involved she would have been tigerish in its and my defense. Whatever else was wrong, our mutual love was right, I could be sure of that. Sometimes I recalled how Clarisse had enjoyed the secrecy of her engagement to Fred and how, as soon as it was exposed to the light of day, it had begun to wither; but with us, I felt certain, secrecy contributed little or nothing to the delight we took in our private world, and I only longed for the day to come when I could be open and honest about everything.

But the job I so badly needed didn't materialize. There were thousands of young men looking for jobs in London and not even the American firms I went to could give me any help. "Come back in a year or so," they said, "and possibly there may be something for you then." I was parting with my drawings one by one and at last Oakenshaw, in a sympathetic mood, said that he would take me on at five pounds a week with a commission on anything I sold. I jumped at it, for at least it gave me a reason for staying in London, and with what Selma earned, and my now reduced allowance, we could get by. I told my father that Oakenshaw would probably make me his partner in time, which I believed to be true, but when he said, "I suppose you're getting around a hundred dollars a week now, aren't you?" I only nodded and said, "Pretty near," and let it go at that. He and my mother urged me to spend every other weekend in Paris, and they took my departure very hard; so much so that when my father said, "I think, Halley, that the very least you can do is to promise me you'll go to New York with me at the end of November," I promised. The time had come, he said, to look out for a new stockbroker, and to rearrange his affairs. He had come to the conclusion that Conrad Falke was no earthly use.

As I half suspected at the time, it was foolish for me to have given Raymond the name of the agent who supplied furnished rooms, for a few weeks later when he and Lucille came to London they went to him and he directed them to Mrs. Reese-Crampton, who happened to have a room vacant. She told them she already had an American "with his English wife" staying in the house and she mentioned my name. Within a few days I received a letter from Raymond from an address near Russell Square.

Dear Halley, [he wrote]:
I am extremely sorry that we intruded, quite by accident, into something that for obvious reasons you wished to keep private. I can only assume that the word "wife" was a euphemism, and that it was used in all good faith by Mrs. Reese-Crampton, your landlady. You are no longer a boy and I am no longer your tutor, but I must admit that Lucille and I were deeply distressed and shocked. Under the circumstances I think we had better not meet, as naturally I do not wish to countenance or

connive at anything that would cause your parents so much unhappiness.

Yours sincerely,

Raymond

P.S. Your father gave us your address as in Chapel Street.

I didn't want to keep anything from Selma, so I showed her the letter and we looked at each other with some consternation. It was the first intrusion into our secret world and it brought with it something that had not been there before: a feeling of shame. It took away some of our belief in our own innocence. Selma said, turning away her face,

"I wish our getting married hadn't made things so hard for you."

I took her in my arms and kissed her.

"As soon as Clarisse's wedding is out of the way," I said, "I'm going to tell them all."

"But that will be terrible for you," she told me. "I know now just how terrible it will be."

"I guess it will," I said, "but that's my fault."

"No," she said, and she held me tighter, "nothing is your fault. I won't let you say that."

I took her to a concert that night and as I listened to Sibelius I thought or tried to think things out. I would go to see Raymond and Lucille, or if they didn't want to see me I would write to them and tell them the truth, and I would tell the family as soon as possible after Clarisse was married. My mother was now in the midst of preparations for an elaborate wedding and it was pretty hard on her that it was a French wedding and that she had to consider and make the acquaintance of a great many of Chico's relations and friends. His aunt, the Duchesse de Marboeuf, she told me, was like a powerful steamroller, and after a session with her she felt flattened out and exhausted. She assured me that she was better, however, and that her heart hadn't troubled her seriously since the day of the opening of the exhibition. She still hadn't told my father, and she kept her medicines in the drawer of her dressing table and took them secretly. I wondered that he didn't seem to notice the new puffiness under her eyes and her shortness of breath, but she was so much a part of him that he could never look at her from any perspective at all.

Clarisse's wedding was to be in the last week of October and I wished I could have found an excuse for not going to it. This time I had no duties to perform, but all the same I dreaded it and couldn't feel optimistic about it. It seemed to me that Clarisse was embarking on her new marriage with a cool indifference that was almost frightening. When I asked her one day if she felt happy about it, she answered,

"Well, thank heaven I shan't be Mrs. Fred Dumont any longer, that's one good thing. It was always like masquerading as someone else. At least I can feel more like myself as the Comtesse de l'Orchat."

She didn't say anything more, and if she had any doubts she kept them to herself. The wedding presents were pouring in, and Chico had signed the lease of the apartment below ours. As far as I could see, my parents were taking it all very well and with more philosophy than I would have expected. Nothing, I think, could have reassured them more than the fact that Clarisse and Chico would be living in the same building. At any rate, he had not made the same mistake as Fred.

XVI

EVEN THOUGH I KNEW RAYMOND WOULD SAY NOTHING, THE FACT
that our address was known to him made me decide to move. I happened to hear, through Frank Oakenshaw, of a furnished bed-sitting-
room with bathroom and kitchenette over an antique shop in George
Street, off Baker Street, and Selma and I wasted no time in going to
see it. The owner of the shop owned the whole of the small house of
which it occupied the ground floor and first floor, and he had had the
upper floor converted into a flat for his own use, but his family had
increased and he had had to move. It suited us perfectly. We could
shut off the bedroom part by drawing a curtain, and the rest of the
room, which was sparsely furnished, had space enough for an upright piano. One of the first things we did was to go out and hire
one and it was when Selma was trying one piano after another that
I heard her play for the first time. She only played a few chords on
each but it gave me confidence, for the one thing I didn't know was
how good—or bad—a pianist she was. It was a big moment for both
of us when they carried the piano up those narrow stairs, and as soon
as it was in its place, and the men gone, I said to Selma,
"Now!"
I watched her spread her skirts, sit down on the piano stool we
had hired with the piano, and turn over the pages of a book of Chopin
Études, and then I went and lay down on the bed. She was a little
nervous at first but presently she seemed to forget she was playing
to her husband for the first time and gained confidence. I lay there
listening and feeling happier than I'd ever felt in my whole life. I
was no connoisseur of piano playing but I knew enough to feel certain it was all right; one day she was going to be a really good pianist,
and I was going to make it my business to see that she got lessons
from a first-rate teacher. Somehow her playing and the pleasure I
took in listening to her broke some of the thousand threads that
bound me to my family. There was a transference of total allegiance

from them to Selma, from *there* to *here*. Here, I felt, was where I now wholly was. If Selma was not, now, the dead center of my life, then nothing was. I waited until she had played the last quiet notes that ended the *Étude* and then, as she looked round at me, I jumped up, ran to her and snatched her bodily off the piano stool. I stumbled back to the bed with her and we fell on it together. She was half laughing half crying, and as we lay there clasped in each other's arms, both our faces were wet. I felt whole and I felt free, and I offered up a silent prayer that I might stay that way.

Clarisse and Chico went to the Riviera for a month's honeymoon and I kept my promise to my parents to stay with them every other weekend. This was, of course, when I should have made my confession, but though I rehearsed the words in which I might make it a hundred times, they simply would not come. There came instead the old feeling of nausea that always accompanied emotional disturbance, and a dread of what I would be precipitating that half paralyzed me. And it was not only that. My mother had had such a severe heart attack after the wedding that there was no keeping it from my father, and now he was haunted by fear.

"If anything should happen to your mother, Halley," he said to me on my next visit to them, "you'd have to take over the responsibilities of the whole family. It would finish me. I only hope that if she goes, I go too."

I tried to cheer him up. I told him that nothing was likely to happen, that plenty of people with heart trouble lived long lives, and I added, "You know Mother is really wonderfully strong."

But all the same it didn't seem the moment to add to his worries or risk upsetting her, and I went back to London and told Selma why I hadn't been able to tell them. She said, "Please don't worry, Halley. There will be a time, and maybe this isn't the right one. I'm so happy now I feel I don't deserve to be any happier."

And she was happy. She loved the shabby little flat; the old-fashioned geyser which, when in the right mood, heated our water, the old bathtub with half its enamel gone, gave her pride and pleasure. And never before had she possessed or even hoped to possess a piano. These things, added to the joy of our life together, made a heaven for her. She had told her boss, Mr. Vining, that she was married and he had taken it well and had even raised her wages by ten shillings a week because she could now write business letters in French. I had given her a book on business French and I had been giving her lessons off and on for more than a year and she was a quick learner. She had tidied up all her own affairs and I wished with all my heart that I could have tidied up mine, but this seemed for the present beyond my powers. In spite of this it was a happy time even though precariously happy, and my delight in her kept growing. Sometimes I was afraid that I made love to her too much, but she was warmly responsive and loving in return. And it was wonderful that there was someone with whom I could be absolutely myself and from whom I had no secrets.

But I couldn't bear that Raymond should go on thinking what he thought, so I rang him up and asked if I might go and see him. He said no, he would rather I didn't, but if I cared to write to him, anything I chose to tell him he would regard as confidential. So in the end I wrote him a long letter. It was hard to write and when I tried to put my reasons for doing what I had done into words, it hardly seemed to make sense. A few days later he wrote to me. His letter was short, and strongly disapproving. He said, among other things,

I think you have made a terrible mistake, whatever your motives were. Until you have found the courage—and I regret to say that lack of courage is something you seem to share with both Clarisse and Julian—to make a clean breast of things to your parents, Lucille and I would prefer not to meet either your wife or you. I am sure you will understand.

P.S.—I note that you propose to tell them before you leave for New York.

I did understand and he was right, of course, but I was sorry. They would have liked Selma, and they would have been people she could have talked to about me when I was away with my father in New York. But I had now postponed any thought of making my confession until after our return. It was important that he should go, and I did not think it wise to upset everything just before our departure. In fact I thought it might prevent his going altogether. It would make, I felt pretty sure, such a to-do that he might even feel he had to stay at home with my mother.

About the middle of November my father was made an *Officier* of the *Légion d'Honneur* at a little ceremony at the *Ministre des Beaux Arts*. My mother went with him, and when I was in Paris, soon after, it was touching to see how gratified they both were and how proud my mother was. After that I don't think I ever saw my father without his little red rosette unless he was in his dressing gown, or in another country.

[238]

"Having been virtually driven out of my own country," he said to me, "it's a great thing to feel I'm welcomed and honored in this country. I hope I shall never have to live anywhere else."

And my mother said to me privately, "I hope we don't make too much of this, Halley, but it really has added enormously to your father's happiness. It's true that he's very much a cosmopolitan, but I know that when we left America he felt like a man without a country. I think that feeling has gone now, thanks to this, and I'm so very glad."

They were eagerly looking forward to Clarisse's return. She hadn't written to me but she had written several times to them and all seemed to be going well.

"It will be wonderful to have her back," my mother said, "with only one flight of stairs separating us. I suppose, darling, I oughtn't to grumble about your being away so much. Angèle tells me that somebody is darning your socks most beautifully and she wonders who it is. Is it your landlady?"

I said it was the housekeeper, which seemed to me nearer the truth, but I think that if she hadn't been lying down, resting, and if she hadn't just asked me to fetch her medicine for her, I might have blurted out everything. Of course I didn't, and a second later she asked me what I thought about Julian.

"I'm a little worried about him," she said, "and so is your father. He seems to have some new interest, but he hasn't told us what it is. It isn't like him to be so secretive. I do hope it's all right. Do you think you ought to talk to him more?"

I said I never found that very easy but that I'd have a try, and I meant to, if an opportunity offered. She then asked, "Are you happy, Halley, in your new work? It doesn't seem to us at all the sort of thing you ought to be doing, but I suppose it will suffice for the present."

I said I liked working in the gallery, that Oakenshaw was a nice chap and that I'd already made some sales.

"I suppose you see a good deal of Raymond and Lucille," she said. "It's nice for you, their being in London."

I had to explain to her that they were busy all day in the British Museum and that I was pretty busy too, but I said that I'd try to see more of them. I thought it was a good thing I was so soon going to New York with my father, out of this "coil" I was in, to use a word he was fond of using, and I made a vow that as soon as we got back I would put an end to this double life which was destroying my peace of mind at the same time that it was giving me so much secret joy.

I only saw Clarisse and Chico once before going to New York. They were staying at the France et Choiseuil until the new apartment was ready for them, but it suited them—or it suited Clarisse— to spend a good deal of time in our apartment on the floor above, and Clarisse wanted my mother's advice, I gathered, pretty frequently.

Everything seemed to be all right and I thought Clarisse seemed happy and confident unless—as turned out to be the case—she was only putting on an act. She said to me that evening, after dinner, "Halley, you haven't seen the apartment since it was furnished. Come down with me now and I'll show it to you."

I knew she didn't want any of the others, but Chico at once said he'd come with us, and then Julian said he'd like to come too. So the four of us went down. The drawing room was the same size as ours, but the apartment as a whole was much smaller. There was no spare bedroom at all, and I wondered what they would do in the event of an increase in the family, unless Chico would be willing to give up his dressing room. Clarisse had no opportunity to speak to me alone until Julian asked Chico to explain to him the workings of a curious clock that was a wedding present from one of the de Marboeufs and was said to have been given by Napoleon to Madame Junot. While they were in the drawing room examining it, Clarisse took my arm and said,

"Come and see my bedroom."

We were hardly there before she said to me, keeping her voice low, "Halley, I must talk to you. There's no one else I can talk to. I do wish you didn't spend all your time in London."

"Is anything the matter?" I asked.

"Yes," she said. "There certainly is something the matter. There always seems to be a catch in everything. Do you know what Chico wants to do? He wants to buy a plane. Did you ever hear of anything so crazy? He can't afford to buy it himself and he wants me to put up more than half the money. I knew of course that he liked flying, but it never occurred to me that he'd want to *own* a plane."

"What will you do?" I asked. "Do you mind his flying?"

"No," she said, "of course I don't mind, he can fly as much as ever he likes, but I never thought he'd expect me to fly too, or that he'd want to *buy* one of the things. He tried to persuade me to fly back from Marseilles with him, instead of coming by train. I simply refused. It pretty well spoilt our honeymoon." And then she said, and she spoke bitterly, "I can only make one generalization about husbands so far and that is that they always want more than one's prepared to give."

I didn't know what to say. I wouldn't have wanted to fly either, and I understood her not wanting to. I tried to comfort her by suggesting that it was only a passing craze, perhaps, and that if she could put off the buying of the plane for a while, he might change his mind.

"If you want to know," she said, "I think flying is the one love of his life."

She was no longer looking serene and happy, she looked really distressed and worried, and I felt sure that there had already been disagreements between Chico and herself about this, and perhaps even quarrels.

"Well," she said, impatiently, "what am I going to do? Can't you advise me? Shall I keep him happy by putting up more than half the money for the plane, or shall I simply refuse? If he does buy it, heaven knows how I shall be able to keep out of it, and the thought simply terrifies me. I've always hated taking risks. You know I'm not brave. This is going to make my life a perfect hell."

"Suppose," I asked, "you do refuse? Then what?"

She looked straight at me and the look in her dark eyes told me more than words could.

"You've never seen Chico in a temper," she said. "Neither had I until I saw what he was like when he was opposed."

I had never seen him in a temper, it was true, but I could guess what he would be like.

"Couldn't his aunt help?" I asked. "Or perhaps you'd better speak to Father and Mother about it."

"It's a little early, isn't it," she said, "to appeal to our relations to settle our disputes? Oh, Halley, you can thank God you're a man! Men don't have to lead other people's lives. They lead their own. Why couldn't he have told me he wanted to buy a plane, and that he'd expected me to like flying? It's so damned unfair!"

We heard Chico's and Julian's voices then, and she went quickly across the room and straightened a picture. I think Chico half suspected that she had been confiding in me, but as she turned around she was once more looking perfectly composed.

"Well," she said to him, "I think we can ask Tante Clothilde to come and look at it now, don't you?"

"Tante Clothilde" was of course the Duchesse de Marboeuf, and her husband was "Oncle Lulu," his full name being Louis Antoine Hercules Remy de St. Clair de Marboeuf.

"We'll bring them tomorrow," Chico said.

"What beats me," Julian remarked, "is why anybody should want to live in a place like this, with all this junk." And he added, "What I'd like would be a room of my own somewhere with a bed in it, a radio and Karl."

"And no washing facilities, dear little brother?" asked Clarisse, laughing. It was a family joke that Julian rarely took a bath of his own accord, or until my mother or someone suggested that it was time he did.

"Oh," Julian said, "our civilization is effete. We take too many baths. We're decadent."

I always thought that Clarisse was at her best with Julian. He amused her and she never lost her temper with him, whatever he said or did. She put her arm through his now and lightly kissed his cheek.

"I suspect," she said, "that it's only thanks to Mother's watchful eye that I can go near enough to you to kiss you."

"Come along," Chico said, and I guessed that such little scenes of family affection jarred on him now. "We must say good night to your father and mother, and then it will be time for us to go."

That was the last I saw of them before I went back to London. I was there for three days, and then I went to Cherbourg to meet my father. We were going to New York by a French boat, contrary to our usual custom, but I suspected that he looked forward to wearing his newly acquired Legion of Honor until he actually set foot in New York.

It was hard to leave Selma, but she made it as easy for me as she could by telling me of all the things she intended to do in my absence. She would give more time to practicing, she would knit me a pullover, she would make herself some new underclothes, she would enamel the bathtub. I hated the thought of her being entirely alone there at night, but she assured me she didn't mind at all. "There's a good lock on the door," she said, "and you know I'm not nervous."

I said to her, when the moment came for me to go, "You're everything I've ever wanted, my darling, and you're a hundred things I must have wanted without even knowing it. And I'll write to you every day."

I thought of her and of little else all the way to Cherbourg, and I planned ways of ending the situation we were in. I would have good opportunities on the boat for telling my father what had to be told, but I didn't want to do this when he was away from my mother, for it seemed to me important to tell them when they were together. I was sure this was right, and not merely another excuse for postponing something I dreaded. And however much I was Selma's husband, when I met my father on the boat I knew I was very much my father's son too. I knew his weaknesses now as well as I knew my own; I had known them ever since that night in Sixty-sixth Street when he had refused to see Fred; but at the mere sight of him my old filial feelings always revived. His anxieties were my anxieties, and we were returning together to the city where I was born. It was all too easy to slip back five years or even more, and if I thought the threads were broken I had only been deceiving myself. They were still there, and they were stronger than I knew, and I asked myself how it would ever become possible to tell them what I had done. Could I ever tell them? I doubted it. I doubted it so much that there was a night on the boat when I even asked myself if it might not be a less impossible thing to give up Selma than to tell them about her. As the thought came to me I broke out into a cold sweat, as if I had already done it or was about to do it, and I said to myself, "Now you have touched the very bottom. You will never think a viler thought than this."

Now that we were on our way to New York, Syl kept coming into my thoughts, and as I soon learnt, into my father's too. One rough day when we were about halfway across he said to me: "Halley, I've been turning something over in my mind and now I'd like to talk to you about it." He gave a little cough and I could see that he was embarrassed. We had been walking up and down the heaving deck but now he stopped and turned toward our chairs. "We might as well sit down," he said. I tucked his rug about him and then the steward saw us and came hurrying up to do the same for me. My father waited until he had gone and then went on, "I don't know exactly what you'll think of this, but don't brush it aside till we've looked at it from every angle. What I want to ask you is this. What do you think—or rather let me put it in another way—how do you imagine Syl feels about us now? Some time has passed, and as a Christian—he's always been a regular churchgoer—as a good Christian, I don't see how he could nurse any hate towards us, do you?" He was stammering a little now. "I mean, that's one of the first tenets of our religion, isn't it, that you ought to try to forgive those you imagine have done you a wrong?"

I saw very well where this was leading, and I couldn't help feeling dismayed. I had been thinking not only of Syl but of Rosie and Helen, and wishing I could see them again. I had been trying to imagine myself picking up the telephone and dialing Rhinelander 0–8889 and saying I wanted to speak to Helen. I imagined myself asking her how they all were and how Syl was, and if she thought—this of course provided she would consent to speak to me at all—that he might let me go to see him. Now, it seemed to me, my father had destroyed any possibility of this by wanting to get in touch with Syl —through me, of course—for his own purposes.

It was some time before I could answer him and then I said, "I don't know, Father. I think Syl is, as you say, a good Christian, but —well, he hasn't got Fred back, has he?"

This wasn't perhaps the best way of putting it, but it summed up what I felt.

"I think," he said, and he spoke with patient forbearance, "that you and I see all that rather differently, Halley. I consider that Fred was an unstable character, or it could never have happened. He ought to have taken it like a man. Anyway it was his fault, right from the very beginning. If I could have talked to Syl, just he and I together, quietly, I think I might have made him see that. Anyway, I refuse to accept any blame at all for what happened." I said nothing, and he went on, "He must know by now that Clarry is married again, and happy. My press-cutting people sent me a number of clippings about the wedding from the New York papers. He adored Clarry; he ought to be glad—that is, if his religion means anything to him at all."

I was watching the tossing gray horizon sink below the rail and then slowly rise above it. We were both good sailors and untroubled by bad weather and now we were almost the only passengers on the deck. I turned to him and asked, "Just what do you want me to do?"

"Well," he said, "frankly, I'd like you to try to get in touch with Syl. I'd like you to try to bring about some sort of a reconciliation. I don't think it's impossible. I refuse to believe that the friendship of a lifetime can't be revived."

"I'd like to think it over," I said. "I had it in mind to ring up Rosie or Helen and say hello, but I don't know if I can do it now."

"Why not?" he asked sharply. "It's extremely important that you should. I've never needed Syl's help and advice as badly as I need it now."

"Yes," I said, "I know. That's just the trouble. That's just why I can't."

"Can't?" he repeated, a little irritably. "My dear boy, you can hardly use that word. Of course you can, if you want to. However, do as you please. It may be that our whole future depends on it—and let me point out that that includes your future too—because there's no one else I can go to for help and advice. Syl always said that Falke was nothing but a stuffed shirt and he was perfectly right. The fellow isn't even trying. Well, if you don't help me I must try to approach Syl in some other way."

He was making the whole thing more difficult and more distasteful to me and I didn't want him to add anything to what he'd already said. I told him I'd like to think it over, and I'd see what I could do. Then I changed the subject.

"Have you had any more offers for the house?" I asked. The only one he had had so far he considered absurdly small.

"Not a single one," he said. "I seem to be in for a run of bad luck, as far as money is concerned. I can't think of myself as really unlucky as long as I have your mother and you children." He threw back his rug. "Well," he said, "I think I'll just go down to the smoking room and see what the news is from Wall Street."

After giving the matter a good deal of thought I decided that I'd better put my finer feelings in my pocket and do what I could, though I hated the whole idea. The fact that I'd been thinking of ringing up Rosie or Helen anyway took a little of the bad taste of it out of my mouth, but some of it remained.

We went to a small hotel in East Sixtieth Street where we'd sometimes stayed in the old days when the servants were on holiday or while the house was being made ready for us. It was a very beautiful day when we arrived, perfect late autumn weather with a sun that still had some warmth in it, though the air was brisk. One of the first things my father asked me to do was to take his key and go around to the house to see that everything was all right there. He said he hated the idea of going into it himself, it was too full of memories. It was full of memories for me too, both pleasant and unpleasant. The library was still, for me, the room in which Fred had died, for I couldn't get the idea out of my mind that though he had put a bullet through his head in that hotel on the West Side, he had in fact died in that room on that dreadful morning. I got out as quickly as I could. If I was going to ring up the Dumonts, it was better that I shouldn't stay there too long.

My father decided to go by himself to see Conrad Falke, and I was very glad, for I didn't want to be present at that interview. When he had gone I sat down on my bed and looked at the telephone. Should I or shouldn't I? I decided that I could at least find out whether or not Rosie or Helen felt they would care to speak to me, and I needn't mention my father until later. At last I nerved myself to take up the receiver and dial the familiar number. A man's voice said "Hello" and I couldn't decide whether it was Irving Dumont's voice or not. It sounded like him and yet it didn't. I said I'd like to speak to Miss Dumont, if she was in.

"Miss Dumont?" he repeated. "She isn't in. Miss Helen Dumont is in, if you want to speak to her. This is Irving Dumont speaking."

"How are you, sir?" I asked, my heart beating wildly. "This is Halley Prentiss here. I don't know how you feel about talking to me, but I just felt I had to ask how you all were. I'm over here for a short time."

"Who?" he asked. "Halley Prentiss? For God's sake!" There was a silence, but he hadn't hung up yet and I took courage from that.

"Yes," I said. "I just felt I had to ring up. How are you all?"

I was stammering, and I suppose he guessed how hard it was for me and took pity on me.

"Speaking for myself," he said, "I've got a cold. That's why I'm here and not at the office. I'd better call Helen and see if she—just hold on a minute."

I could feel my heart thumping harder than ever now and I realized as I waited there that while Helen had kept growing in importance in my mind and memory, Rosie had been dwindling so that I really didn't care much whether I saw her again or not; it was Helen I longed to see.

He was away for some little time, and I guessed they were discussing whether Helen should come and speak to me or not. At last she came.

"Halley," she said, "I never thought I'd hear your voice again. Where are you? What are you doing?"

"Oh," I said, and I tried to speak casually, "I'm over here for a couple of weeks. I just felt I'd like to ask how you all were—that is, if you felt like talking to me."

"I don't know what I feel," she said. "It's all too unexpected. What made you ring up?"

She sounded more natural now and I guessed that her father had left the room.

"I just had to ring you up," I said. "How's Rosie?"

"She's all right. She's engaged. I suppose you didn't know."

"No," I said, "I hadn't heard. That's fine. Is it anybody I know?"

"I shouldn't think so," she answered. "He's a schoolmaster. He teaches at St. Jude's—you know, near Philadelphia. They're getting married next month. He's thirty; he's clever and nice-looking, and they're very happy."

"I'm so glad," I told her, and I certainly meant it.

"Halley," she said, "I don't know what to say to you. You bring it all back so."

I heard her catch her breath on a little sob.

"Would you rather not go on talking to me, Helen?" I asked. "Please tell me the truth."

"Oh," she said, "I don't know. We try so hard to put all that awfulness out of our minds. Perhaps I oughtn't to want to see you, but I do. It's no good your asking to see Rosie. She wouldn't. But maybe you and I could meet."

"I do wish we could, Helen," I said. "I wish it with all my heart."

"No one blames you for anything," she went on. "I don't see why we shouldn't meet."

"Well then we will meet," I told her, "of course we will. But there's one thing I long to ask you now. How is Syl?"

She hesitated, and then she answered, "Well, you'd see a change in him. He's a lot older. Rosie and I aren't much good to him, you know. He lost the dearest thing he had."

"I know," I said. There was a moment's silence and then I asked, "When can I see you?"

"What about giving me a drink somewhere this afternoon, about five?"

"You sound awfully grown up," I told her. "You'd have said tea somewhere before."

"I am awfully grown up," she answered, "but we'll say tea if you'd rather. You sound awfully British, somehow."

"Do I?" I said. "Let's say tea, anyway, and make it half past four."

She agreed, and we decided to meet at the Ritz. I hung up, and the relief I felt was so great that for some time I simply sat there letting the words we had spoken go on echoing in my head. It was better than I could have hoped, and I was thankful, but I made up my mind that I would make no attempt at all to bring my father and Syl together. If by some miracle it came about, well and good, but it would be through no efforts of mine.

[247]

I got a table and sat waiting for her, and I felt as if we had all come back to New York for the winter as we had always done, and that nothing had changed. I could pretend that it was still my home, or at least the place I called home to distinguish it from the other places I lived in. I felt unchanged and I certainly felt no older than I felt when I had left Harvard. I didn't keep reminding myself that in the meantime I had married (though this could still astonish me), because it all belonged to another world, almost another existence, and it played no part in this. I was here, I had gone back in time, and Selma and all that concerned my life with her seemed to have been shut away in a drawer, not forgotten but locked up, the way one locks up a valuable object so that one doesn't have to think or worry about it. One simply knows it is there. And I didn't want to think about it at this moment and the problems that went with it, for what was now happening to me seemed to me almost equally important and extraordinary. I had supposed that I would never see a member of the Dumont family again and yet in a minute or two I would be seeing Helen; and if Helen was willing to see me possibly even Syl might be, and a part of my life that had been broken in a cruel and ugly way might be mended again.

One of the symptoms of a delayed maturity is an unwillingness to let the dead past bury its dead and my longing to return to it was, I am sure, a sign that I was still adolescent. I had known Helen since she was a baby, we had always spent our Christmases together, we and the Dumonts; I had drifted into a sentimental relationship with Rosie—though it had not been a happy one and it had faded out—much as Clarisse had drifted into one with Fred. At the time of the break I could easily, young though she was, have drifted into one with Helen. It was now deeply important to me to do what I could towards restoring, in some degree, these old ties. I even had a feeling that in some way it would make me whole. Perhaps the reason for this was that I found it unendurable to feel that I was hated.

I had forgotten about my father's needs, I wanted to forget them, and it was with wholly singleminded and untainted pleasure that I saw Helen coming towards me. There was no smile on her face, she looked nervous and I am sure she was, and she had certainly grown up, and the subtle transformation from Rosie's younger sister to the finished and highly attractive young woman she now was fascinated me. She was taller than Rosie and her features were better, and it seemed almost unfair that she should have so surpassed her sister. She was wearing a short fur jacket and a little fur cap and I made up my mind that I would get her to take it off so that I could see her more as I was used to seeing her.

She didn't hold out her hand to me; she must have felt that handshaking, between us, was superfluous. We sat down and looked at each other, and it all seemed to me almost too good to be true.

"For heaven's sake say something, Halley," she said, and her lips were trembling with nervousness and with emotions that I could easily guess at. "Say that you're glad to see me, or even 'Hello!' Don't just look at me."

"If you only knew," I answered, "how happy this makes me! It's wonderful. I never believed it could happen."

"Well, anyway, here I am," she said. "I've always made up my own mind about things and I made up my mind I was going to see you. You don't look any different. You look just the same. I'm so terribly glad."

It might have been ten years since we had seen each other and I knew it seemed like that to her, too.

"Do I look the same?" I asked. "You don't. You look beautiful, just the way I always knew you'd look someday."

"You always told me I'd improve," she said. "It was the nearest you ever came to a compliment."

"What are you doing?" I asked, to gain time and to get used to the idea of her being there at all. "I was afraid you might be away at Bryn Mawr. You always said you wanted to go to Bryn Mawr."

"I know," she answered, "but you see I couldn't go very well. There was Daddy, and Rosie was about to get engaged, so I decided to stay at home. I'm going to an art school instead—I always wanted to paint—and I love it. Halley, Rosie came in just before I left and I told her you'd rung up. She tried to persuade me not to come."

"She feels like that about me?" I asked, and I was troubled and sorry.

"Well," she said, "I can understand. She was terribly fond of you. But I think she's going to be happy now. They suit each other very well and it'll be just the right sort of life for her."

I said I was very glad, and we kept on looking at each other. She must have read my thoughts for just then she slipped off her jacket and then took off her cap.

"They keep these places so hot," she said.

She pressed her short, wavy brown hair into place and as she did so I saw that she was wearing a heavy seal ring and I recognized it at once as Fred's. She must have seen me looking at it.

[249]

"Yes," she said, "it's Fred's ring. I always wear it." And then she turned to me with an appeal that moved me deeply. "Oh, Halley, for heaven's sake let's not try to avoid talking about Fred. Let's talk about him as much as we like, and about everything that's happened. At home we never do and it only makes it worse. I loved Fred; he was my beloved big brother and there's nobody I can talk to about him, not a soul. Rosie shrinks from it, and if I speak his name to Daddy or Uncle Syl it's as if I were rubbing salt on open wounds. Let's talk about everything. Tell me about them all; tell me about Aunt Ruth and Uncle Myron and Julian. Tell me even about Clarisse. I want to hear."

"You're a brave girl, Helen," I said, "and you're absolutely right."

"Fred's room," she went on, and I could see she was longing to unburden herself, "is just as it was. Daddy won't let anything be touched. He goes in there from time to time and just stands looking around at all Fred's things, and then he comes out again and closes the door softly. It oughtn't to be like that. It's bad for us all. But there isn't anything I can do. It's as though that revolver shot just keeps on echoing and echoing. . . ." She pulled herself up and I saw her bite her lower lip and blink away some tears. I put a hand over hers for a second and she gave me a little smile and after that she was all right again.

"I don't even hate Clarisse," she went on. "She was like a poor frightened soldier who runs and hides and risks everything because he's afraid to risk anything. We all saw the news of her marriage in the papers, and none of us have spoken of it. Do you think it's going to be all right?"

I told her all about it. I even told her finally about Chico's determination to have his own plane and to take Clarisse up in it, and about the trouble I was afraid it might cause between them. I told her about my father and mother and Julian, and about what my father had done with his pictures. There was so much to tell her that I never got around to telling her about myself, except to say that I had a job in London now and spent most of my time there. It was so good to be with her, talking naturally and freely, weaving past and present together and making it whole, that I felt I couldn't tell her about my marriage then, chiefly because it would have involved all the difficulties of explaining why I had so far kept it secret. I would tell her the next time; there was too much else, now, that I wanted her to know and that I wanted to hear from her. Uppermost in my mind was the question of whether or not she thought Syl might see me, but when I asked her what the chances were she couldn't tell me.

"He just might see you, I think," she told me, "but he certainly wouldn't see any of the others. He believes that if Uncle Myron had shown just the least little bit of firmness with Clarisse, everything would have come out all right."

"I wonder," I said. "For a while, perhaps."

"Yes," she agreed, "perhaps only for a while, but even that would have been better. Fred wouldn't have killed himself if the marriage had just broken up, like plenty of other marriages. He could have taken that. He couldn't take what did happen. Halley, why do people ever despair when they're young? Even if I was heartbroken, I'd *know* that in a year or two I wouldn't be heartbroken any longer. You'd know it too, wouldn't you? Why didn't Fred know it?"

"He didn't give himself time to know it," I said.

It was wonderful that we could talk like this, and it was doing us both an immense amount of good. She'd been needing it the most, of course, but I had been needing it too.

When we got back to the subject of Syl again she said she'd see him the next day and find out how he felt about it.

"I'm afraid it won't be easy for you," I told her.

"Oh, it won't be so hard," she said. "I guess I've learnt one thing and that is how true that old saying is about grasping nettles."

I knew the old saying as well as she did, but I knew I was no good at grasping them.

"What do you know about nettles anyway?" I asked, smiling at her. "They don't even grow here."

"I know all about them," she answered. "Daddy and I were in England most of last summer. We went over at the beginning of May and stayed till September. We got a car and drove here and there and everywhere, and we spent August in Scotland."

"You were in England?" I asked, staring at her. "In May?"

"Yes," she said. "Why? Were you there too? Oh, Halley, I wish we could have seen each other then."

It should of course have been easy for me to tell her at that moment, but I think I was too much concerned with my own thoughts and feelings, and with an instant's wild regret, and the remorse that followed it. Better that that locked drawer should stay locked for the present, I thought, for I was afraid, not so much of telling her about my marriage as of telling her about it as though it were something I wished undone. I thought I had better keep silent.

"Never mind," she said. "We've come together now, and maybe it was the right moment, and please, Halley, let's not be separated like that ever again."

I said, "I hope we never will be, Helen," and I meant it and there was no disloyalty in it. It was only that something that had been broken was now being pieced together, and an old pain had gone.

"Ring me up at lunchtime tomorrow," she suggested. "I'll have gotten in touch with Uncle Syl by then and I'll let you know what he says."

"No," I said. "Lunch with me and you can tell me then."

We decided to have lunch at a small Italian restaurant where I had often taken her when she was still a schoolgirl, and then I looked at my watch and saw that it was a quarter past seven. We had been there talking for two and three-quarter hours. I took her home in a taxi and she sat holding my hand. Suddenly she took away her hand, put both arms about me and burst into tears.

"Oh," she cried, "don't try to comfort me. I'm so happy, I'm so happy! It's just as if some awful ache that has never stopped all this long time had been taken away. Oh, Halley, I've always loved you. Please love me and let's always be together. I do need you. You've taken away all that horror and hate. Isn't love the one single good thing in this world? Isn't it? Tell me it is."

I suppose someone else might have had the courage to say at that moment, "You mustn't love me. I'm married." It would have been like slapping her in the face. I had to let her have her cry because it was what she wanted and needed. And she had more to say.

"It all came at such a bad time for me," she went on, between her sobs. "I was at a difficult age, and I'd fallen in love with you, and then that awful thing happening—it was too much for me. I just felt a lost creature. I had to try to find my own way out. Nobody knew what *I* was feeling, they were suffering too much themselves to see. Hold me, Halley, hold me tight and kiss me, because it's the best thing that's ever happened to me."

I held her in my arms all the way and I kissed her tenderly and without passion. I was certain that when she said she loved me it was a brother she was wanting and not a lover, and I felt no guilt or shame; nothing but a very great happiness and peace. When we reached the apartment house she wiped her eyes and attended to her face a little, and then she put on the fur cap again. She gave a long sigh.

[252]

"It was a good cry," she said, "and it's washed away everything that was bad. Bless you, my darling Halley, and good-by."

My mind was in pretty much of a turmoil as I walked home, but I was young enough to feel that there was a solution to everything, and that somehow things would sort themselves out. And I felt, too, a great deal of elation, as if I had accomplished the impossible.

XVII

WHEN I GOT BACK I FOUND MY FATHER IN HIS BEDROOM—FOR once we had not got a sitting room—busy with pencil and paper, and there were a lot of torn scraps of paper on the floor. He was always the tidiest of men and it told me something of his state of mind even before he raised his face and I saw the harassed look it wore.

"Halley," he said as I came in, "I absolutely must see Syl. I've had the shock of my life. By golly! I had no idea things were as bad as they are."

He suddenly looked to me pathetic and helpless and I had never seen him like that before. There were defeat and consternation in his face and in every line of his body as he sat slumped, as if deflated, in his chair. I bent down to pick up some of the torn paper and I suppose this must have annoyed him.

"Never mind picking up those scraps," he cried irritably, "the maid can do that. Sit down and listen to me." He straightened himself and looked at his writing pad. "I've been working things out. Do you know what my income will be, after taxes are paid, thanks to that buffoon who calls himself my stockbroker? Just over eleven thousand dollars. Eleven thousand dollars a year to support this family. It just can't be done. By golly! if Conrad Falke isn't an out-and-out swindler, as I suspect he is, he's the biggest fool that ever drew the breath of life. I practically told him so this afternoon and then I walked out of his office. I've done with him—finished with him. Halley, you've got to arrange it so that I can see Syl. It's of the very first importance."

I said I was terribly sorry to hear that things were so bad, as indeed I was, but he cut me short to ask impatiently, "Did you see Helen?"

"Yes," I said, "she's fine and she doesn't seem to hate any of us. She's very grown up, and she looks just as I always thought she'd look."

"Well," he said, "she was always the best of the three, in my opinion. What did she tell you about Syl? How is he?"

I told him he was well and that Helen was going to try to arrange a meeting for me.

"But she doesn't think he'd see you," I had to add. "In fact she's pretty sure he won't."

He got up and began walking around the room jingling the change in his pockets and biting his mustache. I noticed that on his bedside table there were two books: a newly published work on French nineteenth-century painting and a volume of Victor Hugo's poems with a letter from my mother in it as a marker. It seemed to me very unfair that he was not going to be allowed to live his life and pursue his interests in undisturbed peace as he had always done.

"If Falke had kept me properly informed," he said, frowning, "and told me the truth about the stock market, I wouldn't have given away the pictures. Anyway, not until things had improved. Well, it's done now, and it's no good crying over spilt milk. I've got nine left—I'd never sell your mother's portrait of course—and they'd all fetch big prices, but I don't see how I could ever bring myself to part with any of them unless it was a case of keeping the wolf from the door. Anyhow, one thing is certain. You'll have to come back to Paris now and live at home, and let me find you a decent job—something that may lead to something. That way we'd save some money, because it looks as if I'd have to stop your allowance altogether. I don't know what to do about Julian; I doubt if he'll ever be able to earn a cent as long as he lives. And there's something else that's certain, too. We'll have to find a cheaper apartment in a less expensive part of town, and as soon as possible. I'm afraid Clarry will be terribly disappointed if we leave, but I really don't see what else we can do."

I agreed with him that we ought to move to a cheaper apartment, but of course I would make no promises about leaving London and going back to Paris to live.

"I simply can't understand why you're so stubborn about this," he exclaimed. "Your home is wherever your mother and I are, and as far as I can see that's going to continue to be Paris. Things always go best when we're together. We've always been a united family and it's right that we should be." He stopped his walking about, went to his dressing table and began to brush his hair. "Well," he said. "I suppose we'd better go down to dinner, though I can't say I feel like eating anything. I never ought to go anywhere without your mother. I feel about half alive."

It was a gloomy meal and it made me no happier to realize, as I did, how painfully my life was divided; and now, since my meeting with Helen, still further divided. I was aware of a wish to stay on in New York and to see her as often as I could. There were of course, I told myself, other reasons, too, why I wanted to spend more time there. René, who after all was my best friend, was coming down from Boston to see me, Bob Lane was now in an advertising firm with offices on Fifth Avenue so that I could see him any day, and Harry Wilson, who had recently married, was living no farther away than Scarsdale. All the same I knew in my heart that it was Helen I wanted to see most of all, and again and again, and the more I tried to analyze and understand these emotions the more perturbed I grew. I was still young enough to feel that what was happening to me was altogether extraordinary and unheard of, and when I thought of Selma it was with a mixture of pity and love and anguish, as if she were someone whom I must protect from my own weakness while at the same time I doubted my ability to provide that protection. It seemed to me that both my own situation and hers could hardly be more dangerous, and though I swore to myself that I would never let her down, that no combination of circumstances could possibly cause me to let her down, all the same I was both ashamed and fearful.

My father urged me to go with him to see a film—"It will take our minds off all this worry," he said—so we went, but I have no recollection at all of what we saw. All the time I was sitting there I was trying to find safe ways out of my dilemmas, ways I could take which would hurt nobody but myself. When I went to my room that night I wrote Selma a long letter. I tried to give her an impression of New York and I said nothing at all that might disquiet her. I told her, in a paragraph, that I had seen the youngest member of the Dumont family and that it had been an unexpectedly pleasant meeting. For the first time since our marriage I was consciously and deliberately not telling her all the truth.

I met Helen at lunch the next day, and by that time she had a good deal to tell me. As she joined me at the table I thought she looked happy and confident, and I knew that the relief of unburdening herself to me had been a blessed thing for her. She sat down beside me, put her hand over mine and looked into my eyes with such frank and undisguised love that my heart nearly stopped beating.

"I saw Syl," she told me. "I saw him this morning before he went to the office. He wants to see you, Halley. I'm so glad, darling, oh! I'm so glad! It makes everything so much better."

"That's wonderful," I said, and it seemed to me that she had worked a miracle. "Tell me what he said. Tell me everything."

"Just at first," she said, "he wasn't sure, then he said he'd always been specially fond of you and he'd never stopped being fond of you. He said that if you didn't stay too long—he gets tired easily, you know —he'd like you to go and see him this afternoon, about five. He said, 'Tell Halley to come around and have a glass of sherry with me. I've always believed that he did what he could.'"

I was moved and grateful.

"And did you tell him I'd be there?" I asked.

"Yes," she said. "I knew you would, so you needn't bother to ring him up. Just go."

After a waiter had brought our drinks I asked about her father and Rosie.

"Daddy said he'd rather not see you just now," she told me. "He said it would bring back too many unhappy things, but that he'd think it over and see if he could get used to the idea. Rosie was furious with me for seeing you. She said I was callous and a rene-gade. I love her very much, but we couldn't look at things more differently if we tried. It's odd, Halley, isn't it, that even when I was a little girl I understood you better than Rosie did? I used to wish and wish that I were in her place and she in mine. You never knew that, did you?"

I looked at that charming face and I knew, beyond all doubt, what I would have been saying to her now if Flavia's father hadn't caught his fingers in the door of his car that night so that I had to go to Queen's Hall alone. And then I was at once sickened by my own disloyalty. I knew, of course, that I ought to tell her everything and tell her now, but I was afraid that if I did I wouldn't see Syl that afternoon, or perhaps ever. Then, mercifully for me, the waiter was there with an enormous menu, and we had to decide what we would have for lunch.

We sat a long time over lunch talking and I was amazed at how much she remembered about the past. She remembered things I had quite forgotten, small, amusing incidents in which we had both taken part and I saw with pain and delight how important a part I had always played in her life. It seems inconceivable that I couldn't bring myself then to tell her about my marriage, but there was the fear that it might spoil my meeting with Syl, and there was my reluctance to shatter this new and happy relationship which was so healing to both of us. I can only say, in my own defense, that I meant well. Like my father, like all my family, I hated the unpleasant duty. There would be a moment, I still believed, when it would be easy to tell her, though my common sense told me that it was becoming every instant more and more difficult. She was a dear and familiar part of my life to which I seemed to have returned as to a safe harbor. When I looked at my watch at last it was after three, and still I did not want to let her go.

"What shall we do," I asked, "between now and five o'clock?"

"I ought to have been back at the art school long ago," she said, "but it's so late now it's hardly worth while. Did I tell you, Halley, that I'm taking a course in commercial art, too?"

"No," I said, "you forgot to tell me that."

"Well," she said, "you never know, these days. I want to be able to earn my living if I have to. Most of the young wives I know are getting themselves jobs, or trying to get them, until the Depression ends."

"Then, I suppose," I said, "there'll be a wonderful crop of babies."

"Oh, millions and millions," she answered with a laugh. "But Rosie won't wait, you can be sure of that. Well, we ought to go, I suppose. The waiter's getting restless. Would you like to go to a movie?"

"Heavens no," I said. "We couldn't talk. Let's go to the Metropolitan."

"Oh!" she cried, "yes, I'm so glad you want to. I'd love to go with you. It's because of you and Uncle Myron that I got interested in painting in the first place. Did you know that?"

"No," I said, "I didn't know."

But it was just one more thing to bind me to her.

We left the restaurant and presently we turned right, up Fifth Avenue. She took my arm and we walked all the way to the Museum like that, talking.

"I used to get furious with Rosie," she told me, "because she scoffed so about your collecting drawings. She used to say it was ridiculous for you not to interest yourself in something really worth while."

"Like making money?" I said. "Well, I think now she was right."

"All the same," she went on, "I was proud to tell her last night that you went straight out and got yourself a job in London without any trouble at all."

"I'm afraid that's not strictly true," I had to confess. "I spent a lot

[258]

of time looking for something, and I'm not earning much now. Only just enough to get by."

"I wish you lived over here," she said, "but anyway, you'll come back soon, won't you, darling? I can't bear it if you don't."

"I'll come back," I said, "but I don't know when. I only wish I could tell you."

The first thing we did when we got to the Museum was to go and look at Renoir's "*Au Bord de la Mer.*" They had been changing things about, but Helen knew exactly where to find it. It had been in the Metropolitan for some years now.

"I've often come here and looked at it," she said. "Partly because I like it for itself, and partly because it reminds me so of Aunt Ruth."

She looked at me and smiled and suddenly I knew that what I had done was to dig a deep pit for myself and fall straight into it, and now there seemed no way out. And then the desperate thought came to me that there was a way out. I could go back to London and tell Selma everything and find out if, loving and generous as she was, she could find enough love and generosity in her heart to let me go. Yes, I would even do that. Because I had committed a youthful folly, partly through pity, partly through the need to have some life of my own, must I be deprived for the rest of my days of what would make me happiest? The family need never know. There would be no necessity to tell anyone, I decided. Somehow, quietly and discreetly, I would undo what I had done. It had been the briefest of marriages; Selma was young, sturdy, self-reliant, and she had the gift of being happy. I was sure I could make her understand. I was even sure that in time she might forgive me. I thought of desertion. I didn't know how long it would have to be, but I imagined only two or three years. I was thinking all this as I stood, with Helen's arm through mine, looking at the little woman sitting in her wicker chair against a background of cliffs.

"That," my father used to say, "is what a woman's face should be like."

It was not unlike Selma's face; but Helen's face on the contrary was finely boned and cleanly modeled, with delicately regular features. What had my father not been mistaken about, I thought. Need I follow his advice in anything?

I said, turning away, "Let's go and look at the Sisleys. I'm not sure I don't like him the best of them all."

Syl had the same two colored women looking after him, Mimi and

[259]

Pearl, mother and daughter, and it was Mimi who opened the door to me. I had known her all my life and she was quite an old woman now. Her thick kinky hair was gray and she wore steel-rimmed spectacles. More than ever, I thought, she looked like the knitting sheep in *Alice*. *Alice in Wonderland? Through the Looking Glass?* I was not sure which, it was so long since I'd read them. She was very glad to see me and she took my hand in both of hers.

"Seems jes' like old times, Mr. Halley," she said, and her eyes were shining. "I'm real glad to see you again. Pearl, she's out, but she said to give you her best."

In the old days she would have asked about all the family but this time she did not, and of course I didn't expect her to. Syl was not in the living room when she showed me in and as I looked about me I saw that, with one exception, everything was just as it had always been. There were the same Currier and Ives prints, the same old maps, the same pieces of early-American furniture, and the only new thing I saw was a big radio-gramophone combination in a handsome mahogany case. I could well imagine—and now I could better understand it—that listening to his favorite records was one of Syl's chief pleasures. I went and looked at the big framed photograph of Fred that had stood on the writing table ever since Fred had had it taken, at the time his engagement to Clarisse was announced. He had given one to Clarisse and I think one to my mother too, but I had never seen either of them since the wedding day. He was smiling a little, showing those fine, regular teeth of which he took such care, and it was a candid, open, still boyish and very happy face.

"Why didn't Fred know it?" I had heard Helen ask only yesterday, speaking of the transience of sorrow, and I wondered if her words were not for me to take to heart too. How long would Selma's sorrow last? And mine? For I would suffer too. For a year? Two, perhaps? I tried to put the thought away.

It was a pleasant room, and there was nothing in it to suggest that it was fifteen stories up, in a modern apartment house, or that from the windows you could see, far below, the ceaseless flow of Park Avenue traffic. It might have been a room in a house in Salem, Massachusetts, or some such old American town. It was as pleasantly old-fashioned as that, and I liked it.

I was looking out of the window when Syl came in, and I turned around quickly and faced him. It was a moment I had dreamed of for so long and had rehearsed in my mind so often that now that it had come I could do and say nothing. But he came straight up to me, not trying to hide the emotions he felt, and put his hands on my shoulders. I put my hands over his and we stood looking at each other. There were tears in my eyes and in his too, and his mouth was working uncontrollably.

"Halley!" he said, and at first it was all he could say. He kept patting my shoulders. Then he said, "Halley, it's good to see you. You can't guess how good. I'm glad you came, Halley-boy."

No one had ever called me that except Fred and I was sure that he knew it and that he was absolving me from blame, both on his own account and on Fred's, and that he knew I would understand.

"Syl," I said to him, "I've wanted this for so long. I've even dreamt about it. I can hardly believe it's happened at last."

He took my arm and led me to the sofa and we sat down.

"My dear boy," he said, "I'm so glad, now, that you're here. I'm so glad. When Helen told me, I wasn't sure. I'm getting old, and—"

He broke off, and I said, "But Syl, you look just the way you always looked, to me. I can't see any change."

He took out his handkerchief and blew his nose.

"There," he said, putting it away, "I'll be all right in a minute. I get worked up. That's the worst of being an old man." He smiled at me then, and it was the smile I'd always known. I knew that I loved him as I had always loved him.

"Well, well," he said, "you look fine, my boy. Tall and handsome, tall and handsome."

"I'm only just five feet eleven," I said.

"Well, maybe I've shrunk," he answered. "You look taller to me."

I had told him he looked just the same, and in a way it was true because everything about him was so familiar to me, even his way of blowing his nose and the sound it made. His hair was even thinner and he stooped more, but his eyes had not lost their look of humor and of shrewdness and now that I was with him again the years seemed to fall away. It was hard to believe that he wouldn't be coming around to Sixty-sixth Street the next day for afternoon tea with my mother, with some little gift in his pocket for me or for his "little sweetheart." My being there with him must have made him feel much as I felt.

"My boy," he said, "I'm happier to see you than I can say, but all the same this isn't going to be easy for either of us. I never wanted to pick up the threads again, even supposing there were any left to pick up. Too much was broken and destroyed. When I left your house that day—you weren't there—it was just as if a whole life had ended. And then, when that terrible thing happened—well, there wasn't much left. My friends have been mighty good to me, they've done their best, but nothing will ever be the same again."

"I know, Syl," I said.

"I wiped you all out of my heart and out of my life," he went on, "the whole lot of you. Do you know why I'm seeing you now?"

"No," I said, "but I hoped with all my heart that you would."

"Well, I'll tell you. I wouldn't have risked getting myself worked up like this if it hadn't been for Helen. She wanted it, and she wanted it badly. That girl makes up to me for a good deal, Halley, and I'd do pretty near anything for her. She wanted me to see you and that's why you're here. And now that you are here I'm glad."

He took my hand and held it on his knee.

"I keep thinking of you all the time, Syl," I told him. "You were always terribly important in my life, and you still are."

He smiled at me, showing those big teeth.

"You talk just like a young Britisher," he said, "but never mind about that. Halley, I want to tell you something. You're the best of them all. You won't like my saying this because you're loyal, and that's the way it ought to be in a family, but keep your loyalty within limits, my boy, keep it within limits. Do you know what I mean?"

I nodded.

"I ought to have said it to you before," he went on, "and I ought to have said it often, but maybe it wouldn't have done any good. Don't let loyalty to your family go too far. You've got your own life to live. Well, for God's sake go ahead and live it. What are you doing now? Still tied up to your mother's apron string?"

"Well, no," I said. "I don't live at home now. I live on my own in London. I've got a job there in a picture gallery. I go home quite often, of course. Every other weekend."

He was looking at me closely and he still kept my hand in his. I thought, "Now I can tell him," but he gave me no time.

"Don't you let them run your life for you," he said. "Stay away. They've got Clarisse—yes, I know she's married but I'll bet they've got her just the same, and they've got Julian. You keep out."

"Syl," I said, "I know very well what you're trying to say to me. You think I'm blind to everything, but it isn't so." And then I went on to say to him what I never thought I could say to anyone, but it was something I wanted to clear up once and for all. "I know that Clarisse did a terrible thing. I knew it all the time. And I know how wrong my father was in the way he backed her up."

"And your mother," he said. "Both of them."

"All right," I answered. "Both of them."

His hand tightened on mine.

"They never in all their lives looked an unpleasant fact in the face," he said. "Never once."

"I know," I agreed, "and I'm just the same."

"No," he said, "not you, Halley. You're all right. I always knew you would be if you had the chance."

"I'm afraid I'm not," I told him. "I'm afraid I'm just like the others. We're all the same. That's one reason it's so hard for me to criticize them."

Syl raised my hand in his and brought it down sharply on his knee.

"Then get out," he cried. "Get right out while there's still time. Get out and come on over here and leave the lot of them. No, don't interrupt me—" (I thought I saw my chance then to tell him everything)—"just let me say my say. Just you listen. You come over here and I'll fix you up in a good job. What you're doing over there is no sort of job for you. I'll get you something better than that. Mind you, it won't be easy. You haven't got a college degree, you were snatched out of Harvard halfway through. Well, that was partly your own fault, I guess. You could have stayed if you'd wanted to badly enough. If you'd been mine you'd have finished at Harvard and then you'd have gone to the Business School. Well, all the same, I'll fix you up in something. You've got brains if you're willing to use them, and I'll see you get a good start. Now just you be quiet a minute longer. I haven't finished yet. There's a whole lot I want to say to you. It may be that I'll never talk to you or even see you again, because you've got some of your father's stubbornness in you and maybe you won't take my advice. What I'm going to say to you now is something you've never heard before. I knew your grandfather well. He was a damned unpleasant old curmudgeon but he had his good qualities too. He had perseverance and he had courage. He got to love money too much but his story is the story of plenty of small-town boys who've got on in the world. Your father despised him. He didn't despise his money but he despised him, and he only got on with him after he came back from Paris because he wanted what the old man was going to leave behind. Well, you think back sometimes to that tough old spitting, swearing vulgarian, but think back to him with some respect. He made the lot of you. He bought your father's pictures, every darned one of them; he gave you your easy lives; he got that sister of yours married to her French Count, and much good it'll do her; he made you the agreeable young gentleman you are and he made Julian the poor good-for-nothing he is, more's the pity. Your father has told you a lot of funny stories about the old man and he's taught you to despise him too, but I'll tell you one thing about him that maybe you don't know. He was honest. He was honest to the bone. Now I believe you've inherited one thing from him; I believe you've inherited his honesty. If I didn't believe it I wouldn't have said to Helen what I said to her yesterday."

He paused only long enough to allow me to say, "I wish that was true, Syl. I'm not honest, and I'm a coward. I—"

"Stop running yourself down," he broke in, "and listen to me for a minute or two longer. You'd better hear everything I've got to say. I told Helen I'd see you because you were the best of them all, and I told her at the same time that I wouldn't see your father if he came crawling to me on his hands and knees to beg my help. And I guess that's what he'd like to do, isn't it? I guess he'd like to because he's in trouble right up to the neck. That's so, isn't it?"

"Yes," I answered, and I let it go at that.

"All right. I knew he must be because I know that Conrad Falke is a stuffed shirt and doesn't know enough to come in out of the rain, even though it's been raining since the fall of 1929. Moreover, he's in a peck of trouble himself. Well, there's just one thing I'll do for your father. You can pass the word along to him that he'd better get out of the hands of C. Falke and Company and get out quick."

"He has got out," I said. "He went to see him yesterday. He's finished with him."

"About time," he remarked. "Then there's nothing at all I can do for him. I'd hate to see every last cent of old Gideon's money go down the drain."

"I guess about three-quarters of it has gone already," I told him.

"Well, better men than your father have taken worse knocks during these last few years." He broke off to say, "Do you want any sherry? I forgot to tell Mimi. I never take it myself, but if you want some go and ask her for it."

"No thanks, Syl," I said. "I don't want anything."

"All right," he replied. "Now let me finish what I've got to say because I'm not going to let you stay very much longer. Now listen to me, boy. I'm not going to beat about the bush, and here's what I've got in my mind. I never bore you any ill will because of Rosie. I understood about her, and it was one of those things you were pretty likely to drift into, seeing each other as much as you did. You and she didn't suit each other and you never would, and thank heaven she's found the right person for her now, though he's a Goddamn bore. But Helen's another matter." He hesitated here and looked closely at me, and then went on, "It seems to me she's got pretty well everything a girl ought to have. She's got brains and good looks and common sense, and—well, let's come straight out with it—she's been crazy about you, she tells me, since she was fourteen years old. She said this morning that she thinks you're pretty fond of her, too. Well, now here it is. Maybe I'm just talking out of turn, but if you want to marry Helen and come over here and live, and take that job I'd get for you, I'll help you in every way I can. How about it? And maybe, in time, we could patch things up. I mean all of us. Your father and mother too. I want to forgive them, I've prayed over and over again for the power to forgive them, the way I know I ought to do. I've prayed that my heart might be emptied of all hate. I tell you again I wouldn't help your father *financially* if he came to me on his hands and knees, but if he came to me and said, 'Syl, Halley wants to marry Helen; what are we going to do about it?' I'd give him my hand. I'd give him both hands. There's been sorrow and misery enough, and if it would make you and Helen happy—"

He broke off, and now at last I had a chance to speak and I had no alternative but to take it. I loosed my hand from his and got up and went to the window, feeling as I always felt at moments like this—miserably stirred up inside. I was pretty sure I wouldn't be, but I felt as if I might be sick.

"Please, Syl," I said, "don't say anything more until I've had a chance to tell you something. Please!"

When I turned and went back to the sofa he was wiping his pince-nez and he looked up at me with a puzzled frown. I stood squarely in front of him. I didn't want to sit down again because I had a pretty good idea that I wouldn't be there very much longer.

"Syl," I said, "here's what I have to tell you. In May of this year I was secretly married in London to a girl named Selma Jackson. None of the family know it yet. I haven't had the courage to tell them. Nobody knows—I told you I was a coward and I am. Will you please let me tell you the whole story?"

He slowly settled his pince-nez back on his nose and slowly put away his handkerchief. His eyes were staring and his mouth was tightly pursed up over his big teeth. He said, never taking his eyes from mine and speaking slowly and carefully, as if he had to, to keep his voice and his words under control, "I think you've seen Helen twice. Is that right?"

"Yes," I said, "but—"

"Twice," he interrupted, "yesterday and again today. She said she was lunching with you today, and my guess is that you were together until you came here to see me. Is that right?"

"Yes," I said again.

"That means that you've been with her, if I'm not mistaken, four or five or maybe six hours. Is that correct?"

"About six hours," I agreed. "Perhaps six and a half."

"Long enough for her to fall in love with you all over again and for you to give her the idea that you were just about ready to fall in love with her."

"Yes," I said, "I guess that's true."

"*And you didn't tell her.* I don't want to hear what your reasons were. I just want to tell you that you'd better get out of here and get out quick."

"Syl!" I cried out, and I was desperate, now, to be heard, desperately anxious to make him listen to me. "Syl, just give me a chance to explain why I couldn't—"

"Just get out," he repeated, staring at me. "Get out. You're all the same, the whole lot of you."

"If only you'd let me tell you," I cried, but he only said, once more, and with a sort of anguished ferocity, "Get out" and he suddenly covered his face with his hands and slowly bent his head, almost to his knees, as if he were praying.

I saw that as things were I hadn't a hope of explaining away those hours during which I could have told Helen the truth and hadn't. I saw that I could only do him harm by staying. I said, in a low voice, "Good-by then, Syl," and turned and went out of the room and into the hall. I couldn't make a quick exit because Mimi, in the way of American servants, had taken my coat and hung it on a hanger in the coat cupboard, and my hat was there too. When I had found them and put them on, I glanced back into the living room and Syl was still sitting there, bowed down, with his hands over his face. I went out, closing the front door as softly as I could, and rang the bell for the elevator, and it was the worst moment in my life except one. The elevator was slow in coming and as I waited I watched the lights indicating the floors it was passing flashing on and off until it reached the fourteenth and then the fifteenth floor. The doors had opened and I was just stepping inside when I heard Syl's voice behind me.

"Wait a minute, Henry," I heard him say. "I want this young man back again."

I don't believe I have ever experienced such an overwhelming feeling of relief and pure gladness as I felt then, and as long as I live I shall never forget it. We went back into the apartment again and as we went through the hall I just flung my hat and coat on a chair. It was like a joyful homecoming after years of absence.

"Sit down again," he said. "Sit right down on the sofa and tell me the whole story. I was wrong. I was judging you without a hearing, and nobody's got the right to do that. I was adding to my own burden of sorrow just when I needed most to lighten it. You haven't turned from the boy I'm fond of into a villain just because of what you've done. Now go ahead and tell me why you did it."

I was there for another hour or more. We talked my situation over and over. It was unspeakably good to have him for my confessor and no one else could possibly have filled that role as he did.

"Well, boy," he said, "what you've done isn't as surprising as it looks at first glance. I guess it was just your way of breaking away without breaking away. I see it now, and it's all part and parcel of the way your family always tries to conduct itself. It's the damnedest thing and it runs right through each one of you. What worries me most is your not telling Helen. How are you going to stop acting like a coward?"

"I just don't know," I answered, and it was true that I didn't know.

"Maybe your marriage will do something," he said, "but only if you stick to that girl and do the right thing by her and make her happy. Are you prepared to?"

"Good heavens, yes!" I told him, and I was absolutely sure that I meant it.

"You know," he said, "thinking it all over I don't believe it would have worked, if you'd married Helen. You'd only be returning to the past again, both of you, and anyway, you're too much alike. You were brought up pretty much the same in some ways. Helen would have got out of that apartment with its closed-up bedroom and gone to Bryn Mawr as she'd always meant to do if she hadn't been the way she is. But no, she had to stay at home with Irving. She couldn't break away. Well, I guess there aren't many left like that today, and maybe on the whole it's a good thing. And there's another reason why it wouldn't have done. I don't believe the two families could ever have got together again. I was ready to try it, I was ready to do my best, but do you think your mother and father—let alone Clarisse—could ever have looked any of us straight in the face again? They couldn't, and you know it."

"No," I agreed, "I don't believe they could."

"All right," he said. "That's my opinion and I'm glad it's yours too. Now, what I want to know is this. Are you ready to tell Helen?"

I answered at once, "Yes, of course I am. I'll tell her tomorrow."

"That's all I wanted to hear," he said. "Well, you're going to leave the telling to me. You'd both of you get all emotionally worked up and God knows what would happen. Before you knew it you might be promising her that you'd go back to London and get a divorce. I'll tell her. Don't you see her again."

I knew that he was right and that he wasn't just letting me off. It was best that I shouldn't see her again.

"And if you'll take my advice," he went on, "you'll tell your father going back on the boat. He won't jump overboard, and you can get away from each other if you want to. There's always something soothing about a sea voyage and he'll take it better there than he would here. Of course," he added, and he looked at me shrewdly and with his face close to mine, "he'll try to arrange a divorce for you if it takes the last cent he's got. You know that, don't you?"

"Yes," I agreed, "I suppose he will."

"He won't leave a stone unturned," he told me. "He'll make every appeal there is to be made. He'd be as glad to get you away from that girl as he was to get Clarisse away from Fred."

"I suppose so," I agreed again.

"And your mother will do her best too," he said, "in her own quiet way."

I made no reply. Again I knew he was right.

"Well," he said, "you've got some bad times ahead of you, and I'm glad."

We looked at each other and I knew that in a sense I was glad too. I was feeling something of that rare inner elation and excitement that I had felt long ago that day on the Thames, when my father had shown me what I wanted to do. Everything now seemed to be resolving itself; I could begin to see my way, and I felt in some odd fashion newly born. All the difficulties I would have to encounter began to seem to me, if not trifling, at least well within my power to overcome, and I was eager now to meet them. Everything had been changed for me by Syl's coming to the door and summoning me back, and I wished there were some adequate way of showing him my gratitude. I even felt that there was a certain nobility and grandeur in my renunciation of both Helen and the life Syl had held out to me, but it was all a part of the joy of having told someone what so greatly needed to be told, and the elation only lasted until it was time to say good-by.

"I've always been the luckiest of men," Syl told me, "and in that one way I was like your father. I always expected to get by without that kick in the pants that everybody has to get sometime in their lives. Well, I got it, and I needn't tell you that it was a good deal worse than any mere kick in the pants could be. It was as near, I guess, as anyone comes to getting their hearts broken. You know how I loved Fred and counted on him, and looked forward to his taking my place some day, and having children that would grow up to be fond of me. And you know how I loved my little sweetheart. Well, there isn't much left now, and anyway I guess I ought to be taking a little more thought for what I've done with the opportunities that have been given to me and with what it's all about before it's too late."

"Syl," I said, moved, "I hope there'll be years and years still."

"Well," he said, "I don't care whether there are or whether there aren't. I only know one thing. I'm damned glad I called you back a little while ago. I'm going to be glad of that all the rest of my days."

As I walked back to Sixtieth Street afterward my elation dwindled but I am glad to say that my resolution remained. I didn't know whether I was really regretting having to leave New York (and for who could tell how long) or not; I only knew that in losing Syl I was losing something I needed, something that was totally lacking in my life: guidance, a shrewd sane outlook, a salty humor and honesty, the capacity to call things by their right names. Sentimental, yes, almost embarrassingly so, and I winced and always had done at his calling Clarisse his "little sweetheart." But all the same there was no one like him, and as I reached the hotel I realized that Syl was the nearest thing to a father I had ever had, and that he had handled with sure wisdom and healing this crisis in my affairs. I had for a long time been seeing myself as a pretty poor thing: weak, blundering, contemptibly cowardly. I had come very near—in my heart I had actually come—to betraying Selma, whose place in my life and in my affections I had believed to be permanent and unassailable. The discovery that this was not so was horrifying. I suppose that in everyone's life, if it could be searched out, there comes a feeling of

[269]

almost total abasement, such a disintegration of self-esteem that anything may happen. After that there may be a rapid descent into a quagmire of ineffectualness and self-pity unless something from within or without arrests it. What had happened to me that afternoon was quite possibly crucial. And not only crucial; it was, in a way, deeply and darkly enjoyable, as if I had at last cast off some horribly unbecoming and shameful garment and knew that I need never wear it again.

I think in fact it marked the beginning of my adult life.

XVIII

To KEEP A PROMISE THAT GOES AGAINST EVERY DESIRE AND EVERY
natural instinct is no easy matter, but I am glad to be able to say
that I kept my promise to Syl to the very letter. I neither wrote to
Helen nor telephoned. Syl had been right and it was better to make
the break a clean one. I could trust him to explain my silence and
even to deal gently with my sins, and my punishment was to know
that I was cut off from her perhaps forever. I half hoped she would
despise me, but I knew that she would do no such thing; I knew
that she would guess easily enough why I had found it impossible
to tell her about my marriage; she would understand that I could
not bring myself to spoil the happiness of those two meetings. She
would know that I was a moral coward, but she would also know
that the time I had spent with her had been pure delight to me. "He
who bends to himself a joy"—well, I had certainly done that, and
we were both going to suffer for it, but I thought that some of the
joy would remain, with her too. And she, at least, was free from
any guilt.

My father asked me several times if anything was the matter, and
at last, to keep him from further questionings, I told him I wasn't
feeling very well. He at once suggested ringing up Dr. Medlicott,
but I managed to put him off. I said we would soon be on the boat
again and if I didn't feel any better by that time there was always
the ship's doctor close at hand. This satisfied him, but he kept watching me with anxious eyes.

As soon as I had convinced him that there was not the faintest
hope of a friendly meeting with Syl he was ready and eager to be
off. New York held nothing for him and he was pining to be with
my mother again. He spent an afternoon at the Metropolitan and
a morning at the Frick Gallery. The latter, he said, had been quite
painful to him as he considered that the pictures were overcleaned,
overvarnished and altogether—as he put it—"dolled up as if they

were new." He never once went near the house in Sixty-sixth Street, he said it was more than he could bear, but he told Mr. Dimlock, of Dimlock and Wineberg, who looked after his affairs, that he would accept any offer for it provided it bettered, by at least three thousand dollars, the only offer he had so far received. He said this was little enough in all conscience. He didn't, this time, get his friends together for a dinner party—he talked economy as never before—and he rejoiced to be on the boat again. It was the same boat we'd come over on and he had hardly got on board before the little red rosette reappeared in his buttonhole.

"By golly!" he said to me as we sat down to a very good dinner that night. "It amazes me that anyone who can live in Europe goes on living in America. Would you care to live in America?"

I answered that I really didn't know, that I supposed I was too used, now, to living in Europe to want to go back permanently, but that I was sure I could always adapt myself to living on either side of the Atlantic.

I said this, I realized afterwards, because of a feeling of loyalty I had towards the place of my birth. It was not exactly patriotism —that was something I had never felt—but I was aware of a bond, and one that I had no wish to break. I suspected that someday I might have to make up my mind and choose, once and for all, a permanent allegiance and a permanent home, but I was far from being ready to do so now. The question of where I had most friends did not arise, for I had few friends on either side. Like my father, who was certainly no mixer and only asked to be allowed to spend as much time as possible with his family and in pursuing his own interests, I felt no particular need of close friends. All the same, I had parted from René with a good deal of regret. He had spent two days with me in New York, days when I was thankful to have someone to distract my thoughts, and I liked him as much as ever. I almost envied him his extreme ugliness, which set him apart, and when I asked him if he contemplated getting married, he smiled and said,

"My ugly face and bat ears settled all that long ago. However, all the arts, to have beauty and meaning, must exist within certain boundaries and limitations and you'll see—my life will be an artistic triumph."

He spoke, of course, with his usual irony and not without bitterness, but all the same I thought that what he said was at least partly true. He was now studying nuclear physics and he told me he found it completely absorbing. He said he was like a dog with its nose to a fresh, strong scent, and that he meant to follow it wherever it led him. It was never easy to know when he was speaking seriously and when he wasn't but he told me that, for him, God existed in the atom in His dual role of giver of life and death.

"And nowhere else but in the atom?" I asked.

He shrugged his shoulders and said, "Why not the atom? It is everything and everywhere. What more would you have?"

I told him about my marriage because I now found that each time I told someone about it, it came more easily to me. I had now told Raymond and Syl, and in telling René I felt I was rehearsing what I would presently have to tell my father. I began to find more and more reasons for what I had done, reasons, I am afraid, that were perhaps nonexistent, or at least unrecognized at the time.

I nerved myself to tell my father on the second day, as we were walking about the deck. In spite of my recent rehearsal, I found telling him a very different matter. I began awkwardly and badly and only succeeded in puzzling him so that he burst out, as I delayed getting to the point,

"For God's sake, Halley, what is it that you've done? Robbed a baby's bank? Come out with it. You're only making me more and more nervous."

"All right," I said, and I felt the usual sinking of the stomach, "I will come out with it. I'm married. I got married in London, in the spring. I've been married since May sixteenth."

He was incredulous, too stunned and shocked to take it in or believe it. He seemed to think I was preparing some sort of stupid practical joke, or just pulling his leg. It lay so far outside the bounds of probability that he simply could not credit it. We kept walking round and round the deck, meeting and sidestepping the same people—once again it was rough and promenaders were comparatively few—and he kept telling me, over and over again, that he refused to believe what I said, that no son of his could conceivably do such a thing.

"You can't mean *marry*," he cried, and he looked so terribly distressed that one or two people stared at him curiously.

"But I do mean it," I said.

"You can't possibly mean it. What you mean is that you've been having an affair with some girl and you've gone through some foolish ceremony to please her. I've felt all along that there was something queer about your wanting to be in London, away from us. Well, other young men have had these affairs. I thought myself in love once or twice before I met your mother. There was Isobel Cléry— I don't mind admitting this now—but of course I knew I wasn't ready for marriage and hadn't met the right woman."

"But, Father," I interrupted, "I mean what I say. I was married at Caxton Hall, in London, by special license. It's legal. I'm *married*."

He persisted, in a bewildered way, "You can't mean it was a proper marriage? Legal and binding?"

He looked as if someone had pulled from under him everything that had seemed to offer a safe foothold. More and more I hated what I was obliged to do.

"Father," I said, and I managed to keep on speaking quietly, "I may be a fool. Perhaps I am, but I'm not a scoundrel. Of course it was a proper marriage. What do you think I am?"

"I don't know what you are," he said slowly, and he looked as he always looked when confronted by a hard, unpleasant and inde-structible fact. "I feel I don't know anything about you. What, in the name of heaven, made you do such a thing? You've ruined your life just as it was beginning. And in ruining your life you've ruined your mother's and mine, to say nothing of the others. I can't go on walking up and down. You'd better come to my stateroom and we'll talk there. This is too much for me."

I followed him down to his cabin on B deck (he had an outside cabin and I an inside one). As soon as we were there and the door shut he sank down on the bed and said, looking at me as if he'd never seen me before, "But were you crazy, were you drunk? That is, if you're telling me the truth and you actually married yourself to a girl like that?"

"But, father," I said, and I sat down in the only chair, "I keep telling you, she's a girl you and Mother could be fond of, and proud of. She's worth fifty of me. She's talented and attractive. She's got a job and she earns more than I do."

"Out of an orphanage," he said, for I had told him this, know-ing it would have to come out sooner or later. "Out of a home. Heaven knows what her antecedents were. Could you have been in posses-sion of your senses? How in heaven's name can we ever tell your mother this? It will kill her."

We were still talking an hour and a half later. I had kept my temper throughout and we had not so far had any really angry words. He was shocked, bewildered and terribly hurt. I thought at last it was best to leave him to himself; I hoped that during the day or in the night some palliative thoughts might come to him; he might say to himself, perhaps, "At least the boy isn't dead. And he hasn't actually disgraced himself or us. It might possibly be worse." What gave him the most anguish was the fact that I had never told them in advance what I proposed doing; had never given them the chance to make me see the folly of it, as he was certain they could have done.

He even said, as Syl had known he would, "I'll tell you what I'll do, and I'll do it if it costs every last dollar I've got in the world. I'll put up the money for a divorce if you'll promise to leave her and come back to us. You've been trapped, like many another young man. But I'll manage somehow. Your mother and I would make any sacrifice rather than see your life ruined like this."

"Thank you for the offer, Father," I said, "but I don't want a divorce, and my life isn't ruined. I love Selma and I want to stay with her, and I'm going to. I'm going to make her a good husband if I can. Now I guess it's time we ended this."

I got up, and he lifted a stricken and despairing face to me.

"You can't mean this, Halley! Do you want to kill your mother and me?"

"I do mean it," I told him. "There's only one thing I'm ashamed of, and that is that I felt I had to do what I did secretly."

I went to the door and opened it. He threw himself down on the bed, his head in his arms, and I heard him give a dry sob and say, his voice muffled, "It will certainly kill your mother. How can we ever tell her? It will kill her."

I went back to him and put my hand on his shoulder.

"Don't, Father," I said. "It'll come out all right. I'm sure it will."

He made no reply but shook off my hand, and I went out and shut the door.

After that we each kept pretty much to ourselves and were silent at mealtimes except that he begged me, again and again, to agree to a divorce. It could all be done quietly, he said, my mother need never know anything about it. When I rejected this once more and told him he was wasting his breath, as at last, after the fourth or fifth try, I did, he avoided me altogether and walked the deck alone, looking pale and strained, and I could see that his anger was growing.

"All right," I said to myself, "if that's the way he wants it." But I

[275]

was as unhappy, I think, as he was. Just before we docked at Cherbourg, he came up to me and said,

"I've got just one request to make of you. I want you to promise me not to say anything to your mother. With her heart as it is, anything might happen, and I presume you don't want to be responsible for her death. I prefer to tell her in the way I think best, and in my own time."

I said I thought he was making a mistake, but that if he insisted, I'd promise. But on thinking it over later I understood. He felt that in this way the whole hateful thing might somehow disappear; that by refusing to recognize it himself and keeping it from my mother it might gradually dissipate, come to some unforeseeable and painless end. It was in fact his way of not dealing with it at all. It was like a nasty boil, to be hidden from all eyes and in time, he believed, it might heal itself and disappear, unseen.

But he had after all one more request to make of me and that was that I should first go back to Paris. This went very much against the grain, for by now I wanted nothing in life so much as to see Selma again, believing that I had only to be with her to rid myself of all my disloyal thoughts. I wanted her to drive Helen out of my heart and my mind, and I was certain that I had only to hold her in my arms to be cured. But my father's appeal, after the blow I'd dealt him, was hard to resist, and I sent Selma a telegram from Cherbourg. He stood beside me as I wrote it out, and he watched me print the words, "Mrs. Prentiss, 241 B George Street, Baker Street, W.1."

"Oh, what a tangled web we weave," I heard him say with a sigh, and I answered, as lightly as I could, "Yes, I guess I'm something of an authority on tangled webs now."

He made a last try.

"I'm ready to help you untangle it," he said, "whatever it costs me."

"Would you mind," I asked him, "never saying that to me again, please? If you do, I swear I'll stay in London and never come back to Paris at all."

He made no answer and we took our seats in the train side by side without another word.

My mother seemed on the whole better. She said she had had no heart attacks, that everything was all right, and that, warned by my father's gloomy letters, she had assumed we would have to move, and had already seen several cheaper apartments, one off the Avenue Victor Hugo that she thought might do.

Clarisse had gone down to the château with Chico, to take possession, as the old man and the remaining daughter had now vacated it, but they were coming back the following day at lunchtime, and we were all to have lunch together. Julian was out when we arrived, but he came in soon after, Karl at his heels. I don't know if what had been happening to me had sharpened my perceptions, but he looked to me as if he had something pretty serious on his mind. He was pale and he had lost weight, and as he was always inclined to be too thin he looked like a candidate for T.B. But I knew this couldn't be so. My mother would have known if there was any danger of it, because the doctor, a clever old man named Rastignac, made Julian come to him for a checkup regularly once a month. I made up my mind that I'd have a talk with Julian before going back to London. He was even more silent than usual, and didn't seem much interested in anything we had to say, except that he looked down at his feet and moved them nervously on the rug— that lock of fair hair falling down over his forehead—when my father was telling him and my mother exactly how he stood financially. Suddenly he looked up to remark,

"You can stop my allowance if you like. I don't care. What you give me isn't a lot of good to me anyway."

"Darling!" my mother protested. "It ought to be quite enough for a young man living at home. Why, you've no expenses at all."

"Money just goes," Julian said. "Anyway, I never seem to have any."

"You aren't even put to the expense of feeding your own dog," my father said to him, sharply.

"I'd feed Karl all right if I had to," Julian said, looking at the smooth, muscular brown body at his feet. "I'd gladly starve myself to do that."

"I wish you wouldn't talk nonsense," my father said irritably. "Why don't you keep an account book? Try budgeting. Find out where the money does go."

Julian murmured something unintelligible. It sounded rather like "You never taught us to think about money," but I wasn't certain, and anyway my father chose to pass it by.

No mention was made of my having seen Syl. His name was not spoken and I concluded that my father would tell my mother about it privately.

I sat looking at her and I was thinking that my father was most probably making a mistake in not telling her about my marriage or allowing me to tell her, but if so, then I had been still more mistaken, and for a longer period. She had taken the news of the alarming decrease in my father's income amazingly well, and had even gone ahead of him in preparing for a change of apartments. She had, I was pretty certain, more resilience than we realized, and I thought she probably possessed more courage than any of us. Dressed as she nearly always was in a simple but skillfully made "little" black dress, she looked to me much as she had always looked, though she was undeniably a trifle heavier, and her pretty face and dark, expressive eyes had hardly altered at all. I wondered at that moment what would become of my father, of Julian, of Clarisse, if anything were to happen to her. I was the only one in any way equipped to do without her, though there was anguish in the very thought of it.

The next morning we all went to look at the apartment off the Avenue Victor Hugo. It was certainly a comedown from the one we had, and it was on the ground floor, which my father didn't like, but the street was quiet enough and the rent was surprisingly low. There was a fair-sized drawing room, a dining room big enough to seat six, or even possibly eight at a pinch, three bedrooms, two bathrooms and a rather dark kitchen.

"What about Arnaud and Angèle?" I asked. I couldn't imagine, even then, having to do without them.

My mother smiled at me.

"Come down to earth, darling," she said. "We'll have to part with them. I've talked to them about it already, and they're quite prepared for it. Arnaud is over seventy, you know, and Angèle wants him to retire soon anyway. She has a sister in Limoges, and I think they'll go there to live."

"Good heavens!" I said. "You move fast, don't you, Mother? Somehow I'd never even thought of you and Father doing without Arnaud and Angèle."

"Well," she said with a sigh, "nothing goes on forever. If we decided to live in the country, they'd like to come with us for a few years, but I can't imagine your father living in the country, or Julian either."

"No," my father said. "Not the country, for me. I'm not dead yet. And you wouldn't like it either, Ruth."

"Perhaps not just at present," my mother agreed.

[278]

One thing worried my father about the apartment. There were no bars to the windows.

"I expect the landlord would put them in for us," my mother suggested, "or we could have them put in ourselves."

"With my pictures," my father said, "and your jewelry, it just wouldn't be safe."

"I don't see why," Julian remarked. "There aren't a lot of burglaries in Paris. Not nearly as many as there are in New York."

"There are plenty of burglaries in Paris," my father insisted. "And anyway, I'm not going to risk it. The value of the pictures is mounting all the time, and it would cost too much to insure them even at their present value."

"Why don't you sell them," Julian asked, "now that you're hard up?"

"Darling," my mother said, "your father has made sacrifices enough. He only has ten pictures left and I hope he'll never, never have to part with any of them as long as he lives."

"They oughtn't to be in private hands at all," Julian said, in a sort of aside. My father merely looked at him and made no reply.

I was anxious to see Clarisse and Chico now, and to see them together. My mother had referred to Chico's passion for flying, saying how much it worried Clarisse, but the way she put it, it sounded as if Clarisse was worried about Chico's safety, which I knew well enough wasn't the case.

"Has he bought a plane yet?" I asked.

"He hadn't actually bought it before they went down to the château," my mother said, "but I had the feeling that he had almost made up his mind to, and that only Clarisse was holding him back."

"Well, I hope she goes on holding him back," my father said. "The whole thing is crazy. And I don't like the way he kept it all dark until after they were married."

"Is that quite fair, darling?" my mother asked. "He talked to us a great deal about flying."

"He never said he wanted to buy a plane," my father argued, "or that Clarisse would be expected to find at least half the money for it." (For Clarisse had told my mother this, and my mother had told him.) "I'll have to have a talk with Chico. It's beyond all common sense."

I didn't know quite what to make of Clarisse when I saw her that day. She looked different, and the difference wasn't of a reassuring kind. For one thing, she was a good deal more made up than she had ever been before, and this gave her face a hard look that I wasn't used to. She had put mascara on her eyelashes, which made her eyes look startlingly big and her face smaller and paler, while her lips were brilliantly red. I thought she looked like a combination of the Blessed Damozel and a Hollywood vamp, and I couldn't take my eyes off her. It was easy to see that the gaiety she had worn on arrival was put on and that she and Chico were a great deal less friendly than they had been. This, I thought, was probably the aftermath of many quarrels. It isn't always easy to tell whether married couples are in love or not because the state of being in love may wax and wane, but liking, affection, friendship are easily seen, and in Clarisse and Chico I could feel their absence all too well.

I wondered, anxiously, what was going to happen. Clarisse showed my parents, even Julian and myself, far more affection in two minutes than she showed Chico in the two hours they were there. Most of the time they didn't even look at each other, and when they referred to each other their words held barbs.

"You know what Clarisse is like when she's decided that she's feeling nervous," Chico said once, and later Clarisse remarked,

"Of course Chico and I never *discuss* anything. He *tells* me what he wants, and that is supposed to be that."

She said it with a little smile, but her eyes were not smiling. At last my father broached the dangerous subject.

"Well, Chico," he said, "I hope you've given up all idea of buying a plane. I heartily disapprove of it."

"Not at all," Chico said looking pleasantly at him. "I have bought it. It belonged to my friend Georges Cartier, but his eyesight is not very good now, and he offered it to me. It is an American plane with two engines. In excellent condition. I am delighted with it. He keeps it at Le Bourget. I saw Georges—he is a neighbor of ours in the country—and bought it from him yesterday. So now I am happy. I am like Julian," he said, with a laugh. "All his life he wanted a boxer. All my life I have wanted my own airplane. Now we are both content."

My mother and father looked at Clarisse, and I did too, but she didn't raise her eyes from her plate.

"Yes," she said. "He's bought it." And she made no other comment.

"Well," my father remarked, and there was a general feeling of awkwardness and constraint, "I suppose if the worst comes to the worst and you find it too expensive or too troublesome, you can always sell it."

"I shall never sell it," Chico said, showing his smile again, "unless I sell it to buy a newer one. I expect to use it constantly." He turned to me. "Next time you are in Paris, Halley, and want to go back to London, I will fly you there. It will take about two hours and you would love it."

"Thanks, Chico," I said, "but personally I prefer traveling the way I always do."

"It's astonishing," he said, in mock surprise, "that no one in this family wants to fly with me. Why this dread of the air? In a few years you will all be flying. Everyone will."

"Never," my mother said. "Never, never, and I do hope, Chico, you won't try to persuade Clarisse to fly."

"Yes," my father said. "I wish you'd promise us, Chico, never to urge Clarry to go up. I know she's nervous about it, and it would be torture for her. It would be torture for all of us."

Chico laughed gaily.

"Aha!" he said. "So I see I shall be obliged to find a flying companion, shall I? A sort of air wife? Well, if I must, I must. But I would prefer it to be Clarisse."

Clarisse put her elbows on the table and rested her chin on her hands. She gave him a long dark look.

"You can absolutely leave me out of all your plans for air travel, Chico," she said. "I give you permission, here and now, before witnesses, to take anyone else up you like, but I shall stay on the ground. And that's my last word on the subject."

"Well," he said, looking round at us, "you all heard."

It was an uncomfortable moment, and I said, hastily, hoping to tide it over, "Flavia seems very fond of flying. I don't know anyone else who is."

"Flavia's an odd girl," my mother said. "I like her, but her tastes seem to me extraordinary."

"And mine too, *Maman?*" Chico asked, and he put a hand on hers, affectionately.

"Yes, yours too, Chico," my mother answered, "and if you wanted to please us, you'd give up flying altogether."

"*Mais,*" he said, and he gave her hand a little pat, "*c'est mon métier.*"

Clarisse did not take the news that my parents were planning to move very well. She kept insisting it couldn't really be necessary, and Chico showed a surprise and concern that were obvious to us all.

"It just means," Clarisse said, "that I shall live in taxis, getting from here to there and back again."

"Come, come," Chico said, "I agree that this is bad news, but you still have a home of your own, you know."

Once again she gave him one of those dark looks.

I knew she wanted to talk to me alone, and I am sure Chico knew it too, for he gave us no opportunity. When she asked me if I'd like to come down and see a tapestry they'd brought back from the château, Chico at once said he'd come too, and when she asked me to walk to the nearest drugstore with her later to buy some aspirin, he came with us.

At last she managed to whisper to me, "I'll write you at the gallery. Be sure to look for a letter there, won't you?" (I had urged them to use this address on the grounds that I never knew when I might move again.)

I did manage to have a short time alone with Julian, however, because he drove me to the Gare du Nord later to catch the train for the night ferry. My mother begged him to be careful, because he'd had a slight accident a few days before, a not too serious collision with a taxi. He got me there all right, and with plenty of time to spare, so he parked the car and came with me to the train.

"It's a long time since we've been able to talk, Julian," I said. "Tell me what's up? You seem to me to have something on your mind."

"I've got plenty on my mind," he answered, as we walked up and down. "Who wouldn't have with things as they are?"

"What do you mean?" I asked. "Do you mean Father's affairs?"

"Goodness no," he answered. "Much I care about them. It's the world at large that I mean and the state it's in and the next war, and all that. Father's affairs can go from bad to worse, I don't care. He's nothing but a parasite anyway. Sometimes I'm ashamed to be my father's son."

"Are you?" I said, and I was trying not to be angry. "Then do you know what you ought to do? You ought to stop being a parasite yourself and get out and earn your own living. You make me ashamed of being my brother's brother."

"Well, you needn't get so indignant," he protested, "just because I tell you what's on my mind. You asked me, didn't you?"

"All right," I said, "go on, I suppose you've taken up with 'Peter' again. Am I right?"

"Yes," he said, "Peter and lots of others like him. Well, not like him exactly because there's nobody like him. He's the best and the finest person I ever met. I'd do anything for him."

"And just what are you doing?" I asked.

"Helping the Cause as well as I can," he replied, and he wouldn't meet my eyes.

"How?" I asked. "And just exactly what is the 'Cause'?"

I saw the same embarrassed look on his face that I so often saw on my father's.

"I guess you know all right," he answered. "We're making the Revolution. Every sou that I can scrape together goes towards helping. I tell you, they're a fine lot of people, and they're all good friends of mine too. They like me. They're the only friends, except Henry and Vera, that I've ever had."

"Poor little orphan boy," I said. But I knew sarcasm was no good. Julian was helping himself with both hands to something I'd helped myself to, and equally secretly; something of his own, something that hadn't been given to him by my father. I understood only too well how and why he'd got himself involved in all this. I promised him I wouldn't be sarcastic again and I got him to go on talking till it was time for me to get on the train. He believed, now, that Russia was going to save the world. He said he hoped to live to see the dictatorship of the proletariat and that he was ready to die for his beliefs. He said he had a perfect right to do what he was doing and still live at home. If he was a parasite on my father it was in a good cause, while my father had been a parasite all his life long for his own selfish purposes.

"What has he ever taught us?" he demanded with a ferocity that seemed to me as unreal as all the rest of it. "Nothing but lies. Bourgeois lies. I feel sick when I think of them. I feel as if I could never get myself clean. The only way I can justify my existence is to do what I'm doing. And now he talks of cutting down my allowance! Well, if he does, I'll have to find some other way of helping, that's all."

Silly nonsense, I thought, but I knew he was getting something out of it that he badly needed. I couldn't believe there was very much harm in it or that it was ever likely to come to anything. I even suggested to him that his friend Peter, if he valued his services and his friendship, might at least give him some sort of paid job.

"There aren't any," he said. "We all give what we can, freely. I don't know how some of them live. They're heroes! Peter's got a nephew about my age, his name's Peter too but they call him Peterkin, and he sells papers, but still he manages to give so much a week for the Cause."

A light attack of measles, I thought, and by no means uncommon at his age. I had heard talk like this at Harvard. All the same I felt it might involve him in some sort of trouble and I urged him to give it up and interest himself in something nonpolitical.

"There's nothing else in the world that interests me," he replied.

I even thought, as we walked up and down the platform, that I would tell him, the next time I was in Paris, about myself and my marriage, and urge him to come to London to stay. I thought he might even lend a hand in the gallery. But then I remembered Karl, who was sitting waiting for him in the car. Julian would never go anywhere without him and he would never consent to the necessary six months' quarantine which bringing him to England would involve. I gave the whole thing up, said good-by, begged him not to commit any follies and took my seat. I thought he looked very pathetic as he stood on the platform waving to me. He was a prisoner (as I had been and in some respects still was), though he was a prisoner who was trusted a little way outside his prison, and he was snatching at his freedom as best he could. I felt deeply sorry for him, but there seemed to be nothing I could do. I had plenty, besides, to occupy my thoughts, and I believed that I too deserved some pity. But even my private anxieties failed to keep me awake for more than an hour after I got into my berth, youth and sleep being the good allies they are.

XIX

Selma, as i had guessed she would have to be, was already at the office when I got back. There was a bowl of chrysanthemums on the table in the sitting room, reminding me that a London winter was well under way, and the little shabby place was as neat as a pin. There was a note for me on the dressing table where I went at once to look for it. She had written:

My dearest darling, welcome home! I'm coming back for lunch. There's plenty to eat, cold meat and other things, but will you please go out and buy a head of lettuce? I was horribly disappointed that you didn't get here on Sunday, but I understood why. I'll be back at one, and I'll tell you then how much I adore you.

Selma

Everything came back to me now, everything of her and her personality and all that there had been between us. Her face, which had eluded me lately, was before my eyes now as clearly as if I were actually looking at it. And as I took possession again of Selma and my life with her I wondered sadly and with shame at the errant disloyalty of the heart. For a while I had not wanted to go on, but to creep back. Helen had been a part of my too happy and untrammeled youth; she was a part of that charmed circle in which I suppose I had secretly wanted to stay forever. No new face could have tempted me as hers had done, and she had had the dangerous power to lead me back to the place in time where I most wanted to be. That I understood this now was at least something gained.

I found in the cupboard the half bottle of gin I had left there and the remains of some Noilly Prat, so I mixed a cocktail, and when I went out for the lettuce, I got some ice from the fishmonger's. I knew my way around lower Baker Street pretty well now, and knew the shops that Selma went to. By the time she got back I had unpacked, set the table, washed the lettuce, made the salad dressing

—as taught me by Angèle—and everything was ready for her. Then I heard her come in. She gave the street door a pretty good slam to announce her arrival and came running up the stairs, breathless with hurry. She came in laughing, dropped her handbag on the floor, and flung herself into my arms, and that sturdy body and those kisses, frantic with joy, gave me back what I feared I had lost. Here and now were together again, and all-important, and I could even forgive myself all my late disloyalty because it was a part of my adolescence, and had nothing to do with what I was and felt now.

After our first kisses and embraces she put her face on my shoulder and sniffed my coat.

"I can smell New York," she cried, laughing. "New York and Paris too. How lucky I am to have a husband who brings me back the places I'll never see."

"You will see them," I said, "and Paris maybe, sooner than you think. I've told my father."

Her head came up quickly and her eyes were wide with amazement.

"You've told him? Oh, Halley, I never expected that. When did you? I don't know how anyone could be so brave!"

I told her the how and the why of it as we were having lunch. She asked if my father had been as shocked and horrified as I had thought he would be.

"Quite as much, I'm afraid," I answered. "Even more."

"He doesn't want to see me, just in case he might find he likes me?" she asked, trying to smile.

"No," I replied, "and let's not deceive ourselves. It may be a long time before he does."

"Well," she said, "I wish you hadn't made him that promise, that you wouldn't tell your mother."

"I wish that, too," I admitted, "but I had to."

"Suppose your father just decides to keep it to himself?" she asked.

"I'm afraid that's exactly what he will do for the present," I answered.

"Well, anyway," she said, "things *are* better, aren't they? Somebody in the family knows now."

"Yes," I replied, "and a lot of good that does."

"Never mind," she said. "I'm glad. Your father knows, and Raymond knows. Soon there may be others."

"Two other people know," I said. "But I'll tell you about that to-night."

I spent the afternoon at the gallery and found Oakenshaw very depressed. He said he thought he had an ulcer and might have to go into hospital. He certainly looked ill and I could see he was worried.

"I hope you won't go away again," he said. "Things are improving. A lot of people are getting it into their heads at last that there's no better investment than pictures. I even sold those Tiepolo drawings, and for the price I wanted."

I congratulated him. We went over the accounts together and certainly things were looking up.

"If I have to go to hospital," he said, "you'll have to carry on alone. It won't be for a fortnight, if they do decide to operate, so now that you're back I can go to some sales I don't want to miss."

"I hope you'll let me go, one of these days," I said.

He'd never yet trusted me so far as to let me buy anything, but now to my surprise he said I might.

"It was you who advised me to hold on to the Tiepolos," he said. "You were quite right and I'm grateful. After this we'll take turns at going to the sales."

He didn't say anything about raising my pay, but all the same I was hopeful. The trouble was that the gallery was too small. There was room to build on at the back but Oakenshaw thought the moment had not yet come to spend money on enlarging the premises.

That night I told Selma about Syl, and when it came to telling her about Helen, I was honest. If she was seriously troubled she didn't show it.

"I hope it's the very worst wickedness you'll ever have to tell me," she said, and she put her arms around me.

"Maybe I haven't made it sound as bad as it really was," I answered. "It was pretty bad."

"I'll tell you a funny thing," she said. "Whenever I choose a dress I daren't look in the shop windows for a long time afterwards for fear I'll see a dress I like better."

"And what's the moral to that?" I asked, amused by her simile and knowing perfectly well what she meant.

"Well," she said, "after I've worn the dress for some time it becomes mine. It's me, or part of me, and after that I'm not afraid to look. What happened only shows you haven't worn me long enough. I don't believe it would have happened a year from now."

"No," I agreed, "I don't suppose it would." But I wasn't as sure as all that. I suspected that any time I saw Helen again might be a dangerous time for me.

Selma hadn't finished with the subject yet.

"I'll tell *you* something now," she said. "You know my mother's cousin's husband, the one who taught me to play the piano? Well, I went there for a lesson last week, and do you know, the most terrible thought crossed my mind?"

"What was it?" I asked. "I didn't know you ever had terrible thoughts."

"Oh yes I do," she said. "He told me that his wife—she's ten years older than he is—had a serious illness, and might not live very long. And the thought came into my mind, just like that—" she snapped her fingers—"'If she dies, then you can marry me.' You see," she explained, "for a moment I quite forgot I was married. It's true! And I don't even like him very much."

She began to laugh, and I laughed too, and in the end we went to bed happy, and that was one more thing behind me.

I'd taught Selma to prefer a Continental breakfast, and all we had was coffee and rolls and marmalade. She had just put them on the table one morning a few days after this, and I had just finished dressing when the telephone rang. We had only recently got it put in and I wondered who on earth it could be, for the only people who so far had the number were Raymond, to whom I'd sent it on a postcard, Oakenshaw and Edna. I thought it was most probably Edna.

It was Raymond, and he sounded a good deal perturbed.

"Halley," he said, "I hope I haven't done a terrible thing. It suddenly struck me that I might have done, so I'm ringing up in the hope that you can reassure me."

"Why?" I asked. "What's the trouble, Raymond?"

"You may remember," he said, "that when we last talked on the phone I said Lucille and I would rather not see you until you'd told your family about your marriage, and you said that you were going to tell them before you went to New York. May I ask if you did this? I assumed that you would."

"Well, no," I said. "I didn't. The fact is we were still worried about my mother and I didn't like to, then. We just got back from New York the other day. What I did do was to tell my father on the boat, coming home."

"Oh," he said, and he sounded relieved. "Then I presume your mother knows too by this time."

"No," I answered. "I don't think so. I left that to my father, at his request. He may have told her, but I rather think he hasn't yet. Why?"

"Good Lord!" he exclaimed. "What a dreadful thing I've done, then! I've just written to your mother, remembering that tomorrow is her birthday—I wrote yesterday morning, to be exact—and I said that I hadn't seen you lately but that I was looking forward to seeing you soon and to meeting your wife, at the same time. I said I thought you had been very foolish in marrying in the way you had done, but that I hoped it would turn out well."

I couldn't speak for a minute. Then I said, "Well, I guess that's done it."

"I'm extremely sorry, Halley," Raymond went on, "sorrier than I can say, but you see, don't you, that I'm not altogether to blame? I was so sure you meant what you said."

"So I did," I told him, "when I said it, but things got in the way. I'll have to think about what to do. I guess I'd better ring up Paris right away."

"It never even struck me till this morning," he said. "I suppose there's nothing I can do?"

"No," I answered, "except hang up now and let me try to get through."

He hung up at once, and I started trying to get Paris. Selma had already guessed what had happened, and she came and put a cup of coffee on the writing table for me. The connection took about ten minutes, and then Arnaud answered the phone. I said I wanted urgently to speak to my father.

"Angèle has just taken in their breakfast," he said. "I'll call him."

That meant, I knew, that the letters had been taken in too. I broke out in a sweat. In a minute my father came to the phone. I told him as quickly as I could what had occurred.

"Wait a second," he said. "Your mother was just opening her mail. I hope to God—"

He hurried off, and I waited. I went on waiting. Five minutes passed, ten minutes, a quarter of an hour. I sat there with the receiver pressed to my ear, feeling sick with fear.

"She's dead," I said to myself, when twenty minutes had passed. "He'd have come back if something awful hadn't happened."

"Darling," Selma said, with a look at my face, "don't be frightened.

He'll be back soon." She put another cup of coffee at my elbow, and a piece of toasted roll, but I didn't touch them. "She's dead," I said aloud, and I had a terrible ache in my stomach. "I know she is. This is it. This is what we dreaded. Oh, God! Oh, God! Damn Raymond! Why couldn't he mind his own business?"

"If he doesn't come in five minutes," Selma said, "hang up, and try to get through again. You may have been cut off."

It was a comforting thought, but I was sure it wasn't so. There is usually an audible click when a connection is broken. I waited five minutes, hung up, and tried again. After a long wait, the operator said, "I've been trying to connect you again but I'm afraid the party at the other end has left the receiver off. I'll try again in half an hour."

"You'd better go," I said to Selma. "You'll be very late, and Vining hates that. I'll ring you."

"I hate to go," she told me, lingering.

"You'd better go, darling," I said. "If I can't get through in half an hour I'll have to go to Paris myself. Don't you wait."

She went, reluctantly, and I sat there alone. I prayed hard that my mother might not be dead, and I made a vow that if she weren't, I'd never deceive her or anyone again. Before the half hour was up I asked the operator to try again, but I got the same answer. I was just about to ring up Selma to say I was off to Paris when a call from Paris came through. It was my father at last.

"Is that you, Halley?" he said. "I suppose you've been wondering what had happened. The fact was that I've been with your mother all this time and forgot you were still on the phone."

"Is she—how is she?" I asked. My long wait and my fears didn't matter now.

"Well," he said, "better than I could have expected, but she took it very hard, terribly hard."

"In what way?" I asked. "Is she ill? Did she faint?"

"No," my father said. "It was a severe shock—she was reading Raymond's letter when I went back to the bedroom—but she's stood up to it better than I could have hoped. That is, she didn't have a heart attack, thank God, but she just doesn't want to see you. I'd better tell you that right away."

"What?" I cried. "You don't mean never! It just isn't possible."

"She says never," my father answered. "I understand just how she feels. She says if you'd ever felt any love for her at all you could never have done such a thing. She says she trusted you completely. I've done my best, I've tried to soften it down, I've even tried to find excuses for you, though that's the last thing I want to do, but she just doesn't want to see you, at present, and she will not see your wife at any time. She's—I've never seen her like this before. I'm sending for Clarisse."

"But I want to come," I pleaded. "Tell her I long to come. I must see her."

"Out of the question," my father said. "I don't want her upset any more than she is. She's quieter now. I never saw your mother really angry before; she was white hot with anger. She says you've killed all her love for you. I'd feel happier if she were to cry, but she hasn't cried once. Angèle is with her, and I've sent Julian downstairs to fetch Clarry. You might have killed her, you know. I hope now you realize what you've done. To help you to realize it I've stopped your allowance altogether from today. You thought you could get along without us. Well, now see if you can. Good-by."

Dozens of times I had tried to imagine how the news of my marriage would affect my mother, but I had never imagined this. I had been afraid—very much afraid—of what the shock might do to her, but it had never occurred to me that she would prefer not to see me. Her love and forgiveness had easily been elastic enough to cover what Clarisse had done, but I saw now that Clarisse had not sinned against the family, as I had. She had run back to it; my sin was, in my parents' eyes, that I had tried to escape from it.

I bestirred myself at last and rang up Selma to tell her that there was no need for me to go to Paris. Then slowly, in a kind of daze, I put on my hat and coat and went to the gallery. It was lucky that I got there when I did, for I found Oakenshaw doubled up with pain, his face a ghastly greenish white. I rang up his doctor, who arrived twenty minutes later with an ambulance, and I saw poor Oakenshaw taken away to hospital. Altogether it was quite a day. The weather, too, was doing its worst. A bitterly cold rain was falling and as it fell it covered the streets with a thin layer of ice. I shut up the gallery at five and went home and lit the gas fire in the sitting room. It had stopped raining by now, but a black fog had come down, the worst I had ever seen. I was beginning to feel worried about Selma when I heard her shut the front door and come running upstairs, about three quarters of an hour later than usual.

"I came part of the way by bus," she said, "but it was so bad that I got out and groped my way to the Underground, and walked from Baker Street Station. Well, we're cozy here anyway."

I told her all the news. I think what I had to tell her about my mother was a real blow to her, but all her sympathy was for me. She refused, however, to be downcast.

"Darling," she said, "no mother could hate her own son for long. In a month or less, you'll see, she'll forgive you. I know she will."

She was on my lap, her arms about my neck. She always wanted to be close to me when we were discussing anything, in actual physical contact; perhaps just holding my hand, or with her shoulder against mine. That she was warmly demonstrative was to my liking, for I was equally demonstrative myself, but tonight I could not bear to be touched. I put her off my lap.

"Play something to me," I said.

At once without a word she went to the piano. I watched her spread her skirts and sit down on the piano stool, open a book of Schumann's *Études Symphoniques,* look round at me as she always did, and then start to play. As a rule I loved to see her sitting there, the light shifting on her smooth brown hair as she moved her head, but now I closed my eyes. The piece she had chosen seemed to express better than any words could have done all that I felt. It awoke all my self-pity and tears came to my eyes. They were for myself and for lost joys. It had now come home to me with overwhelming force and certainty that I was to be deprived of everything I cared for that was not actually in this room. I realized as I had never done before that my mother had all along been the constructive element in the family life. She, in her quiet way, was the ruling spirit, and I had failed to realize her strength. Always gentle, always loving, there had been something softly implacable behind it all. She possessed a will that more than made up for my father's amiable lack of purpose, and hers had always been the driving power. All this I had now turned against myself and my marriage, and it seemed more than likely that I had destroyed all her trust in me and even her love. The thought was unbearable. And that loss was not the only one, though it was by far the greatest. My life had narrowed down and down, and now there was only this; what I would see when I opened my eyes again. This, and the gallery. I had better like it, I told myself, because there wasn't going to be anything more.

As Selma played and the fog blanketed London, I counted over all the things I would never do or have again. I could never again cross the Atlantic in a fine ship, first class, my fare paid as a matter of course; I would never again be able to go back and forth between London and Paris as other people might take a bus or the tube to Piccadilly Circus and back. I could no longer take taxis when I was in a hurry or wanted to get out of the rain. I could no longer go to good hotels and restaurants, or even take Selma out for the evening unless we chose to go to the Hammersmith Palais de Dance. The theater would only be possible at long intervals, and then in the cheap seats. I could never again order a suit from a good tailor. I was chained up; I was hobbled like a goat in a field. When I had told my father that if necessary he could stop my allowance, I had never believed that he really would. But most of all, worst of all, it had never seemed to me even remotely possible that I might be cut off from him and from my mother. For I knew that whatever line she chose to take, he would follow.

Finally, I thought that in all probability I would never see New York again.

XX

A FEW DAYS LATER I RECEIVED A LONG LETTER FROM CLARISSE, addressed to the gallery. It was about her troubles and mine, and she began with mine.

When Father told me about what you'd done [she wrote], I could hardly believe it. Of course I guessed long ago that you'd got interested in some girl in London, but I thought it was just an affair with somebody and wasn't anything important. I suppose you were tricked into marrying her, though Father says you deny this: I still think it must be what happened as I can't imagine you doing such a thing of your own free will. I'm terribly sorry about it, Halley. I hope I'm not a snob but good heavens! You could have married anybody. Please, please think over Father's offer. If you don't, I'm awfully afraid Mother will never get over it. She says you've done an unforgivable thing, and though she keeps up a brave front, I know this has wounded her as nothing else in the world could have done. She feels that in marrying this girl you've deliberately insulted her and all of us and she says she will never see her as long as she lives.

Julian, when he heard about it, said just about what he might have been expected to say. "Halley never tells me anything, and he gets indignant if I don't tell him everything. Well, I don't care. Let him go his own way and I'll go mine." He seems very depressed about it all.

I suppose the truth is you got carried away by some sudden passion, and now you're having to suffer for it. Well, in a way I almost envy you. Why can't I feel that for *someone?* As you know, I never felt anything like that for Chico and what I did feel for him has almost gone now. I don't think it's my fault, and I never dreamt things would turn out like this. Halley, the truth is he's as hard as nails. *Hard,* all through. He only showed me a softer side before we were married, and I suspect that was put on. The odd thing is that he does seem fond of his aunt and uncle, and I sometimes think he's genuinely fond of Mother, but I don't think he really loves me at all. If he did he wouldn't behave as he does, or make life impossible for me about this business of flying. Why should I fly, if I hate it? He says I won't know till I try. Well, I'm simply not going to try. The whole thing has become a nightmare to me. "If I loved him I'd go up with him." "If I loved him I'd want him to do what he cares about most." And now there's still another thing. "If I loved him I wouldn't mind paying his debts." Yes, that was sprung on me about a week ago. I didn't know he had any debts, he certainly never told me and he was careful not to let Father know. I suppose they aren't enormous, but he insists he can't pay them himself, and he says his creditors are pressing him hard. And yet he put up nearly half the money for that miserable airplane! It's too infuriating, and you wouldn't believe what it costs just to keep the thing at Le Bourget. Now he's gone off to Marseilles in it, and from there he means to fly on to Genoa, so I'm here all alone. I don't know who he took with him, he never told me, but I have a suspicion that one of them was an actress named Georgette Lefèvre. I really don't believe I care. Oh, Halley, how happy I'd be just living at home again, away from all these problems and annoyances!

Father has found someone who wants the apartment—I didn't think he'd have any difficulty in subletting it—and they're going to move into the other one as soon as they possibly can. I hate the whole idea, of course. If Chico is going to leave me alone here, I don't know what I shall do! How sad it is that everything had to change! We were so happy before.

I've been down to the château again, just for a night—I took Phoebe with me and Ben Marshall—and we all three decided it was too dismal for words. Of course the country is always horrible in winter, but the château is gloomy at any time, and now that Chico's father and Madeleine have taken so much out of it to furnish the little house, it looks terrible. Phoebe says I'll never be able to do anything with it, and I'm afraid she's right. I suppose if Chico were different and I were really in love with him, I'd manage to make something of the place, and a few lively young people in it would help, but as it is, I simply haven't the heart to try. And not only that, now that Chico owns this plane he'll always want to fly there—he says he can keep the plane at the airfield near Orléans—and that will make more trouble because I won't go with him.

I know one thing: that if this marriage goes on the rocks as it probably will, unless Chico decides to behave better, I shall never, never marry again as long as I live.

Don't be too unhappy about Mother. I'm sure she'll see you in time when she gets over the shock a little. Nothing will ever make them believe that your wife is anything better than a tart, or that you weren't somehow trapped into it. I'm sorry to have to tell you this, but you can't deny that it's all your own fault—not that that ever makes anything any better. Mother told me she'd had a letter from you and that she does not intend to read it. She says that perhaps in a few months she can bear to read a letter from you, but not now. If you want to know my opinion I think that after a while you'll be able to see both Father and Mother when you like, provided you come without *her*. I'm afraid this is all the comfort I can give you.

Your affectionate sister,
Clarisse

At this period I must have been pretty difficult to live with—indeed I know I was. But Selma seemed to find within herself inexhaustible sources of patience, forbearance and sound common sense. She kept her good temper and her serenity, and she never stopped loving me and letting me know that she loved me. She must have realized that I was like a cutting taken from the parent stem and newly planted, and that time was needed to allow the new roots to form. It was lucky for me in a way that poor Oakenshaw was in hospital for nearly two months so that I was kept very busy. He had had a narrow escape, and when I first went to see him he told me, with a pale smile, that he had no business to be alive. During his absence I managed to make a satisfactory number of sales and whenever I could I went to Christie's and Sotheby's and even now and then to country-house auctions. This was made possible for me by the presence in the gallery of Oakenshaw's niece Theodora, and she was certainly a "gift from God" to me at that time. She weighed, as she was fond of telling me, "just thirteen stone," or a hundred and eighty-two pounds, and she was only eighteen. She had helped in the gallery from time to time in the past when she wasn't acting as nursemaid to a whole brood of younger brothers and sisters, and she knew the regular customers. I don't know how I'd have managed without her.

Early in February I wrote to Clarisse—I had not heard a single word from my parents, who had recently moved into the new apartment—suggesting that she might like to come to London for a while and that during her visit she and Selma could meet. She replied that she was expecting to come to London to stay with Flavia and her husband at the flat in Mount Street, as Chico was away again, and that she'd see me at the gallery, but she preferred not to meet "my wife" as it might make trouble between my parents and herself. She was quite firm about this. I then wrote and asked her if she would at least be kind enough to bring over all the drawings that remained in my diminished collection, of which I thought there were about twenty-five. She said she would, and that she'd be in London in ten days' time and would bring the drawings straight to the gallery. She added,

I don't think my marriage will last very much longer. Chico has gone off in his plane with that actress, Georgette Lefèvre, just the two of them, alone. Phoebe, who knows her, found this out. The truth is, I don't honestly care if he has, but I'm going to find out for certain because I don't think the time is far off when I shall decide to end the whole thing. The Marboeufs can hardly bring themselves to be polite to me now. Having got all the money out of us they can, they've lost interest. I don't think I care much, and I really dreaded having to go there to lunch or dinner. Their dinners, especially, were awful, and they're incredibly mean. The last time we dined there we had the thinnest of clear soup, one small cutlet each with some spinach, and, as a final course, the thing I hate most in the world, a caramel custard. Imagine it!

Flavia's husband, Alex Moray, was now attached to Guy's Hospital, and she was working there too. I wrote and asked her if they would both come and have a drink with Selma and myself and named an evening. I had written to tell Flavia about my marriage some time ago and she'd had Clarisse's account as well, so I wondered if she would come. I needn't have worried my head about it because she rang up accepting at once and asking why I had waited so long to invite them.

Selma was always rather in awe of people she considered "in society," by which I found she meant the sort of people whose photographs appeared in *The Sketch* and *The Tatler,* but she was delighted at the thought of meeting the Morays. Flavia was charming to her and I could tell, without her saying so, that she thought my family were behaving very badly. She and Alex (whom I found I liked very much) went all out to be friendly, and I hoped that they might be able to convince Clarisse that I was not in fact married to a "tart." When I went into the little kitchen for more ice, Flavia followed me out and closed the door.

"But what an absolute little charmer!" she cried, the moment we were alone. "You're a million times luckier than you deserve to be. It's one of the most taking and amusing faces I ever saw. It's the sort of face I'd like always to have about just to keep me cheerful."

I kissed her from sheer gratitude.

"Well, thank God," I said, "that you see her the way I do!"

"But don't be silly!" she said. "Who wouldn't? Anyway, I can tell Clarisse now, and you can be sure I will, that if they choose to go on ignoring her it's their loss rather than yours. Only why in the name of common sense, if you wanted to marry that charming girl, didn't you tell them at the very beginning?"

I thought of Mr. and Mrs. Jackson, and especially of Mr. Jackson smoking his cigarettes, and it was all too complicated and too difficult to explain.

I said, as I put the ice into the bowl, "I guess the reason for it will just have to remain a mystery. I'm not sure I altogether understand it myself, but that was the way it seemed to me it had to be."

"Well," she said, with her usual frankness, "I always considered that you were all a bit odd, but I thought you were the least odd of the family. Is it true, what Clarisse says, that her marriage is breaking up?"

"It looks that way," I said.

"And it looks," she remarked, "as if you Prentisses were pretty good at sticking to one another but to no one else. What are you going to do about that child in there?"

"Stick to her," I replied.

"If you don't," she said, "it's all over between you and the Morays."

They stayed till nearly eight, and then they took Selma and me out to dinner. It was a good evening in every way; my spirits lightened, and Selma kept looking at me to see if I were pleased with her, and was boundlessly happy that I was. We got to bed about midnight, and she went to sleep in my arms like a contented child.

There are few things that so tear at the nerves as the sound of the telephone ringing at some unlikely hour. Ours kept on ringing and ringing that night until we were both startled into full consciousness and I switched on the light, saw that it was just after three and scrambled out of bed to answer it.

It was a call from Paris, and I thought of course that my mother had had a heart attack and I sat down to take the call with all the usual sensations. Then I heard my father's voice.

"Is that you, Halley? Oh, thank God! I thought I'd never get through to you. There's been a terrible accident here—no, not your mother—it's Julian. I'm nearly out of my mind. The doctors are here now, two of them, but they can't say whether he'll live or not. Halley, for God's sake get here as quick as you possibly can. He wants you. We all want you."

"But what is it? What's happened?" I asked, bewildered.

"Never mind that. I can't possibly tell you now. Just get here, somehow. I'm afraid he's sinking—" His voice broke. "Maybe I oughtn't to have rung you up till the morning, but I had to let you know. I thought perhaps you could find some way of getting here. Could you fly?"

"Yes," I said, "of course I could fly, but not till the morning."

"Oh, God!" he cried, and then he sobbed, "If Julian should die—"

"Father," I said, "I wish there was something I could do. Tell Julian if you can that I love him and I'll be with him soon. Tell him I love him very much—"

We could neither of us say anything more, and my father hung up. Selma was beside me in her dressing gown, her eyes startled.

"There aren't any planes to Paris at night, are there?" she asked.

"No," I said. "Not until morning, I guess. How can I find out?"

"Ring up Croydon," she said. "Perhaps there'll be someone there."

"It isn't likely there's anybody there now," I said, "but I'll try."

She was quicker at finding telephone numbers than anyone I ever knew. She had it in about eight seconds, and I asked the operator for the number. He must have known there would be nobody there, but he rang it all the same and then told me there was no answer. I couldn't sleep, and Selma wouldn't go back to bed without me so we made coffee and sat up, playing backgammon, till six. I tried again then, and once more at seven, and that time I got an answer. The first plane to Paris was at nine o'clock. If I hadn't booked a seat, I was told, I'd better turn up there at eight and chance my luck. I said good-by to Selma and took a taxi to the airport, and to my unspeakable relief, it wasn't foggy. When I saw the strange-looking object I was to fly in waiting on the field I knew I would never have wanted to get into it if it hadn't been for some such crisis as this. I had never had sufficient curiosity about the air to go either to Croydon or Le Bourget, as some people did, and whenever I heard the sound of airplanes and looked up to see them in the air, I regarded them as something with which I had no possible concern.

There were ten other passengers on that bleak morning and a bitter wind was blowing across the airfield. The plane had a curious sort of superstructure that looked odd to my eyes, but it seemed solid enough—in fact it seemed to me far too solid ever to get up into the air at all. But as soon as we had left the ground and were up and headed for Paris I felt an odd sort of elation. I was doing something I had never dreamt of doing or wanting to do and liking it, or I would have done in other circumstances. The noise seemed to me pretty bad but I managed a brief conversation with the man next to me, who told me it was his eighth flight. I took considerable comfort from this and tried to read a morning paper but I couldn't keep my mind on it or cease to wonder what could possibly have happened to Julian. If he'd had an accident in the car, I knew my father would have said so, but whatever this was, he had felt he couldn't put it into words. I wondered if it were conceivable that Julian had tried to kill himself. I couldn't believe it of him. For one thing he would have lacked the necessary courage. And why should he want to kill himself—unless, of course, he had got himself involved in some serious trouble? But this seemed to me very unlikely. I tried to stop thinking and to concentrate on the flight and my own sensations, and I looked down and saw, between gaps in the clouds, the wrinkled channel far below. At the end of two hours and a quarter we were in sight of the Eiffel Tower and as the plane began to come down we took what seemed to me a terrific bumping, but to my surprise I wasn't sick though there were others who were. I only had a toothbrush with me and wasn't detained long by the customs authorities, and by twelve-thirty my taxi was slowing down for the turning off the Avenue Victor Hugo, and I was nerving myself to hear something pretty dreadful. The door was opened by a woman named Marie who had sometimes come to help with the cleaning at the other apartment. She looked thoroughly frightened and without speaking to me she ran off to tell my father.

I felt I was at home as soon as I was inside the door. The old atmosphere of home was there, and the familiar furniture, and going into the drawing room I saw the paintings on the walls, and the portrait of my mother facing me as I went in. But I had barely time to observe these things before my father came quickly into the room. His eyes were red and swollen, and he looked as if he'd come to the end of his endurance. I went to him and he held out his arms and gave me a sort of awkward embrace, and then said, in a breaking voice,

"I've just got back from the hospital. Your mother sent me for some of Julian's things. She's there with him. They think there may be a chance of saving his life, but they've got to operate before they can be sure." He looked at me wildly, his hands on my shoulders, holding me at arms' length. "I'd better tell you," he said. Then he turned aside and covered his face with his hands.

"Father," I pleaded, "tell me what happened. Please, quickly, tell me! I'm completely in the dark."

He looked at me again, and his face was anguished and wet with tears.

"I shot him," he cried. "I shot him. I shot my own son!"

I said, as quietly as I could, "You can't possibly mean that."

"I did," he told me, and he took my shoulder and shook it. "I did, I tell you I did! Last night, at two o'clock, with a revolver. It was a revolver Aristide Bloch lent me when I told him I was worried about burglars." He took out a handkerchief and for a moment he buried his face in it. Then he wiped his streaming eyes and looked at me again. "I wasn't sleeping, and at two o'clock I heard a noise in here. Our bedroom's through that wall. I listened, and I heard a window being softly pushed up. I didn't switch on the light because I was frightened for your mother's sake. I took the revolver out of the drawer of the bedside table and crept up to this door. I opened it very softly, and I could see a man's body outlined against the window, which was wide open. I thought he was escaping, perhaps with some of my pictures or your mother's jewelry. I fired and hit him. I heard a terrible scream. I switched on the light and ran forward and, oh God! it was Julian. He was on the floor. I had shot him in the back, and the bullet had gone through the right lung. It's there now."

He could scarcely stand, and I drew him to the sofa, keeping an arm about him.

"But what was he doing?" I asked, and I thought, "This can't have happened to us. It can't."

"I suppose you'll have to know." My father had now got himself more under control, but he couldn't keep back his tears. "Poor boy, he'd got some crazy idea into his head that he had to have more money, I suppose. If only I'd known—if only he'd told me. You know your brother isn't a thief as well as I do. It was just some lunatic idea. He must have been half out of his mind. He had all your drawings wrapped up in a newspaper. He was in his pajamas and he must have been going to hand them to someone waiting outside. Oh, my God! If this is a punishment, what have I done to deserve it? How could I guess it was Julian? What made him do such a thing?"

I kept my arm about him. His grief and remorse were pitiable. It still didn't seem possible to me that this thing had happened in this very room a few hours ago. My mind refused to accept anything so fantastically dreadful. My father raised his hand and pointed.

"It was that window," he said. "Why did he do it? What was in his mind? Can you explain anything? I think I'm going mad."

"It'll be all right," I told him, though I doubted it even as I said it. "Julian won't die, and he's welcome to anything I've got."

"Your mother's wonderful!" he said. "I wish I had half her stamina.

She's bearing up in a way I wouldn't have believed possible. If only she doesn't suddenly collapse."

"If she survives this," I thought, "then she'll survive anything." I asked him where Clarisse was.

"Here, in the spare room," he told me. "The room that ought to have been yours. She's lying down, asleep. The doctor gave her something to quiet her, she was in such a terrible state, poor child. Halley, I must go back now. Do you think you'd better stay with Clarry?"

"No," I said. "I'm coming with you."

"Do you think she'll be all right?" he asked doubtfully. I saw that he hated to leave Clarisse but was anxious to get back to the hospital as quickly as he could, and that he wanted me to come too.

"Marie will be here, won't she?"

"Very well," he said. "I'm all ready to go."

He had some things in a small suitcase in the hall, and we went out and found a taxi.

Julian was in the hospital where Clarisse had been born, the American Hospital at Neuilly. My mother had been determined that he should be taken there and nowhere else, my father told me, and I remembered that she had a distrust of French hospitals that dated from many years back, though I knew of no reason for it.

On the way to the hospital, my father sat staring silently out of the window. I wondered whether or not I ought to tell him what it was that had impelled Julian to do what he had done. I guessed he had hit upon the idea of selling my drawings because they were not sufficiently valuable to cause my father to go to any great lengths to get them back, and also because he could tell his friends they were his own but that in order to avoid being questioned as to his reasons for selling them, he had had to stage a burglary. I could even picture "Peterkin" waiting below to receive the parcel. But apart from all this I knew he would never have dreamt of taking anything of mine, however much he wanted money, if he had not been bitterly hurt. It was a gesture, a way of hitting out at me, of showing me that now he was beyond caring what he did. He had never replied to the letter I wrote to him after my mother had received Raymond's letter, but I had been too wrapped up in my own affairs to trouble about it much. I felt that my part in this disaster was almost equal to my father's, and I knew that his burden would be lightened somewhat by this knowledge. So I told him, and his reproaches were bitter and hard to bear. That Julian had made me promise not to tell carried no weight with him at all. For the boy's own protection I ought to have told.

And then he said something I can never forget.

"It seems to me, Halley," he said, his head bent, his hands hanging between his knees, "and I'm sorry to have to say it, that everything that's happened to us that ought not to have happened is your responsibility and yours alone. Even Clarry's marriage—Fred's death—all that. The break with Syl. Now this. All these things could have been prevented by candor on your part. Then, in addition to everything else, you have to go and secretly get married. Why? Why?" He shook his head. "I don't know what to say to your mother. I just don't know what to tell her. I could so easily have talked to Julian, shown him the folly of all this—and now—oh, God! It's too late, it's too late!"

I was silent. I decided to say nothing more. He could be right, and yet I was perfectly sure he had it all wrong. Discussion, argument, were out of the question, and if I had tried to point out to him his own responsibility, I could never have found the right words, or known how to trace it back to its beginnings. I was condemned, and yet I felt I was entirely innocent. I longed for an impartial judge, but there was none, and there never would be. Nor could I ever appeal from this, his final judgment.

EPILOGUE

My father looked very frail and his thinning hair, his mustache, the blue of his eyes, his once fresh complexion had faded. But every now and then there would be a return of his early gaiety, and he still had much of his old charm. When he took out his handkerchief and I smelt the lavender water he always put on it, I was taken straight back into my childhood.

In most ways my mother was wonderfully the same, though she was now a round little woman with gray hair. She would always be a pretty woman as long as she lived, with her still coquettish feet, her charming features and her great dark expressive eyes, though these last, partly, perhaps, because of the darkening of the pigment around them, looked to me full of tragedy. She and my father and Clarisse had just got off the boat that morning and they were dining with us. Clarisse had gone to someone's house for a drink and would be coming later. Meanwhile we sat and talked and drank sherry, for my father would never touch cocktails.

It was June, 1953, and it was only the second time they had been to Europe since the war. They lived now near Oyster Bay, Long Island, where they had gone in 1939. Soon after Julian's death they had left that ill-fated apartment off the Avenue Victor Hugo and had taken a small house at Versailles. They had stayed on in France as long as they dared, hating to leave until they were sure of what was to come, but Hitler finally settled their destination and now my father had no regrets. His views about many things had changed and I think he and my mother only came to Europe now because Clarisse was restless. They really couldn't see, they said, why anybody shouldn't be content in America nowadays, and on their previous visit—they had stayed three months—they had taken an English couple back with them at wages I could only guess at, so they were well looked after.

My father went to New York once or twice a week and was a

trustee for one or two museums and art galleries. He had written a book on French nineteenth-century art—he began it during the war—and it had had a moderate success. The improvement in my mother's health (I have often wondered how much of her trouble was due to heartburn and Angèle's too excellent cooking) and the fact that Clarisse lived with them kept him happy, and this happiness was increased by the steady rise in value of his remaining investments, particularly industrials, which had reached new heights, though he still bitterly regretted all those stocks he had been forced to part with at rock-bottom prices during the Depression. He had another regret, and that was that he had given his collection to Paris and not to New York. But he still had the ten, and he was toying with the idea of beginning a new collection, though a very much smaller one, of "moderns." He had consulted me about buying a Marc Chagall and a Fernand Léger, but he admitted that he didn't really care for them.

It was nearly time for dinner when Clarisse arrived. She was certainly an extraordinary-looking woman. Her hair, instead of growing darker as most blond hair does, had faded like my father's, but hers—and I am sure it was not wholly due to natural causes—had faded to a strange ashen hue, really no color at all. She was wearing a dress of very bright green silk, cut rather too low, I thought, for the daytime, and the lightest of high-heeled sandals. Her eyelashes were thick with mascara which made her eyes look enormous and dead black, and her lips were scarlet. She was now La Belle Dame Sans Merci but she had no one in thrall so far as I knew but my mother and father. The truth was that she was frightening to most men. She loved clothes and she had bought an interest in a well-known fashion house in New York. The three of them usually spent their winters in Florida.

She kissed Selma very affectionately, leaving a touch of lipstick on her cheek, and then me. I wondered how many martinis she had had, for she undoubtedly spoke with a lisp.

"You're looking marvelous, darling," she said to Selma. "You could be a grandmother and you look about twenty-eight. That's because you don't suffer from nerves."

"Oh, come, Clarisse!" Selma protested. "Dick's only nineteen. Give him time."

"Well, you both look too placid and happy for any words," she said. "Where are the children?"

"You just missed Dick," my mother told her, and she spoke of the children as if they were her own; "he's dining out with some young friends and Paul doesn't get back from school till tomorrow, when he goes to the dentist, but you can see Harriet. Selma's just put her to bed."

Harriet was the youngest, our postwar child. She was only six and Selma liked to get her to bed early as she had had what was mercifully a light attack of polio in November.

"I'll go and see her," Clarisse said, and went out of the room. She moved with all her old grace and elegance, and she had not lost the power to charm me even now.

"How do you think Clarry is looking?" my father asked. He always spoke of Clarisse as if she were some wonderful work of art and he were her proud showman.

"I wish she'd give up that horrible mascara," I said. "It makes her look ghastly."

"Well," my mother said, "I don't like any make-up, but Clarisse says it gives her confidence. It's curious she should say that but it's true, she does lack confidence. And by the way," she went on, speaking quickly and in a low voice, "don't mention George Hambleton. That's all off. He's just married a girl from Pittsburgh. I'm afraid Clarisse minded very much."

"Hasn't he been married rather too often already?" Selma asked in her gently candid way.

"I can't honestly say that either Myron or I liked him very much," my mother answered, "but curiously enough he did attract Clarisse. There was something rather impressive about him. But it's true, as you say, that he's been married too often."

"Clarry's well out of it," my father said. "I don't know how she got it into her head that she wanted to marry him. Just a foolish idea."

He got up and went to look at a framed drawing by Constantin Guys that I'd had since my earliest days as a collector; it was of French cavalrymen riding in helmets and shakos. He must have remembered that it was among the drawings that Julian had taken out of the cabinet that night and wrapped in a newspaper, for he passed it by without a word and stopped to look at the reproduction of Pissarro's "Approach to the Village" that I'd given to Selma long ago and that she liked to keep in the living room.

"Come here a minute, Selma," he said, and she jumped up and stood beside him, her arm through his. "I wish you wouldn't hang reproductions," he remarked, "but if you must, this was a good choice. Now I'm going to give you a little private talk about Pissarro and nobody else need listen. He was a remarkable character and a very fine painter, hardly recognized at all until after his death though he lived to be a very old man. He was a great family man, like most Jews, and he brought up five painter sons. Gauguin learnt from him; Cézanne learnt still more from him; he learnt, first of all, to throw away his tubes of black and dark brown—"

He dropped his voice still lower and my mother smiled at me and we went on talking.

"How are things in the gallery, darling?" she asked. "Have you got a good assistant?"

"Yes," I answered. "Two of them, and on the whole, things are going very well. You must all come and see it tomorrow. I've just had it redecorated. Also I have some things to show Father that I think may interest him."

It was still called the Black and White Gallery though I bought and sold paintings now as well as drawings. It was the name Oakenshaw had given it and I didn't like to change it after his death. It was now in Davies Street. The rent was enormous but the move had been justified by the increased sales.

"Halley," my father said, returning to the sofa with Selma and keeping her hand in his, "I often wonder if you realize how much of your success you owe to this girl here. By golly! when I think, Selma, how you toiled away in that office for years and years, and kept on pinching and saving in that miserable little flat you had near Baker Street so that Halley could keep on at the gallery—do you realize all that, my boy?"

Selma and I couldn't help exchanging a quick, amused glance.

"Do you imagine I could ever forget it?" I asked.

"But I loved that flat," Selma said. "Don't you say a word against it. I loved it, and I was terribly sorry to leave it when Paul was born. I even loved that old gas geyser."

"Well, you're married to a remarkable young woman," my father said, "and I can't tell you so too often."

"I think Selma's outstanding achievement," my mother remarked, "was that she managed to stay in London right through the war all the time Halley was away in the Air Force. I simply can't imagine how she dared to do it, and with the two children, too."

"Oh," Selma said, "I may be a Tartar, as Halley often calls me, or a Magyar, or whatever you like, but first of all I'm a Londoner, and quite honestly it never occurred to me to leave. I don't deserve any credit for it."

My father gave a heavy sigh.

"I just wish," he said, "that you'd all come back to America. I think this country is in for a bad time, financially. The two boys would have far better chances of getting on over there, and Paul could go to Harvard. I wish you'd think seriously about it, both of you. Your mother and I hate your being away over here all the time."

"We have thought about it," I said, "but we don't want to leave, partly because we can't bear the idea of uprooting the children."

Clarisse came back then, saying as she joined us, "Really, Harriet looks simply too marvelous. And she remembers everything about our last visit, every single thing. She really is too sweet for any words."

Nothing more was said about my parents' desire to get us to go to America until later, when my father and I were sitting alone at the table finishing our wine. As he held his glass I couldn't help noticing how his hand trembled.

"Apropos of what we were saying before dinner, Halley," he began. "Why don't you at least send the two boys over, if you don't feel you can come yet yourselves? Your mother and Clarisse and I will look after them. I'd see that Dick got a good start in some business, as he's so keen on getting a job now, and I'd like Paul to go to Harvard. I feel sure it's the right place for him. You must realize as well as I do that the future is with America."

"No, Father," I said, "we couldn't part with both the boys."

"Didn't I hear last year," he asked, "that Dick wanted to come to America?"

"He's never said so to us," I told him, "but if he did say he wanted to go, I'd let him. After all, he's nineteen."

"Well, I can't help worrying about you all," he went on. "You've got a welfare state here and that's all very fine, but it's going to break the country's back one of these days. And besides, America is the one strong bulwark against Russia."

"We're getting along all right," I said, "and I want the children to have a settled home."

"You know, Halley," he said, "you always did think you knew best. I hate going back over the past, but please remember how often you've been wrong. I know you aren't a boy any longer—"

"I'm forty-three," I reminded him.

"But all the same," he continued, "I think I can see rather further than you can. All my life I've been used to taking long-range views. You don't mind my saying all this, do you?"

"Of course not, Father," I said. I saw him put his left hand over the right hand that was holding the wineglass to steady it.

"You're American, after all," he told me. "Europe is exhausted by the war, and personally I don't believe NATO and all the rest of the treaties and agreements amount to a hill of beans." (This was an expression Syl had often used, and I wondered if he knew it.) "And there's another thing. Your mother and I aren't getting any younger. Of course we both enjoy coming over here for a visit, but I'm not sure how long I'll be able to make these journeys. They take a lot out of me. I wish you'd listen to me, Halley. I can say this to you because I love you and Selma and the children, and I want you all to be happy: don't rely too much, my boy, on your own ideas of what's best and wisest. Just cast your eye back over the past sometimes and think of all the things that went wrong—things that never need have gone wrong—and ask yourself why they did go wrong. For God's sake, Halley, don't give yourself cause for any more regrets. I know I don't have to cross the t's and dot the i's with you, but when you think that if you'd trusted my judgment instead of your own, Julian would have been alive and happy now—"

His wineglass was empty now and I pushed back my chair.

"I promised Selma we wouldn't sit here too long," I told him. "Mrs. Packer's waiting to clear the table before she goes."

"Well," my father said, getting up, "we've had a very good dinner. I must congratulate Selma. An excellent dinner."

He and my mother went back to the hotel fairly early, and my mother clung to me with emotion as they were leaving and kissed me again and again. I told her we'd all meet tomorrow.

"Yes, I know," she said, "but I can't help feeling unhappy about the way we're separated. It's terrible, terrible, being three thousand miles apart!"

Clarisse stayed on for another hour or so, talking, but I don't think we talked about anything that mattered. She said she'd take a taxi back to the hotel, but I said of course not, I'd drive her back in the car.

On the way she suddenly burst out, in a voice sharp with bitterness, "I suppose they've told you about that devil George Hambleton?"

"They only said," I answered, "that he'd married somebody from Pittsburgh."

"The dirty cad!" she cried. "God, how I hate him now!" With a quick, despairing gesture she put both hands over her face.

"Don't, Clarisse," I said. "He isn't worth it. Why on earth did you want to marry a man who's been divorced three times?"

"Oh, don't be so superior!" she exclaimed, dropping her hands, and I was glad I had made her angry. "Just because you had the good luck to marry the right person at the start. You always did love to take a superior attitude with me. I told you before that I liked the big fool, he could have made me do anything he wanted me to do, and that's more than anyone else ever could." And then her tone completely changed. "Halley, what have I got to look forward to? Tell me that."

"A peaceful middle age, I hope," I answered.

"I'm middle-aged now, and I've never been so wretched. I'm nearly forty-two, and what have I got?"

It was too difficult to answer that, and I didn't try.

"What's become of Chico?" I asked.

"Oh, I don't know. I never hear anything. I only know he's married again and has a family. Why did things always go so wrong for me, Halley?"

I was silent. Once more I wasn't going to try to answer.

"I know exactly what you're thinking," she said. "I know as well as if you'd said it out loud. Well, at least that wasn't my fault. They could have made me go back to Fred so easily if they'd wanted to. I only needed a little push. I'd lost my nerve, that's all, and home was so near."

"Home is near now," I said, as I rounded the corner of Arlington Street. "You're back at the Ritz, my girl."

"Yes, I know," she said, with a break in her voice. "We're all back at the Ritz now, aren't we? And a lot of good it does."

"Selma and I aren't," I answered, "and we never will be."

"Anyway," she said, "how long can it last? Father's living on his capital now. He says he doesn't see why he and Mother shouldn't be as comfortable as they can for the rest of their lives."

The commissionaire came down the steps and opened the door of the car. Clarisse put one foot out and then turned and kissed me.

"Oh, well," she said, "who cares? *Je m'en fiche.* One place is just like another to me now, and if you want to know, one man is pretty much like another too."

She was the proud and defiant little girl, tossing her long blond hair, and I knew I loved her in spite of everything and always would.

[310]

I knew that in spite of everything I loved them all, and as I drove back to Chelsea I wondered whether, perhaps, there might not be a good deal of truth in what my father had been saying; whether perhaps, taking the long view (and if Selma agreed), I ought not to make up my mind to go back. Only in that way could I help to close the ugly gap in the circle made by Julian's death.